TWILLYWEED

TWILLYWEED

A CLAIRE BRESLINSKY MYSTERY

MARY ANNE KELLY

MYSTERIOUSPRESS.COM

OPEN ROAD

INTEGRATED MEDIA

NEW YORK

Copyright © 2015 by Mary Anne Kelly

Cover design by Mauricio Díaz

978-1-5040-1667-4

Published in 2015 by MysteriousPress.com/Open Road Integrated Media, Inc.
345 Hudson Street
New York, NY 10014
www.mysteriouspress.com
www.openroadmedia.com

To my beautiful mother, Helen Kelly,
who remembers Sea Cliff when . . .

TWILLYWEED

PROLOGUE

Rain blew sideways across the lid of the sea. There'd be no boats out there today. Noola tweaked the spiny parts from her geraniums. Still alive from last year, they had that tomato red you could see in Tyrolean window boxes. A wistfulness, the flowers were. All beauty spoke of yearning, she remembered, rocking in her chair.

A gloved hand sliced the kitchen door apart in a blade of dark. Alight with pinpricks of intent, cold eyes attended her.

Noola pulled the plaid rug nice and warm across her lap and sipped the fancy tea someone had brought. That abandoned lullaby from the beach blew up the cliff and through the grate. It had gone on every morning for so long that it was almost routine now. But this time there was an unfamiliar rasp of mournfulness—significant somehow—and Noola rose halfway, the hope that it was Weedy always in the back of her mind, weighing. It wasn't Weedy, though. It was only the wind rattling the gate. Weedy wasn't coming back.

Distracted, the old woman tasted the unfamiliar, peppery cardamom of the chai, the almost nasty smack of cloves. There was something she must do. She nibbled a chunk from Patsy Mooney's Pascal cake. Ah, that chewy moisture was a delight. Then, still gazing off into the grizzle of foul weather, she remembered and opened her phone. She must tell what she'd discovered about the moon dial before—but Noola felt her heart stop once. And then again. She clenched the cup and there it went a third, overpowering time. Turning with the whelp of pain, she caught sight of the enraptured, leering face. Her hand opened and the cup slipped down, cracking on the tray, the browny liquid falling, falling onto and into the Donovan plaid.

Behind the door a quiver of satisfaction released, then stirred and slipped, unclean, away.

CHAPTER ONE

JENNY ROSE

The young girl was thrown against the seat as he navigated the turn.

"From where are you coming?" he asked her as they settled into a straight line.

"From Ireland, sir."

"Is that right?" He wobbled his turban. "Is this your first visit to America?"

"Yes, it is, sir."

"How lucky for you to arrive in the rain," he said.

She found nothing to say to this.

"And," he continued, "to arrive on the day of the new moon."

"Is it?" Jenny Rose peered out into the lumbering traffic. It occurred to her that he could be taking her anywhere. "That would be fortunate," she agreed. "We Irish do know a bit about fortune." *Both good and bad,* she reminded herself wryly. But she'd heard the prim tone in her voice and was instantly sorry. Music fluttered from the radio and she relaxed, just a bit, in her good raincoat, for fortune she was seeking. Many a sullen child's nose had she wiped to afford it. It would last her a lifetime if she looked after it properly, though. *You get what you pay for,* Aunt Brigid would have said—*and hide what a naughty girl you are,* she would have thought. Jenny Rose opened the well-crumpled paper. Twillyweed. Sea Cliff. Long Island, New York. With the heel of her hand, she wiped at the fog on the window. There she was with her pale little face, the spiky, cropped black hair in every direction, the fighting lips. She felt more than saw the driver glance over his shoulder. He was frightening looking, with his unibrow extending one ear to the other.

"Who's that?" she asked now about the music on the radio, curious because it sounded trickly and drumming, like the rain itself.

"Debussy." His smile was sweet. Then, "*Claire de Lune*," he informed her, his reflective eyes glazing over. He went away in his own mind and she was reassured, reminded that art touched all souls and belonged to no one. Finally they came to the exit and headed north over ugly terrain. There was a disappointing train station set in a section of derelict houses. At first she was taken aback, the roads and buildings were so broken down. FOR RENT or FOR SALE signs peppered the walls. Fatigue and disappointment overwhelmed her. But then the road split and the sign indicated Sea Cliff off to the right. One good thing, there were soft pink trees wherever you looked. A locust grove, she thought. She hadn't imagined the place to be so tipsy with hills. She liked hills. They bumped up and then down a quaint road overgrown with elm and reaching willow. Willow. So they must be nearing water. Antique shops, a library, and a museum indicated they'd come to a town. Ghostly, once-lavish Victorian homes with rickety porches and arts and crafts bungalows clung to slanting properties, their tulips drowsing in the rain. A grim real-estate office and a couple of old Irish bars, uphol-sterers, and cabinetmakers. A curiosity shop, pottery, paintings hung, fishing nets on candles, a used-books store. They made a wrong turn and found themselves down at the foggy beach where a long-haired, disheveled old man appeared like a vision at a grimy window. Fretful, the taxi turned and chugged painstakingly up a steep hill. Jenny Rose had the wary, slow-climbing sensation of a roller-coaster drop yet to come and clung to the maroon plastic of the front seat. A low-hanging willow scraped the whole of the cab and they were blinded by a sweep of minnowlike leaves. The sun broke through the trees, a brace of gold illuminating the whiskers on the driver's neck and the grime of the windows. You could see out across the sound then, and a little sailboat, like a toy, glided through the broken mist. A thrill of sudden perspective made Jenny Rose shiver. She was here in the States. On her own in America at last, in this village—Sea Cliff!

CLAIRE BRESLINSKY

I remember I was standing in the drizzle trying to read the paper at the stop on Park Lane South in Queens. There was violence on every page: overseas, at the airport—someone had even bludgeoned a priest for a statue down in sleepy Broad Channel. The rain began to come down hard. I'd just missed the bus to the subway so I was in for a wait. I huddled deeper under my umbrella, reflecting as I did that I'd waited in this very spot facing the woods years ago back in high school, dreaming my young girl's dreams. And then I remembered something else, long forgotten and tucked away: There was a man who used to stand over there up the hill. He'd stand half hidden by the trees and something purple wobbled up and down. In my innocence I'd had no idea what it could have been. It was with a thrill of horror it came to me. And then, with my surprise, it came to him. He'd never approached or even crossed the road. But many an icy morning I'd stand there in my Catholic-school uniform, the skirt rolled up, and accommodate him with the look of shock and surprise he'd required.

Yes, now that I came to think of it, that must have been when arbitrary behavior began for me. It was a sort of a job. I'd felt I couldn't let him down by yawning or laughing. That it was *his* hurt that mattered shows you what kind a life I've led. I certainly never thought to tell my parents. It never occurred to me because in a way, I'd been a participant and so I was to be blamed. As an older woman, I can look back at that spot, at that girl, and have sympathy for who she was. But there are victims everywhere in this world, and the lurking monsters they protect. They sway like the fickle breezes of the past, the wicked ones—and sometimes they wait, squeezing their thighs in lewd expectation, just around the corner.

When I lived overseas, I was a damn good photographer; no doubt you'll recognize the voyeuristic influence. I'm a divorced woman now, two kids away at college. I had a business, a bed-and-breakfast in a gracious old Queens mansion that had just been starting to take off when it burned to the ground. I lost a romantic home, but the insurance money wound up funding college for the kids—a divorce complication that let my ex-husband so utterly off the financial hook it made me see, if not red, then a simmering menopausal orange. My children still had health insurance from their father's police department coverage, so at least they were taken care of. And I was back where I'd started. Except, luckily, now I had Enoch, the fireman who'd saved my life—my compensation for all of it the way I looked at it. But what was I doing with this life? Going to apply for a job in Manhattan where, after taxes, I'd make enough money to save nothing. How had Enoch described it? "Get me out of the house . . . Make a little pocket change." Surely if Enoch thought this enough for me, then I should, too. I ought to be grateful. . . . And it wasn't that anything was wrong. It was just when we made love I was simply always *right there*. I don't know. I never lost myself. I'd never want him to see any signs of regret, though. He to whom I owed so much.

I stood there at the bus stop with the flimsy résumé he'd dictated. It told so little of me really. None of the good stuff, or at least none of the things of which I was most proud. Amateur sleuthing. Living in India. Thirty-eight successful hours in labor. Reconnaissance. This job to which I was applying was to be a temporary thing until I could get back on my feet, but already I could sense a dead end. To be working as a receptionist for a photographer who would have, in my old life, barely qualified as my assistant? Pocket change, indeed. The rain petered out and the sun shone through like in that catechism picture where they put God. I stood watching the reflection of the clouds race by in the puddles. If I'd had my camera with me, I would have shot the striking image. But I never had my camera with me anymore. Come to think of it, I hardly did anything I loved anymore. I stood very still, knowing this. I snapped my umbrella shut. I should have been marching around with my own book of photos. Why *was* I always trying to be less than I was? Because of guilt for failing at a risky business—for which I'd been warned? But that hadn't been my fault. For my mother's idea of how a woman should spend her time? Of course not. My mother didn't care about things like that anymore. As a matter of fact, lately she was more of the "let's take the day off and go to a yard sale" ilk. My ex-husband? He'd lost that right when he'd waltzed off with his actress friend, hadn't he? Enoch? Kind as he was to have arranged this interview, the truth was he'd probably be more pleased to have me at home. He was, after all, crazy about me. *I ought to remember that*, I chided myself, *when I start feeling discontent.*

Another thing; every morning at 10:45 the dog was used to being let out. I couldn't bear the thought of Jake standing, uncomprehending, legs crossed in distress at the back door. Just then the bus groaned across the 112th Street Bridge. The driver pulled over and cranked open the door. "No," I told him cheerfully, "I've changed my mind." I turned and walked determinedly down the hill that goes from Kew Gardens all the way to Myrtle Avenue. I reached the ugly house we'd been renting since Christmas—a hideous little narrow aluminum-sided rental, I'm afraid—in no time at all and was surprised to see the dog out in the yard. My heart lightened at the sight of Enoch's truck on the driveway. There would be coffee and sympathy. I opened the back door and moved automatically to the pantry to get Jake a biscuit. Hearing Enoch in the dining room, I went in. He was standing with his back to me. There was someone there with him. I remember this struck me as off because whenever we had company we sat in the kitchen. For a moment I thought they were adjusting the radiator that spewed heat no matter how you wound it down. The other man bolted upright, adjusting his suspenders. We saw each other's face at the same moment. I wouldn't have known what was up but for his rattled expression.

I don't think I stopped to make sure the dog was in the gate. Fortunately, Jake was so used to being locked in that he stayed where he was out of habit. All I can remember is running down the block through the puddles, all those shining, purplish abalone oil puddles sucking life from the dirty one-way road. Then suddenly Enoch behind me. I must have shrieked at his approach because the lady across the street dropped her shopping bags. His hand on my arm and me wrenching loose. The picture in my mind of him with that . . . I thought I might be sick. I pulled away and kept running toward the trestle where I imagined I'd be safe. Safe from what—from knowing? Enoch's voice and what he said. And here was the best part . . . or in this case, excuse me, the worst part. "Claire," he called after me frantically, "Claire, I was just," and it was the way he said this rather than what he said—his voice, though tight with pleading, sounded, if you can believe this, justified, almost dismissive. "It meant nothing. . . . Nothing more," he insisted and then, gasping, out of breath, "than emptying a hose!"

JENNY ROSE

In Sea Cliff, young Jenny Rose stood with her back to the sea. *Like a house in a story*, she thought, looking up. It was one of those resort monstrosities for the rich that someone had plugged heaps of money into at the turn of the last century. A contrite form stooped beneath an umbrella at the front entrance. A butler, she thrilled, restraining from smoothing her hair.

He was a startling-looking fellow, short legged, with great flaring nostrils, massive shoulders, and bulging muscles. His skin bore the gray-brown shrivel of an olive branch. He looked like an aging trapeze artist. Suddenly he was jostled aside by a hefty woman tiptoeing down the steps, holding a dishcloth over her head. Blustery and at the height of her blood pressure judging from the rosy hue of her skin, the woman then squeezed her cream cake–stuffed frame into the taxi, inspected Jenny Rose's bags, wriggled her body back out, and gave orders. The fellow who'd been flung aside had recovered and emerged now at a stately pace. He was bent forward with self-imposed subservience. He minced his way over, crouching through the rain to assist the driver with Jenny Rose's trunk. The stout woman kept giving orders in that unmistakable New York accent.

Then the butler—in a reserved Patois lilting English—indicated the porch, wanting the trunk out of the rain. He paid the driver and the driver climbed into his cab, but not before folding his palms and bowing to Jenny Rose. She blushed. The sharp-eyed, stout woman saw that and yelled disapprovingly, "Hey! None of that paganism stuff." She bent her cabbage knee to kick off a smatter of sopping tulip leaves from her wet shoe, then ushered them up the front steps. The driver and his lingering music drove off. Jenny Rose watched the taxi turn the curve in the batting rain, then saw it again around the second curve. She hadn't said thank you or good-bye. A senseless feeling of loss overwhelmed her as she was led into the house.

Inside, holding a pail like a purse, was a lanky, honey-colored girl with unkempt hair. She was pretending to polish an alabaster table lamp with a limp chamois rag.

"Take the new girl to her room, Radiance," the stout lady said, then, under her breath, muttered, "Dear diary, I forgot. I'll need the key. Hold her here with you." She blustered away. The butler had come in with the trolley and wheeled Jenny Rose's rain-running trunk off to the kitchen for the time being.

Jenny Rose, left alone with the girl, took in the smell of polish and flowers, tall wooden beams and sloping eaves. It was as grand as a Dublin hotel, but there was something quiet, looming even, like a rectory.

Radiance made a face but put down her rag, pushed her soft crimped hair in a useless gesture with her wrist, and circled Jenny Rose, looking her over. Jenny Rose had never seen a girl quite like this. She had all the features of a tall black girl, but her long hair was almost blond and her eyes were light and gray and grainy as fried cat's-eye marbles.

"Like to kick the tires?" Jenny Rose said.

"Eh?"

"Quite a house," Jenny Rose revised her approach.

"Everyone paints it," Radiance informed her in what sounded to Jenny Rose like a French accent, indicating the series of oils and water-colors of this very house one after the other up the grand stairway.

"Well, then," Jenny Rose said, "there goes that idea."

Radiance looked over her shoulder and lit a bent, yellowed roach she'd had stashed away behind her ear. She took a deep drag and squinted at Jenny Rose. "So you're an artist?"

Jenny Rose said truthfully, "I'm not sure what I am."

"Everyone's an artist in Sea Cliff," Radiance informed her in a bored voice as she blew out a rivulet of smoke. "An artist or a writer or a wannabe."

"Really? What about you?"

"I'm the princess, can't you tell?"

There was a noise behind them. A small, scurrying noise, like a surprised squirrel in a winter garage, and they both jumped and looked around. That was when she saw the little boy for the first time. He had a mop of fluttery hair atop a large head, giving him the appearance of intelligence, with inquisitive, timid eyes that looked away when he saw you notice his meandering eye. The eye was evident at once. Enormous ears, poor thing. So this was Wendell. Jenny Rose liked him on sight. She knelt down and offered him a peppermint from her crowded pocket. The little boy was about to take it but saw the heavy woman coming back and he hesitated, changed his mind, and stepped back and away from her, clearing his throat in anguish. The heavy lady waved him back up the front stairs with a warning look. But Wendell held something in his closed hand, some offering of welcome, Jenny

Rose imagined, so she leaned in his direction without taking a step and tried to make her eyes tell the child it was all right. The boy was sensitive, Jenny Rose could see that, and she remembered her own agonies of childhood, the times they'd paraded her out and wanted her to know what to do, to say . . . how in the end she'd always seemed to fail. *Well, never mind*, she told herself, shaking her cropped, spiky, dark hair, hoping, for a moment, that this child would like her even though she knew it wasn't about the liking. She'd have to master him if she expected to stay. Otherwise, they'd send her back. And she couldn't go back.

"What's that?" The stout woman marched across and grabbed hold of what the little boy had clenched in his fist. He went to cover it, but the woman snatched at it gruffly and with all the unthinking insensitivity of the ignorant went on to berate him, "What's that ya got? Is that what they teach over there in that fancy school? I'll show ya! Turning into a thief now, eh?" The woman ranted on, "Not in this house! What did I tell you about that, eh? Give it here!"

Jenny Rose was appalled. To humiliate the child in front of her! But the damage was done. She must assert herself with an interference of some kind if they were to respect her place over this housekeeper's. She stood up very straight and, in a voice she acquired from she knew not where, though she suspected upon hearing it that it came from that exotic taxi driver, she extended her hand and announced, "Give that to me, please."

They all turned to her in surprise. Before any of them could object, she'd snatched the crumpled silk scarf from the housekeeper's hands and thrust it into her raincoat pocket. "This matter will be dealt with at the appropriate time."

None of them knew how to take this, but while they made their faces of conspiratorial surprise, Jenny Rose slipped in a wink to the little boy and began the slow walk up the stairs.

She was almost to the top when, "Not that way, miss," the butler at last advised. "You'll be down the stairs, not up."

"Oh," she said and meekly trotted back down. This error had

caused her to lose face with them, she realized. But not, she felt sure, with Wendell, who, appraising her with his one good eye, looked at her with interest and concern.

The heavy woman with the broad New York accent took the child away and returned almost immediately, sprawling one hand down over her hefty belly and pinning her lank hair back with the other. "I'm Patsy Mooney. And this here's Radiance. Now you've met there's no reason you shouldn't call each other by your first names," she said, insinuatingly demoting Jenny Rose to cleaning lady status. But Jenny Rose did not move, and the hefty woman urged her on with a bossy but conciliatory, "Let's get going, Miss Rose."

"It's Jenny Rose Cashin," she said clearly as she was led into a huge kitchen with an indigo Aga and a wall of shelves displaying glistening white plates. Lead-paned windows were heavy with rain-drenched ivy and a charming grandmother clock ticked loudly and cheerfully from the corner. A collection of antique white and blue porcelain milk pitchers lined the mantel. It felt like an English country kitchen of long ago. At the plank table the child returned to his seat and nibbled black bread and green salad and cherry pie. Jenny Rose's mouth began to water. "It's all so British," was all she could think to say.

"Boss likes everything foreign," Patsy Mooney told her. "Makes him feel important." She sniffed. Then, realizing she'd said too much, she nicked her head toward the entrance hall and added in a joking way, "But you can't always locate a nice British girl right away." She'd meant Radiance, who was from Guadeloupe, but Jenny Rose, misunderstanding her belittling tone, took it to mean that she herself was after all just another Irish immigrant. It dredged up all the trouble she'd left behind, all the gossip and rude remarks of thoughtless villagers. Her eyes filled with tears and she dropped her head so no one should see. But the sharp-eyed Patsy Mooney softened and tactfully turned away, saying, "You gotta be tired, coming all that way. Want me to show you your room?"

"I am tired," she admitted.

"Okay, just leave the big trunk. Mr. Piet'll bring it along when he's had his lunch. And I'll bring you a tray." She hoisted Jenny Rose's flight bag onto her shoulder. "Watch out you don't trip on that cat. That's Sam—he leaves a nasty smell if he takes a liking to you—right through that door there. That's it. And it's a devil to get that smell off. I don't know why they won't have him fixed. Keeps off the rodents, Mr. Cupsand says . . ." But instead of heading for the back stairs as Jenny Rose had expected, they wriggled through a doorway. "When you live near the water, there's always rats," she informed Jenny Rose with pleasure. "Down these back stairs and you'll see your own room at the bottom. There. Ain't it pretty? He just had it recarpeted. When I came here, it was so slippery. Nothing but the best for the boss. And feel how soft and plushy with your feet!" To demonstrate, Patsy Mooney slipped off her battered clogs and wriggled chubby toes into the pile.

Jenny Rose's heart sank. All the grand views from every window and she was to be stuck away in the basement? She looked around. It was all faux-finish pinkish cream, like being in a ladies' room or a funeral parlor. How would she ever put an easel up on this carpet? Even with a drop cloth. They'd kill her if she spilled a bit of paint. And she always did.

Patsy Mooney went trilling on, "Catch the TV! Mr. Cupsand got himself a flat screen and put his big one in Mr. Piet's. When I want to see my shows on a big screen, I've got to skedaddle down to Mr. Piet's quarters and ask myself in. It's supposed to be for all the help but you know the way it goes; you get to think it's yours when it's in your digs." She touched the ugly television longingly.

I'd have preferred any small window, Jenny Rose thought but didn't say. She sank onto the bed. Gone was any thrill of anticipation.

"'Course I got my own tiny TV, a little feller up on my dresser, but"—she made a face—"reception's no good. . . . Fuzzy! And just look at the bed, they give the latest installment." Patsy Mooney could barely keep bitterness from her voice now as she plumped the firm mattress with a deft mitt. "It's one of them pillow tops. You got the luck." She stood still, her bosom heaving with the strain of yearning and the steps. "Say! You're not disappointed, are you?"

"Oh, surely not. Really! I expected nothing," Jenny Rose fibbed.

Patsy tipped her head suspiciously. "But?"

"No 'but.' Honestly. I just . . . well . . . sort of would have loved to have had a window."

"You'll be glad not to have one when the storms rage, I'll tell you!"

Jenny Rose smiled tiredly. "I love a storm."

"Safe and snug you'll be down here. No one'll get you here."

"Get me?"

The woman peered into the gaping suitcase then looked at her doubtfully. "That all you got? Paints and brushes and stuff?"

Jenny Rose hoisted the other bag up onto the bed and snapped it open. "See? Plenty of duds."

Patsy Mooney's grabby eyes lit up. "Hmm, what's that nice old glittery thing you got there?" Jenny Rose recoiled. "My music box." She stashed it away in the top drawer.

The woman stood there for an indignant moment then took the hint. She wet her lips. "Well. I'll leave you then." She shut the door.

Jenny Rose sank down onto the bed and wearily took it all in. She pulled the white wicker pail toward the bed and laid everything out beside herself, emptying her flight bag and her pockets of boarding pass, gum wrappers, and magazines. The apricot print silk she'd taken from Wendell toppled open like young cups of May leaves. And what was this? A folded paper the size of a tea bag. She kipped it open and onto the coverlet spilled two rocks of blue candy. Goodness, they glowed! They moved like gemstones. She picked them up. But these weren't candy; they were glass. She peered closer. She was certainly no expert, but these looked like something precious. And they were matching. They looked for moment like bright blue eyes. She looked at them—and they looked at her.

Outside her door she heard a sound. Someone was there. A chill went up her spine. She cleared her throat. "Mrs. Mooney?" she called.

But there was no reply. *Maybe just the cat*, she told herself. She looked back at the stones. They were so changing and pearly. "Moonstone," she whispered aloud. That's what they were. Milky blues and greens that moved as she beheld them, watery with color and light and set into almond-shaped and antique, intricate works of silver.

There was something radiant about these stones. Had Patsy Mooney been right? How on earth had Wendell got his hands on them? *And what do I do now*, she pondered, *turn the poor kid in?*

The rain outside came down with delicious force, like blue linguini, keeping him safe and hidden in the cluttered room. Who would come here now? Languidly, on hands and knees, he found his way through the blankets to Noola's personal things. But there wasn't much to interest him. Just artifacts. He thought of the statue and wondered blankly what had become of the eyes? He simply could not remember. But that was not his fault. There'd been so much going on . . . His gaze fell upon Noola's books. She'd had so many books! He picked up the tattered Webster's Universal Dictionary *and thumbed carelessly through it. He should look something up. What? Something relevant to this place.* Murder? *No, not today. Ah, yes. Something enchanting.* Masturbation? *Why not? And here it was in black and white. So how vile could it be? Production of the venereal orgasm by friction of the genitals; self-abuse, onanism. Hm. What was that? One-ism? How true. He looked carefully at the words, fondly, almost, because there was beauty in truth, wasn't there? And he could afford to be sentimental now. It seemed he'd passed that greenish pubescent phase. Now that he'd at last found his way to satisfaction with a mate.*

He decided to look up his new best friend, torture. *It was French. How fitting, he mused. "LL tortura, a twisting, torquere, to twist. 1. Extreme pain; anguish of body or mind; pang; agony; torment." Yes, he agreed, stretching over the bedclothes, how well defined. He read on, aloud, now, savoring the sound of the words. He stopped. Where was that little cat? That was the thing. Once they knew you would hurt them, they were so hard to catch. He returned to his page.*

"2. Severe pain inflicted judicially, either as a punishment for a crime, or for the purpose of extorting a confession from an accused person." Ha! Even they said it was judicious.

"3. The act, operation or process of inflicting excruciating physical or mental pain." He groaned with pleasure. Perhaps, he relented, tossing the heavy book aside, a little self-abasement, once or twice again . . . in this sentimental hollow, just for old times' sake . . . ?

CLAIRE

In Queens, I answered my cell phone. No doubt it would be Enoch. He'd chase me down now. But it wasn't him after all; it was my sister Carmela. "Claire," she said, "you've got to help me."

"I can't help anyone right now, I'm afraid." I performed what I hoped was a tearful snort to emphasize the seriousness of my distress. "It's Enoch. You won't believe what happened."

"Is he dead?" she said.

"No," I said.

Because she grunted with what sounded like disappointment, I hesitated and she made use of the moment. "Claire. Please listen."

She'd said *please*, which was a word she never used, and because she was not impressed by my anxiety, I let her go first. But she always went first. I call it the sense of entitlement the firstborn utilize constantly, but it's more than that. It's a mechanism of timing they have, the selfish ones. There is no courtesy moment ingrained in them. They just plunge on because feeling has nothing to do with it—unless it's their own. You find my attitude cold? Wait. Let me explain.

Back when I'd first started going out with my husband, Johnny, the detective, part of the attraction I'd had for him was that he never really looked at Carmela. His way to put it was a disinterested shrug. Then he'd say, "Too many years doing vice to get caught up with a girl like that."

This I'd found utterly charming. Imagine: a man who hardly noticed when my glamorous sister would walk in the room! Perfect. Or so I'd been fool enough to believe.

Because now, after years of being left out of pertinent information, I knew why.

When she was fifteen (and I was eleven—years before I'd even thought of dating), Carmela, with her excellent fake ID and all gussied up to look like a bombshell, latched onto a bevy of flight attendants and

snuck into the local cop hangout in Kew Gardens. Who should be sitting at the bar but rookie Johnny Benedetto? From what I understand, he
took her to the band shell's parking lot in Forest Park in his convertible.
Johnny always had a great car. Over her head and under the influence
of three gin and tonics, Carmela surrendered her virginity. She'd been
looking for someone to lose her virginity to, she'll tell you. But she was
just a girl, a foolish, miscalculating girl, and she got pregnant. That was
not part of her plan. To be fair, Johnny didn't know this, what with her
going off to Ireland to have the baby. He'd chalked the episode up to a
one-night stand and hadn't even seen her again until years later, the night
he'd come through the door of my parents' house to court me. Neither
of them had batted an eye. And I'd been definitely watching for signs of
interest. Every guy I'd ever brought home went gaga for Carmela. And
they'd recognized each other, all right. Carmela wouldn't forget the man
who'd cost her five months of her junior year at school and put her on
a trip to rainy Ireland—a trip where she'd given up her daughter before
she'd even seen her. As for him, well, no one would be able to forget Carmela's bewitching face. But in our living room that night the both of them
had simultaneously chosen to feign uninterest. Oh, they stayed far apart
all right, sidestepping carefully away from each other the entire duration
of my marriage. It wasn't until recently he'd found out he had a child,
because this secret had been kept even from me. Or, as my family likes to
say, they'd carefully protected me from this knowledge.

If I'm honest with myself, me finding out about it certainly had a lot
to do with our final breakup, at least from my end. That really put the
bow on it.

I stood now on the corner by Holy Child Church. My marriage had
fizzled, we know my relationship had fizzled, and if I moved, my cell
phone fizzled.

"Claire!" Carmela spoke with harsh, attention-getting spleen. "Listen carefully. I'm outside Rome."

I looked down at the soggy, elegant pumps I'd "borrowed" from her while she'd be gone and was still wearing and had better be careful of. I wiped their soles on the wrought-iron gate.

"And now," she went on, "I got a message on my cell that Jenny Rose is in New York."

"Jenny Rose? Your daughter?"

"Stop saying my 'daughter!' I don't even know her!"*

"Well, now's your chance," I muttered.

"Claire, those aunties made me swear on the Bible I'd have nothing to do with her when I let them have her." Carmela lowered her voice. "You know they wouldn't have taken her if I was going to waltz back into her life. I had no choice, for God's sake! Claire. Just listen. She's left the name of a place. I've written it out. Take it down before I lose you. Can't you just go find her? She's on Long Island somewhere. It's some artist colony . . . used to be a posh resort town on the North Shore. What the hell's the name of the place? Hold on. Here it is. Sea Cliff."

Sea Cliff. The way Carmela said it, with that Ida Lupino English lisp of hers, it made it sound so alluring. The very name made me think of sailing boats and high winds.

"She says she's working as an au pair. Look"—she sounded a touch frantic now and I pictured a handsome Italian coming within earshot—"she wants me to meet her out there at noon tomorrow, at a place called Once Upon a Moose. I couldn't make out her number for all the dead spots in the call and so I can't call her back. Can you go?"

"Jesus, Carmela, she'll be expecting *you*!"

"Well, I can't very well fly home in time, can I?" she shouted, then reasoned, "Look. She met you the time you went to Ireland for that funeral years ago. Can't you do this one little thing for me so she doesn't sit there looking at the door and no one comes?"

I could see the logic in this. Of course I'd met the girl. She was just a kid. Cute. But also very clearly a handful. I was actually glad Carmela showed some signs of feeling for her daughter, but I could already imagine the look of disappointment that would cross her face when she saw me instead of Carmela.

"You and Enoch could take a ride out," she suggested, already triumphant.

So I laughed. What else could I do?

JENNY ROSE

In the morning, Jenny Rose felt stronger. She'd slept well, despite the stuffy, claustrophobic space. It was new and clean enough, but whoever had designed the basement must have been a stranger to the rest of the house. She showered gingerly in the convenient pink washroom allotted to her and while she stood there dressing, her eyes fell upon the twin jewels. She'd best keep them safe. She did have a little green satin sack in the music box in which she kept a tiny pearl she'd bit into while eating clams in Ephesus. She took the music box out of the underwear drawer, opened it, and wound it. When it didn't stick, it played the haunting "Waltz of the Flowers." It hurt her just to hear it because the boy who'd broken her heart had given it to her. She should have gotten rid of it. But it was so old-fashioned and expensive looking . . . And she wasn't ready—yet. She shut it. She placed the blue stones in the sack carefully, pulled the drawstring shut, and dropped it into her pocket. Then she made her way up to the kitchen. Ascending from her fluorescent-lit cave, she was startled by the sunshine in the windows. It was a relief.

"Good morning," she greeted Patsy Mooney, who jumped guiltily and sprang to her feet. She'd been holding the *Newsday* and doing the Jumble. Nibbling delicately at a slice of cinnamon toast, she set another place for Jenny Rose. She danced around the table, light on her feet, the way some heavy people are. She had dainty hands and feet and unblemished skin, and very little, darting eyes.

"Coffee?" She held up the pot.

"If you don't mind, I'd love a cup of tea. I could make it myself if it's too much trouble."

"Do I look like it's too much trouble?" she said sharply.

"Oh! My, no. I'm sorry. Yes. I'd love a cup of tea."

"Oh, all right. I'm sorry, too. Start fresh, all right? I'm not much for the morning."

"Neither am I," Jenny Rose said, relieved, although she loved mornings, but she didn't want to start off on the wrong foot.

They sat together and waited for the pot to boil. A collection of white seashells rimmed Patsy Mooney's workspace and her jars of wooden spoons. Jenny Rose studied her with her artist's eye: the woman's arms short and hairless, the skin of a beautiful woman stretched like a balloon over a sly face. Stupid, but sly. A taste for the flashy. This morning she wore a dress of cherries dancing over cotton cream. Her chubby wrist strained under a bauble of red and white poppets and her eyes strayed back to the paper. Jenny Rose realized she'd destroyed the woman's happy solitude and decided from now on to bring a book to the table so as to restore her peace. She knew she'd been staring at her, but kept memorizing her just the way she was so she could draw her later. There was no eye like that of a first glance.

In an odd, falsely cheery voice from left field, Patsy Mooney pried suddenly, "Didn't like things at home, huh?" It was like she'd heard it from someone else and had been saving it up. "Nowhere else to go?"

Jenny Rose didn't see why she always had to be so cross. She extended her spine and settled her most forbidding look on the older woman.

Catching on to this new restraint, Patsy stirred her coffee counterclockwise. "Seems to me"—she spilled a little and sucked a tooth, revising her approach—"most young girls stay close to home . . ." She let that hang in the air.

"It's true," Jenny Rose said pleasantly. The woman was just being friendly. "I like to travel, though. Are you from New York, then?"

"That's me. Born and raised in Oceanside." She paused. "That's the South Shore. You won't see much of that." She nudged her chin, indicating the rest of the house. "This here is the fancy North Shore.

The gold coast, they call it. They think anyone lives on the South Shore ain't worth the time of day."

Jenny Rose laughed politely and inquired, "When will I see the little boy?"

"Look at that! Almost forgot what I was supposed to tell you! Dear diary, I'm thick as a post! Now. Wendell's adopted. They told you that, right?"

"No," she answered simply, delighted. Now she liked him even more. But she wasn't about to tell busybody here that her reason for coming to the United States was to find her own birth mother. She smiled pleasantly.

"Right. Well, he is. But that's neither here nor there. He goes to school every day, see. I get him off to the bus and that'll be your job."

"School? Isn't he just four?"

"Almost five. You wouldn't want him to yourself the whole day, believe me. He's a job. You'll find him sleeping on the floor with the cat. You can tuck him in good as you want but come morning, there he'll be curled up like a dog on a rug at the window and the window wide open. Don't ask me how he gets it open but he does. And not a word out of him! That's seven twenty, now, remember. They pick him up here at the end of the drive. He's a cinch to get up so you won't have to be worrying about that. Opens his eyes and he's up. It's just getting his shoes on that's the problem. Takes a long time. Once you get that done, he'll be ready and waiting, smart as a pin. All dressed and teeth brushed. Not talking. And we know he can. But he won't. Stubborn, he is, that's all. That's what I say. You'll see."

"What do you mean? He can't talk?"

"Oh, he can, all right. Ungrateful. He just won't."

"Who's been putting him to bed?"

"He goes by himself."

At four? Jenny Rose felt a rush of outrage.

"Now, I'll help you out at first—being there's a time difference in your system—but after that, you gotta be up at six thirty to check on him. Here's your tea." She scowled and plopped a decrepit tea bag into a mug and crashed boiling water over that.

Jenny Rose made a note to buy some loose tea and a pot, if there was none. "Mrs. Mooney, what will I be expected to do today?"

"It's Patsy Mooney, dear. Just Patsy Mooney. No 'Mrs.' anymore." She raised her eyes dramatically and crossed herself. "Thank God that's over. Mooney's my maiden name and please God I never have to lay eyes on that man again! You're free as a bird for the morning. At two forty, you gotta be here to meet the bus. Make sure you're not late. The driver won't let him off the bus if no one's there and then there'll be hell to pay." She glanced to the side. "It's just the kid's never easy." She shrugged. "He don't want to get on the bus and then he don't want to get off!"

Jenny Rose paled. Seven hours off on his own! A child that age. Of course he was confused.

"Mostly the driver yells at him loud enough and off he comes."

"I'll make sure to be there," Jenny Rose promised, her eyes out the window, hungrily taking in the spectacular view. "And when will I meet Mrs. Cupsand?"

Patsy Mooney stood with her cup stopped before her mouth. "Nobody told you that part?"

"Sorry? What do you mean?"

She lowered her voice. "Nobody told you what happened or nothing?"

Jenny Rose regarded her attentively.

Patsy Mooney sat back down. "Annabel Cupsand took off with another man, hon. That's the honest truth of it. There's no other way to put it. Well, that's why you're here!" She winked. "Made off with plenty of the family loot, too, from what I heard."

"Oh! Really? Gee, I'm sorry." Jenny Rose stretched to reach for the honey and the green satin sack tumbled out of her side pocket. Guiltily, she slipped it back in.

Patsy Mooney narrowed her eyes. "What's that?"

Jenny Rose reddened. Now was the moment to say something, surely. But some reservation held her back. "Just a little private thing I like to keep close." She smiled. "My rosary," she lied.

Patsy Mooney leaned conspiratorially closer. "Keep your private stuff on your person, like I do." She pulled her collar aside and revealed three silver chains around her neck. A locket, a little key, and a golden heart dangled there. She gave a sly wink.

"Ah!" Jenny Rose smiled. "Faith, hope, and charity."

"Not really." She looked over her shoulder and moved her tongue into her cheek. "The heart's from my father, rest his soul, the locket's got my mother's strand of hair, and the little red key's just for the clock. Keep your friends close and your enemies closer. So, like I was saying, good riddance to bad rubbish, when it comes to Annabel Cupsand, her and her long, showy red hair! He's better off without her if that's the sort she was."

"Was?"

She stopped, seeing something far off Jenny Rose couldn't. "It's just sad. You know. For the little boy."

"Yes, of course."

"And she wasn't such a bad person. . . . It's just . . . she didn't hardly have Wendell here and she goes and takes off . . ."

There was something about the two of them sitting together that opened some intimacy. Jenny Rose inquired carefully, "What exactly *did* happen with Mrs. Cupsand?"

"Annabel?" Her face softened and she relaxed. "She always had me call her Annabel. The day she left . . . it was snowing. I remember exactly. It wasn't three weeks ago, and snow covered the cliff. The wind was moaning and carrying on! In the morning, the sun was shining and everywhere clean and white as a marshmallow. And cold! The town was covered and there was icicles everywhere. Cars are sliding off the road. It's so treacherous because Sea Cliff is nothing but these steep hills, see?" She leaned in close. "It was early, before breakfast even. I come down . . . Mr. Cupsand was standing in the great hall. I thought that was funny, like, because he's not one to use that way. He comes through the kitchen mostly. But there he was holding a pink letter in his hand and I thought, what's that sound?" She leaned in close to Jenny Rose. "Well, dear diary, there's Mr. Cupsand, howling like someone's cutting off his foot! I come running in and it's like he don't even see me. He just stands there crying out loud and his sister, Paige, come running in and she couldn't do nothing with him, neither. Then she picks up the letter out of his hand and—I'll never forget it—she reads it and then she says to me, she says, 'Patsy, go call Mr. Donovan. Mrs. Cupsand has left us. Tell Mr. Donovan to come here straightaway.'" Patsy gave a knowing nod, relishing her tale, "It was like she was afraid he was gonna shoot himself, see? Oh, it's been bad days, let me tell you. Like someone died. And the little boy, well, he don't seem to get that she's gone. He don't talk no more, neither. Not a word since that day! And he was a regular little chatterbox—had a way with words, he did!" She gave a mighty shiver. "So sad, what people do to people. And after all the trouble she went through to get him, too."

"Yes, that is dreadful."

"Well, she knew he'd be taken care of. It wasn't like she dumped him in a garbage bin or nothing." She made a face. "Took off with a doctor from St. Francis right over here in Roslyn. Her doctor, you know. Fertility." She cocked a brow meaningfully. "*Woman's* doctor."

"Oh, dear."

"I knew she liked him from the very start, the way she'd come back from seeing him all aglow. Talking what a wonderful doctor he was! I smelled something fishy right from the start." Her fat face crumpled. "She isn't a bad woman. Just . . . silly, you know? Likes pretty things." She leaned in and gave a scornful snort. "Oliver—Mr. Cupsand—he likes them, too. Anything beautiful he likes. That and the Red Sox. He thinks *art* is the end-all, see? That's what sold him on you as an au pair, if you want to know. It was my friend Darlene at the rectory told him you was an artist from her village in Skibbereen."

"Oh, I must go and see her."

Patsy's face grew thoughtful. "Sometimes I think she felt like she failed him somehow, you know? Annabel? Because she was content all along just to be a housewife. Trouble was, all she ever did was spend money and fancy the place up. Shop, shop, shop. And she'd drag the kid! Americana Mall. Home Goods." She licked the cream cheese from each finger with a smack. "'Course his sister's supposed to be filling in and all. Mr. Cupsand's sister, Paige. You'll meet her soon enough."

"Oliver and Paige." Jenny Rose scoffed. "Nice, that is. Shame on their parents naming them British, like that, and them being Irish! But that's typical of your self-loathing Irish, naming their kids what they think are the King's English highfalutin' names. Disgusting."

Patsy Mooney eyed her carefully. "You should know. Jenny Rose isn't what you'd call an Irish name, is it? Eh?"

"Oh. Well. You're right there. My adoptive mother was utterly enchanted with anything at all Italian."

"Anyways, like I was saying, Paige—the sister—just moved right in after the wife, Annabel, took off. It's only she . . ." She hesitated. "You can't say she don't try with the kid. The truth is the kid just don't take to her. Like he don't warm up to her. . . . She don't have no maternal instinct, if you get my meaning?"

But this was running too close to gossip. "When will I meet Mr. Cupsand, then?"

"Maybe not today. He stays in Manhattan some nights. More often than not he's on the boat. Got a fancy sailboat right here in the port." She shivered demonstratively. "They race them things, too, now spring's here. Fly like the wind!" Patsy Mooney chattered on and Jenny Rose tuned out, wondering how to throw away the ghastly tea without offending her.

"You won't get me on one of them, though. Not me. '*Come along*,' he'll say sometimes, '*Come have a ride on the boat.*' But I won't. Not me. Things go wrong in life. Well, they do. And I'm no swimmer." She leaned her head in confidentially. "That was the last straw for the missus, if you ask me. He took her out on that boat of his and she didn't want no part of it. She told him time and time again but he would insist . . ."

"Me, I'm a great swimmer," Jenny Rose bragged.

"All that money." Patsy Mooney shook her head, ignoring Jenny Rose's remark. "Hundreds he spends on gas when there's no wind! Brings trouble along with it, spending like that, you mark my words. . . ."

This reminded Jenny Rose of the stones in her satin sack. She wasn't keen on hiding something. She'd report them to Mr. Cupsand straight-away. That's what she would do, she decided, present the stones to him the moment she met him. Suddenly, at the thought of a morning all to herself, she had no jet lag at all. She walked her plate to the sink, shooting the tea down the drain. "Mind pointing me in the direction of town? I'd like to buy some things."

"Buy?" Patsy Mooney frowned disapprovingly. "Before you get your first paycheck!"

"Just necessities. I'll have a jog. And I must find the rectory and thank Mrs. Lassiter."

"Darlene?" Patsy Mooney gave a guilty look. "She was here yester-day, bringing the soda bread for you. I forgot to mention it." She made a sullen, cud-chewing face, having finished it off herself late last night. "Pretend I told you right away. She won't know the difference."

Jenny Rose looked her steadily in the eye. "She's a pen pal of my adoptive mother, Mrs. Lassiter is, if you must know."

"I know that. We play bingo together Wednesdays. Who do you think told her we needed someone here?"

"Oh. Then it's you I should be thanking."

"Not me. I just put the word out." Patsy Mooney laughed then turned away. "Don't thank me yet. Plenty of heartbreak in this house."

"Is it right or left when you come to the end of the drive?"

"Well, it's left. Town will be east of us. Not more than a ten-minute walk." She stood with her hands backward on her hips. "Stores won't be open yet, though."

Jenny Rose washed out her cup and placed it on the drainboard. "I'll be back well before one." She smiled and took hold of her red jacket and was out the back door and whistling before Patsy Mooney could object.

Patsy Mooney lifted the white lace curtain and peered out the sink window at the departing figure. *Hmmph.* Not much to her. Washed-out little thing. Pretty smile, though. Light up the room. You had to give her that. She sat back down at the table and buttered her toast, then went back to reading the paper. Where was she now? Excitedly, she rode her pointer finger down the column to where she'd left off. Here it was, that doity business down in Broad Channel.

CLAIRE

At Salerno's appropriately dark and red Italian restaurant, Enoch stirred his coffee. It's an old-fashioned, Fellini movie-look of a place in Queens, tucked away under the Montauk Line trestle. The local politicians come here, judges from the Kew Gardens courthouse, detectives with two hours to kill between hearings. In celebratory debacle, Enoch and I—who'd both long ago switched to green tea in the afternoons—drank fierce espressos today. I was miffed and tight. He was not, I thought, sufficiently contrite for the occasion. I began, "Look. I can't believe this. My children have just let you into their hearts!"

"Claire," he said, "your children are grown. They're both away at school. It cannot have harmed them to have had a decent human being in the house after their father's drinking and gambling knocked them off their hinges. I gave them nothing but encouragement and support. Be honest, all they ever saw from me was decency."

I flinched. It was true. "How am I supposed to be engaged to you and then find out the truth about you and just let you, let you—"

Enoch smiled a sad old smile. I realized I couldn't hate him. It was my ex-husband I hated. I couldn't hate the both of them. It would be overkill. I slumped, exhausted, in my seat. Enoch was supposed to have been my refuge. I'd thought we were settled. I didn't want to start all over again. I was tired of trying, tired of paying all that money up on Austin Street for highlights. This was all such a jolt. And yet, heaven knew Enoch had never asked to be gay. I slithered down still farther in my seat, abandoning all attempts at good posture.

"Claire . . ." He frowned, reaching across the table in his concern.

At that moment, it occurred to me that maybe I was overreacting. He was a nice man. He gave the most wonderful backrubs. And he didn't scrimp the way some people I knew did. He kept on, kneading and plowing through the stress knots. We'd had such fun together. Really. Staying up late eating rosemary, garlic, and olive oil popcorn and watching Bette Davis movies. And he'd enjoyed it just as much as I. Oh. Yes. I see. I should have seen.

"You know," he was saying, "I could keep Jake with me while you look for a place."

I stared at him in disbelief. "Thank you," I said, "but Jake is my dog and I'll figure out—"

"Claire," he interrupted harshly. "You can't just take a dog Jake's size to your mom's house. He's just too big. It's not fair to her. And not fair to Lefty."

Lefty is my parents' dog. He is so named not because he is south-pawed but because he was always to blame whenever someone *left it*. I know. It's crude. We're crude. "It's a little inappropriate for you to be telling me what is and isn't fair, okay?" I asserted. "And what makes you so sure I'll go to my mom's?"

"Where else would you go? He can come to the firehouse with me. He'll love it. And he might be your dog, but I gave him to you," Enoch said in a tit-for-tat tone of voice I'd never noticed. I realized what was happening. He was letting his guard down. No reason not to now. And the truth was, Jake would be fine with him.

What had happened to me? At one time I was thought to be the next Diane Arbus. True, I was the only one who had thought that, but my photography *had* taken me around the world and given me access to the flow of easy money. For a while I had been flush, but both these advantages, my career and the money, had withered early on the vine. What was wrong with me that caused husbands to betray me, houses to burn down around me, boyfriends to change entire sexualities on me, and people to get themselves murdered while I visited their towns?

"Have the eggs," Enoch urged. "You always like them. C'mon. Feta cheese and spinach, with salt and pepper and tomato on the side. It will do you good. It's early. You've got the whole day to work it off."

He was right. This wasn't about what was wrong with me. I might as well eat. I ordered the eggs. Enoch specified to the waiter exactly how I liked them. He would have an artichoke. My cell phone rang. It was my sister. I told you about her: Carmela, the bitchy one, the one in Italy. I have two sisters, actually. One's a peach, a cop on leave of absence—she recently married an Italian landowner; the other, Carmela, is a writer—or so she claims—and is as cantankerous as a woman can be. But Carmela is beautiful and so gets away with everything. She looks like Gene Tierney but underneath that Catholic schoolgirl face lies a Machiavellian heart. I say this not in good fun; she's sort of a sociopath. But people don't get it because of the beauty thing. *Beauty is as beauty does*, they think. But it's not true. Anyway the call came and went, and by the time I answered it, she was off on another. I know this not because her number climbed to the screen of my cell phone—I can never find my glasses quickly enough to read the numbers and answer it in time—but because she hangs up all the time if you don't pick up quickly enough. So I know when it's her—or isn't her, as it were.

The eggs arrived in all their glory. I regarded Enoch's innocent expression and decided to be frank. "Enoch, you asked me to marry you. Just when were you planning to tell me this?"

A crease appeared between his gentle eyes. "Claire. I keep telling you. It's nothing. These are things that men do. It's just . . ." He hesitated, looking for the right word, finally saying, ". . . release." He pierced a slender fork hole in my egg and dappled it with A1 Sauce.

It was then I realized that there would be no end to the misunderstandings. Was I the last sexually loyal person on the planet? Suddenly I didn't care. I stood, upsetting my eggs.

"Come on, Claire," he exclaimed, losing patience, "sit down and attend to your brunch."

Maybe it was that fussy stipulation that finally did it. Brunch. How right he was. It wasn't breakfast and it wasn't lunch. It was brunch.

"I'm counting on you to watch the dog until I can make other plans then, all right?" I relented. Even as I said it I felt I was betraying my dog, but what could I do?

He bit his lip with those white-white uppers and lowered his head in acquiescence.

I spent that afternoon and night on my parents' lumpy sofa with their farting dog Lefty and by morning—feeling gritty, discombobulated, and in shock—I was anxious to shower and be off. I made my way over years of doggy saliva-coated toys to the kitchen. My mother, who mostly loves serial-killer stories but will settle for any horrific crime in a pinch, was enthusiastically relaying the details of a particularly gory heist out loud to my father. I caught the tail end. It was the follow-up story of that priest in Broad Channel who was whacked over the head for some holy statue. She reluctantly handed the paper over to my father when she saw me and, humming, set about making my breakfast. I had a soft-boiled egg in a blue cup painted with pagodas and fences and wise little men fishing from delicate bridges. Strips of buttered toast sprinkled with cinnamon my mother refers to as "soldiers" were presented on a cake plate from Vienna. I thought, *Gee, maybe I will stay here.* From the paper, the beat-up priest's brave smile grimaced up at me. My shoulders sagged and I heaved a downhearted sigh.

"Don't look so worried," my dad said, pushing my foot under the table with his. "Is anyone shooting at you?" This was the prerequisite with which he, valiant survivor of World War II, would qualify any predicament.

My mother stood, her lips pursed. "I take it by your presence you've quarreled with Enoch."

My father covered my hand with his own beefy mitt. "Everybody fights, Claire. A good fight clears the air."

Look, I reasoned with myself, *I'm alive and healthy and so are my kids. I've been through worse than this. Nobody's dead or dying—or shooting at me.* This realization did me good.

My mother hovered, hefting a pie dish of crullers above my head. "Are you going to tell me what's up with you and Enoch or are you not?'

"Have you done something wrong?" My father eyed me carefully.

"No."

"Then you'll be okay." He bit into his toast. "A clear conscience has the strength of ten men."

My mother wasn't so quick to let it go. "At your age, you're better off making up. Plenty of lassies with their tongues hanging out just waiting to get a lick at a fine man like Enoch."

"Mom," I said, changing the subject, "Carmela told me Jenny Rose is out on Long Island."

From the calculated look of self-satisfaction that crossed her face, I concluded it was she who'd sent Carmela's cell-phone number to the auld sod. She's cautious when it comes to her sister Deirdre in Ireland, though, and you have to watch what you say, Deirdre being a lesbian and an elderly one at that. *Artistic,* Mom safely dubs her. My mother is Catholic first and Christian second. I caught a glimpse of my reflection in the china cabinet. I was wearing Carmela's clothes from yesterday, the grown-up-find-a-job outfit that was meant to say I was reliable and Republican. But that wasn't me at all. I'm more of a used-to-be-pretty, dangling-earring, oriental-jacketed, befuddled-but-refuse-to-be-pigeonholed woman. So where had the real me gone? Was she ever coming back? I looked out the window.

"Take a chance." Dad looked up from his crossword and instructed the president. "Try something new."

I decided then. The days of running home to Mother were at last at an end. I got up to go and I told her, "Ma, save me the paper. I'll be looking for an apartment when I get back."

JENNY ROSE

Jenny Rose was taking her jog past the marina when she caught sight of a really cute guy on a black boat with red sails furled. He had dark, silky hair like her own, only longer. Crafty eyes. Cheeky. Skinny. Weird. You could tell. He made quite a sight, cool as a rock star up on his deck on the cell phone, but his full attention was on her, watching her move. She moved faster, letting him see what a fine, healthy specimen she was and she pushed her short hair behind her ear and laughed at herself when she got far away. *What a country*, she thought, smiling to herself, out of breath, looking up at last to an authentic American blue sky, great dark clouds in the distance looming in like bedroom comforters. Sea Cliff's wooden houses gripped the steep hills. She took each hill, spending an hour exploring the up-and-down terrain. Old branches heaved and toppled from the weight of all the recent rain. So many trees! The light was dappled and moving and she ran, intent, a good long while. She could hardly wait to paint it all. She was really in the country here, she realized, pleased, turning to head back. No one about. She came to a dense bit of forest, a shortcut from the look of it. The real path stuck to the outskirts, meandering off in the wrong direction, so she took the shortcut. The light was momentarily obliterated by green and dark and branches from the fury of trees. She slowed down. She could hear the birds bicker, the rude barking of some gulls, smell the pine and moss, but she was quite alone in the dark.

Suddenly all was silence. The shush of her sneakers on the pine carpet floor was the only remnant of sound. She felt the hairs on the back of her neck raise up and her heart quicken. She was being watched. Not the common watching of a strolling woodsman or an admiring pair of eyes. A hound, she thought first, feeling her body go cold. It was the calculated intention of some purposeful force. She kept her pace and never turned her head. Some deep sense of preservation kept her stalwartly moving forward; some instinct took over that knew if she hesitated, she would be the wounded gazelle and danger would strike. She'd be lost. She bent under low branches and passed into a gleam of sunshine, then almost laughed with relief. It had occurred within a minute's space of time. And yet she knew she'd perceived something distinctly malevolent, something . . . foul. She looked this way and that, breathed the fresh air hard, rubbed her arms, and trotted on beneath the lowering sky.

It wasn't difficult to find Twillyweed again. You could see it from anywhere. She made her way nervously across the cliff and found her way, glancing now and then over her shoulder, back across the vast property. There were green bent rods turning into day lilies and huge rectangles of screeching yellow forsythia. The feet of the stone wall borders were thick with rain-trodden daffodil and hyacinth, and the scent of their perfume lingered like darkening water. She felt, rather than heard, someone close by. Still jumpy, she cried out and turned.

There, on the other side of the yard, was Radiance wrapped in a heavy sweater, her voluminous hair now dragged back and knotted in place with a chopstick. Silver hoops reaching to the middle of her neck dangled from her ears and beside her was a folded turret of sheets and towels in a basket and a hardcover book opened up on her lap. She remained looking at Jenny Rose, poised and disdainful with a cigarette in one hand and a pack of matches in the other, her eyes limpid and unimpressed.

"Fuck," Jenny Rose exclaimed with relief, "you scared the shit outta me!"

"Better not let the boss hear you using language like that, missy."

She closed the book and stuck it in the laundry like a secret. "He toss you right out."

Jenny Rose nicked her head good-naturedly. "Ah, come on over and have one of mine."

Radiance peered at her suspiciously, then, deciding it was cheaper to oblige, she tucked her own back in the pack and came across in a roundabout way, circling the hedge and perching herself delicately on the other side of Jenny Rose's bench.

Jenny Rose studied her. Radiance looked a few years older than she—and so somewhat interesting. Her fingernails were painted red and perfectly maintained while her feet, naked in flip-flops, revealed a mangled, calloused wear. Her neck and legs were long and pretty and she wore a lot of silver bracelets that sang when she moved. She was, by Jenny Rose's standards, spectacular. Also, she seemed like a tough girl, always a plus. Jenny Rose lit them up.

"That's drop-dead gorgeous, that nail color. What's it called?"

"Persimmon." Radiance pulled her hand back and twiddled her nails in the air, admiring them. "I swiped it from Patsy Mooney." She saw Jenny Rose's look. "*Phh*. She didn't need it. I found her painting things with it."

"What's that you were reading?"

"I'm not reading anything," Radiance's tone was inappropriately spiteful. "I just look at the pictures." She sighed, looking somehow defeated, away. "And they tell me nothing."

"Oh." But she'd seen the gold letters peeking out upside down from the eyelet. It was the *Rubaiyat of Omar Khayyam*. The wind moved the branches just above them and Jenny Rose leaned back, enjoying the sky through the shimmering canopy of leaves. "What's this, then, a beech?"

"*Phh*," Radiance snorted derisively, "that's a box elder. Don't you know trees?" Softening a little, she added, "Just wait till the linden trees bloom. The smell is intoxicating." A monstrous black-and-white cat strode across the garden, not bothering to give them a look.

"God, there are so many rosebushes! Like the grounds of a palace!"

"Noola and Annabel," Radiance murmured dreamily, "they planted them."

Jenny Rose gave her a blank look.

"Annabel is Mrs. Cupsand. Wife of Oliver." She twisted the hem of her skirt, looked up quickly, and informed her, "And you don't have to bother learning about her, Miss Nosy, because she's gone. They're both gone." She shook her head and looked out to the sea. "Hard to believe, but they are. Annabel took off and Noola's dead."

"Dead?" Jenny Rose moved closer, alerted by the catch in Radiance's voice. "Oh, I'm sorry. Was she very old?"

"Not that old. . . ." Radiance looked off moodily. "The thing is, she was fine the day before . . ." She cleared her throat. "She lived up there, Noola. In a little cottage just on the edge of that cliff. You can't see it from here. Just from the beach. Only in winter you can see it from here. . . . She—" Suddenly she stopped, unable to go on.

Interested, Jenny Rose leaned forward, concerned, "You loved her, did you?"

Radiance turned her back. "You are *such* a busybody! Can't a person just enjoy her privacy?"

Jenny Rose didn't buy the routine, however, for she utilized cantankerousness herself as a cover for loneliness. Undeterred, she peered with Radiance into the distance.

But Radiance stood and turned her back, remarking dismissively, "Why am I talking to you anyway?"

"The cat can well look at the queen," Jenny Rose shot back, hurt.

Misunderstanding, Radiance sputtered, "You make fun of me? Why? Because you think I'm a cleaning lady? I'm not just some cleaning lady. I'm a dancer, *comprende*?" She preened and lifted her long neck like a sassy crane.

Jenny Rose kicked her feet up and down like a child on a swing. "This is good," she protested out loud, determined despite herself. "I can't believe it. Here I am outdoors in the US, making friends."

Radiance said disdainfully, "Don't be so sure, Irish girl. Because as far as I'm concerned, you're just another white ass. Look how white you are. You're so white you're almost green!" She made a face and twisted it back and forth and imitated Jenny Rose's assertive tone the day before to Patsy Mooney: "*I'm Miss Jenny Rose Cashin!*" Well, I'm *Radiance Marie-Claire Piet.*"

For a moment Jenny Rose was frightened for Radiance. There was some desperation in her voice that was not equal to this conversation. She seemed possibly unhinged.

Radiance took a last theatrical drag on her cigarette and flipped the butt to the dirt with spite. "Why would I let some little painter wannabe take up my valuable time, eh? Look. Women, I don't like. They don't like me and I don't like them. Okay? You got it now?" She saw the crushed look pass on Jenny Rose's face and justified in a rush, "You just gonna stay for a minute then pick up and leave like the rest of them anyway." She gathered her things in her basket and got up to go.

The big cat Sam came around the ivy wall and sidled near. Jenny Rose wrapped one trembling arm around her knees and stroked the cat, then called after Radiance's back in a hurried afterthought, "That says more about you than it does about me, you know."

She sat there in the sudden emptiness, blinking. She would certainly not let this girl upset her. Today was a special day. Lightheartedness returned to her as she scanned the cliff path toward town. A thrill of anticipation propelled her happily forward and she stood. Today was the day. She could feel it. She would see her mother at last. All the bitterness of years gone by would be forgotten. She was grown up now, and understanding. She took the well-worn picture from her pocket and scanned it for the millionth time. It was a high school graduation picture, cracked and rubbed almost to oblivion, but it was her image. Her mother, as young as Jenny Rose was now. She could see her own reflection in the crackled plastic and she hugged herself and laughed and hurried away.

. . . It was always pleasant here between the dogwoods, he mused, lingering, pressed secretly against the bluestone wall, having enjoyed listening to the two silly bitches prattle on while he'd had his brunch. For they were candidates, weren't they? Or they would be. He would have to groom them first. He'd have to be careful. Move slowly. He turned his face to the sun. A shame not everyone could enjoy it.

He took the hansome gray glove off carefully, so as not to get it dirty, and trailed his fingers across the gritty surface of the rocks, picking up the blobs of sap fallen from the maples. He liked sap. He'd cut the maples deep, in slivers, to get at it, then bring it, sticky, up to his nose.

But it was getting cold. Time to go. He picked his bag of takeout up and tucked it under his arm, then took the rock path carefully so he wouldn't slip. Couldn't slip. Oh, no. So much to do. And now with the old bitch gone, there was nothing more to stand in his way. . . .

CHAPTER TWO

CLAIRE

I drove into Sea Cliff with no trouble at all. It was so wildly pretty and old-fashioned, I couldn't understand how I'd never been to this place; but we were South Shore people, I supposed, my Irish mother drawn to the bleak, raging, free-to-the-public ocean. This was shady and remote, off the beaten path. Only one road in and out. It was almost another world, yet it was just a mile or so this way and that with hedges and mammoth rhododendron sufficing as borders instead of fences. I was transported by the light, the mood, the screened-in porches, the names of the lamp-posted streets: Winding Way, Dubois Avenue, Bathway, Littleworth Lane. Even the trees were preposterous: oversized and elderly. I thought of Enoch, who loved trees, and for a moment before I remembered, I missed him. But I did remember, and I would be jolted into heartbreak often in the near future, I knew, until I'd gotten used to the idea. But somehow, a broken heart never seems to hinder my appetite. I parked and looked around for a place to eat. The deli looked all right. There was a good, sturdy fellow in there and he hooked me up with an eggplant, mozzarella, and roasted red pepper on brick-oven olive bread. Coffee, you helped yourself. I took it outside and passed up the benches on the square of grass before the library, instead taking the short walk past the shops to

the overlook. Benches were placed there, too, jutting out over the blue
sound. The air was charged with particles of ozone and silt and though it
was cold, it was just warm enough in the steady sunshine so you could sit
and eat. But the sea! Oh, it was glorious and navy blue.

When I finished my sandwich and coffee, I just sat there for a
while. You couldn't read the paper—it was too windy—so I decided
I'd make my way down the breathtakingly steep steps to the beach. At
the very bottom it was almost still, protected as it was in a cove. I took
off Carmela's shoes and went out to the beach. There was no one in
sight. It was cold and the wind blew fiercely, which I enjoyed. I didn't
stay there long, but I could imagine what summers here would be like.
Early morning walks. Picnics on the beach. I returned to my shoes and
hunched over to put them on, leaning against a sizable boulder. The
sound of someone playing piano drizzled from one of the far-off houses.
You can always tell if it's a real piano rather than a tape or the radio. I
don't know how but you can. I thought of Enoch, warmhearted and
courtly. I tried to conjure up some melancholy again but, at the risk of
sounding frigid—which my sister tells me I am—I didn't feel it in this
early morning change of scene. I didn't feel anything. If I was honest
with myself, I had to admit to a certain coldness on my part as well. For
hadn't sex between Enoch and me been, if friendly, also somewhat utili-
tarian and singular, like two pals getting off? You can't be someone's
back unless they are your front. And there's a safety to that. I wondered
for how long I had been this numb. Since I'd seen the light for another
woman in my husband's eyes? Yes, that could have done it. That had
hurt. So much so that I'd closed myself off. I looked up at the bright
sky with its promise of spring and I remembered that at that moment I
felt almost glad. I don't know what it was—getting away from Queens,
maybe just being in such a dramatically pretty place—but I felt free.
I heard the tight, intense hum of bees. Bees indicated life, and I was
struck by the heady, almost sickening fragrance of hibiscus. Out in the
bay, a picturesque little orange boat, empty, bobbed up and down in the
fast churning sea.

I took the steep footpath, stopping to catch my breath, and at the very top, edging over the side, a stab of red wobbling color caught my eye. A FOR SALE sign, meant to be seen from the beach, had come loose and was wriggling and about to fly off its hook. I leaned out and hitched the sign back up and looked at the tiny house. It was pale blue, no, gray, a pale gray but with a hue of blue and it had peeling white painted sills. An old-fashioned porch stole the show. The house wasn't in the least bit fancy or beautiful. Except for the porch, it was plain. Tiny. Solid. It had to be, clinging to the edge of the cliff like that. A small bird landed on the front gutter with a gathering of weed in its beak. Just beneath the porch light was a battered plaque, the way some houses announce and portray themselves. It was spelled in an antiquated hand: THE GREAT WHITE. I smiled—someone had a sense of humor—and hoisted myself over the steps to the walkway and then something in me turned me back around and I thought what the heck. . . . I scribbled down the number.

A gray-haired woman next door on the inland side was hanging a rug over the hedge. She peered at me suspiciously.

"Just taking down the number," I called.

She tipped her head in understanding and proceeded to swat her rug with an antiquated beater.

I ventured a little closer. "I don't suppose you know what they're asking?"

"Better not be much," she said in a heavy Italian accent. "She was a clutter bug. Place is a mess." She gave me the once-over, sizing me up. "Needs new gutters, too. And the boiler's all the time on the blink." We both listened to the chirp of the nesting bird.

How cold could it get? I asked myself. After all, spring was here. Why, it would soon be summer. I asked the woman if she thought they might rent. "I'd love to get a look inside."

Swatting abated, she squared her stance and scrunched her face up. "Might have missed your chance. I think the son's fed up. Said he's looking to sell. Told me he gave the house to a realtor just the other day."

"Oh." Acquiring a house on the water, even a paltry one, would be way above my budget. Feeling oddly let down, I thanked her and started to walk away.

"Of course, if you want to go talk to him, he'll be down the marina. . . . Still might be there."

I hesitated. My better judgment warned me, *Don't you go starting all over again with one of your harebrained schemes.*

"Hey!" The woman put one hand up to shade her eyes and another heavily on my shoulder and she gasped, "Look there! It's a blue heron!"

Just above our heads an impossibly heavy, prehistoric-looking bird flew low above us in a slow-motion, long-stroked way. It looked right at us. "Wow!" I said.

"*Madonna mia*," the woman said as she grabbed hold of me. "You don't think it's a spirit of someone?"

"I've never heard that. I've never even seen one!" I cried. "And so close!"

"Did you see? She looked right at us!"

We stood watching the empty sky long after it had passed, both of us enthralled. I looked back at the little house. This whole place would be transformed by summer to a tourist town. Suppose I could think up some sort of business. . . . Well, what? Stranger things have happened. Let's face it—nothing wonderful was waiting for me back in Queens. I dug into my purse for a pen. "What's the man's name?"

"The man?" She was still frightened by what seemed to her a mythological apparition.

"Who owns the cottage?" I prompted.

"Oh. Donovan," she said, returning to the real world. "Noola's son, Morgan Donovan. You ask anyone for Noola's son's—Morgan's—boat. He owns the house now. But I got to warn you. Noola's ghost"—she thought she'd help me out by adding—"she's come and go with the fog. Late at night, I hear . . ." She leaned in, close and garlicky. ". . . something bad!"

The first happy aspect of being on my own took shape. No sensible man to put an end to my dream just because of something so provincial as a ghost. After all, I harrumphed to myself, knowing more at that time than I realized, it's not of the dead we must fear, but the living.

In no time at all I sat in the Once Upon a Moose and waited for Jenny Rose. You've never seen a place like the Moose. There are antiques and white lattices and climbing ivy, glittering curiosities and collectibles, and ladies' old-fashioned hats along the walls. This afternoon it was practically empty; one elegant couple sat at a wrought-iron table at the other side of the room. The man, I noted, was prosperous looking, gleamingly Rolexed, a certain sort of handsome. Norwegian looking. A scant portly. I couldn't see his companion as she had her back to me, but she wore a green loden mantle and hat, the sort of thing you'd see in Germany. Very attractive, I thought idly, and then was amused to see him glance furtively to the side and pass her a short stack of bills. She took it without hesitation. At once I turned away discreetly. The young woman in the loden mantle stood, slipped out the door, and hurried up the street. I'd chosen the cozy bay-window seat at the far end that looked out at the town square, had ordered tea, and was thinking Jenny Rose was going to take one look at me and her face would fall. That's basically what happened.

The glass door sprung open, jingling with a rope of bells, and in she walked. Her eyes took several seconds to adjust to the dark, then swept the room and she caught sight of me. Her face didn't change, but her hazel eyes went sort of dead. She looked so young. Well, she is so young. I stood up, tripped over my own two feet, and made it across the room to give her a hug. She hugged me back all right. But on her way to my shoulder she let her guard down and I caught a clear glimpse of her disappointment. It didn't take her long to adjust her face into a pleasant expression. We sat down. I took my time explaining, giving her a chance to get herself together. Jenny Rose chewed her lip and listened as I rambled on. Finally she shrugged. "I didn't really expect her, you know."

You knew the kid was lying and her nonchalance was put on. "Well, she didn't know," I defended Carmela.

"Yeah, I just thought I'd take a chance." She lit a cigarette and the owner—an interesting-looking lady with Veronica Lake hair and red lipstick—clicked her tongue and frowned pointedly.

"You can't smoke in restaurants," I hissed.

"You're joking. How do you eat?"

I patted my hefty tummy. "We manage."

Jenny Rose stomped out her cigarette and, still pulling herself together, stared out the window. I tried not to focus on the henna brace-let and the chipped blue nail polish, the black eyeliner and mascara. Actually, I was relieved there were no piercings other than the three in each earlobe. "I see you got a new tattoo." I sighed, regarding the color-ful rock star on her arm.

"Actually I painted it on, with makeup. Looks real, right?"

"Yes, it does," I marveled. "Listen, Jenny Rose, Carmela's expected back in a couple of weeks," I said hopefully. "My sister Zinnie got mar-ried to a fancy Italian, I must say. Carmela was having a difficult time finishing a book, and Zinnie invited her there to work on it. Do her good. You know."

"Uh-huh." She whittled away at a last strand of blue nail polish with her teeth.

Together our heads turned to the empty piazza across the way. We watched the flags and window-box petunias ripple in the high wind. "Doesn't feel much like spring yet, but Memorial Day's coming up," I encouraged. "Everything changes."

We both moved unfamiliarly in our chairs. Outside, the cold sun glared on the empty road. Here in the Moose it was dark and cozy and smelled of butternut soup. A young man brought the tea in a sweet pot with roses. The cups were delicate, thin lipped and roomy.

"Oh, at last." Jenny Rose smiled gratefully. She drank it down scald-ing hot.

I sipped my tea. I'd had enough of polite discomfort. "Jenny Rose, I'm not glad this happened, that Carmela wasn't here, but I'm so incred-ibly pleased to see you. My children are both away at school and—well, your coming happens at a perfect time for me—"

Suddenly she took out her pad, knocking half the contents of her bag onto the floor in the process then scrambling to throw them back in untidily, and I thought she was going to write down my number, but instead she began sketching the interior of the restaurant. She did this with one foot up on the rung of a chair but otherwise inconspicuously and with an almost furious intent, reminding me of myself when I was just starting out, always photographing everything, no matter where I went. At last she said, "Wait until you see Twillyweed—the house where I'm working. There are onion-heads on turrets! It's a trip."

"May I come? Are you settled in?"

"Not really. They've stuck me in the basement. Well. It's not as bad as it sounds. It's just—"

"My sister said that you've taken a job as an au pair." I realized I'd said *my sister* instead of *your mother*, but no need to start things off on the wrong foot.

"Yeah. They hustled the little boy off to bed before we could have much of a gab." She scratched her cheek. "Cute as a button. They have him in school all day, can you believe it? At four! Well, almost five. He's adopted. No sign of the mother. And no one about but the help. Where do people get off having kids if they're not going to stick around and bother with them?"

We both thought of Carmela, who'd done neither.

She frowned. "And it's kind of creepy. Like there's a *secret* up there or something." She shrugged dismissively then glanced at her watch.

I cleared my throat. "Do you have to get back right away?"

"I must stop in and show my face to a Mrs. Lassiter at the rectory, Deirdre's old kick from back home. I ought to bring her flowers or a bottle of perfume, what do you think?"

"Oh, flowers are always nice."

"Yeah, right. And I thought I'd look around for some drop cloths and turpentine and rags."

"I passed a hardware store coming into town," I said.

"That'll do for a start."

The good thing about somebody else's troubles is that you quickly forget about your own. Watching her swift movements with the pencil, I mentioned, "When I met you, you were just a teenager, but even then you showed the promise of becoming a really talented artist."

"Yeah. Real talented. Couldn't even pay the rent it turns out."

"Jenny Rose! I can still remember that painting of three fish you did! So full of imagination and color and depth! Please don't tell me you're not painting all the time!"

She shrugged. "I'm painting. I've just lost my cocksureness, I guess." She grinned, looking me dead in the eye. "That would be a good thing, you'll be telling me."

"No. You need to be brash in this world of hope dousers."

"Yeah." Her voice was bitter. "There'll be plenty a them."

Together our heads turned to the empty piazza across the way. *Funny*, I thought, *she doesn't have Carmela's knockout beauty, but she's captivating. She has charm. She's not burdened with self-consciousness but has that sporty, boyish way about her—not masculine, though she is graceful as a young boy is graceful.* She just didn't have girlish airs, probably because of the ways of those two Irish lesbians from the countryside who had raised her. There was something about her. It made me furious to think she'd been hurt. I knew Jenny Rose was quick to answer back. She had a sassy edge and a fresh mouth that was sure to get her into trouble, but she was a good-hearted kid. You could never say she wasn't.

I thought of something else. I ventured, "There was a guy, I seem to remember?"

Jenny Rose shook her head. "*Ach.* There was him and there was me and there was the girl I was painting. This all was in the south of France, mind. Him speaking French and me not." She gave a false laugh of bravado, then her eyes clouded, childlike and vulnerable. "Aw, I might as well tell you. I'd been having a terrible time of it, got turned down by a gallery in Cannes, the one gallery I really wanted. Like I had this dream my stuff would hang there in the window, you know? The gallery owner held my paintings up and ridiculed them." Her eyes glazed over in misery at the memory. "And then I came home, really down, see, only to come in and find them not talking. You know what I mean . . . that loud silence that says something's been going on before you walked in. Then there's the bed made that's never been made before." She shrugged. "And the smell of it. It was there in the room like a thing. *Ach*. I just knew."

"What did you do?"

"I beat her up."

We looked at each other for a long moment and then I burst out laughing. I love the Irish part of my family with all my heart. I really do. I wiped my eyes. "So where is he now?"

"Oh, wait. Here's the best part. He was so worried about the poor dear—Chantal, that's her name—when I knocked her about, he drove her to the hospital. And there's me standing there watching him drive her away."

"Well . . . er . . . how badly was she hurt?"

"Sure, it was nothing. A couple of teeth. It was my hand he should have been worrying about, my selling my pictures was what kept us in baguettes and Brie if the truth be told." She looked at her fist. "I was dead certain I'd busted it."

"But it's all right?"

"Yeah." She turned it around admiringly. "No harm done. It was his ring knocked her teeth out, not me poor knuckles. I left the fuckin' thing in one of his shoes and the both of them to it. Took my painting stuff and hitchhiked around the Mediterranean, got a job as an au pair down there with a lovely Turkish family, on the southern coast near Ephesus. Side, the town was. I thought he was out of my system by Christmas and I went home. Don't you know he was there in Skibbereen with her! They'd opened a pub. A pub!" She snorted with disdain. Then she muttered, "His mother had set them up. She never did like me, the mother. Never thought me good enough, me coming from a house of raging lesbians and no money to speak of. And him with all his talk of becoming a great chef! I couldn't bear to walk past their bloody love nest. And there's everyone boasting about how grand it was. Even my own adoptive mum, Deirdre. 'Ooh, you'll get the tastiest salmon in three ports at the White Tree!' She'd rave about the place! That's what they called it: the White Tree. After his mother's family." She paused and added, "Protestants," and I hoped she wasn't going to spit. But she only gave a morose shrug and said, "That's when I got to thinking it was time I looked up my blood mother." She put her tongue in her cheek and winked. "She might be bad and all, but I can't imagine her eating at the White Tree. I had this feeling it would stick in her throat."

I said a silent prayer that when Jenny Rose did meet Carmela, she wouldn't be too disappointed. Carmela had a way of making you think you were going to be best friends and then you might not see her for months. I suppose it would have been the perfect moment to confide what had happened to me with Enoch. But I didn't. I'm not sure why. Still very raw, it was, I guess. And—you know me—a part of me feeling guilty, maybe, like I was involved in a conspiracy. I kept it in.

Jenny Rose busied herself with her pencil. "And here I am. So."

"Well, how did you come upon Sea Cliff anyway?" I changed the subject.

"That was because my adoptive mother, Deirdre, is pen pals with the rectory lady here, and Mr. Cupsand—that's my boss—needed someone because the wife took off with another man!"

"The old story," I interjected bitterly.

"Yeah." She lowered her voice. "And on top she made off with the family jewels!"

I gave a low appreciative whistle. "Want something to eat?"

"Nah." She made a face.

I leaned across to the neighboring table for some more of the tasty honey. But with the gesture I caught sight of what Jenny Rose was doing. She'd dashed off the whole other side of the restaurant in deft strokes, capturing all the curious paraphernalia in perfect detail.

"Your turn," she was saying. "Did you make your comeback as a photographer like you planned?"

"Well, no. I guess you heard about my divorce and my catastrophe of a bed-and-breakfast?"

"No." She looked up, frankly interested. "Not a bit of it."

"Nothing's turned out exactly as I'd planned, either. The truth is, I'm unemployed. I have no idea what I'm going to do with the rest of my life and I just found out my fiancé is gay."

"You don't say!"

"I do."

"Couldn't you tell, Auntie Claire? How daft can you be?"

I'm embarrassed to say my mouth quivered. "It seems you can live with a person and never know a single thing about who they really are!" I could feel the tears getting ready to let loose down my cheeks.

But Jenny Rose encouraged, "That's it. Cry. It will do you good." With permission, it's almost impossible to cry so I did not. I blew my nose into my napkin. Jenny Rose made a face. "We're a fine pair, we are." But my news seemed to have cheered her up. Together we had a rueful laugh, and I knew things were going to be all right between us. I noticed the young fellow who'd served us the tea was banging his tray lightly against his knees while he stood watching us. He had a handsome face with light blue eyes and dirty blond hair.

"British, are you?" he asked us.

"Fuck, no." Jenny Rose scowled. "We're Irish."

"Oh," he said.

The other customer, disgruntled that the server was paying him no attention, threw his left arm out to examine his watch in a display of irritation, gave an adamant call for his check, paid, and left. Then three more customers came in so the young man didn't say any more, but when we were about to leave, he came over and asked Jenny Rose if he could see the drawing she'd done.

"Sure," she said, handing it over as she stood.

"But," he marveled, "this is wonderful!"

"Keep it."

"Oh, but I didn't mean—"

"No, really. Keep it."

"Thank you," he murmured wonderingly. He stood watching her go, she oblivious to his admiring expression. She sauntered off in that way she had, generous and carefree and good in her skin, unselfconscious, a kid on a soccer field.

"He was very keen," I remarked when we stood squinting at each other outside in the sunshine, "and good looking."

"Sweet." The way she said it explained him away with all the worldweary offhandedness of the young. I looked back at the young man, conscientiously returned to his work now. He wore no earrings or tattoos or other bad boy accoutrements to signal and lure a young girl artist like Jenny Rose. He wasn't cool, but serious and intent. Nice. The kiss of death.

"Well . . ." Jenny Rose hoisted her backpack up onto her shoulder and smiled. "It was grand to see you. Do you think you'll come out here again?"

"I was thinking I'd poke around Sea Cliff." I remembered the cottage but decided it would be silly to mention it. It would most likely come to nothing. I shrugged. "Wait around for you to get off tonight. Take you to dinner, if you're not too tired."

Her hazel eyes lit up. "I thought you said you had no money."

"Oh, I have money. I just don't have *money*."

"Oh. Okay. Yeah, that'll be great."

We traded cell-phone numbers and the both of us hurried off, the young man watching us go from the window.

JENNY ROSE

She took the long way down to the pier. Her knees were trembling, and her heart thudded with disappointment. She'd just lollygag pointlessly around the marina, she told herself, having no heart to go shopping or visit the rectory. Aunt Claire was great, a real doll, but—Jenny Rose stopped on the shore and lit a cigarette—she'd been so sure she'd get to meet her mother. So sure! She pressed her back against a piling, sank down onto the dock, and looked up at the moving sky. There was no comfort. She felt nothing but desolate. If she'd had a joint, she'd have smoked it. Feeling herself watched, she looked up. There was that guy again. That cute guy on the pirate ship, now tethered to the dock. With something like rebellion, she jutted her chin out and stared right back at him and with no more encouragement than that, he hoisted himself over the prow of his boat and came across to her, moving with an elegant, catlike poise.

"What's your name?" was the first thing out of the side of his mouth. The emphasis was on the *your*. Like she was next in line.

"Jenny Rose," she answered, her eyes on the level of his worn, black jeans, "Jenny Rose Cashin. What's yours?"

"Malcolm McGlintock. But you can call me Glinty."

She looked him up and down with more coolness than she felt. He was, she smirked to herself, right up her alley.

"Here on vacation?"

You could get arrested for working without papers. "Sort of," she replied, smiling.

He tipped his head. "Irish?"

"Yeah. Scots?"

"That's right." His eyes circled her slowly, assessing her, taking in the tattoo, the devil-may-care eyes. She was thin, but curvy. Suddenly the sun broke through. Liking what he saw, he said, "Wanna see my boat?"

She let him pull her up. "Why not?"

They walked together across the reach, the glare so bright you could hardly see. Jenny Rose followed him along the heaving dock and onto his sloop. The boat was a two-master, painted all black, *The Black Pearl Is Mine*, with a white stripe of a railing, pine-colored wood on the deck with faded Moroccan red sails when they were unfurled, tied up neatly now. Jenny Rose felt herself go weightless with the ebb and flow of the deck, the sound of the bay sloshing against the prow. She followed him, this perfect stranger, beautiful as he was, down the hatch and into the cabin, with his long, lustrous black hair, and for a moment she thought of her mother, never there, never there for her, not even now after she'd come so far across the ocean. She touched his sleeve and he turned around and she raised her chin and opened her mouth and, understanding what she wanted, he kissed her. Through the grinding cloth she felt the stirring of his erection. Their eyes caught in the dark and now, winding into the rickety tight galley and before she could catch her breath, he fell with her onto the bunk, pinning her under him, kissing her neck while they undid each other's jeans. His skin was milky white and dense, almost silver, with a fray of black hairs in a silky trail leading down. She saw him only swiftly, his pendulum toward her, as he lifted her leg and moved forward into her, his wet eyes catching hold of hers in the dark cabin. There was a moment when she flew away, propelled, and then, brought back to that elegant moment of staggering bliss, erupted. She'd felt that before, but never with someone, always alone under covers in her bed, and she pivoted into a frenzy of stillness, a clenching and then a gush without warning.

"Jenny Rose," he whispered and flinched.

She was still in a spasm. She locked her knees up and she rattled again. "Oh, my God," she breathed out, trickling down.

"Wow," he said, turning her face. "Most girls don't get there so quick."

And she shuddered again.

"That was awesome," he said, getting up. He went into the head.

She got sober quick. "Fuck," she said, remembering. Patsy Mooney would be waiting, wondering what she was up to. She reached for her jeans. He was still in the loo. "I've got to go," she called in.

"Okay," he called out. No *Hold on, I'll walk you home.*

She felt in the dark for her boots, grabbed her jacket, still trembling with the spinning of it, into the blinding brilliant sunlight. Just get away quick was all she could think. On the ladder over the side she hesitated. Just in case he would call up to her. No. No sound. She'd left her panties on the floor. Damn. Nobody around. A crass sound made her jump and she looked up on the prow, but it was only a crane, a small rangy one, watching her. A baby one, maybe. She buttoned up her jean jacket. She ran, footfalls muffled on the deck, past the spot on the beach from where she'd first seen him, alluring and smirking. The wind hit her and she was cold again now, so she continued running, under the cover of sunlight and end-of-May wet wind, up the hill, way, way up the hill to somewhere else, anywhere but here and who she knew she was.

CLAIRE

I hung around, spent the day poking around the town, exploring the shops and the library, thinking I might run into Jenny Rose, but I never did. The low clouds had moved along and the evening was sunlit by the time I made my way down to the marina. It was a good way by foot and I was reminded again just how out of shape I'd become. There was a parking lot and then seven or eight rows of boats. I went into a restaurant called the Hideaway that catered to the sailors and occasional townies. It wasn't serving dinner yet but someone who looked like he might be the owner—collared shirt and mildly prosperous looking— was sitting there with another man, a delivery man in a route uniform.

"Excuse me." I approached their table in the sudden dark and asked if they knew Noola's son's boat. They both shrugged. Behind the bar a wiry old fellow in an undershirt was carting a full pail of calamari entrails. He dumped the slimy lot into a bin, covered it, and shut it tight, then pulled a stogie from his mouth, and said to no one in particular, "That'll be Morgan Donovan's boat."

"Oh, *Morgan!*" they both said at once, sitting taller with the sure air of respect. They pointed me over toward the third dock. "He's got that forty-foot sloop out there, the *Gnomon*. She's docked right next to the schooner, the *For Sail*. Get it?" The route guy spelled it out. "For *S-A-I-L*?"

"Ha-ha. I get it. Thanks." I took off down the walkway and checked off the names of one pretty boat after the next. I don't know anything about boats except I like to be on one. This sloop was navy blue and white and clean as a whistle. The *Gnomon*. It rocked gently in the flood of evening gold. "Hello!" I called. "Mr. Donovan!" There seemed to be no one there. I didn't like to peek below deck. There was a bell, a big brass one, up on the deck and I climbed on board and pulled its cord so it clanged.

A man's head popped up, surprised, and whacked on the beam. "Jesus Christ!" he shouted, rubbing his head. He was a onetime red-headed, now amber-haired fellow, weathered tan from years of sun and fuzzed with gold. My first thought was, *Uh-oh, he looks like a golfer.*

"What the hell's wrong with you?" he yelled, and in what sounded to me like a Scottish accent he raved on, "Can't you give a cry out before you come on board? You scared the crap out of me!"

"I did." I took two steps back. "You're wearing earphones!"

"What?" His eyes were greenish gold.

"I said you're wearing earphones!"

"Oh!" He slipped them off and threw them violently down on his bench. "Well, you've done a fine job messing up me varnish!"

I looked down and behind me and saw my own footprints. "Oh my gosh! I'm so sorry."

"Women." He shook his head scornfully. And with that he picked me up bodily, flung me over his shoulder, and put me over the side.

"Hey! Let me go!" I protested, but he already had.

"It took me two hours to finish that job!" he flashed angrily.

"Well, you should have put up a sign!" I shrieked with injured pride.

He held up the pertinent sign he must have been working on when I'd surprised him. Only the last *N* and *T* were missing. His face was all sucked in with fury. "What the hell do you want, anyway?" he growled.

I spat on a tissue and wiped his red paint print from my arm. "I was wondering what you're doing with the cottage up on the cliff."

He searched my eyes for a long moment and held them. Then with this crushed look he turned from me. He sort of sagged.

I remembered what the neighbor had said. His mother only dead three weeks. "Look . . ." I stammered, "I'm really sorry. I sure know how to start off on the wrong foot. I'll come back later." I don't know what I thought he'd do. Say something conciliatory, I guess. But he whirled on me and shouted, "Just don't come back at all. Just leave well enough alone!"

"Okay. Okay." I tried to sound soothing and I tripped, backward, away up the deck. *Sheesh*, I thought, rubbing my arm, *what a grouch!* I cleared the marina and stomped back up the beach road, but for the life of me I couldn't remember which cliff stairs I'd come down. All I could think was what an unnecessarily rude, cantankerous man he was! And so strong, picking me up like that! He'd made me feel like a foolish little girl. I realized I was trembling. I stopped walking and sank down onto the nearest bottom step and as I did so I heard a harsh ripping sound. It was my pants. Or should I say, Carmela's (that I hadn't yet mentioned to her that I'd borrowed) good interview pants. They were split soundly up the back. If I'd have had a cigarette, I think I'd have smoked it. And now the best part, Carmela's fancy shoes—the ones she was so finicky about—were absolutely crusted with varnish. They looked caramelized. It all seemed to catch up with me. My marriage. Now Enoch. I let my head down and this time I did cry, cried my heart out, my face cradled on my knees at the bottom of the dock shelf. I just collapsed and crumpled into a mush of mascara raccoon eyes and tears. Then, just to make everything perfect, the man from the boat, Morgan whatever his name was, came up the road. He was carrying my purse.

"I believe this belongs to you," he said and plunked it down at my feet, removing his eyes from the sorry sight of me. But I was beyond caring. My nose, he didn't have to tell me, was running like a hose. A hose! I collapsed again into wretched sobs.

He handed me his handkerchief and squared his fists to his hips, seemingly oblivious to my hysterics. "I keep telling you people to leave me alone. Don't you have any respect?" he went on. "You people think all I'm interested in is the lure of your money."

I reared up in dismay. "Hold on a second." I snorted disdainfully, for I, too, am (or was) a hotheaded red-head. "While *we people* demystify our-our-our tantalizing allure." I gave a meaningful good honk into his pristine handkerchief, dredged up what was left of my shreds of dignity, and stood to go. My feet, however, were already stuck to the ground with his quick drying varnish and I fell like a tree on my nose.

JENNY ROSE

She hung up the phone. No answer. Again. All evening she'd been calling, and here it was night. This was odd. She wouldn't have pegged Auntie Claire as one to let you down. She went upstairs to the kitchen. Wendell was still sitting at the table with Patsy Mooney. He was eating creamed corn with a spoon and picking at a saucer of torn-up little bits of deli ham. He was having trouble with the spoon, however, and the creamed corn leaked onto the tablecloth.

"Not like that." Patsy Mooney picked his little hand up and smacked it.

The little boy did nothing. Said nothing. He was locked in a shell.

Jenny Rose strolled in. "Hello." She smiled and sat down next to him.

"He don't like to be talked to while he's eating." Patsy Mooney leaned over and mopped the table around Wendell's plate. "Don't you get up until you finish every bit of what's on that plate, mister," she said, aiming her pointer finger at the boy.

"Oh, go soak your head," Jenny Rose said.

"Excuse me? What was that?"

Jenny Rose batted her eyelashes innocently. "What? No, nothing. So. Wendell. Would you like to go for a stroll?"

"A walk?" Patsy Mooney shrieked. "In the dark? He gotta finish his supper!"

"Where's your jumper, cookie?" Jenny Rose took the boy by the hand. "Your sweater?"

"And he got his programs to watch!"

Wendell slipped to the floor and they went out into the hall where he pointed to the mackintosh hung on the coat tree.

"Close enough," Jenny Rose said and unhooked the thing and put it on the boy. It practically reached the floor, but he'd be warm.

Patsy Mooney trotted after them and ranted on, "I'm not taking this crap just because Mr. Cupsand is in the city and isn't here to see! You doing whatever you feel like! Radiance taking off without even asking! Mr. Piet taking the car! What the hell do I look like? What'll Mr. Cupsand say?" She sank onto the hallway chair. "Now Noola's dead it's all gone wrong."

He wasn't sure what would happen next, the boy, but Jenny Rose had the distinct feeling he was game. He watched them both from behind his thick glasses, his bad eye dancing with the stress and his lips pulled tight, like closed purse strings. Jenny Rose put her own soft beret on the boy's feathery hair and out they went, down the great steps. They walked along, hand in hand, under the glittering branches. Jenny Rose could smell the earth, rich and loamy. She wasn't going to bring up the stones. Not yet. One thing at a time. There were plenty of houses to look into. The moon was a sickle but bright. "That's an American sky, Wendell. And a new moon," Jenny Rose informed him, remembering her Sikh driver. "Good luck."

She began to hum. And then, just when she thought the kid had started to cry and she felt her heart sink, she heard the shred of a tinny sound of a sort of a hum. Like a song. Not a song, but almost.

CLAIRE

He'd driven me very swiftly, I must say, to the hospital. I'd telephoned my mother on the way to tell her I'd be staying out here with Jenny Rose.

"Jenny Rose, is it?" My mother flew into a rage. "You've been drinking! I can hear it in your voice. Drinking and driving! What kind of a good influence is that?!"

I'd shifted the paper towel wad soaked with blood from my nose so she'd understand me. "Yes, Mother," I'd agreed, just to spare her a sleepless night, "that's why I can't be driving anywhere. I'll call you tomorrow."

Morgan had stuck me on top of a blanket in his car—his precious upholstery to be protected—maneuvered me into the emergency room, stayed at my elbow while they'd signed me in, and then he'd walked out and left me there. He should have called an ambulance because then they take you first. I was good and sorry for myself, let me tell you, and I wanted, for the time being, to stay that way.

They did their battery of outlandishly expensive, agonizingly long tests that go on sporadically through the night and always just when you're dropping off. I checked my cell phone. Not one message! I yearned for a toothbrush and a change of clothes. It was my second day, now, in Carmela's go-to-the-city-look-for-a-job clothes. But I couldn't call her. Both my sisters were in Italy, remember, dining on anchovies and Gorgonzola. Drinking wine from Orvieto. I was all alone. *Nobody cares*, I thought as I sniveled. I waited and waited, crackers from painkillers, for the plastic surgeon to come and have a look at me. Sprawled on my creaking gurney, I floated in and out of a doze while the night passed in white emergency light North Shore noise.

JENNY ROSE

She woke up with a start. Something . . . God! What was it? From the scant green luminescence of the clock she could make out the form of the big cat on her chest. He was standing on top of her, looking into her face. Sam. For one groggy moment she looked back at him. "Jesus!" she cried out and knocked him off her. "What the fuck are you doing in here?"

She'd been dreaming she was standing on a chimney and the chimney was going to give way. There'd been a squirrel in there, making a terrible sound. The chimney had melted, sort of, and then crumpled beneath her. It must have been the cat making that sound. She looked at the clock. Five thirty-three. She'd never get back to sleep now. She sat up, swinging her legs over the side. Was it morning or night? She hated this room. Hated it. You couldn't tell if it was dark or light out! She threw off her bedclothes and shivered, then dressed in a pair of jeans and a warm sweatshirt.

She crept up the stairs and creaked open the door. It was almost morning but too early to go bonking around the kitchen. She'd wake someone for sure. She put her socks and sneakers on. The cat streaked past her, almost knocking her over. She went to let him out the back door, bumped into a stool, tried again for the door, but then a sixth sense made the hairs stand up on her neck. "Hello?" she whispered. She waited. No one. Outside the wind sent up a pale whistle. "Shite, I'm daft!" she cursed and went to open the door. The knob would not turn. She looked over her shoulder then tried the knob again. The cat waited and slunk between her legs. She remembered you had to turn the lock left. It made a crunching sound and opened. The fog slipped in. The cat went out and disappeared into the dark and she followed. For some reason she felt safer outside. She kept a cap crumpled in her sweatshirt pocket and popped it on her head, then stood still for a moment getting her bearings. The rose garden was loopy with fog shrouds. She found the cliff with her eyes and went the other way toward the road. It had rained and a sense of relief filled her as her feet sunk into the drive; she broke into a run. That was it. She'd have a fine run before the day began, one up on the rest of the world. She took the beach steps down and wangled her way over the salmon-bright rafters of buoys left out there to dry, then trod with heavier footfalls along the sand.

Jenny Rose ran for as long as one could go without coming to the outward jut of the marina, the end of the point, then circled and made her way back to the cliff. A wisp of light in the east congratulated her. She was in fine shape. Wherever she'd lived, she'd run whenever she could. You had to make yourself—that was the thing. The madder you were at the world, then the faster you ran. She scanned the marina for *The Black Pearl Is Mine* but it wasn't there. Good. A loose sailor, that's what he was. She must have been out of her mind. She hoped to God he hadn't given her syphilis. Of course it was better this way. What kind of a girl would he think she was? The kind she indeed was, it turned out. She laughed out loud with caustic unfamiliarity and heard herself. The light was coming swifter now, a dull and unconfirmed color. A dog was out in the bay swimming in the lapping waves. A golden. She smiled, running, and sparked her step. No, it wasn't a dog. She stopped where she was, bent from her waist, gasping hard now. She was tired. It wasn't a dog. She stepped forward, her head before her, trying to make it out . . . A momentary flash of something. It looked like . . . a person!

Whoever it was disappeared and for a moment. She told herself it must have been a seal. That was it. No one swam in this weather. But she peered harder, straining her eyes and craning. Then, far out, an arm came up, reaching. A glint of bracelet caught the light then dropped and was swallowed up. Jenny Rose scudded forward. It was a woman. Drowning!

She looked frantically left and right, but there was no one. "Oh, my God," she said and waved back. But now there was no wave, no answer. She looked again right and left for someone to help, but seeing not a soul, she skipped to the shoreline, hopping on each foot, yanking off her sneakers and red sweatshirt and jeans, casting them into the sand.

The shock of the cold water was nothing in comparison to the fear of what she would do when she got there. What if the person pulled her down? That's what they said happens. She was so scared she didn't even think to pray. Getting there seemed to take forever. It was like in a dream when you move so slowly, so slowly. She kept going, giving it all she had. When she got to the place she had aimed for, there was nothing. God. Nothing. She flailed around, feeling for life. Nothing. Nothing. A hank of seaweed brushed her and she grabbed hold of it to fling it away, then pulled it up and screamed with fright when it came with a face like a watery grave, eyes open, gaping at her, then suddenly it vomited bracken and choked with a horrible but living gasp and she saw it was Radiance. Radiance!

Jenny Rose was ready to punch her to keep her from pulling them both down, but then Radiance slunk in her arms, passing out. Jenny Rose grappled for a hold under her arms. She tried to tow her in. She kept going under, though, so she had to hoist Radiance faceup onto her shoulders and tread water toward shore. She was aware the tide was going in. Thank God for that. She couldn't have done it with the tide against her, she knew it. She kept having to stop and lurch upward for air. Twice she thought it was hopeless, she'd never get her in. Once Radiance half rallied and struggled wildly, but Jenny Rose got hold of her hair and pulled her by it until she dropped, giving Jenny Rose moments to get her hand under Radiance's chin and then, sideways, she swam them both in.

When she got near the shore, she thought they'd be safe, that someone would come, but no one was there. Her heart sank. She could just see the sun breaking into the eastern sky—it was just coming up—and she staggered, pulling them both onto dry ground. They lay there for moments, maybe minutes, Jenny Rose gasping and Radiance now waking with the feel of solid ground beneath her, stunned, retching onto the sand on all fours then collapsing. Jenny Rose staggered down the stretch of beach to where her jeans and red sweatshirt lay, praying her cell phone was still in her pocket and not landed in the water when she'd flung it off. She flinched, her foot cut by something, but she staggered on, crab-walking, crouched over, to get to the red fabric landmark. The phone was there. She was trembling, shaking so hard now, the slippery wet cell phone lurching up into the air the moment she clutched it. She caught it by reflex alone, barely able to hold on to the thing while her purple-and-yellow cold finger frantically hammered out 911.

CLAIRE

It was early next morning when the plastic surgeon finally arrived, looked me over, and declared me fit without professional reparations. The medics were bringing in a drowning and the whole place was in an uproar, so I gathered my stuff and moved to the waiting room. I was about to call a cab to get me back to Sea Cliff, when the reason for all my troubles strode into the hospital lobby. He sidestepped and navigated easily through the turnstile door.

"How's the nose?" he greeted me cheerfully.

"Great. I always wanted a nose job."

"They said it wasn't broken." He frowned, the lines around his eyes crinkling. He'd shaved and showered, it seemed. I scowled at his alert, well-rested self, his clean shirt and leather bomber jacket, his big chunky head and small ears. He was as tan as an overdone biscuit and had eyes the color of . . . well, I'd never seen eyes just that color. I didn't know what they were. All I knew was that they weren't going to get me in trouble. No, sir. I wasn't sure why I was so mad at him. He had, after all, brought me here after my fall, but he prickled me in some visceral way. I vaguely remembered hollering crazily at him yesterday. And he'd then left me here. Well, he didn't know me from Adam, did he? But, I realized, he must have called to inquire about my nose. All right, so it wasn't broken, but I did have two black eyes. My pants were still ripped.

I was glad, at least, that I was wearing a long blouse under my jacket, untucked now, pregnancy style, which covered my tailpipe. The young lady at the information desk was tapping her hair—always a giveaway. She twinkled admiringly at this, this big lug, and he smiled charmingly back. I had no idea why such behavior would catapult me into a rage. I clung to my prescriptions and my purse and drooped unhappily. She could certainly have him. All I wanted was to get out of the place and go—where? Where was I going?

"C'mon." He hoisted me into an about-face and escorted me out the swivel door.

"Stop *doing* that!" I yanked my arm away from his, but I went along with him. He did owe me a ride if nothing else.

Not bothering to park in the lot, he'd left his car right in front of the ER. He drove an old black Saab 900 convertible and hadn't bothered to put the top back up.

"It might have rained while you were in there," I scolded sanctimoniously.

"Nah. Won't rain. Rain's over."

"Ah." I looked up at the filthy sky and shivered. "And you know this because . . ."

"Got one a those weather sticks from Maine. Never wrong. So. Where to?"

I blinked indecisively, caught between wanting to know about the magical weather stick and wondering where I should go first. He had his brawny arms resting on the steering wheel, the wrists furry with dark gold. He looked about my age. I knew his type. Men like him always dated girls in their thirties. Not that I cared. Yesterday morning at just this time I'd been treated to a visual of Enoch's diverse tastes. Was it only yesterday morning? No, it was the morning before, two days ago. *I must change these clothes*, I reminded myself, past tiredness. "If it wouldn't be too much trouble, back to Sea Cliff." My cell phone rang.

"Hello?" I shouted.

"Aunt Claire! It's Jenny Rose. I'm fine," she shouted back.

"Oh, good. Look, I'm sorry about last night," I blurted, "but something happened—"

"To my mother?"

"What? No. No, of course not. You sound upset," I said, covering my ear to the wind.

"I waited for you. I've been calling and calling! So much has happened!"

"Really?" I held my phone out to look at it. Twelve messages had popped up at once. Then I realized cell phones don't work in the hospital. "I'm on my way to Sea Cliff. Are you free?"

"I've got the kid," she shouted. "Come over later to Twillyweed, if you can."

"Okay. Are you sure you're all right?"

She laughed. "Bloody freezing. I've had quite a morning! But I'll be glad to see you!"

"Me, too." I closed the phone. "My niece," I explained but said no more. Once he dropped me off I'd never see him again. We were on open road and the fresh wind made me shiver.

"Too much?" he asked.

"No," I admitted, resting the back of my head on the leather. It felt wonderful. He handed me a scarf—his handy, girl-of-the-moment scarf, I presumed. I thought of my ex-husband and his actress girlfriend and all the heartache they'd put me through. Enoch and his present fancy. He was a snake. Men. They were all the same. "You can just let me out near the square."

"I can't very well dump you in the square, now can I? You're on painkillers. You can't drive. Look at the trouble you got in yesterday."

"Excuse me. What has one thing got to do with the other? And who got me into trouble? You did." That wasn't exactly true. I softened my tone. "Look, I'll be completely fine. My niece—that was she on the phone just now—is here from Ireland working as an au pair right in town, at a place called, if you can believe it, called Twillyweed."

He burst out laughing. "Of course she is. Where else would a niece of yours be working?"

"I don't get the joke."

"You're right there. There is no joke." He raked his fingers through his hair, "However, in light of what's happened to you, I think you do deserve an explanation."

We both settled into our seats. He began, "Ever since my mom died, these real estate people have been sending buyers over to look at the cottage. I simply *mentioned* I might want to sell. Jesus. You'd have thought I was giving away platinum bars. I thought I'd go berserk. They won't leave me alone. The phone always ringing, women like yourself climbing onto the *Gnomon*."

Women like myself!

"It was enough to make a grown man cry! Women everywhere. While I was eating. While I was in the head, for Christ's sake. It started in the funeral parlor." He evoked a high female voice, "'I'd just like to get a quick look inside!' they'd say. Is every woman on Long Island a real estate agent?"

"But I'm not—"

"I know you're not. But, you see, you certainly looked like one."

He meant my tailored conservative suit, I supposed. "These are not my clothes," I protested absurdly. "I borrowed them to go look for a job, but then—oh, what's the difference!"

He studied me with those unnerving green eyes for a moment and then went on, "I was up at the cottage and spoke to my mother's neighbor last night. She said you'd noticed the sign. You see, the thing is, I don't know what I want done with the house yet. I don't know if I want to sell or keep it or what. What I really need is to rent it. Until I can get it cleared out, though, I can't." He scratched his head. *In five years he'll go bald*, I thought with satisfaction.

"I live on the *Gnomon*," he went on, "but that doesn't mean one day I wouldn't want to have a cozy port in a storm. It's a good structure, that. Built to last. And on the water, isn't it?"

I said nothing. My brain was going ahead of me a mile a minute. Imagine I could stay there for a while, it was telling me. But of course that would be too good to be true. . . .

"Suppose . . ." He hesitated, then finished, "I were to make you an offer?" He glanced at me as we sped along. "Maybe work out a deal where you could stay at the house while I figure things out."

I straightened my spine. "How long were you thinking?"

He shrugged. "I don't know. Till the fall anyway."

"But how much were you thinking?"

He looked at me. "I wouldn't be able to pay much. It would be more like a house-sitting job till I could sort through the tons of stuff she's got. I'd need a lot of help with that."

Then idiot me says, "Hold on. Pay? You mean you would *pay* me to stay there?"

"You said you were looking for a job."

"I was," I admitted.

"Well, I'll be needing a woman's help. I can't go through all her things. I just can't. I don't like to use the locals. They're all so nosy. My mother's death was so"—he paused—"sudden. And people in town love to talk. I thought I'd ask at the convent but now you've turned up . . ." He threw another glance my way. "It'll take time to sort through all her stuff. She loved antiques, and the place is in a mad bit of clutter." We'd turned off the highway and the road flew by in bursts of Bradford pear. "To be honest she was turning into a pack rat. I couldn't accept rent. There's hardly room in there to swing a cat." He frowned at me over his shoulder. "But like I said. I couldn't pay much."

Jesus, Mary, and Joseph, I thought, *sounds like my ship's just come in!*

"However," he went on, "I think it only fair you see the inside before we talk a deal." Then, "Is there someone I could call for references?"— he assessed me with those piercing eyes.

"There is my mother," I joked. "Once you talk to my mother you'll know all the bad things about me. Or," I proposed, rambling on flippantly, "there's my ex-husband and his girlfriend. Or my ex-fiancé and his boyfriend . . ."

"There must be some sort of official who could give you a character reference?" he said, scrutinizing me doubtfully.

I thought of Swamiji. Nah. That wasn't what he meant. I shrugged. "Not really." And then I remembered Jupiter Dodd. Years ago, before I was married, I was a sort of successful fashion photographer. For ten years I poked around the continent and in India. Jupiter Dodd was my New York contact and he'd made quite a name for himself editing several prestigious magazines. I smoothed my lap. "I do, actually, know someone of consequence who would speak for me."

"Good."

"I think I might even still have his card somewhere." I grappled through my purse. "I always have one. I just haven't— Ah! Here it is. A little dog-eared and bedraggled, I'm afraid."

"Doesn't matter." He took the card and pocketed it without his eyes leaving the road.

"I have to be honest. I thought I'd be paying rent."

He grabbed a look at me. "As it happens, that's my one prerequisite—I'll be needing someone honest. My mother had some valuable pieces amid the junk." He cleared his throat. "The thing is, the house is in such bad condition—I wouldn't want you to sue me because I'd rented you an unstable environment."

"Oh. You mean like if I fall through a hole in the floor, it will be my tough luck."

"That's it." He grinned.

"A gentleman's agreement, then?"

"Yes."

Our right hands went instinctively toward each other. They clasped in a perfect fit. For one moment we held on. Embarrassed by what felt unnervingly like intimacy, I pulled away. "It couldn't be any worse than the house I just lost." I sighed, gazing out the window.

I blotted my nose. No blood. At least there was that. I told him,

"I had a bed-and-breakfast in Queens that burned to the ground. But when I bought it, it took forever to get it livable. I did, though. I fixed it up. My children helped me." I felt his look. He'd be thinking they would join me. "They're both away at college," I said.

"I never had to raise kids," he murmured. From the way he said it I took it to mean he'd escaped lucky.

"Really?" was all I could think to say. I watched his profile. It was a fine, manly nose he had. But despite my scrutiny, he gave nothing away but the facts, ma'am, no sign of emotion; still, I sensed a cool retreat. I said, "Look, if it makes a difference that I have children just tell me now because I can go back to Que—"

But he interrupted me. "You don't have to apologize for being a woman. Some people have no idea what that takes. Some people think in order to be a lady one has to give up being a woman." He shot me a reluctant look. "And in the end it does nobody any good."

At the time I thought he was talking about his mother. Only later would I find out what he meant. And my thoughts had turned to coffee. I checked my watch. "Look, I'm free until eleven."

"Anyone else you want to call?" he asked. "Your ex-husband? Your gay fiancé?"

I gaped at him. What did he think, it was a joke? My life was a joke?

"Why don't we go see it, see how you feel about it," he suggested. "Figure out if it suits us both." He gave me the once-over.

I must have blushed. I knew what I must look like. My two black eyes. No doubt by now I smelled of perspiration. I moved a little farther away from him. He was probably thinking I would go very well indeed with that dilapidated cottage.

We drove up and down the unfamiliar hills, then approached the cottage from the roadside, which was an experience in itself. It went almost straight up. The steep lane had my stomach in a knot as we reached the top. I held on to the door and was prepared to jump out when the car slipped backward, which I felt sure it would. He glanced at my hand on the door and laughed. And then we were there. We pulled the car onto the drive and came to a halt. He literally jumped over the door like someone in a movie. The cottage could hardly be seen from the road, barricaded by low-hanging branches dripping with white petals. The path was strewn and covered with things grown wild. Braided wisteria husks the size of saplings lounged across the roof. Thinking to show off my house-hunter savvy, I suggested, "If you're thinking of selling, you might want to clear the front. That way, people can see the cottage."

He searched his pockets for the key. "Some people treasure privacy," he said in a cold tone.

I shut up and followed his broad back down the overgrown path. What had once been a garden in rows had fallen to plunder. A verdigris sundial sat prettily on a pedestal and I trailed my fingers across its cruddy surface.

"Sundials have been telling time for three thousand years," he remarked. "She's missing her gnomon, that one," he muttered. Then, "Never got around to repairing it."

"Gnomon?" I tasted the word. "The name of your boat, right?"

"That's right. Shows the direction."

There was a ruckus of birdsong. It stopped suddenly when we came to the door. "Damn key," he muttered and then dropped it. He winced and grabbed hold of his wrist. I saw that he was wounded somehow, so I knelt and retrieved the key from a drowsy of chamomile between the slates. The birds went back to singing. He swatted his arms. "Cold enough," he grumbled, embarrassed by his clumsiness.

"When I hear the birds singing, I don't mind the cold." I slipped the key in. "I always figure if they can take it, so can I."

"They're cold-blooded," he said wryly.

"Oh, so am I," I assured him, acting big.

The door hesitated then swung open easily. It was dark inside, but a huge window across the cottage was filled with the lit-up sea. I'd never seen anything like it. It was utterly magical.

"Hang on," he said as he reached for the light switch.

The house tipped to one side, into the direction of the sea. Along one wall a series of silent clocks hung in disorganized rows like in an old-fangled clock shop, abandoned and neglected. Unlocked cabinets on the land's side swung open as if on a tilted ship.

"What the—!"

"The place looks like it's been ransacked," I said.

He cut straight across the room to a particular standing closet, one of those Bavarian stenciled cupboards, struggled with the painted cabinet door, and seemed relieved when he got it open. Inside was a funny-looking instrument. He picked it up, cradling it.

"What on earth is it?" I came up behind him.

"It's a gilt bronze dial," he said. "Polyhedral. Do you like it?"

"I guess so."

"It's from France." He smiled at the thing admiringly and blew the dust from its pointed top. "About 1660. Luckily, not everyone knows how valuable it is."

There was a lot of dust and I sneezed. He lowered the dial gently into a leather bag, zipped it up, went to the kitchen windows and opened them, then went around shutting the opened drawers and cabinets. A fresh cold breeze traveled in, fluttering the worn faded curtains. They were made from lawn. *Lawn*, I thought. Such old-time stuff. He moved to the other side, to the west-facing windows and opened them too. The fresh air was a relief. "Do you believe this? This is what I'm talking about." He strode about, outraged, picking up things that had obviously been thrown around. "I leave the cottage unlocked one day and this is what happens!"

I touched some upside-down herbs in bunches that were tied to a line of ribbon. The flowers crumbled and I sniffed and flinched. "Valerian," I said, watching the dust of the petals land on a pair of brass jewelers' magnifiers.

"My mother," he explained wearily, "was thought to be something of a witch."

"Really?" I looked up, interested.

"Yes, but it wasn't organics, it was things; people would bring her old broken watches and she would fix them, presto chango—like magic . . . things no one else could fix. She could repair any clock until recently. And of course she was more than that." His arm swept the wall. "She was a first-class collector, as you can see. She'd studied clock making at Eton, you know. That's where she met my father. They'd both come specifically to study horology."

He saw my puzzled expression.

"Oh. That's the science of precision timekeeping. She even taught some of the locals. Her eyes were good until the end. She could count the hairs on the back of a fly. Just . . . she began failing of late . . ." He cleared his throat, reviving himself. "And a great sailor she was. At one time, anyway." He caught the look on my face. "Of course if that bit about sorcery changes your mind about staying here, I'll fully understand."

"On the contrary," I admitted. "It only makes it more compelling. I wear my white light around me anyway." I asserted, looking around. In such a crammed space, it was hard to make anything out. I tried to disassociate myself from the incidentals and see through to the essence. Basically it was an almost square room with two adjoining walls solid with books and a kitchenette. In the opposite corner was an adequate pantry. The old stove was small but gas. I like gas. A collection of dusty but unchipped English teapots decorated the shelf above. There was a record player, an old one but that at least seemed in good repair. At least there was no dust on it. In a small drawer I discovered dozens of pen tops and no pens. I pushed aside some boxes and found iron pans, six of them, one fitting into the next. They were gritty but could easily be scoured out with sea salt and steel wool. Now some people like to go to the gym and lift weights. Me, I'll take a couple of iron pans to swing around the kitchen any day.

Across the room—if you could see past the rubble—was a full-size bed with a wonderful rosewood headboard, with harps and ten-stringed lyres carved into it. *It would look incredible if someone took the trouble to clean and oil it*, I thought. Rugs were piled in varying layers, and I lifted one to check the condition of the floor. It was very bad, pitted and uneven; I didn't think much could be done for that, but as I lifted the rug, the thickness and texture of it struck me. I recognized it right away as Tibetan and of the first caliber: silk and wool. There were lots of them, smaller ones piled on top of one another on one side of the room, evening out the tilt of the floor, some of them precious dark red Afghanis—really old. If they were aired and given a good swatting, they'd reveal their magnificent jewel-like colors, I had no doubt of it. I might have had no knowledge of clocks, but first-class carpets from particular obscure villages make my heart go pit-a-pat. Did I mention I once drove in a van from Munich to India along the Silk Route? Oddly, as I stood there in this cockeyed little house perched on the edge of a cliff I had the same shiver of excited anticipation as when I started out back then. Like I was going to have fun.

On one edge of the room were some doors, each of their faded frames hand-stenciled. I opened the first. A tiny bathroom appeared with an ancient claw-foot tub. This, at least, was in good condition. The eaves were crooked and rugged as a pirate ship's cabin. I'd never seen anything like it. I went in and turned on the faucet. A glob of rust sputtered out but soon ran clear. There was an actual porthole for a window. I crumpled some toilet paper and swished around the dust until you could see through. You could sit on the toilet and feel as though you were in a ship of olden days, look out and on a good day see clear across the sound. Wow. I opened the latch and pushed the window out. Down on the otherwise deserted beach below, a young woman walking past was singing. I craned my neck to look. She was walking, crooning to a newborn baby. *Too cold for a baby*, I thought. But it was a strange and lovely sound. I sat down to listen. There was a little two-tiered white metal table beside me with cat's paws at the bottom and little women's heads at the top. Books were wedged onto each shelf. And the toilet seat was padded. *This*, I thought, laughing to myself, *is what I call living*.

I shut the porthole and went back to the main room. Morgan Donovan had his back to me, looking over a stack of papers on a very promising-looking French writing desk. Evidently his mother had a good eye. All the stuff, once attended to, held promise. There was a weird sound and we both looked up at once. I remembered the Italian woman's words. A ghost? I wouldn't mind a ghost. Or at least a mystery. But no, of course it was nothing. Old houses on the sea are filled with noises.

We gazed together at the rows of books askew, crowded in upright and every which way. "She never could get rid of a book she liked," he said. "She'd loan them to anyone, but she never gave them away." He confided unnecessarily, "She was a hoarder," then pulled a little ceramic box from a top shelf and opened it with a worried click of the tongue. "She never kept this up here! Lord knows what else is missing," he groaned. "Not that anyone would ever know. She had so much crap." He gave up with a heave and a rueful smile and parked himself on the arm of the bumpy sofa.

I looked through the old journals, labeled with pictures of clocks and watches, some of them very old, and some with the innards hand drawn and personal remarks scrawled beneath.

"She certainly seems to have been a good witch." I tried to smile.

"A *timely* witch," he joked wryly.

I smiled gently. "How did she die?"

"Heart," he answered quickly. Then, "Well. The truth is she took too much of her medication. Overdosed." He looked at me. "I might as well say it first—there are those who will say it was intentional." I noticed his hands tighten on the book he held. "But"—he hesitated— "she never would have; that was so against her religion. And she was staunch in her beliefs. If I'd been here, of course—" He stopped himself. "She got confused sometimes, you see. Forgot." He sighed. "Forgot everything. Spent the last months in a terrible muddle. Drove everyone crazy."

You know me. My ears perked up. She wouldn't be the first troublesome elderly person to be disposed of medicinally. Easily enough done. But no, I thought of my own parents. If they didn't stick to their little categorized cubes of pills marked with the days of the week they might overdose as well. Morgan Donovan stayed put where he was. I don't think he could move. He just stood there, every once in a while emitting a huge sigh. I remembered that such sighs accompany grief. I turned away, trying to busy myself so as not to embarrass him, but I realized he'd simply forgotten me. There was a part of the wall not obscured by clocks and I guessed it was a door. A wood knot halfway up turned into a doorknob, and I attempted to open it. It stuck but gave way after a hearty yank, opening onto a horrible green-moldy shower curtain. I was already dirty and swished it aside. There was nothing behind it, just a wall. And then I thought, *That's not right, from outside the cottage must reach the side porch.* There had to be a reason for the door. I gave the wall a shove and, sure enough, it moved, opening onto—goodness! What was it, a tiny notions room? There was a sink and a ceiling lamp and then the entire addition was given over to tiny wooden porticos, square drawers, really, from floor to ceiling, and each one had a button, an old-fashioned button, sewn onto a loop to pull on. I pulled one of the buttons and the drawer slid out to reveal a handful of the same buttons inside. But they were wonderful! I opened another, this one green and glittery, making me think of my mother's old coat she still kept from when she was a girl. Sure enough, inside was the rest of the set. I rolled it back into its cubby and went for a red Schaffhausen—a sort of Heidi-in-her-dirndl button. There they were, eleven of them. And next to that was a brass Knopf of edelweiss. There must have been thousands of buttons. She even had them sorted by country! "Mr. Donovan!" I called. "Come look at this."

He put down the paper he was reading. "Yes"—he strode across the room—"I know all about them. That used to be a mudroom. Sink still works, I think."

"They're a trip!"

A pained, half-humorous, half-wincing expression took him and he turned away. "She used to let me play with them when I was little," he murmured. "Took them away, though, when I tried shooting them from my cannons." He scratched his head, dazed by the childhood memory. Perhaps stirred by these childhood memories, he became suddenly the host, venturing back to graciousness and hospitality. "Oh, and," he added with sudden charm, "be so kind and call me Morgan. The only one calls me Mr. Donovan is Patsy Mooney up at the big house."

Embarrassed by this sudden warmth, I turned away and dislodged two fancy buttons left on the top of the cabinet. They dropped to the floor and I picked them up, saying, "They seem to be all sorted and labeled, except for some in a basket and these two." I held them up to the light. "But aren't they lovely? Like little jewels!" We watched them glimmer in the half-light.

"Keep them," he said gruffly. ". . . if you like them."

"Oh, I couldn't."

"Claire,"—he raised his eyebrows dismissively—"they're only buttons."

I felt the blood in my cheeks. He'd not yet said my name. Defensively, I said, "Yes, but someone loved them once." I realized even as I said it I'd passed the mark. That's the trouble with me. I give too much too soon. "I'll make them into earrings," I stammered. "Thanks."

He turned away and I, chagrined now, returned to my assessment. But I knew now that he was not entirely mean. I'd seen the crack in that cold shoulder. And I liked it—liked him—that he wouldn't sell his mother out, belittling her by saying she was crazy. She'd probably been an old dear, just too feeble to keep up. I focused on the buttons in my cupped hands. "It's a wonderful collection, though. I've never seen anything quite like it."

"Yes. My inheritance. Buttons by the dozens . . ." He flipped the papers in his hand like a deck of cards and sneezed from the dust. ". . . and clocks after clocks . . ."

The scornful way he said it. I turned and busied myself reading the titles of all those books. There were two rows of clock repairman's guides and a group of herbal and gardening books. There was even a guide called *Collecting Buttons*. I would investigate them later, alphabetizing and categorizing, I thought, my mind already taking on the job at hand. I spied a pen, an expensive, glistening affair with a golden nib. It lay on top of a pile of decaying antique maps and somehow did not go with the room, too new and shiny to belong here. I imagined someone had left it behind. *An intruder*, I thought, my heart beating quicker. Shy, I didn't touch it. I didn't mention it either. I still don't know why.

Morgan held his arms up in the air and cleared his throat. "Well, as you can see, it's not a palatial dwelling."

I smiled. "No. Not palatial. But so imaginative!"

"So." He watched my face. "Too big a job you'll be thinking? They're not all repair books and research," he assured me. "Do you care for novels?"

My eye scanned the other shelves of books. There were lighthearted novels and mysteries by the dozens, most of them outdated and romantic. I was surprised to see they were, almost every one of them, my own cup of tea. I ran my finger over the alphabetized names: Brookner, Drabble, Du Maurier, P. D. James, Lively, Mansfield, Maugham, O'Brien, poetry, V. S. Prichett, Jean Rhys, Rohmer, Shaw, Muriel Spark, Steinbeck. Oh, yes. I could stay here. Morgan Donovan and I regarded each other with a strange sort of satisfaction.

With the relinquishment of his crankiness the entire atmosphere had changed, lightened. And suddenly I knew what it was about his house that reminded me in a funny way of the house I'd lost. It needed me. It was old and decrepit, and without me it would never regain its quaint charm. It would be torn down or renovated into something else. What lay beneath the clutter, the dear antique pieces this woman had spent a lifetime accumulating, would be sold at a tag sale, the clock journals cut up for quaint picture frames and then someone else would come along and turn the place into a modern granite beach house surrounded by pavers. "Oh, I love it so," I cried out emotionally. "I'd love to stay here!"

He gave me a screwy look and I realized he might think me nuts. Well, I am nuts.

And I remembered I must go find my car. But on the floor a box

moved. I think we both jumped. It moved again. Both of us half expecting a rat, Morgan stretched a long leg out and lifted the milk crate cautiously with his toe. It was a leggy kitten, milky gray and cowering.

"Oh, the poor thing!" I cried, kneeling down to pick it up.

"A stowaway!" He laughed.

"How long has it been here, do you think?"

He leaned over and I caught his scent, salt and canvas and leather.
"I've no idea. My mother had a cat. Yellow eyes just like hers. But she
went missing just before Mother died. For a moment I thought it might
be her, but her Weedy was a hefty size."

"Ooh," I crooned and carried it over to the sink. "It's scared to
death!" She just stood there blinking her yellow eyes, shaking her head
with outrage. I cupped some water into my palm and held it to her. At
last she figured it out and took it, lapping at it with her little pink tongue.
I knew I still had the deli paper my sandwich had come in. I'm not one
to litter and any small animal could probably live for days on the entrails
of snacks in my purse. I opened the white, waxed crumple of paper and
scraped the cheese shreds and offered them to her. Very daintily she
sniffed them. Surprised, she looked at me as if to sum up my trustworthi-
ness, then nibbled at it skeptically. I don't know if you've ever heard a cat
talk. But the little nipper let out something between a yowl of complaint
and a sigh of relief. It was the same groaning sound we'd heard when we
came in. *Mystery solved*, I thought. *No ghost.* I can't stand cats. I really
can't. I don't like their torturing ways with mice and birds. But I picked
her up into the curve of my arm and she didn't try to jump away. She sunk
in compliantly, no doubt exhausted from trying to right the milk crate. I
stroked her back with a knuckle. Pure velvet. She turned over on it and
looked right at me as if to say *A little to the left, please*. I could feel her
ragged breath through the skin. I looked up at Morgan, standing there
with his straight face, his arms barricaded across his chest. He shook his
head, charmed, despite himself. "Well, you can't leave now," he said in his
gruff way. "Who's going to feed the cat?"

I became aware that I was alone in a house with a man. Suddenly unsure, I asked him, "Well, what should I do now? Stay here?"

He scratched his ear. "I don't exactly see how you can. It's such a mess."

I shrugged. "Now or tomorrow. No reason for me not to start right in." I scrunched down on my haunches and peeked into the GE. "Do the washer and dryer work?"

"They should. I had them put in just over a year ago."

"Well, that's good." I stood up, mentally beginning my list. "I'll drive to a store and buy some new sheets. I can't bear someone else's. Oh! I didn't mean—"

"Don't worry," he assured me, "I'm not that sensitive. And neither was she. At least . . . not when she was well. She'd have been the first to see you set up right." He hesitated, giving me a quizzical look. "But wouldn't you like to get yourself some new, uh . . . duds?"

I stood, self-consciously backing my rear against the wall. "New clothes. Right. That's just what I'll do. Because I simply don't have the courage to go back home and face Enoch."

"Enoch?"

I tried to laugh. "You know, my gay fiancé."

This time he didn't laugh. He shrugged his leather jacket off and rubbed the dirt from his hands. He put them under the faucet in the sink and lathered them with dish detergent. I don't know why I stood there staring at his hands, the workman's veins like ropes climbing his forearms, so able and alive, but he looked up suddenly and caught me looking at them with a stupid look on my face. They were beautiful, his hands. Luckily, heartbroken, I was immune to his charms. But evidently I wasn't blind to beauty. That I never was.

"I'm sorry," he said in a way that he hadn't spoken to me before. A gentle way. The mocking tone was gone and I felt for this reason worse. He grabbed a dishtowel and dried himself, then put a strong, brotherly hand on my shoulder.

I was wrong about immunity to men's charms. I felt his touch right down to my toes.

"It's only natural that you're upset," he said.

"You know, you're a funny guy. I can't figure you out."

He gave me a lopsided grin. "That's because I'm all mixed up myself."

"You?"

"When I was in the seminary, I was told—"

"Hold on," I interrupted. "You were in the seminary? As in studying for the priesthood?"

He made a pained face, "That's it."

"Oh" was all I could say, thinking, *Aha! That's why no kids.*

He stood abruptly. "But that's a story for another day."

"I can't wait to hear it," I said, meaning it.

He stood at the open window, looking out reflectively, squinting into the cold light. "Odd," he remarked at last, "our meeting like this."

"How do you mean?"

"We're both at a crossroads, aren't we?"

I tried to smile. "Yes. That's it exactly. And I'm sorry if I was rude. Hopefully we can help each other out. Shall we start fresh?"

Again we shook hands. There was the cry of gulls as they swept by just outside the window. What a place! You could hear the waves lapping against the sand. All at once I was so grateful. This sort of opportunity didn't fall into your lap often. Morgan jammed his hands into his pockets and turned in a circle, looking around the room. "She wasn't always like this," he remarked. "It was just this last year . . . She was always sharp as a tack . . . then all of a sudden"—he shook his head sadly—"she just went senile. Senile and deaf at practically the same time."

I waited.

"The thing is"—he bit his lip in an effort to stave off emotion—"I really regret losing my temper with her. I didn't realize at first what was happening. And you had to repeat everything. I know that's no excuse . . ." He looked away.

"I'm sorry," I said and I meant it. But he didn't like anyone being sorry for him, you could tell that right off. He grimaced at his chronometer watch. "That's it for me. I've got to meet the harbormaster in ten minutes. Big regatta coming up."

I shut the window and firmed the latch. "Okay," I said, "so how shall we do this?"

The shrill of his cell phone cut me off. "Donovan," he answered. He listened intently to the person at the other end. "Right," he said, seeming to change his mind about something. Scowling, he hung up. "Well, it seems I'm to dine at Twillyweed this evening. Why don't you find me there and we can talk about it. I can't make heads or tails of anything now. I'm too distracted." He turned abruptly and, becoming the captain again suddenly, ordered, "I'll expect you no later than sixteen hundred hours. Give you time to see your niece. Will that suit you?"

I laughed. "Aye, aye. Four o'clock." I saluted. "Got it."

"Now I really must go. Draw up a list of things you'll want. Oh. You'll be needing money." He reached into his pocket.

Horrified, I pushed his fistful of bills back at him. "Don't be silly. I have some."

"Well, then, keep the receipts and I'll reimburse you." He took hold of his leather satchel and went out the door, the screen slamming with a friendly bang. He loped down the path. "Bring the list with you to the Cupsands'."

Scooping the kitten up, I followed down the windy path and called after him, "But I don't even know the Cupsands!"

"Nobody does." He laughed with his back to me. "Least of all the Cupsands."

When the sun leveled with the horizon, he washed out the gray gloves, his agitated hands inside them. He worked them feverishly, with a mixture of mild white soap and fabric softener. It seemed to work. The water ran foamy and clear. He relaxed, leaning on his outstretched arms, his wrists and palms against the old grain sink.

A job well done.

He consulted himself inside the broken mirror and was comforted by the conviviality and composure that greeted him there. He winked. He drew his legs up on the bed and rested now, clicking on the TV to watch the news. He liked channel 2.

Beside him, the gloves lay neatly out to dry—one on top of the other, palms down like hands in repose—away from the heat on a polished table. It was a small, elegant table with feet, each foot holding tightly on to its own mahogany sphere. Each rigid foot had claws painted abalone and verdigris, claws pearly and expectant with their greenish talons.

CLAIRE

I stretched and raised my arms above my head to reach the sky and realign my spine. The wind in the boat sheaves wailed and you could just hear the harbor bells clang. If you had to pick a place in which to be miserable, I thought, stepping over the ruins of daffodils—*I must locate a broom*—you couldn't find a better one than this, overgrown and mysterious and far away from it all. What better place to sort one's self out? And things were looking up. Morgan. Good name. He must be just my age. A little older, I thought hopefully. I didn't see why I should always be the oldest one around. I'm not going to play coy and say it didn't occur to me that he might not be someone in my future. A friend. A good friend, maybe. When you reach my age, you know right away when someone is interesting to you or not. *Well, just wait and see*, I reminded myself. A priest! I couldn't get over it. I hopped over the puddles. On my way back up the path, I noticed the neighbor, Mrs. Dellaverna, hunched over the fig tree wrapped in potato sacking; her iron-gray helmet of hair stayed in perfect chunky waves despite the wind. I put the kitten in my pocket and leaned on Noola Donovan's creaky lattice gate. "Hi!"

"*Oomph!*" She affected a jump. "I didn't see you there! Was that Morgan?"

"Yes."

She stood back, an apron over her coat, her crafty brown eyes inspecting her hacked-up square of earth, wiping her brow with her forearm. "I'm not planting yet. Just clearing away the dirt for when it gets warm." She gave an impish shrug. "I can't wait to get started." Then she sat back on her broad haunches, up to her knees in boots, her face still smooth for a gardener's. "Of course"—here she frowned, shaking her head, looking a bit puzzled—"now that Noola's gone, it will all be different. We used to have a big competition with our flowers." She rocked in the hard dirt and her little eyes filled with peevishness. "My tomatoes were always better than hers . . . and my figs." She sniffed, then, remembering me standing there, she added, "I never told her my secret." When I didn't bite, "Anchovies," she volunteered, making a shrewd face. "That or sardines. Whatever's on sale. Now that she's gone it takes all the fun out. Death," she whispered. "It's so final."

"Yes," I agreed. "I wanted to say thank you," I went on, changing the subject before she ran away with herself, "you know, for mentioning where I could find Mr. Donovan. And to let you know—you won't believe it—I'll be staying here for a while!"

I was sure I detected real disappointment in those nut-brown eyes. But she hoisted herself from the soil and brushed the dirt from her knees, out of breath from the exertion. There was something cold and off-putting about her now, and I wasn't sure if I should back off. But I introduced myself properly, and we shook hands over the hedge. From my pocket, the kitten gave a hearty mew. "Oh," I explained, pulling her out. "Someone left her in the cottage."

Mrs. Dellaverna's expression turned to mush. She scooped her away from me, huddling it to her breast. However cold I'd thought her expression, the iciness dissolved at that moment. "*Dio! Una gattina.* Noola used to have one looked just like her. Weedy. She never came back." She narrowed her eyes. "It kind of looks like Sam, too—that nasty big boy cat at Twillyweed. Son of a bitch! Eh!" She stroked the kitten, shaking her head suspiciously. "How come you're going to live in Sea Cliff, eh? I'd like to know."

"It's so funny." I shrugged. "Everything just fell into place. For some reason it suited us—Morgan Donovan and me—both."

"But you're not going to move in yet?" Mrs. Dellaverna sniffed the air. "Place is too crazy."

"I haven't decided yet what to do. I might have to drive back to Queens tonight and stay at my parents' house," I said, thinking out loud. "I'm not sure."

"You're gonna need a team of a cleaning ladies for that place," Mrs. Dellaverna cautioned.

"That's a good idea. Do you know anyone?"

"There's Radiance. She does housework. I wouldn't trust her, though."

"Oh? Why not? I'd like someone local."

"She's more interested in the showbiz!" She wiggled her nose with distaste. "I'm from Ischia and I know that type!"

I shrugged and gave my own tender nose a tentative feel. "If I could have her number . . ."

She watched my two black eyes now with interest. It was clear to her they were the traces of the fight she was sure had gone down.

"Oh, this!" I touched my face. "It's from falling," I told her.

"Sure," she said too fast, clearly not believing. She could just see the cad who'd beat me and she'd never mention it again because she knew in her heart that was why I was out here in Sea Cliff, running away from a man, *un diavolo* of a man. She put one hand on a hip and twirled the other wrist in a Mediterranean flourish. "I wouldn't worry about anything, *cara*. Claire, is it?"

"That's right."

Her nose wrinkled, and her voice was thick with understanding. "You were right to come here. Get away. You wouldn't be the first to look for sanctuary here. I have my friend, Patsy, that shit of a motorcycle-driving husband, he beat her up good. Eh. She came here and she slept on my sofa. Got a good job now and she'll never go back. *Basta.* Don't you worry."

"Hmm. I'm sorry." I edged away from her tirade. "I was just really hoping to find someone to clean." And then I thought, *Hell, the woman is right. I am here running away from a man, a devil of a man.* Suddenly I was exhausted and just wanted to rest.

Mrs. Dellaverna stood ruminating, inspecting me and sizing me up head to toe. She nodded with a closemouthed smile. "That's like Morgan to come up with a nice house sitter like you! Out of the blue! Eh?"

"You know him well, I guess. Living next door and all."

"Sure." She leaned her chin against the handle of the tall wooden hacker with a thick pick of iron. "When he's not in Scotland, he's here. Nice little boy he was."

"He was in the seminary, he mentioned," I pushed.

"Ah! No more." Her tongue clicked. "Noola, may she rest in peace, she drove him to that."

"So he is a priest?"

She laughed.

I ventured, "So he isn't a priest?"

"Morgan? *Dio*, no!"

"Lost his faith, did he?"

"His faith? Ha! More like he discovered the earthly pleasures."

"Oh."

"No"—she got rid of her coat—"he never made it that far, to the priesthood. Not that Noola she didn't try and hound him into it. I shouldn't speak bad of the dead now, I know. But there was nothing she wanted more than for Morgan to join the priesthood. From the time he was a boy she'd be marching him off to church for one thing or another. First, he had to be a paten boy. Then it was an altar boy. After that he was a—what do you call it?—Eucharistic minister. Nothing wrong with all that, I don't mean that. But it's sad, you know, when someone pushes their own ideas onto a child—won't stand back and let the child find his own way." She sighed. "Morgan was so heartbroken over the separation, see."

"Oh. His parents were divorced?"

"Not she!" She gave a snort. "In her mind, you didn't get divorced. He was from Scotland, the father—they're Protestants—and she was Irish, the Catholic part. They shared him up, the two of them. Tom couldn't take her religious ways. Ooh, he hated the Catholic Church! Of course he loved her, he just hated what she was"—she tapped her noggin—"how she *thought*. Anh. It's hard to describe."

But she didn't have to. My flamboyant mother, convent educated, clandestinely paying for indulgences; my father, intellectual and conservative, spiritual as she was but scornful and wary of the politics within the church, the secret cover-ups, money changing hands. I knew the wars that went on without words. I knew the anguish it could cause in children. There was no divorce in homes like ours. Misery, even, some-times. But you stuck it out.

"He went back to Scotland in the end," Mrs. Dellaverna confided, leaning comfortably on her pick. "A *piccolo* village called Invergowrie, that's outside Dundie, Noola always tells. Morgan spent half his days there and half here; went to school at Edinburgh, near the father. That was the deal. All the way across the sea in Scotland!" She gave a quick look off to the side as if to see if someone could hear. "The poor boy didn't know if he was coming or going! The only peace he had was taking out that little boat of his. That's what he loved most, all the time. Any moment he had to himself, if there was just a bit of a wind, you'd see him scoot right down the hill. Ten minutes later his *piccolo* boat would be shooting out from the cove. That was what Morgan loved. The wind and the sails."

"So no divorce . . ."

She closed one nostril with her finger. "Uh-uh. She was a *veramente catolica* and wouldn't even let the word *divorce* cross her lips. There'd be none of that. She was Mrs. Donovan until the day she died. Sad, really. I think she always thought one day he'd come back to her. I really do. And here she is dead." She shook her head.

"How did she die?"

"Heart," she answered quickly. She frowned, looked over her shoulder toward the cottage and chewed her lip. "Too much digoxin. She took too much. I thought one day she'd do something wrong—I wor-ried she'd fall off the porch. You know, she shouldn't have lived by her-self. Not anymore. Bang. She dropped dead."

I asked, "Who found her, then?"

"Me. I found her. That's right. You know"—she scratched her chin thoughtfully, wanting to change the subject—"seems like a yesterday Morgan was little, out there sailing around . . ."

We both looked out over the hedge to the sea, as if expecting to see the small boy and his boat. But the rash wind belted us and there was only the flap of the flag and the clang of the pole links. She threw her apron over her head. "But that's me, talking about it when it's none of my business! And all you wanted was the name of a cleaner!"

"If you have it. Or if I might just have Radiance's number?"

"I have the number." She turned and, elbows out, took off. She raised an arm. "Come in my house," she ordered. I followed her in. "It's cold outside." She rubbed her arms briskly and kicked off her clogs. "Let me warm up some milk for that puss. Eh?"

The house, after the one I'd just been in, was a pleasant shock. Highly polished Mediterranean furniture and clean windows. Petit point embroideries of violets lined the walls in oval frames. A woman living alone. Mrs. Dellaverna's house wasn't dead on the water, but you could see a little chink of it, blue and white capped with wind. "Rest yourself," she invited, pointing to a thronelike chair at the table.

I sank onto the plush cushions still covered in vinyl. Heavy, amber velvet drapes muffled any sound, and the miniature, expensive furniture gave the room a loungelike feel. There was smell of something wonderful bubbling on the stove. "What's that, gravy?"

"Gravy? No, it's sauce!" She paused in the doorway, catching me. "Ay! You look done in." She eyed me suspiciously, coming back to the table with a recipe box.

"I have had a rough two days," I admitted.

She frowned, placing a leathered hand gently on top of mine. "I'm gonna make you a cup of coffee."

Sometimes a perfect stranger is just that—perfect. And so I told her my whole sorry saga. She didn't bat an eye, just sat there stroking her flimsy mustache until I was done.

"It's so crazy it's got to be true. The whole house burned to the ground? Unbelievable!" She shook her head. "All your clothes and all your shoes?"

"Yup. Well. It's not that tragic, really. After all, everyone's alive. So it's just me, really. I suppose it's up to me now to start a new life." When I got to the part about Enoch and his, uh, "diversion," she grabbed her chest and the kitten flew out.

"*Mama mia!*" she cried dramatically and blessed herself. I almost laughed. She held out her hand and made me hand over my trousers. "I looked at you in these pants"—she held her fingertips against each other and shook them—"and I'm thinking, what's she doing walking around like a vagabond?"

While I waited for the strong bitter coffee to percolate, she mended the pants on her machine in the bedroom, her knees bobbing up and down from the doorway, the kitten on the floor at her feet tackling a spool of emerald thread. "You gonna have a quick rest on the nice sofa while I finish these off," she said, snapping the thread with her teeth.

"Oh, I shouldn't. I have to go to Twillyweed. I'll never wake up."

"What time you want to leave?"

"I'm to be there at four." I gave a lion's yawn.

"Never you mind." She led me to the sofa. "I'll make sure you're up by three. You can use my shower. Let's see if I can fix these for you to wear by then. Hey! What's about you stay here just for the night?"

I supposed she figured if Morgan Donovan trusted me, she could, too. I looked up hopefully.

"Eh. Then you can start up fresh in the morning. Let's face it. You can't sleep in a dump like that." She gave a warning look. "But just for the one night, eh? This is not a *pensione*."

"Are you sure?" I lowered my head and yawned again, sniffing with pleasure the percolating coffee and clean linen pillowcase she'd maneuvered beneath me.

"That's what the neighbors are for." She smiled, her little acorn eyes glittering with kindness. "Noola—she taught me that." She went to the stove and stirred her sauce.

I gazed at the beautiful religious souvenirs from Rome on the bottom shelf of her fancy glass *armadio*, the cloisonné paraphernalia, the ornate gold clock under a glass dome, and I half listened as her voice became muffled and faraway. Enoch's self-satisfied words echoed in my ears above the shush of the waves beating the shore. *These are things that men do. It's just . . . release*, he'd explained. The last thing I saw before I fell off to sleep was Mrs. Dellaverna folding a copper-colored silky comforter over my shoulders then turning off my cell phone and tucking it into my purse.

JENNY ROSE

She waited at the end of the drive for the school bus. At last it came, crunching to what Jenny Rose thought was an excessively rash halt. Anyone sitting unbelted would lurch! Determined to start on the right foot, she smiled hopefully up at the driver, who opened the door with a hefty lever and then sat there chewing gum, looking straight ahead, not signaling the little boy that he should move. Jenny Rose poked her head in the bus. There was no obvious head peeking back down the aisle. She stepped onto the bus.

"Hey!" the driver snapped. "No parents on the bus!"

"That's good then 'cause I'm not a parent," Jenny Rose sassed him and marched past. There were no other children. Jenny Rose had to walk to the rear until she reached him, his little arms around his blue knapsack, scrunched up tight as though he were waiting to be smacked.

Jenny Rose lowered her head very close to the child—good Lord, the air was thick as a closed-up car park! Why, it was suffocating! She whispered the start of a song to get Wendell to open his eyes and then gently took him up in her arms. He didn't weigh a thing! Wendell stayed rigid and stiff, but he let himself be transported. Jenny Rose was thinking if the child left the school at 2:10 and it was now 2:40, he'd been driving around in this wretched air for thirty minutes. Thirty minutes! Intolerable! An agony of time for a child. And God knew how the other little mites had tortured him! She knew how vicious little kids could be. She'd been one herself. As she carried the boy still scrunched into sitting position past the driver she said, "What's about opening a couple of windows in here, aye? The rear of the bus is claustrophobic! It's awful."

"Can't do it, lady. One a them kids will stick their head out."

Trying to be reasonable, Jenny Rose suggested, "Well, then, how about cracking a couple of them so the kids don't suffocate!"

The driver yanked his lever so the door whipped open and the bus lurched and she practically lost her footing. "Go on. Move it."

Jenny Rose muttered, "I thought we were on the same fuckin' side here."

"Wadja say?" The driver leaned toward her back in a threatening way.

Jenny Rose's eyes flashed and she turned to him, her hand protectively cradling the back of Wendell's head. "I'll tell you what I'll say if you don't pay heed to the child's good health! It's criminal not to, I'll have you know!"

"That's it. Off the bus."

"We're going. Don't worry."

She put Wendell down and the bus took off before they were even clear of it, spattering mud onto Wendell's hat and Jenny Rose's rough-cut black hair. It was filthy weather again and difficult to see beyond the road. Wendell stood there, his bad eye veering off in an uncontrollable spasm. Jenny Rose, her foxy face clenched in a glare at the disappearing bus, whispered, "Wendell, do you know what a poem is?"

As he didn't answer she went on, forcing herself to walk slowly, "You make a word at the end of a sentence sound like a word at the end of another sentence."

He walked beside her, his eyes on his shoes.

"Listen. It's fun!

> "There was an old man from the west
> "He wore a pale plum-colored vest
> "When they asked, 'Does it fit?'
> "He replied, 'Not a bit.'
> "That uneasy old man from the west.

"See? That's from Aesop. It's a poem."

"Going home," Wendell said.

"We'll be there soon." She hurried along beside him.

"The cat and the spoon," replied Wendell.

"Oh," Jenny Rose realized, catching up. "Huh! That's very good!" He'd spoken! And not only that, he'd answered in rhyme. They walked along up the short, flat expanse of road. She picked a stick from the ground and swung it casually. "Darlin', remember you gave me that nice scarf when I came to Twillyweed?"

He smiled. No teeth, but a smile. Then a nod.

"Well, there's something I've been wanting to ask you. Do you remember where you got it?"

"Noola," he said right away. "Boola boola."

"Good rhyme!" Jenny Rose congratulated him, "You've got the idea, all right! Say. What about the pretty blue stones? Did Noola give them to you to hold?"

Wendell shifted his haversack but he didn't answer. *Oh, well*, she thought. *Two out of three.*

Twillyweed, humped and dark up there in fog, loomed before them and they hiked on, abandoned but together, toward its jutting turrets. Wendell would twist his head to see if she was still smiling. She didn't seem to mind him at all. The wind blew at their backs and the mist separated, the sun broke through just a crack, and the sea down the hill was a still shimmer of glass. "Tell you what," Jenny Rose said, changing her mind. "It's a fine, soft day—not a day to be inside. What do you say?" She crouched to his level. "We'll take a walk to the shore before you've had your nap. Or we'll bicycle for a treat! How's that?"

Wendell jumped up and down in answer, and they took all their stuff to the porch then went to the garage for some bikes, of which there were many.

They pedaled along the coast road, carefree, she on a rusty old maroon Schwinn and Wendell on a squeaky bright red tricycle. Wendell, thrilled with the unexpected fun of it, head down, knees out, kept up. At Duffy's Bait Shop he hopped off his tricycle, determined to go inside.

She pulled their bikes over to the side of the building and followed him in.

Leaning over the cash register and busily counting coins from a purse stood Malcolm McGlintock—Glinty—to Jenny Rose's horror and delight. Even with his back to them he was slinky. She stopped dead in her tracks, but then, fueled with confidence by Wendell's presence and resigning herself to Glinty's taking one long look at her and scramming out of there—for what else did she deserve—she greeted him softly. "Hello," she said, her cheeks darkening.

It was the girl! The one who'd got away! "Hey!" he cried out before he could stop himself. "It's you!"

Jenny Rose's heart took flight at the smile in his eyes. You couldn't lie with your eyes.

"What's up?" He smoothed over his delight with a touch of cool.

"Just following my boss here." She indicated Wendell with a nudge of the head.

"Well, if it isn't Wendell!" He veered to the side with a grimace.

"You two know each other then, do you?" Jenny Rose said.

"Oh, aye. We're old chums."

"He seems to like the place. What about you?"

"Readying to pay for a new mizzen. Just doing a jury rig."

"What's that?" Wendell pushed his way through Jenny Rose's legs.

Surprised, Glinty glanced up at Jenny Rose. "Talking, you are now, is it?" he leaned over and said to Wendell. "Well, now. That's fine. A jury rig is a sort of a temporary repair, mate." He rose back up to the shopkeep and said, "Oh, and give me one of those cleats, will you? That'll be it. What's the damage?" He paid up, carefully doling out the bills with almost comical care, and the three of them walked from the store into the daylight. "So, little man"—Glinty crouched down to be on Wendell's level—"what is it you've been up to?"

Wendell thought for a moment. "I can tell a rhyme," he boasted.

"Really? Hmm. I've got a couple of them up the sleeve, meself." He lifted his eyebrows at Jenny Rose. "Got a couple a good filthy ones, too."

"Take hold of yourself!" She smacked him playfully.

"Say, how would you two like to go for a ride?"

"Yeah!" Wendell shouted. "Yes! Yes!" He arranged himself into an obedient little boy and looked pleadingly at Jenny Rose.

"What about that fog?" She eyed the distance, unconvinced.

"Aw, we'll just stay close to the shore."

"He's supposed to be having a nap . . ." She wavered.

"He can have one on board." Glinty looked in her eyes. "We can all have one."

"Don't be silly." she retorted. "It's hardly the weekend."

He stared at her. She had the spookiest eyes. "You're a wee sheedie, you are."

"Oh? And what would that be?"

Disarmed, he smiled at her crookedly, "A faerie, you might be."

"I should have guessed you'd be superstitious," Jenny Rose sallied, pleased despite herself. "You've got to get us back in time for supper, though."

Glinty rested his burden on the ground and looped up the length of a rope he always seemed to be holding. "We can manage that." He watched her with his eyes like slits guarding against the sun.

"And no funny business," she warned, still unsure.

He grinned and opened his hands beseechingly. "What do I look like, some sort of a monster?"

She hesitated a moment, just to tick him off and then smiled. "All right. We'd love to."

"Here, mate." Glinty handed Wendell a bag. "You'll have to work for your pudding." He scrounged around in his pocket and came up with a whistle. "Here you go, laddie. Keep this with you at all times, now. A whistle can save your life if you're lost in a fog." He slung his package romantically over his shoulder and started toward the dock.

They hauled out their bikes. Jenny Rose whistled a tune and Glinty whistled, too. Wendell, his one good eye eager with trust and hero worship, cheerfully lugged Glinty's brown paper bag in his backpack and pumped along squeaky as an engine at the rear. They went the beach way, passing the row of shabby, old-time cottages.

An unkempt hand wiped circles on a dirty pane, alert eyes observing their progress.

CLAIRE

My new neighbor woke me up as she'd said she would, then gave me two wrung-out tea bags to soak my eyes. After that she pointed me to the shower, which was terrific. When I emerged, I saw that she'd lain out a shimmering blue-green sheath. I stared, uncomprehending, at the old- fashioned dress. Was she going out? I looked up and there she was, her hands clasped across her belly, her eyes twinkling. She spread her fingers wide and circumnavigated her middle. "You won't believe it now, because look at my belly, but once a long a time ago, it fit me *bellissima!*"

I stared at her, still not getting it. Had she imagined it would suit me?

"It will make you look like a real *jezebella!*"

I was speechless. What was I to do? She'd gone to so much trouble.

She leaned so close I could smell yesterday's broccoli rabe. "You're going up to Twillyweed you better look like you got some *bumpalena*, eh? Like you're somebody!"

I sat down on the bed. Already it seemed we were in cahoots. She removed the dress from the hanger and attacked me with it forthwith, roughly picking up my arms and negotiating it over my head. *Don't ever tangle with an Italian woman*, I thought, stifling a laugh. I saw that the seams were beautifully sewn. All by hand. Simple but elegant.

She'd even lain out a pair of black tights and sturdy shoes. These were, however, flats, which, surprisingly, almost fit. A little snug for my gondolas, plain as they could be, but good. On closer inspection they turned out to be vintage Salvatore Ferragamos. When I stood up to see myself in the Venetian mirror, I feared I looked like the queen done up for tea—but I didn't care, not really. The dress was nice and clean, had good lines, and at least was slenderizing. The hem reached below the knee, a flattering if dated style. I don't know what I was worried about. Anything was an improvement. And it was heaven to be clean. Then I struggled into the tights. I knew this would be trouble because I've got these long pegs. However, due to the miracle of modern fabric, when I pulled hard enough, they just about reached my crotch. I couldn't go bare-legged, I'd freeze. I gave them another good yank so they'd stay up. There. Not bad. I said, "I don't suppose you have a shawl?"

"I got a thousand tablecloths," she said, throwing open the sideboard, wild-eyed with relish. "Take your pick."

"Hmm." I knelt down and sorted through the neatly ironed, squeezed tight piles. They were white or ecru lace, but one was fringed antique gold, sort of velvety. I yanked it out and unfolded it. It was nice and soft. "May I borrow this?"

"Sure. They don't like you, come back and we'll have a bowl of macaroni and gravy."

"I thought you called it sauce."

"No. When I'm making it ready, she's sauce. When she's all dressed up with the meatballs, the *braciole*, the sausage, she's gravy." She gave me a nice smack. "What's the matter? Don't you know nothing?"

I threw the tablecloth around my shoulders and snuggled into it. It still looked like a tablecloth, but it was warm and a feeling of well-being overtook me. I looped the buttons Morgan had given me onto the small hoops I always wore in my ears and they hung perfectly. The truth was, they dressed my ears with the glitter of a new set of earrings and I admired myself in the bathroom mirror. There. Refreshed from sleep, I would have looked almost terrific if I didn't have those two black eyes. I thought of my landlord seeing me now in a different light. For there was one thing of which I was sure, Morgan Donovan was not gay.

JENNY ROSE

Here it was evening. Jenny Rose and Wendell sat on the floor in a small corner of her basement apartment. Wendell had lugged down the plaid bolster pillow from his bed and arranged it like a counter. He had his toys lined up across the top as if for sale. Jenny Rose bought several of these toys, paying him with bobby pins and sample packages of Q-tips and wipes and pretzels she'd got on the plane and which Wendell seemed to covet. When she ran out of these, he required she pay him in limericks, which she ran off easily. Her mind was somewhere else . . . worried about whether or not she'd get the boy in trouble. When she thought he was relaxed and happy, she thought she'd try again. "Oh, by the way, where was it you found the fancy blue jewels, Wendell?" she asked him in a casual way. "Remember the pretty stones you gave me, Wendell? When I came here? You slipped them in the silky scarf. Bright blue and sort of moving with light—as blue as the sky."

Wendell frowned and went back to concentrating on sorting his merchandise.

Jenny Rose remembered a documentary film she'd seen once of a neglected baby who'd lain with no human contact in a crib all day long. All the child could see from morning to night was a moving construction crane out the window. And all the child would do, with grand sweeping gestures of one arm and then the other, was imitate the long moving arm of the crane, gliding in majesty against the cold gray sky. Every time Jenny Rose remembered this black-and-white documentary her eyes would fill with tears. It was like that with Wendell, she thought. Poor kid. All he did was prepare shelves of merchandise. Was that all he'd witnessed from the deserter Annabel? Shops?

Wendell looked up suddenly. "Wiggly, wiggly, just like my eye."

"What?"

Impatiently, he pursed his lips. "As blue as the sky! Wiggly, wiggly, just like my eye!"

At last, she understood: He was rhyming her last words again. He was very good at this rhyming game. She leaned over his make-believe store and grasped him in her skinny arms and rocked him. Surprised, Wendell let her hold him. She wouldn't let him go, she promised herself with passion. The room was strange, so strange. She heard herself crying like a child until she realized it was he who was holding her.

CHAPTER THREE

CLAIRE

In the dark I made my way to Twillyweed, grateful I'd thought to wear the cozy tablecloth. The wind blew and I heard below that long, platinum-haired girl singing to her baby. It was a deep, mournful sound I thought, remembering at once the all-encompassing loneliness of having an infant and the banging-into-walls fatigue. I stopped for a moment, listening, determined to meet her and invite her over first chance I got. But tonight was to be about Jenny Rose, and I hurried along. In the drive, a red Alpha Romeo convertible was parked. Wow. I resisted the temptation to reach in and caress the butter-soft seats.

The door to Twillyweed was propped open with an antique black iron shoe form, size four. One compelling seascape above the mantel in the grandiose foyer caught my eye and I stood there looking up. White sand and way off in the distance a blue ribbon of water sparkled with sun. Simple boats ferried this way and that. Captivated, I unwrapped my shawl, admiring it. I heard voices and the tinkle of glass from the living room. I took a deep breath—well aware of my two black eyes and inappropriate outfit—and though unannounced, I decided to go in. The grandiosity of the place was intimidating. There could be no mistaking Jenny Rose's employer, Oliver Cupsand. With the perfect lord of the manor air, he poured drinks from a whimsical decanter. I had the feeling I'd seen him before.

"Ah! Claire Breslinsky!" He set the goosenecked crystal container onto a burled walnut Biedermeier bar almost as tall as himself and said in a blustery voice, "Welcome to Twillyweed!"

I knew right away by the respectful way he came forward that Morgan had made his investigatory phone call to Jupiter Dodd, and Jupiter, bless his little heart, had told him all sorts of exaggerations about my uproarious past. "Mr. Cupsand," I said, shaking his heavy, forthright hand.

"Call me Oliver." He smiled with charm. "Please. Come in. We're celebrating."

Well. Things were certainly looking up. Oliver was all Brooks Brothers navy blue, gold buttons, and expensive smile. He cocked his head and regarded me quizzically, shaking my hand. The heft of him was an indication that one day he would run to fat, but for now he was simply manly, even chanticleer.

"We've met . . . where?" He took hold of his big chin and pointed at me with the other hand.

"The club? No, I remember. Once Upon a Moose! I was alone. Yes, having my tea on my own. You were with Jenny Rose!"

"Of course!" I smiled, for now I remembered him, too. The handsome man at the table in the corner at the Moose where Jenny Rose and I had had tea. Before even they had met.

"I never forget a face." He grimaced as though this were a burden. He was white blond, Norwegian looking, booming voiced, even boisterous, but nice. He seemed to like me. Smiling eyes. Debonair. He gave a half turn toward someone standing behind him and said, "And this—Of course you will have met Morgan's fiancée . . . my sister, Paige Cupsand."

Morgan's fiancée? "How nice!" I gushed insincerely, my head spinning. I tried to sound delighted. And here I'd been imagining him just out of the seminary! That would have been fast work. But the quick vision of a lithe female flitted by and was gone through the doorway into another grand room with a glimpse of an armload of flowers. I smiled at Morgan with new respect. I had no idea why this should bother me. And of course it didn't. Not a bit. What had I been thinking? He was too old to have just left the seminary. Just left the priesthood, more likely. After all, he was my age. Sometimes I forget how old I am and then it hits me, like a shovel.

Oliver Cupsand said, "Oh. Well, she'll be off to locate a vase." His lips moved up and down in a meditative consideration as he inspected me, weighing, no doubt, the outdated wench before him against Jupiter's mythical icon. "I hear you'll be staying at the Great White." He said it in a sweet way, yet I felt his eyes surveying me skeptically as I turned to see Morgan. "Paige, by the way, is damned good at decorating."

"Yes," Morgan agreed, moving forward, "I'm sure she can give you some tips."

I felt myself standing between the two big men when a square-cut black man with gray hair, short legged but with the huge shoulders of a Portuguese fisherman, rolled over with a tray. Oh God, I thrilled, hummus and olives that took you to the Mediterranean. And baba ghanoush and tabbouleh! I helped myself.

"You're very lucky to find a house on the cliff." Oliver made do with careful nibbles on his hors d'oeuvre, blotting his mouth with his napkin between each one so as not to dribble on his starched shirt. "It's not often one comes up. Of course, Paige will have found you the cottage . . ." he wrongly surmised, his eyes wet with appreciation.

Morgan Donovan handed me a cut crystal glass of scotch as he said, "Paige is a real estate agent."

"Oh. No, I see. I misunderstood. The way you said it earlier I thought you had it in for all real estate agents . . ." I tried to laugh. I hate scotch. I put it on the sideboard and left it there, hoping someone would ask me what I liked to drink.

"Not *this* agent, I hope," a seductive voice chortled from the doorway and high-heeled into the room.

And then there she was, every woman's favorite nightmare. I won't bore you with the details. No, I will. If you stood beside her, you felt every one of your joints was oversized. Her blond hair was turned and perfected into a frizzless French twist. As big as Oliver was, his sister was equally petite. She wore a string of pearls and a grass green cashmere sweater set. Her nails were wedding-bells pink. And yes, she wore a ring. It was a tasteful yet eye-catching blue-white diamond. Her hands were lovely. She came over, sleek as a cat, and snuggled up into Morgan's armpit. We all stood there grinning. A perfect fit.

My first impression was intense dislike. We all love to hate the blonde. But as the evening wore on, I realized Paige Cupsand was not only cultivated and charming, she was that infuriating mix of goodness and worthiness as well. So try as I might, I couldn't hate her. First impressions, it turned out, were not always correct. Well, after all, what did I care? Nothing, that's what. The reader will know that I hadn't a reason in the world to be troubled by this match. If I was lucky, I chided myself, we would all become friends. Yes. Friends. Don't think you know so much. Paige helped herself to one heaping cracker after another. I was amazed by the voracity of such a little thing's appetite. She gavooned like a cattle rustler.

At last she swallowed. "How long will you be with us in Sea Cliff, Claire?"

"Until the fall, I hope. Six months, to start. After that I don't know."

She seemed to consider this. "Are you a gardener?" she asked. "Because we have a club. Just local women, I'm afraid, no one very exciting. Just us, digging around getting filthy."

"Don't be so modest," said Morgan.

I said, "I can already see what fabulous gardens you have here. Just the bulbs alone are—"

"Yes, isn't it awful," she interrupted. "Now everything's going back under with this cold."

"Don't let Paige try to trivialize what she does," Morgan said with pride. "She raises more money for charity than most people earn in a year."

"All the niceties." Paige shook her head modestly. "It's easy. You know. For children. Orphans. Our organization gives girls who aren't looking to get abortions an alternative."

Oliver put in, "They house them during their pregnancies and provide them with affiliated classes at nearby universities. So when it's over, even if they don't want to keep their babies, they have some sort of an education going on, somewhere to head."

"That's great," I said.

Paige picked a thread from her brother's jacket and rolled it between her thumb and forefinger. "Oliver's connections don't hurt," she teased.

"And, no," Oliver put in, "it's not funded by the church."

"I didn't—"

"It's just that everyone always thinks it is," Paige said. "That's usually the objection. We've been able to buy a quite large house for the girls. Oh, by the way, Oliver, the wind knocked off some more of the roof tiles." They shared a pained grimace.

"I'll have Mr. Piet look into it," Oliver assured Paige, then he leaned toward me and touched my arm. "Lucky we have Mr. Piet. There aren't many who know how to fasten the things." Then he added. "'Battening down the hatches,' that's what our Mr. Piet does. If you had to hire a fellow to do it, any other man would charge an arm and a leg."

I looked around the corner for Mr. Piet. He would roll in and out every little while.

"It won't be cold much longer," Morgan said easily, parking one haunch on the olive leather divan and extending his long legs out into the room. Then, thinking better of it, he placed his feet back in front of himself on the floor. He caught my eye and I looked away.

"You could take Noola's place at the Garden Club!" Paige enthused. But before the words were out of her mouth she looked feebly around the room, "Not that anyone could fill her shoes. I just mean—"

"We know what you meant, Paige," Morgan comforted her graciously.

"What I really meant was"—she smiled at Morgan with all her

charm and her eyes shone, then turned to me—"we would love to have you."

I was touched. "I'm afraid I'm not much of a gardener," I warned.

"Oh. Really? Pity. Noola had such a lovely garden. Oh, well. We'll find something for you to join," she said, smiling prettily at me. "We wouldn't want you to feel left out. Such a little place we are, Sea Cliff."

"Almost a throwback, it feels like," I said. "And so remote."

"How did you drive in?" Paige asked, perching herself neatly beside me on the couch.

"Glen Cove Road," I said.

"When you've been here awhile, I'll show you how to take the switchback road down by the water. It's roundabout, but it's so pretty. And faster when there's traffic."

The butler made himself known with an almost imperceptible shifting of the feet.

Paige said, "You'll be joining us for dinner, Claire."

"Sure. I'd love to."

"Nothing festive. Just us, you know." She indicated Morgan with a warm smile. "Morgan's still in mourning, of course."

"Yes, of course," I said, remembering with regret my indelicate behavior the day before.

"Our nephew was supposed to come, but . . ." Paige let this hang in the air.

Just then Jenny Rose, with the little boy by the hand, came into the room.

I was surprised to see her, though of course she was the reason I'd come. But there was something about Jenny Rose that you couldn't quite put your finger on, a shining vividness that brought the whole room to life. It wasn't just that she was young. There was something else, something good, despite all the macabre accoutrements she could come up with to make herself look otherwise: the spiked-up hair, the eye makeup, the henna tattoo, the dark blue nail polish, the naughtiness. I walked over and gave her a kiss on the cheek.

"Here she is," Oliver Cupsand said, thrusting his glass into the air, "our hero!"

An enthusiastic round of applause followed this. I thought, *Wow, they must really be glad to have her!* I thought this with relief because Jenny Rose was notorious for getting canned. The little boy tried to step back in shyness but Jenny Rose held him fast.

"It was nothing," Jenny Rose stood behind the boy, petting his hair flat.

"It certainly wasn't nothing!" Paige cried, and they all joined her protest. I realized I hadn't a clue to what was going on and it must have shown on my face because Morgan said, "I take it you don't know, do you? Jenny Rose here saved a girl from drowning this morning."

"What?" I gasped.

"Radiance. Our Radiance," Paige said.

"While you were languishing in the emergency room," Morgan teased.

"Emergency room?" Jenny Rose jumped up. "Auntie Claire! What happened to your eyes?"

"Oh, it's nothing. I fell, that's all. Down at the marina. I'm fine now."

"Mr. Piet saved some copies of the late edition here somewhere." Oliver fiddled with his desk.

"Went right into the sound and hauled her out!" Paige said. "Your niece did that!"

Morgan took a firm gulp of his drink. "I didn't know either until I got here. Here it is, right on the table, Oliver. Have a look at this, Claire."

"Crack Down on Illegal Aliens!" the headline cried and I squirmed with discomfort for her. But my eye cast down the page to the next story and I saw where I was meant to look. "Jenny Rose!" I cried, for there she was in a picture with a policeman's jacket draped over her and an EMS driver with his arm around her. "Tourist Saves the Day" the caption read.

The little boy looked with adoration through thick glasses at his au pair.

"So, Auntie Claire, what do you think? Shall we send it to my mother in Italy? Show her what an ace I am?"

"We're all so proud!" Paige sat with her legs gracefully crossed at the ankle. "But whatever made you do it? Jump in, I mean. Most people would have just called for help!"

"She went down." Jenny Rose shrugged. "It didn't look like she had the strength to hold on."

"Wow," I said. And then I remembered where I'd heard the name Radiance. "It's Mrs. Dellaverna's cleaning lady slash showgirl!" I gasped.

"She works for us," Oliver stammered, then he added, "part-time."

"She does *some* cleaning," Paige said. "But she's quite a bit more than that. Radiance's grown up here. She's practically part of the family."

"*Phh*," said Oliver.

Jenny Rose volunteered, "Yes, but she's really a dancer, Auntie Claire! She just does cleaning to make ends meet. She's *always* going to dance classes. Wait until you meet her. She's really cool. Exotic."

"She's Mr. Piet's daughter," Paige whispered. "She doesn't live here, though. She lives in town, over Gallagher's."

"What was she doing in the water at all?" I asked.

"She was out fishing," Jenny Rose answered. "She couldn't start the engine and she was drifting."

"She probably didn't want to get her cell phone wet," Paige said, shrugging, "and left it ashore."

"It was just that wee tub of a boat," Morgan said. "She's very lucky you happened along."

"I told her never to take that blasted cat ketch." Oliver scowled. "And that's another thing. Now I've got to replace it."

Morgan's face clouded. "I'm surprised Mr. Piet let that boat fall into such disrepair. It's not like him."

Jenny Rose went on excitedly, "There was hardly a moon. She cast the anchor over the side and to her dismay it came undone! Everything that could go wrong did."

Bemused, Morgan shook his head. "I don't know what she was thinking. She's a better sailor than that." He looked at Oliver. "And I tied that anchor on myself."

Paige said hurriedly, "You know what it's like around the point. The current's dreadful."

"But surely another fisherman would have seen her?" I asked.

"She said they'd all gone out for blues," said Morgan. "She panicked. She probably thought she was in so close she could make it."

I got the oddest feeling they were covering up for her.

"Thank goodness you're a marvelous swimmer," Morgan said, smiling, to Jenny Rose.

"I've no form at all. I never won a badge at school. I guess I'm strong for my size, though." She sat back, glowing. "It's just luck, really."

The birch in the fireplace crackled. No one spoke.

"I still can't believe it!" I marveled and turned, overwhelmed, to Jenny Rose, "To think we might have lost you!"

Paige swept across the room and reached for Jenny Rose. "A terrific beginning!" She gave her an awkward, standoffish hug.

"Let's not get soppy, now. Children present." Jenny Rose stuck out both arms like a traffic guard, but you could see she was pleased.

"Radiance was actually rather cross when she came to," Jenny Rose murmured thoughtfully.

Oliver, outraged at this, cried, "To you of all people! After all you've done for her! You'd think she'd be grateful! But that's just like her, isn't it."

"No, it doesn't surprise me either." Paige stood, smoothing the seat of her skirt. She opened a can of spicy raw pistachios and handed them around, laughing pleasantly. "Radiance has a chip on her shoulder when it comes to women."

Oliver grabbed for a fistful of nuts and bulleted them into his mouth one by one.

"God, these are spicy." Paige fanned her face.

"Jenny Rose," I said, sitting forward, "it looks like I'll be living here in Sea Cliff for a while!"

"What, here? Really? That's great. How did this happen?"

"To tell you the truth I just fell into it," I said, and Morgan and I laughed.

"Yes"—Paige rested a light hand on Morgan's shoulder—"how *did* you two meet?"

Morgan turned to Jenny Rose, explaining, "Your aunt is going to help me sort out my mother's house."

Jenny Rose said, "Oh! By the way, the air in the rear of the school bus where Wendell sits is absolutely unbreathable! The driver refuses to crack open a window and so Wendell and I shall be walking or biking to school until the situation is remedied." She summed up her speech with a flourish and knelt beside the boy, holding on to his waist and glaring at us as though daring any one of us to argue with her. There was something ferocious about Jenny Rose with which you wouldn't like to mess.

Worriedly, Paige spoke first. "But, Jenny Rose, the weather's still dreadful!"

"Bad weather never hurt a soul," Jenny Rose answered her staunchly. "Does one good to walk to and fro. Makes you strong." She gave her chest a gorilla thump with a fist. "Robust! And I'm teaching him poetry along the way. You say a thing, he rhymes back, don't you, Wendell! A regular bard he is. I've never known a child to be such a quick learner."

"He might have that Asperger's syndrome," Paige said as though he weren't even there. Her eyes lit up. "Or he could be an autistic savant! Those children have remarkable memories."

Oliver said out of the corner of his mouth, "I'm still astonished she got him to say anything at all!"

Mortified with incomprehension, Wendell put his face down into Jenny Rose's lap.

Jenny Rose tousled with the boy. "No, wait. Give a listen. Wendell, stand straight. Come on, stop that. Show them how brave you are."

His neck mottling a prompt red, Wendell let himself be jimmied into a head-lowered, pigeon-toed stance. Jenny Rose pushed him softly away from herself, saying, "Go on then, Wendell, recite that nice limerick."

His scrawny arms plastered to his sides and his eyes shut tight, he recited:

> *"There once was a man from Turgass*
> *"His balls they were made of pure brass*
> *"When he shook them together*
> *"They played Stormy Weather*
> *"And lightning shot out of his ass."*

There harked a baffled pause when all one could hear was the grand-mother clock's loud ticking from the next room. Then Oliver Cupsand whooped and threw back his handsome head in a burst of laughter. Paige moved the cut-glass ashtrays and candy dishes around the coffee table uncomfortably and in a schoolmarmish tone, she declared, "My! That's not exactly what we're used to hearing in this country!"

Jenny Rose, who'd turned whiter still, flustered, "Er, that wasn't the one that I meant, Wendell. However, you do have a brilliant little memory there. We'll just find a different one for you next time, all right? The one about the pale plum-colored vest would do nicely." It was that Glinty! She'd kill him!

Still grinning, Oliver shimmied jauntily. "So! You've turned our lit-tle Wendell into a poet, have you? Well done! No one could get a word out of him since"—he grappled for the words, then settled on—"for the longest time! I guess there'll be no arguing with the likes of you!"

I glanced at Morgan. His eyes were brimming with held-in tears of mirth he'd disguised with a cough.

"Are you always getting into hot water?" Oliver asked Jenny Rose pleasantly.

"Yes, I am," she answered, just as pleasantly.

"Hmm," he said, turning to me. "Good thing you'll be staying nearby."

"You're not at the cottage now, though, are you?" Paige asked me. "It's too grim."

"Actually, Mrs. Dellaverna, the Italian lady next door, has invited me to stay for the night."

"*Lina* Dellaverna?" they gasped in unison.

"You're joking," Oliver said. "She hardly speaks to anyone!"

"Well, it's just for the one night. She made that pretty clear."

Morgan said, "I'm glad she's invited you. This way you won't have to drive back to . . . Queens, is it?"

"Yes, Queens."

"Really? Queens." Paige turned to me. "How charming." She smiled pleasantly. "Our people are from right here on the North Shore, of course."

"She means we don't associate with anyone south of 25A," Oliver scoffed. "And we rarely leave Sea Cliff at all nowadays if not by boat."

"How lucky for you," I said.

"That Lina Dellaverna, she's so stingy," Paige whispered in a gossipy tone, "she even keeps the money she charges on the House and Garden tour!"

"You don't say!" I said, interested. *Good*, I thought, deciding I liked Paige. I could be friends with a gossip. I didn't know how easy it would have been to be friends with the saint Morgan Donovan seemed to think she was.

Mr. Piet stood in the doorway and announced dinner. In a loose knot, we marched through to the dining room. I remarked I'd never seen such a huge and splendid chandelier.

Oliver said, "We just got it. It's French, probably made in Morocco around the turn of the last century. That's what you said, didn't you, Morgan?"

"Yup. Made of bronze. The whole thing. It took Oliver, Teddy, Glinty, and myself to bring it all the way up from Virginia, didn't it? And then to hoist it up! What a job!"

"Oliver won it in a card game," Paige added with disapproval.

Floor-to-ceiling glass doors lined one whole side of the room and looked out onto treetops and the best winter view of the sound—*except for the Great White*, I thought, prematurely house-proud, where the view was unimpeded year-round.

"The house has so many wonderful rooms," I remarked.

"Yes, the Victorians used to come out here from the city for the summer. This was a grand inn, originally." Paige smiled to herself. She seemed happy, satisfied with the way things were going. I got the feeling she liked having me there.

I noticed Oliver didn't talk to Wendell at all and realized he had no clue how to relate to a child. The only one who did was Jenny Rose and occasionally Morgan, who seemed to have a great store of knock-knock jokes at hand.

Once Morgan asked him, "And when you grow up, Wendell, what would you like to be?"

"I'll have a store," Wendell said clearly and we all laughed. He had such an unexpectedly croaky voice. Then he added, "on the seashore."

"Wendell"—Jenny Rose placed his napkin across his little lap—"you don't have to make a rhyme of *every* sentence. That would be boring, see?"

"And what sort of store might that be?" Morgan inquired.

He thought about this. "Pwobably bells and, like, ropes and bait and beer coolers. Stuff for boats."

"Motorboats or sailboats?" Oliver asked him.

"Oh, sail-boats," he replied without hesitation.

They all chimed in their North Shore approval.

Oliver, realizing this was going well, continued, "So you'll probably stay right here in Sea Cliff then, will you?" He made a thoughtful face. "After college?"

"Yeah."

"*Yes*, not *yeah*," Paige instructed.

"Yes." Wendell frowned. Then he lisped firmly, "But I'm not going to college. I'll be working at Duffy's Bait Shop."

"Ah," we all said, butter never melting in our mouths.

"Be careful when you take him over there," Morgan warned Jenny Rose. "Those buildings down the lane toward the water there are all condemned. Stay away from them."

Paige said, "I have an idea! I was just thinking. Why don't I take over the garden at the cottage? That way the value of the property will be maintained." She cocked her pretty head at Morgan, and I had a sudden horrible vision of her crouched behind the sunflower stalks, watching my every move.

Jenny Rose, seeing my face, jumped to my aid. "Aunt Claire is very modest," she announced. "But when she was in Ireland, she revitalized our little historic cemetery." She took a sip of her ginger ale, her lying eyes holding mine for just long enough. "It's never looked so fertile and glorious."

I blinked uncomprehendingly. It was true in a way, I supposed. Hadn't I clandestinely planted a cremated corpse just inside the cemetery gates? What better fertilizer than that?

"Well," said Morgan, "in that case, we'll leave the cottage garden to Claire."

"But you'll have so much to do!" Paige snatched the crumbled Gorgonzola away from Oliver's reach and smiled pityingly at me.

That condescending smile was what gave me the courage to be honest. "It sounds very silly, I know," I said, "but I'm looking forward to having the cottage to myself and putting it right."

In bustled Mr. Piet with a white china soup terrine. Dinner commenced with what looked like a disappointing broth but turned out to be delicious. He whisked the bowls away and returned with a magnificent platter. He started with Jenny Rose, ceremoniously lifting a piece of fish onto her plate. We all looked at that piece of fish. It was the head. It regarded Jenny Rose with one gooey, glassy eye. Mr. Piet stood there waiting for her reaction.

"What!" Jenny Rose exclaimed. "The head for me?"

Mr. Piet gave a grave little nod.

Fearing what would happen next, no one looked at anyone. Paige's fist covered her mouth. With determined fortitude, and a courage with which I shall always be proud, Jenny Rose tackled this great honor with gusto and swallowed the eyes without the slightest outward sign of revulsion.

Mr. Piet, waiting, watched the last flaky cheek flesh consumed, declared, "*Bien, très bien*," then hurried off to deliver fillets to her and the rest of us. He spooned a horseradish sauce with capers over the sweet white flaky fish, caught, as it turned out, early this very morning by Mr. Piet himself, who seemed to be an invaluable man of all trades.

"What is it?" I asked. "Is it fluke?

"The fluke are just coming in," Morgan said. "It's a weakfish."

"Called so for its weak jaw," Oliver informed me, jutting his own strong one demonstrably forward.

"Oh, Mr. Piet is our treasure," Paige stage-whispered to me. "When he retired to Guadeloupe a while ago, we thought we'd lost him forever. But"—she smiled complacently—"he returned to us after only four months. 'How many tourists can one fellow bear?' was how he put it."

This was all very interesting to me because while Mr. Piet had poured I'd noticed a peculiar tattoo beneath his wrist shirt cuff. I'd learned plenty from my detective husband, not the least of which was the sort of tattoo one acquired in jail. *Guadeloupe, my foot*, I thought. However, what's done is done and everyone's entitled to a second chance if you ask me.

Oliver relegated a trim slice of potato to his plate and cornered it at right angles to the fish with his knife, putting his fork on top of it as if he expected it to jump away or as though someone would snatch it. For such a big man, it was curious that he ate so delicately. And then there was Paige, the size of a dime and fingers like rose petals, wolfing it all down willy-nilly.

"Where is Radiance, now?" I asked.

"They've kept her one more day," Mr. Piet said quietly, "just to be sure."

"Don't fill up on bread and butter, Wendell," Paige warned sharply.

Oliver said, "This wine will interest you, Claire. It's local, but fetching. What do you think?"

I took a sip. It was white and crisp and cold. "Good."

He began to tell me about all the vineyards that were established now along the North Shore. At the other end of the table I overheard Paige exclaim defensively, "I only let in one or two potential clients, for heaven's sake!"

Morgan murmured something in an annoyed tone and she answered back in a hasty whisper, "Well, last week you seemed so keen to sell!"

I kept my eyes dancing on Oliver, but I didn't hear a word he said. I was leaning sideways toward the two of them and I caught her sharp whisper, "I'm sure no one took anything!"

The housekeeper, Patsy Mooney, glowing with steam and energy, manned the pantry door. Her little eyes flew around the dinner plates to check who'd eaten what. Panting like she'd run the forty-yard dash, she passed to Mr. Piet, who scudded in and out and intermittently refilled our glasses with the greenish wine. Jenny Rose, I was happy to observe, knew just how to keep Paige—a pious Francophile—in her place, captivating her with naughty south-of-France tales. I love a dinner party, especially when there are servants and you won't have to pitch in at the end with the dishes and the food is terrific and the wine very good. Wendell surprised us and ate enthusiastically. We all did. After the fish, we had lemon sherbet with little flags of mint in pudding cups, and then came lamb chops, three apiece, resting in rosemary and lemon slices and rocking with garlic. There were bowls of asparagus and fresh spinach and candied carrots. We devoured these, too. It was all I could do not to pick up the lamb bones and gnaw on them.

Jenny Rose, who was seated beside me, whispered, "Aunt Claire, I want to talk to you."

"Of course."

"I need some advice."

"Sounds cheap enough."

"Tomorrow?" She glanced warily aside. "I'll just pop by, all right?"

"Perfect." I sketched out a little map for her.

Her shoulders relaxed. "Heard from the fiancé?" she probed.

"No."

"Well rid of him, I'd say."

I had actually just decided that life might not be all that bad without Enoch when Paige Cupsand, who'd been watching us, reached across the table. "What's that in your ears?" She fingered one of my dangling earrings. "Why, are those buttons you're wearing? Darling, I do believe our guest is wearing buttons in her ears!"

The way she said it, for a moment I thought my first impression had been right after all. And then everyone laughed and I laughed with them. I realized she was simply voicing her surprise. I returned to my delicious asparagus.

Morgan Donovan didn't join in the laughter, though. He left his chair to refresh his hard-liquor drink and came over to me from behind, lightly touching the dangling Lilliput along the way. My neck hairs prickled.

Oliver Cupsand, who'd been savoring his food with a closed-mouth happy chew, noticed this exchange. He patted his lips with his napkin and said pointedly, "Jenny Rose didn't mention her aunt was a famous photographer."

Morgan regained his seat. "I had to hear it from your old employer. . . ."

I was a little disappointed to think Morgan acted as secretary for Oliver. "Well, it's been a while—" I began.

"Not only that," Morgan said, eyes glittering, "but it seems our guest is responsible for solving a murder."

Oliver looked up in surprise. "You didn't tell me that."

Actually, it was more like several murders, but who was I to toot my own horn?

Paige enthused, "A famous photographer! You are absolutely in the right place! I'm sure you'll be portraying our little town as soon as—"

And then, to my astonishment, Jenny Rose took it upon herself to interrupt again, announcing, "Auntie Claire needs some time to recoup, I think. Her bed-and-breakfast burned down in a fire and on top of that, she's just found out her fiancé is gay."

Oliver, just loosening his belt, revolved in his chair and gaped at me. This was just the sort of impudent behavior I'd feared from Jenny Rose. Some people you can just count on not to keep their mouths shut.

"Oh, my dear," Paige cried. "How awful!"

"Yes, it was, really," I admitted. Well, what did I care if everyone knew? It was all true.

"Was anyone hurt?"

"Only my pride," I joked weakly, wishing with all my heart someone would pass around the asparagus again without my asking.

"Was anyone hurt in the fire . . . ?"

"Oh. No. Just everything I owned was lost. I had insurance, but—"

"And your fiancé?" Oliver probed, fascinated.

"It wasn't because of the fire. We actually got together because of the fire, if you can believe it." I looked from Jenny Rose's face to my feet in Mrs. Dellaverna's Italian shoes. "Quite recently. It was just this past Christmas. . . . Romantic, I thought at the time. The truth is that I was as much to blame. I gave my love too soon, before I had the chance to know him. You see, he was so understanding and helpful. My ex-husband has always been the guy everybody wants to hang out with. You know, charismatic and fun, but not much use when it comes to real life. He was a loving father, to give the devil his due, but a degenerate gambler, to be honest. I thought Enoch—that's his name, Enoch—I thought he'd be reliable and safe, you know?"

"Don't think about it," Oliver tried to soothe me.

I shook my head. "If I purposely try never to think of him, he'll always be half there, nudging at my consciousness. What happened was that both my children went back to college, my son's at Villanova—he's a biochem major—and my daughter studies philosophy at Providence, and once they're gone . . . it's amazing but it's as though they forget all about you. I know they don't really but that's what it feels like. All those years of love and having them around and then, poof, you drop them off at some ivy-covered building and if they answer your messages twice a week it's a lot." I heard the whine in my voice. "Oh, I know they're all like that in the beginning. It's just . . . hard to get used to. . . ." I looked at my hands. Even I had stopped eating. "Well, anyway, I let myself get involved too quickly with Enoch. I see that now. It becomes now suddenly clear that his . . . tastes lay elsewhere." I felt sorry for myself and had to shake my head briskly so I wouldn't start blubbering. I held my ear in my hand and pressed hard. "And now, because I came out to see Jenny Rose, one thing's led to another and, well, here I am!" And then, looking around the table at these faces and with a gush of sudden clarity, I realized what exactly I was feeling. Not sorrow. I lifted the delicate glass of white wine to my lips and tasted its clear refreshment. What I was feeling was relief.

"My dear, you can count on us." Paige leaned across and covered my hand with her light touch. "We're not going to desert you, are we, Oliver?"

Oliver, fully in favor of such melodrama, poured himself another glass of wine. "Certainly not," he swore, his face steamed and flustered with outrage for all mistreated womankind.

Paige, smiling kindly at me, reached into her sleeve and handed me her lace-trimmed handkerchief. I thought, *This gal's really something. No wonder Morgan Donovan is going to marry her. I'd marry her myself if I were a man.* She was perfect. Ironed lace-trimmed handkerchief at the ready. Who had such things? And of course she was still of childbearing age. He could raise a family with her. What was she, thirty-five? Thirty-six? Still ripe. Still bleeding. Still juicy. What had I been thinking? Dried-up old me. He was just sorry for me. And of course I could be useful. You want something done, you get an old broad to do it. He knew that. That was what he'd said, wasn't it? Well, look, I told myself. I'd had a good run. I felt his eyes upon me. If Enoch wasn't what he'd seemed, then I hadn't been either. How could I have been, having feelings for a perfect stranger right after I'd caught my guy in the clinch? I tried to think reasonably. I wanted to fit in. I should be happy just to be here with these intriguing people. I realized I had to rethink this. Morgan was taken. That much was clear. I had this perfectly respectable, handsome, appropriately aged, funny, rich—I repeat—rich guy right in front of me. So what was so terrible? A movie or dinner would be so bad? People grow to appreciate each other, after all. I smiled wryly and attempted to move on, "Jenny Rose, I was wondering if your paintings had arrived?"

"Oh, yeah. Truth be told, I haven't even unpacked them yet."

I remembered what she'd said about her disappointment at that art gallery in Cannes. Disregarding present company and fortified with wine, I urged, "Don't let some man who knows nothing about you stop your passion from becoming real!"

Jenny Rose blushed furiously. She rolled her eyes and made a face, saying, "Hey! Don't take it so seriously. It's not like I'm Cézanne or something."

It was interesting that she chose Cézanne, because if there were one artist whose work hers reminded me of, it was him. I cleared my throat. "Please, don't get me wrong. I'm not trying to tell you what to do. It's just . . . you're letting one person's judgment interfere with your future—your whole life." And then I heard myself telling these people I hardly knew, "Years ago, when I still thought of myself as an artist, someone told me that I had no talent. I'd just arrived in Germany and still had hopes of becoming a real painter. He was a critic, an art critic. I took what he said to heart and stopped drawing and painting. I stopped right then. I will say he didn't leave me without hope. I had these photos I'd taken of scenes I intended to paint one day. He pointed out that as a photographer I really did have talent. I followed his lead and pursued photography. What I'm trying to say is that I took his word as truth. Even though all my life until then I'd wanted to be a painter, I let a perfect stranger dictate my future—tell me what was meant for me."

Just then, along came an intricate, show-offy salad, all aged balsamic candied pecans and oak leaves and goat's cheese and cranberry bits at the bottom. We groaned appreciatively.

I went on, "It's not like I didn't have a wonderful career as a photographer. But there are times I pass the odd gallery and I peek in and think, wow, that could have been me, you know?"

And from the end of the table, behind Oliver's chair, Mr. Piet, who'd stood perfectly still in the shadow for the last of my soul searching, said, "Like: I could have been a contender?"

"Yeah." I smiled and looked into his deep brown eyes. "Like that."

Jenny Rose, who'd been watching me skeptically, pushed away her salad, fell back in her chair, and yawned and stretched with a great show of nonchalance. "All right, all right. I promise I'll think about what you said."

I added with heat, "Any talent I might have had is nothing compared to yours."

"Hmm. Really?" Paige's fork stopped in midair and she regarded Jenny Rose with new interest. "And do you do portraits?"

"She surpasses herself with portraiture," I told them all.

Paige said to Oliver, "That's perfect. She can do Wendell and you."

"I'd rather do you, to start." Jenny Rose closed one eye and scrutinized Paige.

Well done, I thought.

Mr. Piet hurriedly collected the dishes and returned with a purple cake decorated with nasturtium. "Oh, you must try it!" Paige insisted. "It's raspberry-jam filling surrounded by layers of real whipped cream. Those are edible flowers."

Obediently, we gorged our way through another achingly delectable gamut of textures.

"I have an idea!" Paige turned to me. "You can do our wedding pictures."

If I'd have wanted to do weddings, I'd have stayed in Queens and opened a shop on Austin Street. Still, it would be ungracious to refuse. "Any photographer would be privileged to shoot you," I compromised by saying—a little too late—and hoping she wouldn't exactly take it the wrong way. And, yes, I admit it, sort of hoping she would.

When the meal was done and Jenny Rose had taken Wendell off to bed, the rest of us traipsed through to the living room. I stayed behind and struggled to rearrange the crotch of my tights, which kept creeping down my thighs.

Paige turned in the doorway. "Is something the matter?" she frowned.

"*Tch*. My tights. They don't fit," I confided.

"You have to go to CVS, just south on Carpenter Avenue for tights. That's where I get mine. Here. I'll write it down. Let me get my pen." She went to her desk and riddled through it. Then she went through her purse, but it wasn't there either.

I said, "There's a pencil on the desk."

She wrinkled her forehead, "It's not that. I seem to have lost my good pen."

Aha, I thought. I was about to say I'd seen a fancy pen at the cottage, but something—perhaps the culpability that crossed her face—held me back. She wrote the way to the shop on a piece of stationery with a pencil and then led me through to another elegant room, this one with tall ceilings lined with shelves stocked with fancy books, everything wood paneled and with a fire blazing at one end. Even the crown moldings wore tooled etchings. A grand piano, off center, graced an antique gold-and-ruby Persian carpet. A library. It was certainly one of the most impressive rooms I'd ever been in. I said so.

"The walls," Oliver said proudly, touching them in a downward, loving stroke, "are chestnut and oak. Every panel had to be refurbished. That's how I came upon Mr. Piet. He did carpentry and I was looking for someone to bring them out. Every contractor I interviewed wanted to either polyurethane them or paint them over." He took a satisfied smack of the matching amber liquid and caressed the glowing walls with a glance. "Mr. Piet's idea, on the other hand, was to scrub them down with hot water and Murphy's oil soap, then a mixture of Patsy

Mooney's pecan oil from the kitchen and beeswax and lemon. I hired him on the spot. He got our Teddy to help him and he did them himself! They glow, don't they?"

Paige, handing around after dinner drinks, chimed in, "Teddy is our nephew. Oh, they worked so hard!"

Oliver said, "Yes. Until Teddy walked out."

"For heaven's sake! He had to go back to school!"

"Paige decorated the place." Morgan spoke proudly from his camel-colored leather easy chair.

I held my smile and turned to him. So this was where he belonged. This was his future. Here he would sit on a Sunday and watch soccer, munch pretzels. "It's absolutely beautiful!" I tried to say with genuine feeling. And it was. Morgan's feet, though, were not up on the hassock. They were being polite and long and thin in moss green deck shoes. Old deck shoes, worn and chafed, the tops of his elegant bare feet tanned and narrow. I pulled my eyes away. As lovely as the place was, you'd never call it homey. Gracious, that was it, an elegant family room in a palace.

Just then there was conversation out in the hall and in strode a handsome young man, flushed with the cold.

"Teddy!" Paige raised herself up to be kissed. "Speak of the devil!" The young man went around greeting us all and as he stood before me I thought I recognized him.

"Sorry I couldn't make dinner, Aunt Paige," he apologized, flopping his overcoat down onto a sofa with easy familiarity. It was the same young man who'd waited tables at Once Upon a Moose.

"Teddy lives out on that romantic schooner you see in the harbor," Paige announced, "the *Dream Boat*."

Teddy said, "Well, I'm refurbishing her. I wouldn't exactly call it living."

"We've met!" I said as he shook my hand. "My niece and I were having tea at the Moose."

He continued to shake my hand warmly, but I could see the light still hadn't dawned. Of course he hadn't noticed me at all because he'd been captivated by Jenny Rose. "She gave you a picture," I reminded him, "of the interior of the Moose."

"That girl? Your niece?" His eyes grew wide. He let go of my hand.

"Teddy is studying at Hofstra," Paige added. "He's going to be a teacher."

He didn't seem to hear her but remained before me. "The girl who did the picture is your niece?"

"Yes." I disengaged my hand.

"I still have it," he said. "I put it over my desk. Uncle Oliver, you saw it! I was surprised at the time that you didn't take more notice of it. You, of all people!"

Oliver looked nervously to the side. "Ah . . . yes. My mind was somewhere else. I was having a quick lunch . . . on my own," he said again and I looked up. Because he hadn't been alone. I remembered now. He'd been with that girl in a green loden mantel. I wouldn't have thought of it but that he mentioned again so pointedly that he'd been on his own.

"I'd advise you to hold on to it, Teddy." I laughed. "That's an original Jenny Rose Cashin."

"Jenny Rose," he murmured, tasting the name like she was a sort of dream. He helped himself to a beer, choosing to drink it from the long neck of the bottle.

"Jenny Rose is our new au pair, Teddy," Paige said.

"What sweet news!" Teddy laughed. "Now you won't have to be bothered with the kid."

Morgan frowned. "I've never heard Paige complain about Wendell."

Leaning herself prettily against the Florentine credenza, Paige informed me, "Wendell was Annabel's last purchase."

"Oh, shut up," Oliver said.

"Well, it's true. She had to have this and she had to have that. She was a shopaholic. It all came too easy to her. The only thing she's really passionate about is shopping . . ."

"She certainly had good taste," I said in an admiring tone, looking anywhere but into Oliver's increasingly sodden eyes. Then I thought, *The poor guy. His wife up and leaves him. Why wouldn't he drink too much?* I said, "The house is filled with wonderful pictures. So many maritime oils."

"Yes," Paige agreed. "That was one thing she did have, Annabel. Talent for the right subject." And as she said this she looked meaningfully at Morgan. Morgan didn't react, but I noticed a flicker of annoyance in the tightening of his mouth.

Paige smoothed her neat lid of platinum hair. "Here's a person with every advantage handed to her and she throws it back in your face! It's a pity, really. No, it's a sin."

Morgan spoke up, more kindly. "She knows how to make a beautiful home. She's romantic. We all wish she would have stayed and duked it out, you know?" Then, thinking he'd spoken out of turn, he defended himself, "We all miss her, I guess."

"I happened to make the mistake of taking her out to sea," Oliver said, enunciating his words with the careful spacing of the intoxicated. "That was one thing I wasn't allowed to do. I could wave to her on the shore . . ." He swayed precariously above the addictive spicy raw pistachio dish. "But I dare not take her with me. I forced her, you see. We'd been arguing. I didn't realize how terrified she would be. . . . I put her in her life jacket and she was trembling. I should have listened. You see. So." He collapsed into the leather chair. "I couldn't get her back to shore fast enough and . . . Well, that was it." He raised his unhappy face to me. "And then she left. That . . . next . . . day."

"I suppose all your trips to Atlantic City and the arguments that followed had nothing to do with it," Paige remarked churlishly.

I pretended not to hear the trouble in Camelot, and Teddy, tired of all this, spoke up enthusiastically. "You really would be interested to see that picture Jenny Rose did, Oliver."

"Mrs. Lassiter did mention she paints," Oliver said, shuffling over to the drinks table. He glanced, puzzled, at Paige. "Wasn't that why we took her on?"

"There used to be no end to the maritime oils in this house," Paige commented, somewhat exasperated, crouching down and straightening the flap of Morgan's hassock. "Annabel deemed them all outmoded. Oliver *would* encourage her to take things into her own hands, change things around." She gave a hollow laugh. "She got a bit full of herself and went about changing all the paintings in the house. Taking down every decent old thing, some of them quite unique, and"—here Paige sneered—"replacing them one day, as a *surprise*, with the sort of thing that screams Home Goods! It was a surprise all right."

"You were the one who agreed with her that they were old-fashioned!" Teddy accused.

"Yes, well, James E. Butterworth is old-fashioned. It doesn't mean one donates him to the thrift shop!"

"Is that what she did?" I gasped.

"And we had to make a pretty fancy donation to explain it all away." Oliver pursed his lips. "But in the end we got most of them back."

Paige added, "And then when Annabel left, we had to get rid of the new monstrosities!"

Oliver stifled a burp. "To whom did we give them? I can't remember."

"Mrs. Lassiter at the rectory," Paige said. "That's how we learned about Jenny Rose, remember? Mrs. Lassiter was the one who went mad for the colony prints." She put a hand over one side of her face and cautioned Oliver, "Only let's not go on about those colony prints. Morgan wanted them, himself, remember?" She leaned over and whispered to me, "Rather a sore spot. Even I had no idea what they were worth. Poor Morgan. He'd been counting on them."

Morgan erupted, "They were seventeenth-century English school prints of the Spanish Silver Fleet, and, as if you didn't know, they were my mother's!"

Paige made a chagrined face for my benefit and said, "Oops." She slipped down beside Teddy. "Of course we knew once, but we'd forgotten. They'd been hanging there so long. It was Noola, Morgan's mother, who made us hang them there over our fireplace, remember? Noola said the spot deserved them. I don't think even she knew how much they were worth. We had them in fours. Burled beechnut frames. Until Annabel swept through with her Monet replicas!"

"Where are they now?" I asked.

"Mrs. Lassiter still has them. The one good thing is Annabel kept the frames. She liked them for her Home Goods collection."

"Well," I ventured, thinking it was one of them, "I have to admit I like the one in the front hall."

Paige said, "To be frank, it only looks so captivating because it's in that massive gilt, hand-carved nineteenth-century frame. I've been meaning to move it. It's too amateurish to be in such a revered spot."

"Just leave it," Oliver warned.

"Yes," I agreed, "it does seem amateurish. And childlike. Maybe that's what I love about it. The uninhibited strokes and bright colors. It draws you in. It's like its own little world in there. Maybe the word I'm looking for is fetching. Or fey. Is it a place . . . beyond the boats?"

My little speech seemed to please Morgan and he smiled at me. "I think it's supposed to be Duffy's Point," he said. "A fantasy view, perhaps."

"Evidently," Paige surmised, her leaden tone putting an end to our discussion of Annabel, "Wendell painted it."

Oliver turned away and went over to stir the fire, then, not liking to dirty his hands, changed his mind and implored, "Morgan?"

Morgan roused himself good-naturedly and pulled the fence away and put on another log. He brushed his hands against each other, glancing over at me. "So, Claire, Jenny Rose is your sister's child?"

Before I could answer, Paige murmured, "There was no father there, I believe . .." Then, lifting her eyes to the door, she interrupted herself. "Ah, there you are, Glinty."

Relieved by the intrusion, I turned to see another young man, lithe and fashionable, dressed all in black. I hadn't heard him come in. He was just suddenly there.

"Glinty" strode silkily across the room, took Paige's hand and kissed it.

"I was beginning to think you weren't coming." Paige indicated the chair beside her with an inviting pat.

"Would I leave you high and dry?" he said, smirking. He, like Morgan, had a strong Scottish burr.

"We were starving or we would have waited," Oliver reprimanded him fondly.

"But you know me. I'm never hungry," Glinty said smoothly, "only thirsty."

He was very young and bold and his hair inky black as a rock star's. *Probably dyed*, I thought with sudden mean spirit, my loyalty resting with the clean-cut Teddy.

"Claire Breslinsky, this is Malcolm McGlintock. Glinty, to us. Glinty, say hello to our new neighbor. This is the lady who's taking Noola's house."

"How do you do." He eyed me briskly but thoroughly up and down as I held out my hand. Just a second too short, as far as I was concerned, because his distraction indicated he was unimpressed. He was, to me, immediately disagreeable, druggy thin as a fingersmith, and there was an odd, fancy smell to him, like weed and vetiver or something. And the tiny diamond in one ear looked real. I know what you're thinking. She doesn't like sexy handsome men. But Morgan irritated me in a different way. In a sexual way, if you must know. This one . . . this Glinty, he had something . . . Rolling Stones-y and aloof about him. I couldn't imagine how he fit in with this upstanding crew. And when he heard I was to have Noola's house, he emitted a black silence I could practically feel.

When Jenny Rose came galloping back in, she reared to a sudden stop.

"Jenny Rose"—Paige lifted one gracious hand to the air—"come in and meet our Glinty."

Glinty was quick on his feet. "Well, hello!" And then, still holding Jenny Rose's eye, "We've seen each other, I think, but we haven't officially met."

They shook hands and Jenny Rose's cheeks burned red. I knew at once she was attracted to him. Oy. The wrong one. The bad boy. Of course.

"At the marina, wasn't it?" Glinty grinned way too familiarly at Jenny Rose.

"Yes. I think so," Jenny Rose stammered.

Teddy stood the moment he saw this, knocking over the valuable chess set and making things worse by falling all over himself to pick the things up. Glinty saw it, too.

"And this is Teddy, our nephew," Paige said, and Jenny Rose simply waved a hello. I watched Teddy; his troubled complexion and high-set, pointy ears, his pale, disappointed blue eyes. My heart went out to him.

"Sound asleep, our Wendell," Jenny Rose said, though no one had asked, and she came and sat next to me and smoothed the soft fold of her short purple skirt. She didn't look directly at him but there was the flutter of her lashes in Glinty's direction. Why is it that women go for the bad guy?

From the corner, Glinty watched Jenny Rose. I didn't like the way he looked at her. Now that he saw Teddy wanted her, he wanted her, too, and the game was on. He was luring her somehow, hypnotizing her, and I felt a little sick. He took out a zippered baggy of cigars from his jacket and, handling them with genuine affection, gave one to each of the men for later, explaining how his friend brought them in regularly from Cuba. I was reminded of Roger Hasenfuss on Third and McDougal, who'd assured us senior girls of the potency of his nickel bags and then lured us back to his roach-infested apartment for his roommate's masala dosa. I could still remember that endless ride home on the F train and having to throw up in the garbage pail on Union Turnpike.

"Claire?"

"I'm sorry, what?"

"We were just talking about the big regatta coming up. It's great fun. Anyone can enter."

"And anyone does," Oliver put in. "People build their own tubs. Kids. Teenagers. They rig up anything that floats. Some fall apart halfway through! Do you sail?"

"No, sorry, never learned."

"Too busy pursuing the life of the mind," Teddy volunteered.

I looked up. He offered me his smile. He had sharp little canines. I liked that idea, the life of the mind. I liked him.

"I do." Jenny Rose raised her hand as if she were in school.

"You can tag along with me, then," Glinty said before Teddy had the chance.

"All right," Jenny Rose agreed without thinking, jumping right in.

"How good are you?" He narrowed his eyes.

"The dirtier the weather, the happier I am," she boasted, then thought better of it and looked at Oliver doubtfully. "If I might have that as my day off?"

Paige shrugged. "Oh, Mooney can stay with Wendell. Or Radiance, providing she's well."

"Providing she's not depressed," Morgan threw in.

"I really wanted Radiance to crew for me," Oliver frowned, lolling slightly.

Morgan turned to me, explaining, "She can sail, that girl. But she can't get into the club. She can work there, but she can't be a member. They'll tell you she could never afford it, but they'd waive those fees for a good sailor like her if her name were Coventry or Brickworth or Davenport."

"Not if she couldn't swim, they wouldn't," Glinty said.

"You mean if she were a shade lighter." Paige smiled unapologetically. Then, "Morgan is our Democrat."

Morgan's jaw dropped. "I'm an independent," he corrected. "And I won't be pigeonholed, thank you. Anyway, I don't give a crap about all that. The environment is my issue."

"Oh, here we go!" Paige raised her eyes heavenward.

"Did you know"—he leaned forward—"there's a glut of plastic the size of Texas in the north Pacific?"

"It can't possibly be that big." Oliver looked up over his drink.

"Well, it is. And it's all because of your plastic water bottles and plastic containers—"

"That's horrifying!" Jenny Rose cried.

"There will be no fish on the planet at all in twenty years if nothing is done," he said.

"Yes, we know all about that," Paige said as she slammed her drink down, "but the way we dealt with the extinction of the dinosaurs, we'll deal one day with the extinction of fish. We'll find something else to eat. Anyway, we have problems right here and now, children who need homes—"

"I'd be happy to stay with Wendell for the race," says arbitrary me. "Really."

There was silence. "Well, then," Paige said, "that would be lovely."

"I'd love to learn to sail," I added.

"Oliver will take you out in high winds! You can learn later in the season, when the wind dies down," Paige advised. "Otherwise you'll get turned off."

"I'll take you out soon." Oliver, with his eyebrows raised, had his scotch decanter perambulating above my glass. "I'll see to it you don't get turned off."

"No, thank you." I had to firmly cover mine with my hand. "No, really! I'm a rye and ginger girl, actually."

"Mr. Piet! Get Ms. Breslinsky a rye and ginger, will you?" He looked around. "Where is he? Oh, yes, of course. He's gone back to the hospital to check on Radiance." He turned to Morgan. "Rye and ginger. There's an old-fashioned drink for you."

Taking the hint, Morgan got up and made me my drink.

Teddy cleared his throat. "Not to belabor the point. But can anyone get back to what Radiance was doing out on a boat before dawn in the first place? Because I still don't get it."

Glinty twisted his earlobe and leaned to one side. "These locals are a bit mad. They're all for the fishing."

"Except that Radiance doesn't exactly fit into that category," Paige remarked wryly.

"Of course there's always the obvious reason," Oliver said, leering. At first I didn't know what he meant but then I took it he meant sex and I guessed everyone else did, too, because Paige frowned in a disproving way, "You're disgusting. No wonder Annabel left you."

But Oliver, ignoring her, went on expansively, "Mr. Piet—first name Gilles—originally came from Guadeloupe. He was a vacation guide there. Had his own sloop." He finished his drink and ran his finger around the rim of the glass, warming to the story. "He fell in love with a tourist. That was Radiance's mother. Margaret, or something. She was a Dutch tourist. No, Margriet. That was it. Beautiful woman, apparently. Well, obviously. One only has to look at Radiance and her long legs. Anyway, the woman, Margriet, went home but when she saw the baby was black, she returned to Holland and left Radiance with Mr. Piet. Well, not black. Sort of cocoa."

"Oh, really, Oliver!" Paige exclaimed.

"Truth's the truth. Morgan"—he thrust a presentational arm toward him—"our Morgan here, was down there when all this happened, dropped anchor there for a while when he'd needed repairs and Mr. Piet helped him with his engine so he got to know the story, isn't that right, Morgan?" He kicked the sole of Morgan's foot with his own. Morgan didn't answer him but he didn't say no and so Oliver went on, "He told Mr. Piet about Guardian Angel House up here in Sea Cliff—they'd just opened in a little house over on Kitchen Lane—and suggested he bring her here. But once Mr. Piet got here, he found he didn't want to give her up. She's been with us almost every summer since she could walk, really." He fished around for the bottle at his feet and poured the last of it into his glass. "She didn't always look like she does now, though, did she, Paige? Gawky, toothy thing she used to be. Shot up all of a sudden."

"So . . . she's worked for you all her life?"

"I wouldn't say *worked*. More like made trouble one way or another. . . ." His eyes twinkled. "She's always acting up. No mother, of course. They used to live on Guadeloupe, but he brought her up here for good after a while. She always lodged at Guardian Angel House because it was convenient for everyone. She would stay on long after the infants were adopted because Gilles worked here for us. It's not an orphanage, you see. More like an exchange place. Aboveboard, of course. No scandal anymore. The girls know before their babies are born where they will go." He sighed. "As a result, Radiance's education has been a bit catch as catch can. She'd just get settled up here and he'd take her back. He has a villa, he says." He lowered his voice. "But they all say that. Personally I suspect it's more like a hut, but you wouldn't want to insult him. He's very learned, really. He just doesn't get a word in edgewise with Patsy Mooney around."

"Nobody does," said a grinning Morgan.

Glinty said, "It's no wonder her husband used to belt her."

"Oh, be quiet, Glinty." Paige flung her cardigan at him. "You're incorrigible!"

"Anyway, they used to go back, but she won't anymore." Oliver lowered his voice. "Wants to make it as a dancer, you see. Wants to be a Rockette."

"She's certainly attractive enough," Jenny Rose piped up.

"And she speaks four languages," Morgan added.

"So does every taxi driver in New York," Oliver pointed out.

"I hate it when you say things like that," Paige said. "It's so unkind."

"It's not unkind. It's the truth. The whole trouble is she's turned into something of a bombshell. Thinks she's entitled to all sorts of amenities. She should be pursuing some sort of job at the United Nations, not the cattle calls in the back pages of *Variety*."

"That was another of Annabel's bright ideas," Paige said scornfully.

I took my new drink from Morgan and sipped it, then sat there swimming happily in my alcoholic buzz. I actually like to be around snobs because I have the feeling if I listen carefully, I'll learn something.

"Don't suppose anyone feels like chess," Teddy said hopelessly once he'd reorganized the board.

"Oh, I'll play." Jenny Rose jumped up. "What a magnificent set! Can I be the Moors?"

I knew what she was up to, making herself more attractive to Glinty by not talking to him.

She and Teddy hunched together at the games table and I couldn't help thinking how good they were together, young, healthy, laughing, and natural. Oh, I knew she didn't care for Teddy in that way—which was probably why she could be so easy and fun filled with him—but maybe later, once she saw Glinty for who he really was . . . I crossed my fingers.

"How's work at the Locust Valley Inn, Teddy?" Morgan asked him.

I said, "I thought you worked at the Once Upon a Moose."

"She just fired me," he said, shrugging, not particularly penitent.

Oliver shook his head. "Teddy's had more jobs than anyone I've ever known."

Paige said to me, "He'd have his real estate agent's license, too, if he'd go take the darn test. But between waiting tables and showing houses for me, he has hardly any free time at all."

"And then there was the club," Teddy put in.

"You wouldn't have so many jobs if you could hang on to one for any length of time," Oliver chided Teddy and this time there was an edge to his voice. "You could have made plenty of money this summer caddying if you hadn't broken Doctor Spiegel's putter in two!"

"He had it coming." Teddy yawned.

"That's not your place to judge!" Oliver reprimanded, turning red. Then he added for my benefit, "We all belong to the sailing club, you see."

"Only I'm hired help, not a member," Teddy grinned good-naturedly. "And I don't wait tables at the Locust Valley Inn," he asserted. "I'm tending bar there, now, Paige." His hand went to his head. "I almost forgot. When I go back I've got to put away those beer deliveries. I'll have boxes all over the place!"

"You don't think I could come and get some, do you?" I ventured. "I never have enough."

"Sure. But don't bother. I'll bring some up to you. Noola's cottage, right?"

"Oh," I said, "that would be wonderful! Are you sure it's no trouble?"

He moved a knight cautiously forward and right then caught my eye. "Not a bit."

Oliver parked himself beside me and took the opportunity to change the subject. "I'm unable to draw a straight line myself, not like Jenny Rose here. Or Glinty. But then Glinty can't really create art, he can only duplicate it. . . ." he added maliciously.

Glinty winked, indicating unashamedly the truth of what Oliver was saying.

"But I *value* art," Oliver went on, "art and"—he put an arm behind me—"beautiful women."

I caught Glinty's dejected, off-guard expression and for a moment I felt sorry for him. I wondered if his brashness was all bravado. "Oh, good," I said with a laugh, pretending to misunderstand Oliver. "You'll be happy when my beautiful sisters come to visit me, then."

"If they're as lovely as you," Oliver began, but I stood up, unnerved. I'd enjoyed his tributes at the table, but this fast work at close quarters was, to my mind, a little much. And to be honest I didn't think he meant it. There was a sort of overkill about his flirting, a desperation that made me feel more pity than caution. I ambled over to the bar as if for another drink.

Jenny Rose and Teddy began to sing a pleasant Dave Matthews song none of us middle-aged folks knew the words to and so we all watched and listened. Then Glinty moved in and gave them a three-part harmony, turning a spontaneous, youthful outburst into a professional-sounding song. He really had a good voice, I admired grudgingly.

My tights had meanwhile meandered their way down my thighs and if I didn't pull them up soon, I was going to have to hop home. I waited until all their backs were turned and then I hoisted them up, only to see Oliver catching me at it. His eyes popped open happily.

Embarrassed, I looked at my watch. It was nine o'clock. I wondered what trouble that kitten had gotten into by now. Also, I wouldn't want to keep Mrs. Dellaverna waiting when she'd been so kind. All I had to look forward to was her couch, but, reluctantly, as they finished their song, I announced, "I'll be on my way, then. Thank you so much for dinner."

"Where's that old guitar of Oliver's?" Glinty called out to Paige.

"Just *please* don't haul out that banjo." Teddy shuddered.

"Sure you're all right to drive?" Oliver frowned, concerned, and stood with a wobble.

I liked him at that moment. He wasn't a bad guy, just hurt and uncertain. "Oh, I'm not driving. I walked."

"The Irish walking girls." Paige laughed, linking her arm into mine. "You'll lose that weight in no time here."

Gosh, I thought. What had I done to deserve that? But she'd said it so sincerely, with such kindness and consideration. And I was just a vain old coot to be offended—for who was it I didn't like to hear that, but her fiancé? Yes. I was foolish and calculating. I realized it. And all she was doing was pushing her brother forward because she loved him and wanted him to be with someone who would love him, not leave him. It stood to reason that in her mind the two losers, the two who'd been left so recently, would find each other.

Then she said, "Come over again soon, Claire. You can be our fourth for Scrabble on Wednesdays. Morgan, Oliver, you, and me." And she fluttered out of the room to go look for that guitar for Glinty.

You see? I reprimanded myself. *She's just blunt and friendly and helpful.*

Morgan Donovan stood. "Come," he said gruffly, with that infuriatingly attractive Scottish burr, "we'll be needing to talk about your duties. I'll walk you on my way to the marina."

I was relieved when no one argued with him and moved swiftly before Paige would come back with the guitar and have something else to say. "Checkmate!" Teddy grinned triumphantly and Jenny Rose waved gaily from the board. Morgan and I went through the elegant rooms to the vestibule. He held my tablecloth up like a bullfighter flourishing a cape and I shrugged into it. He slipped into his bomber jacket and we went out the grand door into the night and crunched down the drive.

"Let's take a detour along the water, shall we?" he suggested.

"All right." The air was soft and delicious and I thought how crazy we all are not to live near the water when there is so much of it in the world. Here I was embarking on an entirely different life. And all because I hadn't gotten on that bus.

JENNY ROSE

Jenny Rose went up and checked on Wendell. Teddy followed her. He stood standing just outside the door when he noticed the muck on the soles of his shoes and scraped it off under Paige's fancy French carpet.

Wendell looked like a statue of a child, still as marble. Jenny Rose almost touched him just to see if he was alive. He was. Of course he was. His red mouth moved a little. She went to his closet and touched his clothes. Boy colors. They were so nice. It was hard to believe a woman would waste her time choosing them and then go off like that. She felt as though that woman wouldn't like her standing here going through Wendell's things and she moved away, sensing something preemptory. But that was foolishness. Hadn't the woman deserted Wendell? She took a last look at the little boy and silently went out.

Teddy reared up onto his toes.

"Oh!" she said. "Hi."

"Hello there." He looked at her with eager eyes.

She remembered her horrible stuffy quarters downstairs to look forward to, gave him a friendly smile, went back in the nursery, and shut the door.

CLAIRE

"Penny for them," Morgan said as we walked along.

I looked up at him. How suddenly everything had happened. And here I was to be friends with these enchanting people. Gardening clubs. Wednesday-night Scrabble. I said, "I wouldn't have figured you for Scrabble."

He lit his cigar and took a deep, satisfying pull on it, "Oh, when you're out at sea you read so many books, and you find yourself able to spell all sorts of words you never even knew you knew."

"And do you spend a lot of time out at sea?"

"As much as I can."

"And what do you do?"

"Think, mostly. Crosswords. Read. I read a lot."

"Who do you like? To read, I mean. Novels?"

"Oh, I don't know. I used to love Joseph Conrad when I was young. Let's see, history mostly. And Thomas Merton I loved. I love the Civil War. Bruce Catton. David McCullough. And naval battles. Nothing I like more than settling down with a story about a good fight at sea. Mainly, I just like an entertaining yarn. Morris West was my favorite. Chap who sailed to the Azores? I'll sit a long night in the bar just to wait for someone to come up with one close to that." He stopped to relight his cigar. "You strike me as bookish, a reader, I would think."

"Do I?" Mentally I raced through my store of good stories. "I'm glad because I thought I came off more as a hysterical woman."

"That, too," he said and we both laughed. There was that good silence that follows a shared laugh. Then he said, "It was nice having you with us tonight."

"For me, too," I said, pleased. "So you're from Scotland originally . . ."

"Oh, aye, a small place called Invergowrie in the north. No one's heard of it but for a famous train wreck in 1979. Glinty comes from nearer to Edinburgh."

"He seems an odd man out," I commented. I thought of the one earring he wore. "Kind of like a pirate."

"Glinty?" He laughed. "He is a bit. He'd love the description. He's harmless enough, though. Good sailor. Worked under me in Bosnia. Good soldier, he was. Well intentioned. . . ."

"Really? I would have judged him weak."

"Ah, no. The power is in the intention, isn't it?"

I thought about this for a bit. Then I asked, "You were a soldier, too?"

He spit out a piece of tobacco. "For a while, yeah. Choppers. Helicopters. 'Twas a good while ago." He brushed it off and we were silent. A ferry horn blew. "That's from Steamboat Landing," he said, adding, "Teddy worked over there, too, for a bit."

"He gets around, doesn't he? And why does Teddy never hold on to his jobs?"

"Never finishes anything. Bit of a temper, that lad. But having one myself, I can't hold it too much against him. Glinty, now, he's cool as a cucumber but a bit of a daredevil. I think he crashed more often in Bosnia than I did. But he never broke a bone!"

"And he lives here in Sea Cliff?"

"Well, down there at the marina, yeah. He didn't have much where he came from in Scotland. A fool's trap. I came across him when I was at university there. He was just a lad. He'd lag about on the docks and take work from the fishermen. No mother. His father was a beast. Had a shop where he'd cheat the tourists. A roaring drunk. But he would tell a great story, you see, so they left him about in the pubs—the father, that is." Morgan's eyes became tender. "Glinty learned the shopkeep's business and everyone else's as well. He'd be playing his guitar down on the loch in the freezing cold—that's where I first heard him—and he didn't even have a jacket so I gave him mine. '*Ach,*' he told me later, 'that was just to get sympathy from the old slags. I had plenty a garb!'"

I had to laugh at the thick Scottish accent that perfectly captured Glinty's.

"Enterprising, he is. When his father died, I took him along with me. He's got a nice little sloop now, called *The Black Pearl Is Mine.*"

"Funny name for a boat."

Morgan chuckled. "You'll find there's no name too silly for a boat. Glinty had a shop for a while in Southampton, living off the gentry. Jewelry, he had, mostly. That's his specialty. Made a bundle. But it's seasonal there. The music, that's where he shines. Well, you heard him. A regular troubadour. He could have stayed a musician but there's no money in it. Doesn't want to spend his life doing gigs at the Barefoot Peddler, he says. And you can't meet all trains, can you? He's hungry for the money, Glinty is. And he's very good at what he does. Always up and down the coast doing estate sales."

"Really? That sounds like fun."

"It was. I did it for years. It was that or boatyard repairs. I don't have the heart to work at a desk, or for someone else. Wears on you after a while, though."

"So that's what you do? Antiques?"

"I did, yes. But it's rare timepieces, complex timepieces that are my crumpet, antique ship's compasses with sundials. And moon dials. Especially moon dials. I'm mad for them."

"I didn't know there was such a thing."

"Oh, aye, timepieces actually dictated by the moon. Can you imagine the strength of the pull of the moon? The tides she rules? She's the queen of time, the moon. And yet it's men's science that channels it, actually directs it. It's mathematics, isn't it? Why, you can feel the movement of the earth as the dial shadow moves!" He laughed at his enthusiasm. "*Och*, any antique gizmo interests me. Fine paintings. Some estate jewelry. But not much of that. That's Glinty's department. Almost went into business with Glinty at one point but then—" He stopped. "I seem to work best on me own."

We walked along silently and came to a house set back from the road. There was an old man with a white beard in the window. When he saw us, he jerked awkwardly and went and hid behind the drapes. I thought that's what I should be doing; I had my own elderly parents who could use some help. I vowed to have them out, make a day of it. But first I was going to have to help myself.

I glanced at Morgan, summing him up. "So the priest thing was just a passing fancy . . ."

He winced with something like disappointment. "Oh. You remember I told you I'd left the seminary, do you? Well, it was more the other way around. Booted out, I was. I, um, beat up a feller there. Another seminarian."

"Ah! I thought Teddy was the loose cannon."

"No. It's not just him. All right, if truth be told, I almost killed that fellow. You don't have to look at me like that. Look. He was having it on with one of the kids from the sacristy. Or trying to. Kind of the old story, isn't it? But can you imagine? Well, I came upon them. Under a beautiful dogwood tree they were. I can't so much as look at a dogwood to this day without thinking of it. I tore him off the kid and almost strangled him. So . . . they threw me out. You can't blame them."

"No," I agreed, but I didn't blame him too much, either. "What did they do to him? The fellow you almost strangled?"

"Him? Short stay in hospital was all."

"Was he badly hurt?"

"Oh, aye. But they don't keep them long, nowadays."

"They throw him out, too?"

"Not at all. He went to confession and stayed on, I imagine."

"That's terrible!"

"It is. But then they're more in the forgiveness business than the punishment business. Or at least they were then. That's my trouble, though. I always imagine I'm here to dole out reward or punishment."

We walked along in silence. Then I said, "And now? What will you do now?"

"Oh, I don't know. We'll see."

I took it he meant after marrying money he wouldn't have to. Funny, though, I couldn't fit him into that niche. And then, before I could stop myself, I said, "So. You're engaged!"

"That's right."

I felt like saying, *You might have told me*, but of course why should he have? If I'd thought him courtly, it was only my frenzied wish for it to be so. And so I said, "You'd never find a prettier bride anywhere."

"No," he agreed.

"When's the date?"

"No date set yet."

I couldn't help liking this news. We walked steadily down one hill and then up another. I thought I ought to say something glib or fresh and self-confident so I didn't look like I was after him, which of course I wasn't. "Don't bother coming up the walk," was all I could come up with. "Mrs. Dellaverna's probably watching out for me and she—"

He didn't seem to hear me. He grabbed hold of my wrist and pulled me toward him. I thought he was going to kiss me and I froze. But he didn't. He just squinted at the sickle moon with that cigar in his teeth and held me up close to him and sort of breathed me in. When he let me go, I turned and walked hurriedly away. But my knees, never my most resolute of hinges, dissolved and loosened like slithery Del Monte peaches in oatmeal. Not so dried up, it seemed. Not so dried up at all.

JENNY ROSE

Behind a curtain, a fluorescent-lit Radiance lay with her face to the wall, her big hair a pale jumble on the pillow.

"*Psst*. Hi."

Radiance turned in slow motion.

"How's it going?"

"Oh." She looked disappointed. "It's you."

Jenny Rose smiled. "You look better."

"I feel like shit."

"Yeah. Well. That's something."

"It's the middle of the night. What do you want? I suppose you want me to say thank you."

"Nah. No big deal. Just want to see you're all right. Did you see the papers? My picture's right on the front. I know I look awful but that's not the point, is it. Everyone at Twillyweed is thrilled. It's like I'm a celebrity."

Suddenly remembering her woes, Radiance rallied. "My back. They think I ruptured a disc."

Jenny Rose drew closer. She made a grimace. "That's tough luck, that."

"I'll never be able to dance!"

Jenny Rose pulled up a chair. "Then you'll just have to learn to live like the rest of us. Flat on our feet."

"What's the difference anyway," Radiance mumbled, half to herself. She frowned. "How did you get here?"

"Swiped your dad's truck."

"Eh? He'll kill you."

"Naw. He's out fishing."

Radiance swallowed painfully and took in Jenny Rose. Little face like a heart. Little jerk. She was just a kid. "*Asseyez-vous.*"

Jenny Rose sat down. She cleared her throat. "You jumped off that boat, didn't you? It was for real, right?" She reached her hand across the blanket but did not touch. "You had enough, right? Aw, that's okay, you don't have to answer. I had enough a couple times myself. I just wanted to tell you, if you ever need some extra money—I always have a little something put away—get you out of town like. Not that you think you've got no choice, right?"

Radiance's drooping lids moved to the doorway and Jenny Rose's eyes followed.

"What are you doing in here?" The cranky nurse stood, hefty arms crossed, feet planted apart.

"Just shoving off, I was."

"See here, you get yourself home. Don't you know it's dangerous to walk around this time of night?"

"I'm already gone." Jenny Rose winked and smiled and patted Radiance's hand. "Take good care of her now," she advised the old cow and slipped out cheerfully.

Radiance, alone now and still taken aback by Jenny Rose's words, was almost sorry she'd stuck those moonstones in the kid's pocket.

CLAIRE

I stood on the cliff a good while, looking and listening to the night. You could hear the water lapping at its edge, soft and sweet. The fog was rolling in and I let it surround me. Suddenly I couldn't bear to impose myself on anyone, and, bad as the state of the cottage was, it was like a place of my own now, and I just really wanted to be alone. I opened Mrs. Dellaverna's door and stood there for a moment, Mrs. Dellaverna's loud snores barreling from inside. There was Carmela's blouse washed and ironed on a hanger, the suit brushed, with only the merest shadow of the stain along the hem. She'd even cleaned the shoes! I leaned down to pick them up and, from a box of tissues on the floor, the kitten popped her head out. The dickens had been hard at work shredding dozens of tissues. I swept them and her up before she went and hid somewhere, then left a quick note of thanks on the kitchen table and crept out.

At the Great White, I slipped the key in the lock. The door swung open. I had the oddest feeling someone had been inside. But that was silly. Probably just the redolence of Noola. I felt around for the light switch but couldn't locate it. I knew there were matches on the lantern. I felt my way to it and struck the match. A small but promising light shone. I'd looked forward to this moment. All my enthusiasm died, though, as I saw what devastation lay before me. But this was the deal I'd made, I told myself sternly, and snapped on the radio. Reception was bad until I found a local station. "This will be Rachmaninoff on a theme of Paganini Opus 43," the voice announced. It filled the cottage. Wearily, I hung Carmela's suit on the standing lamp, put a dish of water down for the cat, and opened the window all the way despite the chill. There was a decrepit Noah Webster dictionary in two parts on Noola's bed stand, their spines held together with mending tape. Each book was three inches thick. I took up volume one, A–Lithistid, printed in Cleveland in 1937. The pages were yellow and their edges frayed, but so well made they didn't crumble.

I cleared a spot for myself on the couch, spread the tablecloth I'd worn to the party over the cushions, covered myself with a cozy plaid blanket I'd found in the cupboard and opened the book. I turned to *G.*

Gnomon. From the Greek. 1. One who knows or examines. 2. The index, or triangle of a sundial that casts the shadow . . . From gnome: thought, intelligence. So called from the belief that gnomes could give information as to secret treasures in the earth.

Hmm. A gnome. I supposed that was Wendell. An indicator . . . I removed my earrings and turned off the yellow light, wondering what sort of shadow this gnomon would cast—and which way it was going to point me.

It was the hour the world is asleep. A meandering glove touched and moved across the underbelly of the cottage in the dark. This glove loved the dark. It caressed the west corner, the nubs and the nicks in the surface.

Ah, this little house had caused so much trouble. Tch. Tch. *Who would have thought such a plain little place could foil so many plans? It wouldn't take much to send it toppling like firewood into the sea. Or burn? It would go up like kindling! But no. There were other ways. And there was time.*

The glove cut and unlooped the decaying jute twine holding the elderly wisteria in place. It drew back appreciatively and it would fall, wounded, onto the dirt and sand with the next jolly wind. A vicious boot kicked the roots up and over the earth. The glove dug an angry chunk off from the crumbling sill but then stopped itself, thinking. It was not the damned house to be got rid of, after all, but the intruder within.

JENNY ROSE

She left Mr. Piet's truck in the deserted marina parking lot, placed the key back on the front left tire where she'd found it, and briskly took the cliff steps up to Twillyweed. When he came in from fishing, he'd find it just where he'd left it and never be the wiser. That poor Radiance was in a great lot of trouble right up to her neck. She'd help her, Jenny Rose resolved, jogging swiftly up the cliff. She let herself in, then went up the back stairs to Wendell's door and checked the bed. He wasn't there! She bolted in, frantic. But there he was on the floor, all curled up. The scamp! Still, she'd best not run off and leave him again. She picked him up and put him in his bed. Light little bugger. Feather light, he was. Putting off descending into her cellar, she lay down beside him and watched his dear little face for a minute, lovely in sleep, then got up and tiptoed to the window. She could just make out the outline of the cottage and thought of her auntie Claire all alone in that ramshackle place. She squinted, imagining she saw some movement there along the cliff and under the house. It was a funny feeling she had. No, it was probably a raccoon. Ought she have insisted Claire stay here with her? The Cupsands wouldn't have minded. And if they would have, she'd have told them good!

The sea was close and black and the mist floated over it in eerie scarves. New leaves on the spreading limbs moved in the wind, obscuring her view. *I'm being paranoid.* She sighed and scrabbled down into her pocket for the satin sack. The stones glittered in the half-light. They were cool to the touch and mysterious, staring at her eerily, but they warmed quickly. She knew she ought to get rid of them but something about them warranted care. She slipped them back into their sack, got up, and leaned against the open window. You could barely make out the Great White, now, hazy in fog. *That's my mother's sister in there*, she thought, smiling. And you never knew what life held in store. She yawned and climbed back into Wendell's bed, half listening to the monotonous slosh of the tide as they cuddled warmly like an unmatched pair of spoons, drifting, lime and lemon, off to sleep.

CLAIRE

When I opened my eyes in the morning, the inside of the cottage was thick with fog. At first I lay there, puzzled, but then remembered I'd left the big window open all night. The weather had changed. I threw off the blanket. I felt strangely good, different. I got up and let the kitten out, then, following her lead, I treated myself to a good stretch. I'd get myself in shape, by gum. I did a little Downward Dog, then staggered across the floor to the window and peered through a wall of mist. There I saw it. The magnificent wisteria, old as the hills, had come down during the night. It lay there, tangled and broken off, a vine once as imposing as Jack's beanstalk. I shuddered, glad, at least, that Noola was no longer alive to see its demise. I shook my head sadly. Then I heard it— the woman with the infant! Without even brushing my teeth, I shrugged into Noola's beaver coat and took off, climbing over the devastated wisteria, finding my way down the steep path to the beach by holding on to the rocks. Down below in the wispy fog I saw her slender retreating figure. Now was my chance to invite her over and I trotted across the sand, the water lapping on my right, her keening song keeping me on course as the fog lifted and then again swallowed her up. Charmed with my own generosity of spirit, visions of company for lunch and a young friend to advise and chat with filled my heart.

"Hi," I called. "Hello there!" But even in the stillness she didn't hear me. I reached, keeping up, and tapped her on the shoulder and she whirled around. She was a man! Long, straggly, yellowed white hair blew in the wind crisscrossing his whiskery face and pale blue eyes, an old man swirling in the thick mist, one moment there and the other not, and there was no baby, just a wrapped-up broken doll in his arms! The hairs on my neck stood up. I screamed with no sound coming out. Like in a dream, my legs would not move. Then I turned at last and I found myself running, running frantically away.

When at last I clattered to the top of the hill, I saw Mrs. Dellaverna out digging, looking as though she were kneeling on a cloud. I almost ran into her arms but I spotted Jenny Rose in and out of the mist, leading Wendell up the winding path—little refugees from Shangri-La—and I ran to her instead. I don't even know what I was afraid of, but the vacant blue eyes of the man had terrified me. And that terrible fog . . . I just sobbed on her shoulder, not caring if I frightened Wendell, just losing it completely. Jenny Rose led me into my own place and boiled up some coffee she found on the stove. Wendell held tightly onto Jenny Rose's hand but he didn't look frightened, just curious.

"Sure, you've had a shock," Jenny Rose said as she spooned sugar into the cup.

"Oh, God," I cried, crashing my fist on the table, "I hate sugar in my coffee!"

"All right, all right," Jenny Rose soothed. "Now tell me what happened?"

Mrs. Dellaverna was in the doorway. "You met up with Daniel, I think."

"Yes, it was a man! He's a man." I covered my mouth. "An old man. But he had this long platinum hair." I trickled my hand down my side. "And I only ever saw him from the back. I heard him singing, well, not really singing but humming, like, *keening* and I thought it was a young woman with an infant." I sniffled, pulling myself together. "You know, I remembered how hard it is with a new baby and I thought, oh, let me invite her up to the cottage. My own son had colic," I went ranting on, "and I'd walk him, from seven to nine every night."

Jenny Rose patted my arm. "Sure, you're not used to living by the sea. It does strange things to a body. The fog and all . . ."

"I think you scared him, eh?" Mrs. Dellaverna said wryly.

"Who's Daniel?" Jenny Rose jumped up and down.

Wendell spoke up, "Daniel, he lives just down the road from Twil-lyweed. He's got a lovely cottage. But it's run-down now." Except for the Elmer Fudding of his *L*s and *R*s, Wendell spoke with the vocabu-lary of an adult and I was shocked to normalcy because he sounded so mature—no doubt what comes from a child spending all his time with women.

Jenny Rose put her hands gently on his shoulders. "Do you know him, then?"

"Oh, sure," he said easily. "Me and Mama always go. We take him mozzarella and cheese and parsley sausage when we go to Uncle Giuseppe's." He stuck his thumb into his mouth, clamming up.

Jenny Rose mouthed the word *Annabel* to me. Wendell noticed this and he sunk into his neck.

"*Ach*," Jenny Rose soothed him, "sure, you'll be wanting to speak of your mum, isn't that it? None of us mind, do we, Auntie Claire?"

"No." I felt better and now somewhat foolish. I looked down at my cup. "I have no idea how old this coffee is."

Mrs. Dellaverna reluctantly left to get some fresh milk and I showed Wendell the button safe.

"This will keep him busy for the while," Jenny Rose declared, set-ting him up on a throw rug.

Mrs. Dellaverna returned with the milk. She'd also brought a bell jar, sliced bread, and a salt shaker filled with red pepper flakes. "Oh, *Dio*! You have to have spicy." She nestled it into the condiments group-ing. "It's what makes life good! You got to have the zest!"

"And what's in the bell jar," I asked, "sauce?"

She gave me a hard look. "Gravy."

Together the three of us cleared off some seats. Mrs. Dellaverna said, "One more, we can play cards."

I put WFUV on the radio, cleaned the percolator as best I could, giving it a wicked scrub, and set about to make a decent pot of coffee. We watched Wendell arrange the buttons into separate piles.

Jenny Rose said, "He's making a little shop." We both smiled.

Mrs. Dellaverna popped some slices into the toaster, checking it first for mice.

Jenny Rose said suddenly, "You know, we could rent a little shop in town and sell buttons."

"Too expensive," Mrs. Dellaverna protested sourly, drumming her fingers for the toast.

"No," Jenny Rose pursued excitedly. "There must be *five* little empty shops in town."

Mrs. Dellaverna laughed. "Don't be *pazza*! You can't make no living selling buttons."

"No," Jenny Rose went on enthusiastically, "but vintage button shops are a draw. There's one in Dublin. We could put my pictures on the wall and your photographs and have a sort of gallery. I could make popovers and tea."

"Mmm." I shrugged, not really paying attention, for I was still seeing that man, that Daniel, with his haunted face there alone on the beach. "I could make my sauerbraten," I said.

Mrs. Dellaverna said, "I could make spaghetti!"

"Is that what you really want to do?" Jenny Rose said suddenly.

"No," I admitted.

"What do you really want to do?"

I closed my eyes and saw myself on a clear day sailing past the lighthouse with Morgan Donovan at the helm. That woke me up. What was I thinking? I shook my head to clear it and saw the mess before me. Slowly, I stood to fetch another cup.

Jenny Rose, her little chin in her fist, said dreamily, "You know, I think I know who you mean, this bloke Daniel. When I drove into town the first time, I saw him behind his dirty windows—it must be the same fellow—and I thought how sad. Long silky white hair, just like you said, almost platinum. I'm not surprised you took him for a lass from behind. Dead skinny. Little bat shoulders. Could be good looking, but he's got those awful, haunted eyes. I still remember seeing him and thinking *this* is America? What's wrong with him, Mrs. Dellaverna?"

Mrs. Dellaverna made a face and shrugged. "He's here a long time. Sometimes, people go visit. They got that Eucharistic minister brings him the host. He's not old, he just looks disheveled. What are you going to do? Put people in the crazy house just because they look and act funny? He wasn't born that way, you know."

I said, "What's with the doll?"

Mrs. Dellaverna sighed heavily. "It's a long time ago. *Dio mio!* That was a story."

Wendell put down his turret of buttons and got up and moved close to the table. "He had a baby that drownded," he mispronounced solemnly and nodded his head to affirm this.

Jenny Rose scratched her neck. I could tell she didn't like where this was going.

Mrs. Dellaverna stroked her mustache and leaned back in her creaking chair. I prayed it would hold her. She said, "No! No, I'll start at the beginning. See, this house here she belonged to Noola. She was a great one to sail. Every year, they have this what you call charity regatta. Her boat was the *For Sail*. Noola was so sure she was going to win. Daniel, he's just a little boy, maybe seven, living here in Sea Cliff. He shouldn't have been in the water. But he was spoiled, always up to no good. The family had plenty of money. What happened was terrible. It was a catastrophe! Noola, she ran over Daniel with the *For Sail*. His head, it came apart. He had to have hundreds of stitches on his head. Hundreds. He's in the hospital for months. His brain was . . . He was never the same, never came back the right way. He was without oxygen too long. And he don't hear so good, either. Noola, it's not her fault. The kid was out where he shouldn't have been. It was an accident. But she never got over it, see? And Morgan, he was in the boat and he watched the whole thing! Noola never forgave herself." Here she stopped and, composing herself, took a sip from her cup. "He's sweet. But let's face it"—she tapped her skull meaningfully—"he's *pozzo*. He looks okay. But who's gonna be friends with such a boy? So when he grows up, he meets some junkie girl in the church basement, at one of those meetings. Janet, her name was. You know, one of those can't help getting stoned, then yoga, then getting stoned again, in and out of all those rehab groups over at the church basement. AA. NA. One of them." She tapped her noggin with her pointer finger. "She was smart, she smelled the money. I never liked her. But that's beside the point. Daniel had property, you know; his parents they left him the little house there on the shore, where he lives now. It didn't look like that then. Let me tell you. So anyway, it was a big shock when she got herself pregnant. *Minchia!* She's into her thirties when she had his baby. *Some* people were not so sure about whether those two could take care of a baby. And let me tell you, they were right. Because one day there she was getting stoned and there's the baby with nobody watching. And this after one time I found a needle on the beach." She shrugged. "I'm thinking, who's gonna change the diaper? But everybody figures somebody else is there to keep an eye on them." She paused, not sure if she should go on and then—all of us listening with bated breath—she continued, "There was talk the baby should be taken away. Adopted through the Guardian Angel House. But then nobody wants to interfere, you know? But then something happened that changed everything. I'm outside, hanging up my wash on the line. I just happened to look down. I see the baby alone on the beach and it's getting dark. I'm shocked! I go down. I take him up to my house and I put him to bed. I didn't know Janet made the overdose—how could I know? Make a long a story short, Janet was dead. They found a shoe, a little baby shoe on the beach. And a sock in the water. Oh, *Dio,* it was terrible. Everybody thought the baby went into the water!" She bit the side of her hand. "I didn't know Janet died. How would I know? Even after I took the baby down, and everyone saw that the baby was safe, Daniel, he kept looking for the baby. Always he looked! That was what, twenty years ago? That's why nobody talks to me." She shrugged, not meeting our eyes, but looking, fretful and hurt, out the window. "So now you know."

Jenny Rose and I said nothing.

Mrs. Dellaverna smacked her ear with the heel of her hand. "*Santa*

Maria! I gotta go. I still got my sauce on the stove!" She went out, slamming the screen.

"Look, Wendell," Jenny Rose said. "The fog's lifted! Want to go, now?"

He jumped up in a shower of buttons. "Please can we go to the boatyard?" he pleaded.

"I don't see why not." She bent to pick up the buttons and suddenly cried, "Wendell, a kitten!"

"She's my stowaway." I laughed, savoring Wendell's rapt expression, padding over to open the screen and gathering her up. I lowered her into Wendell's outstretched arms. "I guess she's decided to stay."

His eyes gleamed and he cuddled her gently, lovingly, to his face.

"She hasn't got a name," I said. "Maybe you can think of one?"

His mouth dropped with the shock of this great idea and his glasses steamed with intensity. "I can," he swore. Then he looked worried. "Now? Do I have to say it right now?"

"No," I said as I filled the sink with soapsuds, "she's been nameless so long a little while longer won't matter. But let's keep her here in the cottage, shall we? You can see her anytime you want."

"All right," he agreed solemnly, planting a dry kiss on the little head.

"Auntie Claire . . ." Jenny Rose put her cup in the sink. "You'll be all right?"

"*Tch.*" I clicked my tongue reassuringly. "I'll be fine. I'm a nervous Nelly, that's all. Just don't mention my flipping out to Morgan. He'll think I'm crazy."

"I won't." She kissed me on the cheek. I walked them outside and they took off down the hill. There was no car to be heard, no airplane overhead, just the bright caw of the gulls and the flap of the flag. *I should be grateful for what I've got*, I reprimanded myself, *not thinking about another woman's fiancé!* Back inside, I found Noola's phone book and telephoned Paige.

"Ah!" She sounded happy to hear from me. "I was just thinking of you."

"Really? I wanted to thank you for the lovely dinner. And I thought I might reciprocate and ask you to lunch," I said.

"No, absolutely not. I'll take you to my club. It's Wednesday, Ladies' Day. You'll love it."

"Great."

"Shall I pick you up in an hour?"

"Fine."

"Oh. And no jeans."

The wind flew in. I regarded my one and only suit fluttering respectably on its hanger. "Not a problem."

The club turned out to be one of those prestigious white and navy affairs with touches of polished brass. It was situated in a pretty cove with a half-moon beach at its lip and tennis courts discreetly off to the side in a huddle of bushes. Striped canvas awnings pooled the wraparound porch in shade. In the main dining room, old-fashioned propeller fans whirred and dangled from the ceiling. I was the only human being not wearing white. We helped ourselves to fancy salads and fresh sandwiches at a table indoors and took seats at a round table set away from the clique of other women.

"They won't like that we sat over here," Paige remarked. "The women always sit together at one table. But I thought we might talk."

"Sounds good." I covered my lap with the creamy linen napkin.

"By the way, I notice you've got your camera with you. Please don't photograph anyone here."

"All right," I agreed, hoping no one had noticed me shooting while she was in the ladies' room.

A waiter came over. "G-and-T for both," Paige specified without consulting me, then scrutinized my face. "Are you settling in?"

"Not really. It's a mess. And last night the wind took down that huge wisteria vine. Such a tragedy! I'll have to have someone help me remove it. But I'll get there," I hurried to say, not wanting her to pull out her do-gooder persona and invade my space.

"Just how *did* you and Morgan meet?" She jumped right in—not a girl to waste time.

"I saw his sign from the beach, actually. Then I ran into Mrs. Dellaverna."

She looked out toward the fleet of little sailboats heading into shore. "Good old Mrs. Dellaverna," she said. But it was the way she said it. So she was nobody's fool. Then she added, unnecessarily I thought, "I told him not to hang that sign. He insisted only locals would see it from the beach."

"I see."

"You know," she said, toying with her earring, a tasteful gold knot, "Morgan has a lot on his mind."

"Yes, I realize he's just lost his mother."

"Well, Easter. She died just after Easter."

"When someone dies from a heart attack, it's so sudden—and death is so final."

"Mmm, she'd been failing for some time, though. And the truth is she died of an overdose."

I said, "I know how old people are. They take their medicine then forget they took it. My own parents—"

She interrupted, "There was some . . . *skepticism* about her intentions. There's an unpleasant stigma attached to that sort of death. It was understandable that she might forget and take more than her daily dose, but to have taken *five times* that . . . Well, we all rather *protected* Morgan from her intentions."

Or someone else's, I thought. "No one suspected there might have been"—I glanced around—"foul play?"

"No. No! We all loved Noola. But, you see, she couldn't do the things she loved anymore. She knew she was getting rapidly incapacitated by Alzheimer's. What I'm getting at, as sophisticated as Morgan is, there's something idealistic, almost *naive* about him as well."

"Oh?"

"I wouldn't want to think he was laden with distraction."

Did she mean me? I put down my fork. "You don't have to beat around the bush, Paige. I'm a big girl."

She pursed her lips. "Yes. We both are. I think we understand each other." We were silent for some moments. Then she put in, "I'd like to think we are on the same side."

I turned this over in my mind. So much had happened. It would be unwise of me to burn my bridges before I'd even landed. And I had no doubt this woman would know just how to go about getting me ejected from Sea Cliff.

A boy in an immaculate white jacket stepped in and refilled our water glasses then slipped discreetly away. I gave her my loopy *you're right and I'm wrong* smile. "Okay."

"Good." She sat back. "You know, Claire, we might even be able to help each other. Wendell particularly has been a great problem for us. He and Annabel were always up there with Noola. I don't know if you've noticed, but my brother doesn't have the slightest idea how to raise a child. He's on another planet."

The waiter returned with two iced gin-and-tonics stuffed with limes.

"What about Annabel?" I took a heavenly sip. "Will she come back, do you think?"

"*Phhh*. She wouldn't dare show her face in this town. Refreshing, isn't it?"

"Yes. Delicious. Just the thing. It got warm so suddenly, didn't it? I have to agree with you about Annabel. I think any woman who would leave her own child is despicable. But I was just wondering. If she was such a fly-by-night, why did they give her a child? It seems to me, she started off well intentioned, didn't she?"

"Ah, yes"—she raised her eyes—"the well intentioned."

I thought, *The power is in the intention.* Now where had I heard that? "You sound a little cynical," I said.

"I'm not. And I'm dead serious. The gall of that woman! To keep writing to Oliver like he's an old friend! It's beyond belief." She drained her glass. "Bring me another," she said to no one without raising her voice.

"Yes. You're right," I said, trying to understand. "But it must have been that she'd fallen hopelessly, horribly in love."

She rubbed her arms, chilled. "Love!" She practically spat the word. "That's not love."

"It does happen," I went on. "To just leave like that. . . . She must have been so ashamed."

"*Uch*. Please. Don't go finding excuses for her. You don't know her. She's all excitement and enthusiasm one minute, sadness and sorrow the next. And what really bothers me is that you won't hear a bad word about her from Oliver." A waiter from nowhere appeared with another drink. "He dismisses all her bad behavior as his fault. I can't bear it. He blames him*self*. He left her on her own too much, he thinks. Instead of Atlantic City, he should have 'taken her to more plays and museums,' he told me last week, '*That's* what she likes.' But the truth is he couldn't have done more. She's just selfish and egotistical. Oh, she had us all fooled," Paige went on. "She swept into his life with her goody-two-shoes routine and took everything she could and then swept out of it. Jewelry. Family jewelry. That's the kicker."

"Oh, I see."

"No, you don't. You think it's because I wanted those pieces for myself. But I don't care about them. Not really. All right, I suffer to think those emeralds are gone. But mostly I wanted Oliver to be happy. He was, you know. For a good while. He was luminously happy. You could hear it in his stupid car when he drove up, see it in his eyes when he came in the door, all goofy and merry. The house was like a fairy-tale port in an everyday world. There was music, fires in every grate. He loved a fire. She always made sure the house was perfect, I'll give her that. You should have seen Twillyweed while she was there. She named it that, you know. Silly name from a silly woman," she said scornfully. "The house never had a name before she came along. Romantic. Read those stupid novels one after the other. Always at the library. 'My best customer,' Mrs. Wetjan, the librarian, called her." Paige's face softened, despite herself, remembering. "It was so beautiful last autumn. Every window gleaming. She'd sit on the sill upstairs and Radiance in another and they'd polish the windows—as if they enjoyed it! She *liked* being a housewife, she said. She certainly had the knack. And then with the snow. It was like a fairy-tale castle, all ashimmer. The only thing missing was a child. And then she even had that." Her voice was tinged with desperation. "It was me, if you want to know—*I* saw to that—to my shame. Even though I should have had my doubts—about whether she'd stick with it. Wendell can't have been easy at first." She frowned, cooling her soup with her breath. "But oddly enough she took to Wendell right away. Despite myself, I thought it was the great success, the perfect fit. Until she left. You see? Even happiness wasn't enough. And she *snuck* away." Even across the table I could hear her rasping breath. "And now there's me. Filling the place with loathing."

"Oh, no."

"Yes." She gasped and sobbed. Tears, so long in check, sprang from the well of her blue eyes.

I was completely caught off guard. She always seemed so in control. And she wasn't pretending, that was sure. She, too, had been hurt by all this. Wounded, deeply, from the wrenching look on her face. Quickly, though, she blew her nose and pulled herself together, glancing around to see who'd taken it in.

"The worst of it is she keeps writing to him, torturing him, really. Going on and on in her neat little handwriting on the very writing paper Oliver gave her for Christmas, pale pink with dahlias along the edges. Telling him how happy he should be she's gone and how he should get on with his life. Giving him advice!"

"So at least we know she's not dead, anyway," I said.

She gave me a frozen look that seemed to say it would be better if she were, then she went on, "She's in Virginia Beach. Writes about what a big art center it is now. How he would love it!" She lowered her voice. "I'm sorry, but Virginia Beach is no such thing as an art center. Not by a stretch! And not a word about Wendell. That's the worst of it!" She bit her lip and shook her head. "You'd think . . . If he wasn't the right child for her she could have given him back, you know? Worked with us. Found him another family. There are people who find themselves in such circumstances. It happens." She clenched her napkin and wrung it. "I told Oliver. I said, 'Go down and get her. Bring her back, if you can't live without her!'" She crunched over and shook her head. "Then he showed me her letter. How anyone so sweet can be so vindictive is beyond me." She bit her lip. "Even torturing him about his inadequate lovemaking! It's beyond cruel." She gave me a sharp look. "Yes, I know Oliver is fussy about clothes. But we were brought up to be elegant. Annabel used to make fun of him for it, but to use it to be deliberately vicious . . . and untrue! Oliver is very male, trust me."

Uncomfortable, I changed the subject. "What were Wendell's birth parents like?" I probed.

Paige puffed as if to blow out a candle, indicating her difficulty. But she was too far into her story now to stop. "I shouldn't say . . ." she started and then went on, regardless, "His mother was just a girl. They were from the Midwest. Went too far with her boyfriend, the old story. Didn't know she was pregnant until too late. It was summer. Her mother came with her and left her here. Wendell was born early September. The mother came back and picked up the girl. She never even looked at Wendell. Never went in to take a peek!"

Carmela! I thought. *Just like Carmela.* I said, "One day she'll come looking for her son."

"Who, Wendell's mother? No she won't. They left together like they'd been on vacation and the girl went back to school. No one knew. The mother put her here because she couldn't tell her husband. He'd kill her, she told us. I don't really think that was true, but a baby certainly didn't fit in with their social agenda. She pretended the girl was at camp." She snorted. "French camp! She even paid Radiance to go over there every day and speak French with her. We didn't place Wendell because we always thought one day . . . maybe . . . She never did, though. Not one inquiry! Usually the boy babies are snatched up right after they're born. However, there's little call for a baby with a vision problem. I know he looks frightening with that big head and short little legs and that eye—"

"No!" I protested. "He's just a little boy! He's adorable!"

"Yes, well, you're kind. In Wendell's case it's nothing more than a lazy eye—correctable in time with glasses—but his is particularly grievous."

"That's a sad story." I sighed. "But Annabel wanted to be good."

Paige reared her head. "Oh, no. I'll tell you what she *wanted*; she wanted to fit in with the moneyed North Shore set. She was a nobody from the South Shore. She worked at the gift shop in Locust Valley. She knew what she was looking for, all right. That's how Oliver met her, buying a birthday gift for me if you can believe it; he complimented her bow tying. Told her she'd tied a perfect clove hitch. He teased her, saying he could have her hoisting his mainsail in no time at all. She hoisted his mainsail, all right. The minute she met him she switched gears and became a volunteer. Made herself a peer. Oh, she knew just what she was doing." Paige rubbed her chin along her arm. "I have to admit they seemed to be happy as long as he was role-playing. You could tell they liked each other. As soon as he went back to his regular ways, though, gambling, sailing all the time, things started to go wrong. They began to argue. And she hated the water. But she wanted to come to lunch here, at the yacht club. That she wanted. She came. She sat right there where you're sitting now. Thought it was ever so chichi. But the truth is these women don't care about things like that. Fancy things. They just love to sail. It's in their blood. They live for it. And she doesn't want any part of it, Annabel. It made her a nervous wreck, the sailing. She couldn't do it. When she realized she'd never really fit in, she put on a new dress. One that would fit her better. A runaway." Paige spat the word. "She'll find out she's no good at that, either. It's bad enough about Oliver. But Wendell wasn't a dog you adopt from the pound and then abandon. It's criminal. She's a criminal. And so is Patsy Mooney if you must know, always speaking well of her, defending her, never letting it go, making Oliver suffer, on and on . . ." She actually shook her fist in the air.

I shrank back. "But why didn't she just get a divorce? Surely she would have been better off."

"Oh, that was the other thing. He made her sign a prenup. To protect *me*, he told her. She would have had to stay around a good while to have gotten anything. *That's* why she left. That's why she just took off."

A rugged-looking woman approached the table. "Hello, Paige. Who's this?"

"Hello, Taffy. Taffy Henderson, this is Claire Breslinsky. She'll be photographing the race for *Town and Country*."

"Ah!" She gave my hand a hefty shake. "Don't forget to get a good shot of the *Dauntless*. We'll be the winning skiff."

"Oh, no you won't," Paige promised. "The *Corinthian* will win. She always does."

"We'll see about that. Your luck's changed, I hear." Taffy closed one eye and aimed her tanned face at Paige. "Well!" She turned and hit her hips. "Nice meeting you, there, Kate."

"It's Claire."

"Yes. Claire. Enjoy your lunch." She scuttled off.

I said, "What was that all about? *Town and Country*?"

"I just told her that," Paige said, shrugging. "I lied. Serves her right. She was very rude coming over and asking who you were."

I laughed. "It didn't bother me a bit."

"Well, she shouldn't have. You're my guest. But these women sort of despise me because my outfits are coordinated. You know what I'm saying."

I did.

She squinched up her face. "And they think I overanalyze the wind. They don't think I'm a *natural* sailor. That sort of thing is very important to them."

A terrific-looking, elderly blond woman with blue-white teeth approached our table. She held up her clipboard and pen. "All right. Think about how much I can shake you down for. I'll be over after dessert to sign you both up." She moved athletically off.

"What was that?"

Paige said, "There's a garden contest every September. She's selling the seeds now."

"Oh, I don't care about things like that," I said.

"But it's for charity. You'll want to play! The winner gets half."

"Oh. So what do they usually collect?"

"Twenty thousand, give or take."

"Ten thousand dollars to the winner?"

"Ten, yes. Or fifteen more often. Half to the winner and the other half to her specific charity."

"I'll take a package." I scrounged around my purse. "Sign me up," I said. Just then my cell phone burst out a series of thunderous rings and I shuffled around in there to retrieve it. When I opened it, I realized every single person in the club was staring at me. "*Ach*," I said to loudly to everyone, "it's the pope. He always calls when I'm eating."

Paige lowered her eyelids at me. "Put it away, darling. There are no cell phones at the club. Ever."

I closed it without even answering. We finished a bowlful of fragrant berries and Paige, on her third drink, signed up for the contest, then left. Considering the way she'd been belting them down, I figured she was toasted so I told her I'd drive.

"Don't be silly."

But I slipped the keys from her easily and once buckled up, she nodded off into a cacophony of snores. These were music to my ears, for I could only mean-spiritedly think how unfeminine they would sound to Morgan.

I dropped her and her car off and hiked up my hill.

Teddy, bless him, had been a man of his word. He'd delivered a good twenty big cardboard boxes to the side of the road and had weighted them down with huge Montauk stones from the garden. The boxes were soft from the fog but not wet so I lugged them in. He'd left a thoughtful note on one of them. "Claire," it read, "Will stop by later to help you chop up that old vine. Teddy."

I'd be sorry to see it go, but I was glad for the help disposing it. The first thing I did was seek out those shallow aluminum serving trays from the shed and fill them with dirt. I lined them up along the south window and made little furrows and sprinkled in the seeds. I cut out the names on the envelopes and taped them onto toothpicks. In the back of the pantry I found a tin of anchovies and cut the fishies up into tiny pieces and poked them into the dirt. In three weeks there would be sprouts and not long after that flowers. What, Paige was the only one who could have a money garden?

JENNY ROSE

That night, Jenny Rose sat by herself in the dark at the kitchen table. Patsy Mooney came in balancing a blue-and-white Limoges dish of half-eaten sausages and she snapped on the light. She came to a sudden halt seeing the girl, and the sausages rolled dangerously to the edge of the plate. "Jesus! Holy mackerel, you gave me a start!"

Jenny Rose stirred her soup. "I can't sleep. I hope you don't mind. I've opened a tin."

"Why would I mind? Saves me the trouble." Patsy went to the stove and heated what was left in the pot to a boil. She sniffed the air and made a face. "Oxtail soup? *Uch.* Better you than me." She waited another moment then spooned the rest into Jenny Rose's bowl. She went to the bread box and tore off some Italian bread, got the good olive oil from the shelf, and set it down. She whittled away at the rest of her sausage and, with a great show of kindness, divided the pieces and nudged the other half onto Jenny Rose's saucer.

"Well, thanks."

"Now what would you like special for saving Radiance? Come on, anything you like!" She eyed the vodka bottle over the fridge. "We'll have a real celebration!"

Jenny Rose mulled over this thought, then suddenly her head shot up and she said, "What I'd really like is to switch rooms with you, Patsy Mooney."

Patsy Mooney moved back in her chair, scraping the floor and upsetting a basket of onions, most of them rolling off into corners. She bent over to pick them up with a groan and Jenny Rose sprang from her seat to help.

"That don't make no sense. Why would you want to leave that gorgeous apartment you got? And for my drafty place?" She leaned her fat elbow on the chair cushion and dabbed away at little dustballs from under the stepping stool with her hem. "There's plenty of rooms here. Paige's always saying how 'charming' they all are." She sat back on her haunches, her pinafore straining. "You notice she don't help her nephew Teddy out by offering him a room, though. That she don't do. And here they have this big house." Thoughtfully, she rubbed at a smudge on the floor. "She's always bragging about how smart her nephew Teddy is and how ambitious. Talking him up. Like she's . . ."—she furrowed her brow in thought—"overcompensating. It's like she wants to pawn him off on someone else, like. And here they've got it all. You'll notice she's not so fond of sharing. Sends off a check in the envelope each week. Keeps the poor at arm's length, that's what. That's the rich for you, Jenny Rose. Don't you ever forget it." She sucked a tooth.

Jenny Rose lurched toward Patsy and grasped both her hands in her own. "Oh, please!" she implored. "Let me move into your turret and you can have my cellar! I can't bear that dry, awful space without a decent window! And you said that you love it! Oh, please!"

"But you got that nice bright fluorescent light," Patsy reasoned doubtfully, cringing from the contact, dusting her off. "And my room is cold these nights. It's drafty and noisy in a storm!"

"I told you I love a storm and I can't bear fluorescence and central heating from every direction! It makes my nose stuff up. I really mean it. A drafty turret is everything I could dream of. So romantic! I could wear my Greek cardigan and set up my easel and—"

Patsy leaned suspiciously forward. "Just be straight with me. There's nothing hidden in there with that cable box, is there?"

"What do you mean, hidden?"

"Like dirty movies or nothing . . ."

"No. Of course not. I'd say so if there was. The truth is, I wouldn't know, would I?" She thought guiltily of the blue gems and prayed they wouldn't show in her eyes.

Patsy flattened her mouth and looked over her shoulder worriedly. "All right, all right. If you really mean it. It's just that Mr. Cupsand had that apartment smarted up special for the au pair, he said, see? So I don't know if he'll like the idea. . . ."

"Then we won't have to tell him! I won't mention it if you won't. Okay? If they find out, we'll just say we decided to switch! Once we've moved our stuff they're not likely to do anything about it." She looked beseechingly into Patsy Mooney's darty little eyes.

Already Patsy could see herself propped with her feet up on that comfy couch watching the Yankees. "All right," she agreed. "But not a word to no one!"

Excitedly, their shoulders scrunched up to their ears in happy anticipation, they went to rearrange their stuff.

Radiance, theoretically at Twillyweed to recover, had returned unannounced and was staying in her father's rooms. She was on her sweet way to the porch to light her joint when she saw Jenny Rose and Patsy Mooney cavorting up the grand staircase. She stood now quietly in the foyer, unobserved, enjoying their stealth. They were up to something, those two. There was no one on the main floor now but her. She threw a lemon in the air and caught it. Threw it, caught it. When she slipped through to the dining room, she hesitated. Someone had been looking for something because they'd left the top drawer in the ladies' writing desk ajar. A piece of something was caught there behind it on its way to the floor. Without turning on the light, she felt her way over and grasped it, a sheet of old-fashioned letter paper, a soft shade of pink and edged with dahlias.

CLAIRE

Armed with news, I telephoned my son and daughter. They were very cavalier about my state of affairs, though both of them were pleased I had somewhere to live. For them, Grandma and Grandpa's house could always serve as home base. And how close was I to the water? "*On* the water? No shit!" They forgot their manners and gasped. They liked that, had visions of themselves arriving with carloads of drunken friends on weekends when I wasn't here. And, to be fair, I don't think they'd been entirely sold on the idea of Enoch. Well, they both love their dad. I was very nervous calling my mother, however. I might be a mother myself, but you have to know mine to understand. You see, because she thinks she's the boss of the world, the whole world thinks so, too. I was nervous out of habit, I guess. My father picked up the phone.

"Hi, Dad, it's me, Claire."

"Who is it, Stan?" I could hear my mother over Bill O'Reilly in the background.

"Some lady," Dad said.

"Hello?" my mother said in her tart *whatever yer selling we'll not be buyin'* voice.

"Mom. It's me, Claire."

"What's wrong?"

"Oh, I knew it was Claire all along." My father's voice jollying in the background.

"Nothing. I just wanted to let you know I'm all right."

"Made up with Enoch, have you?"

"No. I'm still out in Sea Cliff. I—"

"Sea Cliff! Are you with Jenny Rose?"

"Yes, actually. You see I—"

Excitedly, she rushed on, "Darlene Lassiter called from the rectory out there. Tell her I've bought seven copies of the *Post*! I'll have them polyurethaned and send them off to Skibbereen day after tomorrow!

Now, you'd better bring Jenny Rose here on Sunday. I'll not have them speaking ill of me back home."

Back home to my mother will always be Skibbereen in County Cork. No matter she's lived here fifty years. "All right, I'll ask her."

"No, you'll tell her. I'll make me famous meatloaf."

"Okay, Mom." I hung up and thought I must go and buy some jeans and sneakers and sweatshirts. And—I sat down to make a list—some lovely new sheets. Anything at all would be better than going back to sleeping with Lefty on that couch.

JENNY ROSE

Jenny Rose, too, had a phone call to make. She waited until everyone had gone their separate ways and then she called.

"Hello, Mrs. Lassiter?"

"Hello, yes? This is Darlene Lassiter."

"Hi, it's Jenny Rose Cashin, Mrs. Lassiter. Brigid and Deirdre's girl. I'm here at Twillyweed."

"Oh, are you, now? Just a minute, let me sit down. I've just come back from sorting out old Father Schmidt and I'm just drying my hands. There. Are you settled in?" Before waiting for a reply she blurted, "We heard all about you rescuing the Piet girl!"

"Oh, that was nothing." Jenny Rose swayed modestly.

"That's not what Teddy Cupsand said. Painted you up as a real hero, he did. And your picture in the paper. What will they think of that back home!"

"No doubt they'll brush it off as just good luck as I did," Jenny Rose said, imagining, anyway, the lot of them leaning over the paper on the bar at the White Tree.

"Well, you've done us proud. Now tell me, lass, have you met the little boy?"

"I have. He's darling."

"Not too much trouble? Because there was talk he's a bit backward."

"No! He's bright as a shiny new penny. He's just shy." *And hurt*, she thought but didn't say.

"That's fine, then."

"I wanted—The reason I'm calling is to say thank you for hooking me up with this job—I'm sorry I haven't come by in person, it's all been a mad dash—and to bring you greetings from home."

"They're all well?"

"Yeah, they're fine. So, I wanted to say thanks and all . . ."

"That's a good lass. I remember you when you were just a wee thing. Hot tempered! Tempest in a teapot, that's what we used to call you, dashing all about the cricket field. Will you come and pay me a visit?"

"Soon as I have a few days off. They're talking about a race and I might be able to sail . . ."

"Oh, you'll love that. All sorts of nonsense these rich folk get into. And the fireworks at the end! If I don't see you before, I'll see you there."

"Sounds great."

"Oh, and be careful of that Mr. Cupsand. He's got an eye for the ladies, that one."

"I will. Thanks again."

"Good-bye."

"Yes, good-bye."

Mrs. Lassiter sat by the phone for a minute more, thinking.

Then Father Schmidt ambled in. "Are you done?"

"What is it now?"

"Come on, Darlene. I've been a good boy and I've eaten all my peas. Show them to me, come on."

"No. Go away with you."

His eyes glowed like coals. "Just this once more, Darlene. Let me see them." He wriggled excitedly into the oak chair.

"Oh, for heaven's sake," she muttered, pleased, unbuttoning her blouse.

CLAIRE

Late at night I heard some noise out in front of the cottage and went to investigate. Mrs. Dellaverna was standing there struggling with the wisteria carcass. She had it lifted over her head. "Don't just stand there!" she berated me. "Help!"

I ran to her. "It's no use!" I cried. "The roots are up. It's no good. It's dead!"

"*Porca miseria!*" she snarled. "Get down on the ground and cover the roots! What's the matter with you? Hurry!"

I did as I was told. I dragged and dumped enough dirt over to cover the naked roots and then helped the old woman hold up the trunk. Believe me, she was strong as an ox! I trembled under the clumsy weight, but she stood there, feet planted, until I got around and lugged the python of a vine up the steps and thrust its thick hulk back onto the roof, trying best I could not to upset the already wilted foliage. Together we wedged it, bypassing the drainpipe, and laid the old torso back home on the generous swoop of the roof. "It's best we do it in the moonlight, so it don't get a shock," she said. She had a crude wooden hacker with an iron hatchet and watched while I dug up more soil with it and tidied the roots over, absorbed in my task. Doubtful, I stood back to look at it, in place but clearly wilted. "I can't believe we did it!" I marveled, but I couldn't see where she'd gone. I caught her unawares beneath the seaside of the house, measures of broken twine in her hands, an expression of panic gripping her face. "What's the matter?" I said.

"Nothing," she frowned, squinting worriedly out at the sea. "Wet the dirt down good now with the hose."

When I finally got to bed, I tossed and turned on the lumpy sofa, far too wired to sleep. There was unease about, some discomfort I couldn't put my finger on. The wind hurled across the bay. It was now that I really missed my dog, Jake. A dog is a comfort. I lay there reliving Enoch's cruel betrayal, gnawing on it, unable to get past the shock of it. And who knew what new wanton carousal my Jake was witness to at this very minute?

Giving up, I turned on the bright overhead light and pulled a couple of clocks down from the wall. None of them appeared to be broken, just neglected. They were each of them the antique, wind-up type and it was kind of fun seeing them spring back to life. I got up and stretched and walked around and decided I might as well take a stroll into town. How thrilled Jake would have been by an unscheduled late-night walk, I thought. I knew he was better off where he was, but still I resented not having him. Funny how a dog steals into your heart.

On my way into the village I passed the local bar, Gallagher's. It was so good to hear people singing like that and such a nice song, an old song, "Charming Billy." I glanced in the window and who did I see but Morgan Donovan, drunk as a post, and Paige, sitting rigidly beside him on the bench. There she was in her pale-green Chanel suit and brooch. She remained at all times the lady, didn't she? He was waving his beer and raucously singing "She's a young thing, and cannot leave her mother!" with the rest of them. I hurried on by, deflated, and found another place, the Tupelo Honey, but it was mobbed. Then I saw Oliver, Teddy, and Mr. Piet at the bar and went in.

Oliver, delighted to see me, bought me some drinks and I bought him a couple in return. He introduced me around. "Teddy," I said after an hour or so, "the wind must have knocked Noola's wisteria vine off the house. I've managed to get it back up. I think it just might live. Isn't that good?" Teddy sucked his chin into his neck. "Morgan will be so glad," he said. A big fellow with a kind face overheard us. He said, "Morgan Donovan? Was over there in Bosnia. Never the same after that. Used to be a lot of fun, Morgan." My ears perked up. Then Teddy said to him, "Well, that's it. He's in a tossup. Mother's a mick and his father's a Scot. No wonder he's mixed up with us Cupsands. He's mixed up completely!" He pulled on his drink and held my eyes, finding himself funny. "That's the thing with the immigrants," he went on, "first they take your job and they take your land and the next thing you know they take your woman. They're all on the take."

Mr. Piet didn't move or flicker an eye. I was a little surprised at Teddy.

Oliver put his scotch glass hard on the counter. "I wouldn't go callin' Morgan Donovan on the take when I was around, Teddy. Not if I was you. Now Morgan, twice he sailed in a race around the world, and he would have won that second time, too, if that whale hadn't walked into him and Glinty. That was a funny story."

"Oh, not now, Oliver!" Teddy rolled side to side.

"And don't forget, he was I4 Implementation force over in Bosnia. Did them exhumations for mass graves. Took it in the hand from a semiautomatic."

"Yeah, yeah." Teddy skated this road familiarly. "But all the ex-army jocks are nuts if they were there in the thick of it. And you saw what happens in the jails. They're all like that. Like the cops. Wall of blue." He was drunk, too.

Mr. Piet turned him about on his bar stool and looked him dead in the eye. "You're not saying Morgan's dishonest, are you? How would you like it if I said all teachers are pedophiles? Huh?"

"Well, they're not. . . ."

"Oh, really? I saw it in the papers what they're up to. I can show you."

"C'mon, Piet"—he held him on the sleeve—"don't be so serious. And don't pretend you haven't heard the scuttlebutt." He glanced right and left. "Plenty of folks think Morgan had something to do with pushing Noola over the edge. I'm not saying it was so wrong . . . I'm just saying."

"I'm not joking with you. One more word about Morgan's integrity and I'll—"

"Okay, okay. Sheesh."

"And get your hand off my arm."

We'd all been drinking like we were going to the chair, so anything could happen. Oliver gave me a nod and we stood carefully. He paid the bill, and he and I stalked off arm in arm. There must have been a thousand stars as we rolled unsteadily up the hill. I hadn't left a light on, and the cottage through the brambles was otherworldly and unwelcoming. "Oliver," I said nervously, "there isn't any truth to those rumors about Morgan Donovan, right?"

"*Phhh.*" Oliver wiped his mouth with the back of his hand and spat meaningfully onto the gravel. But he didn't say no, either. We parted at the cottage path and anyone could hear him singing drunkenly at the top of his voice as he staggered back to Twillyweed.

The cottage was closed and overheated, and I threw open the sea window. I tried to sleep but sleep wouldn't come. I opened a bottle of Bordeaux and, with the aid of the French, passed out. Then, very late, I sat up in bed, wide awake. In the twisted, whirly place where my dreams and the fog came together, I thought I saw a hunched-up figure pass by the window. *A ghost*, I thought, but I didn't screech. I covered my head. Common sense got me eventually and I edged away the plaid blanket to see a small light in the east. And something else. I remembered Morgan's remark about *some people thinking in order to be a lady one has to give up being a woman*. I lay back down and snuggled into my pillow, absurdly reassured, and slept.

CHAPTER FOUR

CLAIRE

Those days passed—like spring days should, I suppose—with rain. It
befitted my mood and the lonesomeness of the job at hand. It was what
I needed, though. And if it wasn't raining when I walked out of the cottage, there would be Mrs. Dellaverna watering down the reconstructed
wisteria vine with her hose just to make sure it stayed soaked. Its ten-
drils remained dilapidated, but if you walked up to it and held the core,
you could somehow tell it was alive. Cupping its stalk, I almost sensed
its pulse. A small, manipulated miracle, but a miracle nonetheless.

All the cleaning people I could find wouldn't be available for a while
so, rolling up my sleeves, I began to do it myself. I worked like mad on
the inside of that cottage, so occupied with discarding and redistribut-
ing I hardly had time to think of Enoch. And all around it was beautiful. At the start, the pale pinks of crabapple and cherry had decorated
the hills; now tight buds of creamy dogwood were loosening. Tender,
impertinent mushrooms sprang up all over. About midday I'd always
treat myself to a break. Sometimes I'd prepare a bowl of oatmeal and
milled flax on the tiny stove, lopping in the five almonds allotted by
Edgar Cayce, some banana and canned black cherries, slathered it
with half-and-half, sprinkled it with cinnamon. I'd take one of Noola's

well-worn novels and climb onto the huge, lumpy easy chair that must have been her favorite for it faced the window like someone else's would the TV. I could knot myself into Noola's chair and stare out at the sea any time I chose, I realized. As the rainy weeks passed, I began to appreciate my own company and didn't particularly want someone around, confusing my steady, slow progress. I'd even managed to patch the leaky roof, climbing up with Mrs. Dellaverna as my ladder holder and watch. Granted, it was makeshift, stuffing heavy cardboard and unmatched socks into the gaps, but it stopped the drips and no one was the wiser. Little by little I was making headway, and I didn't want some thoughtless girl throwing out the mate of an under-the-chair mukluk until I'd found the other. And find it I did, locked between the headboard and the fitted sheet. I decided to keep them for myself. I threw them into the warm wash twice, way overdoing the fabric softener, then stuffed them with paper towels and let them dry slowly, away from any direct heat. They had hand-sewn buffalo leather soles so you had to be careful. It took a few days for them to relax but—I looked down at my feet, admiring them—now they were as soft and cuddly as buntings. The weather stormed and blew, but that was all right with me and I had the windows open almost all the time. It wasn't cold anymore, or if it was, I didn't feel it much because I was working so hard. It was only my hands, red as lobsters from all the cleaning stuff. I took one corner at a time. After a while, I managed to categorize and pile up boxes of antiques for Morgan to come and get, and I had seventeen black bags to be picked up by the St. Mary's by the Sea truck on Thursday. The floor was swept of clutter and scrubbed by yours truly with good old-fashioned soap and water.

Mrs. Dellaverna had been a doll, popping over with unexpected necessities: paper towels when I ran out, a box of matches, a phone book, and plenty of southern Italian dishes. I cranked up the old gas stove and kept it going, telling myself it would be that much easier to clean—and it was. The warm gunk peeled away easily. I spent hours and hours on that stove until it shone, and one day, while folding a big pile of giveaway from the dryer, I realized I was pretty much done with the inside of the house. Ceremoniously, I tied up the last bag and staggered to the porch with it, then looked around with satisfaction. The uncut grass blew in the breeze like an undulating river. Now all at once the rest of the trees seemed to have sprung open at once and my views of the neighboring houses and Twillyweed were obliterated.

I heard someone climbing up the path from the beach and bent over the railing. Why, it was Jenny Rose! And she had the little boy, Wendell, with her. Excitedly, I ran back in and put the teakettle on.

"Hello! Anybody home?" her clear voice called.

"Come in! Come in." I ushered them in.

"Bless all who enter here," said Jenny Rose as they crossed the threshold. "Look who I've brought! Hey! What's happened here? This is fucking great! Oops. Sorry, Wendell. I'm not to curse in front of you, am I?"

"I've been busy," I agreed. "And I did a couple of big shops. How do you like it?"

"Hey, you could take a picture. Looks like a granny house back in olden times!" She'd brought scones and laid them out on the table, light and fragrant in a checkered cloth.

I couldn't resist. "Oh, my God!" I exclaimed. "Where did you buy these? They're delicious!"

"I made them. Simple."

"Mrs. Mooney lets you use her kitchen, then?" I set the table while they looked around.

"I helped myself this morning while she was deep in the arms of Morpheus. Take a deep breath, Wendell! Good salt air."

Obediently, the boy took a deep breath in and held it.

"There's a good lad. All right, don't turn blue. You can let it out." She twirled around. "I swear, you and I have certainly landed on our feet. We've got the two best views of the sea on Long Island."

"I thought you said you were stuck in the cellar."

"I talked Patsy Mooney into trading with me. Turns out she hated it up there. Just wait till you see my turret! A circle of windows! Got my easel set up already. I see you've a hearth, you lucky duck! Do you use it?"

"Not yet. I thought I'd better have the flue checked first. The chimney sweep will be here this afternoon. And then I'll need a cord of wood."

"Oh, the chimney sweep will bring luck to the house, but already it's that cozy!"

"Thank you," I said as I placed a vase of tulips on the table. There was some pound cake left over from yesterday's lunch and I laid the orange marmalade out with it. At the back of a cupboard I'd found honey—Noola's honey. Horrible how life goes on without you once you're gone.

Jenny Rose arranged Wendell with a big cardboard box and a plate full of buttons so he could play store. There was a basket of brightly colored embroidery threads and I let him have those as well. She flung herself onto a chair. "I'm beat."

"Me, too," I said. "I've made a good strong tea. This will cheer us both up." I sat down across from her and lifted an eyebrow. She really did look tired. "You've been seeing too much of that Glinty, haven't you? You know, I think he dyes his hair."

Jenny Rose pulled her knees up to her chest. "It's blue-black like that all over."

The way she said it. "Don't tell me you've *fall*en for him!"

"Well, why not? He's a bit like me, if you must know. He comes from shit. Oh, I don't mean Deirdre and Brigid are shit. They raised me as best they could. But, you see, they're both sort of bats, aren't they? It's not like you, coming from a house with a mom and dad and kids at the table all eating together. A substantial home. I know it's hard for you to understand. But see, it just wasn't like that for me. I was fed in the pantry before they could shuffle me off to bed at eight o'clock so they could get on with it. To this day I stay up later than everyone just to stay up. It wasn't like I was in the way, but I was always aware that

I'd been left behind. That I was someone else's, see? I know they loved me"—her eyes swam and she wiped her nose with her sleeve—"but I was always waiting for my ma to come and claim me."

"Oh, don't!" I cried and tried to reach for her.

"No!" She pushed me off. Wendell, sensing trouble, looked up. Jenny Rose lowered her voice. "It's not that I want you to feel sorry for me. I just want you to understand."

"I *know* how you must be feeling. But just *think* for a minute. We don't know anything at all about him except he's from a broken home! That's no reason to feel—"

"Aunt Claire, it's too late. Look. If you must know, it's that Glinty and me, when we're together, him and me, it's like we make one, see? Like he's got no arms and I've got no legs but together we're a complete person."

"But, Jenny Rose, it's all too quick! You're a wonderful, complete person just as you are. You don't need a boy to make you feel—"

"I do." She cut me short and eyed me fiercely. "He's the moon and stars for me, okay?"

My heart sank. I could say nothing.

She bit her lip. "And there's somethin' else."

"What?"

"And this is between you and me, okay?"

"Okay."

Jenny Rose, with something fidgety in her hazel eyes, took a small green satin sack from her pocket. She checked to see that Wendell was distracted then tipped out two silver-rimmed buttons that seemed to move with undulating color. Baffled, I looked down at them on the plate and I remember thinking, *Hang on, those aren't buttons.*

And then she told me all about it.

On Sunday I went to early Mass. It was a fine, windy day. I parked in St. Greta's lot and was practically blown into the church, then found my way through the regular parishioners to the back. Newcomers have to be careful they don't take someone's pew; the devout are so often territorial. It was especially crowded and I soon saw why: It was the day of the May crowning, when the children who've recently received their first Holy Communion march in wearing their white outfits and veils and the last girl goes up to the statue of Our Lady and places a wreath of flowers on her head. It's lovely, especially the songs, which take you back to childhood. I settled into a dark spot. If ever my faith is tried, I just have to go on a Sunday and watch the family men who manage to get there every week, kids in tow, the backs of their necks bent in reverence at each appropriate moment—there is something so beautiful and true about them, like soldiers relieved from combat. *If it's not too much trouble, Lord,* I prayed silently, *lead me in the right direction in the Jenny Rose department. I don't seem to have the hang of it on my own. Help me know what to tell her, all right?* Then I posed the puzzle of the gems to the Almighty. You never know what might spark His interest—and at that point I didn't look at it as that much of a problem. After Communion, I sat back in the pew and watched the children, unable to be still any longer, acting up. Suddenly I blinked twice, for there was Morgan Donovan over on St. Joseph's side with his head in his hands. Hurriedly, I left by the side door so he wouldn't notice me. He was at least entitled to his private grieving time. Rain had come and gone, but now the wind tore at me. I opened my umbrella but gave up before it blew inside out. "Claire!" I heard Morgan call my name over the bells ringing and the wind. He caught up to me and loomed, moving back and forth above me.

"Hi," I said, hoping my eyes didn't reveal how absurdly significant his nearness was.

"Hi, yourself." He fell into step beside me. "I noticed your front headlight is out."

"Thanks. I didn't see it," I said. "I'll take it in this week."

"No, you'll need to be weeding through the stuff in the cottage." He raised his voice to be heard. "I'll take it to the marina for you and have Mr. Piet put one in."

"I've been finding out that Mr. Piet can do just about anything. But, by the way, I've got quite a few boxes of valuable stuff for you to come pick up."

"Help yourself to anything. It's so depressing in there the way it is."

"Really? I was hoping you'd let me. You won't be sorry," I promised, adding, "I didn't want to overstep my bounds."

"So you're a good little girl," he teased.

Was he flirting with me? "Not that good," I grumbled, not sure where to look.

He laughed cheerfully. "There's enough wickedness in Sea Cliff. You'll soon find that out."

Whirling bits of trash were moving past us down the steep hill, little toy boats in the gutter.

I ventured, "I saw that fellow Daniel. He was walking on the beach, crooning to a doll."

He laughed. "Oh, he's harmless."

"Is he?" I thought of his demented leer. "How can you be so sure?"

Morgan cleared his throat and squinted toward the sea. "Ah, that's a story. I wouldn't worry about him, though. He's afraid of his own shadow, Daniel is. He's even terrified of me! But there's something else I wanted to tell you . . . what was it?" He looked into my eyes, and for a moment the two of us just stood there and I went on that cloud height journey I always went on around him. He seemed to go there, too. It's always reassuring to me when someone else forgets what they're talking about. "Oh, yeah," he said, returning to himself, "I saw Jenny Rose and Wendell bicycling and I thought, *There's a bike in the wee shed beside the cottage.* It's not very fashionable and it only has foot brakes, but the tires are fine."

"I love foot brakes!"

"Good, then. I thought you might. Enjoy it. And what has Jenny Rose to say?" He pushed my hair off my face so he could see me.

"I think she loves the little boy," I said, annoyed that I should be so moved by his simple, tender touch. "So that's great. She's coming with me today to Queens, to visit my parents."

"*Ach*. She'll like that. What about Wendell?"

"We're bringing him with us."

"Oh? Tell you what." He pointed to his old black Saab. "You take my car and I'll run yours down to the marina this morning. You wouldn't want to be getting a ticket."

"Are you sure?" I was doubtful.

"*Ach*, everyone uses it," he said. "Key's under the front seat. Full tank of petrol."

"In that case, it's a deal." I handed him my keys.

"Cheerio." He waved over his head and strode off down the road to my dear little green PT Cruiser, who would have him all to herself. I stopped to lose a pebble from my shoe and leaned against a lamppost. *Now why*, I asked myself crossly, *can't I find me a man just like that? Why?* I found the keys under the front seat just as he'd said I would—obviously the man had no common sense—then went to pick up Jenny Rose and Wendell.

"Nice wheels," Jenny Rose, who seemed to know about things like cars, said admiringly. "A classic." She petted the butterscotch seats.

"Have you any grand shops out in Queens?" Wendell wanted to know as I shackled him into his seat belt. By God, he was taking on Jenny Rose's Irish brogue. I laughed to myself. He looked so cute in his little red plaid shirt. I told him all about the stores I knew and we drove, top down, to Richmond Hill.

Jenny Rose had the stones with her. We'd decided we would tell my mother the story and she would know what we should do. "Take them," Jenny Rose said as she slipped them into my pocket. "They scare the shit outta me." She fiddled with the radio, Morgan's stations all too corny for her. Because I'd spoken so highly of the nickelodeon at the original Jahn's Ice Cream Parlor, Wendell had to see it, so we made a stop there. We sat on stools at the counter under Tiffany lamps and drank from authentic Coca-Cola glasses. I had a bad moment when I looked at the table where Enoch and I used to sit. But children have a way of making you move on. And already the day was a success as far as

Wendell was concerned. We ran out and stood underneath the elevated trains every time one clamored by. Wendell screamed with delight. Whenever you want to entertain a Long Island kid, just drag him with you to Queens.

At my mother's house, the TV blared as usual. In fact, the living room was lined with consecutive rows of chairs like in a theater, my father's hearing and my mother's eyesight not being what they were but to varying degrees. Wendell went right up to my dad in the first row and climbed over Lefty onto the La-Z-Boy with him. My dad must be the last living pipe smoker who smokes in the house in America. With Lefty at their feet, they watched one World War II battle after the next on the History Channel. You might think that sort of stuff harms children but my father believes it arms them for the world. Or, he points out, is Hansel and Gretel a warm and cuddly story? And what about the Little Match Girl or the Tin Soldier?

My mother made a great fuss about Jenny Rose. They stood together and marveled at her picture in the paper. She told her how she'd sent copies home, but as soon as she'd hugged her and kissed her enough she put us right to work. "Just peel these taters for me, darlin'," she said, handing me a pot and a paring knife, and she gave Jenny Rose the apples to peel for the pie. We sat there at that table at the back kitchen window almost all that Sunday afternoon, drinking tea and eating cheese-filled sheet crumb cake from Oxford's on Liberty, my mother telling stories of when she was a girl in Ireland and Jenny Rose asking her questions and Mom drilling Jenny Rose about whether the Gorta Thrifty Shoppe was still there over the bridge from Bridge Street in Skibbereen and what about Paddy's on the cemetery lane and all and Mom running back and forth finding pictures of Carmela at twelve, Carmela at the prom, Carmela with the perilous mumps.

I watched and listened to all this with interest, but on my eleventh potato, I saw through my peels to a picture in last week's wrinkled newspaper. Distractedly, I pushed the peels aside to read the article. There was that story of the priest who'd been bludgeoned for the valuable statue, and a picture of him standing before the statue in happier times. But as I gazed at the picture, I noticed something else. The eyes of the statue—and here the hairs on my neck stood up—looked just like the two set in silver, blue moonstones that were that minute in my pocket! Oh, my God.

"Mom," I swallowed, "it's the picture of that statue."

"Oh, see, now, I kept those papers for you because you said you wanted them for the real estate." Then to Jenny Rose she complained fervently, "Claire thinks she'll be better off without Enoch. Doesn't know which side her bread is buttered, and him the finest man you'll ever meet!"

Jenny Rose and I looked at each other.

"Any red Jell-O left in there, Mary?" my father called through.

"No," she called back.

"Mary?"

"No!" she shouted, clicked her tongue and shook her head, and muttered, "His hearing's worse and worse."

I gave Jenny Rose the warning look, but she snapped at me, "Auntie Claire, don't go giving me no warning looks, now. Who will you be protecting? Enoch? Your mother?"

"What's she mean?" my mother said suspiciously, looking back and forth at both of us.

"The truth is, Grandmother, that that fellow Enoch was prepared to marry your daughter while he's just as gay as a three-penny opera."

My mother raised up. "What did she say?"

"Mom," I said as I hung my head, embarrassed for him, "it's like she says. Enoch is gay."

"What do you mean, gay? Homosexual?"

"Yes."

"He can't be. You slept with him."

"I did," I agreed.

"Well, didn't you know?"

"Mom, he seemed fine. If anything, he was particularly solicitous."

"That should have been your clue right there," Jenny Rose snipped.

From the other room there was a noise and we all strained to listen. My mother leaned in and heard my father demonstrating the times tables for Wendell. She cupped her mouth and sat back down. "He'll have given you the AIDS!"

"Jesus, I hope not!" I cried.

"Well, did he wear a jacket or not?"

"Not with me, he didn't. I mean, not lately."

Wendell stood in the doorway.

"What is it, lad?" Jenny Rose said.

"I've got to go for a little attention."

"You mean you've got to go pee?"

"Yes."

My mother said, "Well, it's right down the stairs."

"He'll not know his way," Jenny Rose pointed out.

"Or up. Go up," my mother called. "Stan, take him upstairs, will you?"

My father rumbled from his chair.

"Hold his hand so he won't fall," my mother instructed. They held hands up the steep stairs. My mother went over and stood at the bottom with her wrists on her hips to watch them.

"Jenny Rose!" I grabbed her arm and whispered a shriek. "Look at this!"

"What?"

"The eyes!" The two of us stared at the picture and gulped.

"Fuck," she said.

"What did you say, young lady!" my mother reprimanded.

"It's an Our Lady statue!" Jenny Rose exclaimed.

"I never imagined it had anything to do with us," I whispered, "but it's the eyes from the statue! It has to be," I cried. "Mom, what's the story with this statue?"

"Sure, that's a terrible, wicked thing. Lust for power, it is." She stomped back in and tapped the table firmly with her pointer finger.

"Those criminals don't know the half of what they've got themselves mixed up in. That there's a miraculous statue."

I looked at Jenny Rose. "They probably just took the jewels and threw the statue away."

"Oh, I don't think so." My mother glanced to the side and leaned in close. "People pray through that statue and miracles happen. Sick people get well. That sort of thing. Really, what's a couple of stones? Stones you can pick up easily enough on the shopping network. It's the statue itself that's of value, the blessing within that contains the mystery of healing."

We stared at her.

"Sure, look at Sal and Terry down in Florida; his father had the pancreatic cancer and the doctors gave him four months to live. Patsy McKenna told them about the statue and the lot of them came up and stormed heaven. When they opened the old man up, what do you think? There wasn't a trace of cancer! And they couldn't explain it. He lived eight years! That statue will find its own way home. You'll see."

"You believe in all that?" I said.

She cracked me on the head. "And for what did I send you to Catholic school!"

I ducked and covered my head with my arms. She never hurt you much. "But we were also constantly warned against idolatry," I pointed out. "And trickery."

"That's the devil, in case you've forgotten. That's his job. You kids! You act like there's no source of wickedness. It's all understanding the perpetrator and Prozac. That's where the Holy Spirit comes in, filling us up with the courage to fight!"

Jenny Rose whispered, "She means it's not the statue that cures, it's the faith it inspires."

"That's it." My mother lifted my chin. "A test. That's exactly it."

I thought of Morgan Donovan. That great hunk of a man, humble in church. If a man like that ever came at me, I doubted I would have the strength or goodness to resist. "You're the warrior, Mom," I murmured softly.

"Not anymore I'm not. It's your turn, now, Claire. My fighting's done." She sighed, worn out, and sat down with a heave, spilling her tea as she reached for more toast. I'd been just getting ready to tell her about the gems and then, for some reason, when I looked at the spilled tea, I couldn't.

"You'd better go collect your clothes, Auntie Claire. I think we ought to be leaving, now."

"What, leave, now?" my mother cried and I cringed at what was to come, but it turned out she wouldn't get as disgruntled as she used to, as I'd imagined she would. It was getting on late in the day anyhow so we packed up and left, my mother only slightly put out that we wouldn't be staying for supper. Sadly I realized I hadn't had much of a fight with her because, and this came as a shock, she was getting old. My ma. The brigadier general, letting things pass. It broke your heart. But tomorrow my father's sisters—the bad aunts renowned to have a fortune but who were tight as string and would doubtless leave all their money to the dog and cat hospital—would be coming in from Ridgewood and this way she'd have everything already prepared.

"You can drop him off here anytime," my father said about Wendell. "He and I get along very well."

"And I don't mind at all that you smell," Wendell rhymed and my father chuckled.

My mother wrapped her shoulders in a peppermint-striped apron and walked us to the car with enough instructions on life to fill a catalog. "Drive slow. Here, take some gladioli, they're the last of them but they're lovely! Watch out there's no one lurking in the backseat. Put your seat belts on. Have you enough gas? Whose car is that, by the way?"

"It's my boss's," I said, looking away. The rain had stopped and the stars were out. It was cold now again, and I found I was still shivering but, in an odd way, ready. It always pays to go home, one way and another, if only for how wonderful you feel when you leave. Jenny Rose wrapped Wendell up in one of my mother's woolen blankets, worn soft and pink from years of laundering, and I overheard him explaining patiently to my mother as she strapped him in, "Paige says you must say a *little* attention and a *lot* of attention when you've got to go make."

"Is that right," my mother answered him without missing a beat, "and I'll be waiting to hear your multiplication tables when you come back next time."

"I wouldn't pass any heat on that," he retorted in a replica of Jenny Rose's fresh way of speaking, and as we set off his eyes batted and struggled to stay open but he lost the fight even as we pulled away. We passed Enoch's and my rented house, but I didn't say so to Jenny Rose. This was my new life, I thought. What was the point? Also, I was ashamed of how ugly that house was. But as we tooled past I caught a glimpse of my dog, Jake, at the window. He was standing up at the glass, his big paws up on the sill and he was gazing forlornly down the road. The house was dark. I only noticed him because of the streetlamp's glare from the huge saliva stain on the glass. I felt an actual tug at my heart. Then I thought, *Hey!* Enoch said he was going to take him with him to the firehouse when he worked. And if Enoch wasn't there, it was a perfect time to pick up some clothes. I turned right at the corner and swung around the block.

While Jenny Rose waited in the car, I went in with my key. You'd have thought I was the greatest person ever invented the way Jake carried on at the sight of me. We hugged each other a good long time and I could actually hear his true pleasure whine groaning from the depth of his rib cage. I was shocked to notice he smelled like he needed a bath. Jake loved his bath. Saturday night, he'd wait by the sink until I would lug him up into it and give him a nice sissy bubble bath. "Enoch?" I called up the stairs. But he wasn't home. I felt my lips tighten at the empty water bowl. Gently I held open the back door and let Jake into the yard to take care of business, which he did with such alacrity and volume I had to wonder just how long he'd been left alone. I stole up the stairs and packed as many clothes as I could fit into Enoch's duffel bag. The hell with him if he needed it. I tossed in my other cameras, cell-phone charger, my electric toothbrush, and my double-duty jar of

Nivea cream. I remain loyal to Nivea because when I was in Germany, the company booked me to photograph the still shots of a commercial in Rio, a job so exorbitantly plush and luxurious and fun, I remain impressed and grateful to this day. I took one last look at the neatly made bed. Fussy, when you thought about it. At that moment I felt no remorse, only anger that he'd left Jake alone so long in the dark, cold house. I lugged the bag downstairs and looked out. Violets were strewn across the clumpy lawn and for a second I felt a pull of regret in my throat. Enoch always said how lovely it smelled when you mowed. But Jenny Rose was moving uneasily back and forth in the front seat of the car—probably worried she was in some scary New York neighborhood. I rinsed Jake's bowl and filled it up with nice cold water and called him back in, explaining in a reasonable way about what had taken me away after I'd promised I'd always be there for him. "Look," I said as I stroked his brown bear fur, pretending to sound happy, "you're better off here with Enoch. Go ahead, now, hop into your beddy-bye. I'll see you soon. I promise. Be a good boy. That's it."

Jake did as he was told. But as I took my leave, he held my eyes with such trusting devotion that I was overcome with guilt. Never mind, I told myself, grown-ups had business to attend to and this was Enoch's fault, not mine. I made it as far as the door and then made my mistake, turning for one last look at Jake's rumpled face, his broken ears that someone had once tried to trim then given up and so they hung like floppy, clobbered leaves. He'd dropped his gaze at the sound of the doorknob, knowing I was really off, and now his gaze held on to nothing, where it would be stuck for hours and then days, no doubt imagining that I'd been devoured by predators and would never come again.

Jenny Rose was alarmed to see me emerge with a bounding, colossal dog, a duffel bag, a doggy bed, and a whopper-sized bag of dry food. "What is it?" she cried in fright.

"He's part pit bull, part Irish wolfhound they tell me. His name is Jake."

Wendell, utterly unafraid, threw open his arms in delight. He scooted over right away and patted the seat beside him. Jake tumbled in.

When we were well onto the Northern State and both boy and dog had fallen asleep, Jenny Rose said sternly, "You didn't tell your mum we've got the stones."

"How could I tell her? She'd worry herself sick. She's got a stent, you know."

"Yeah. It's bad enough she thinks you've got AIDS."

"And now I've got to go get a blood test." I squirmed in my seat. "That bastard!"

"At least you won't miss him now you're so mad at him."

"That's true." I shook my head in exasperation. "As if we don't have enough to worry about with the moonstones! What are we going to do?"

"Beats me." She worried a cuticle with her teeth.

"Well, we've got to tell Mr. Cupsand," I said. "That's the first thing."

"What? And what if he's the one who stole the gems to start with?"

"Oh, don't be silly."

She glanced over her shoulder to make sure the boy was still asleep. "Don't be silly? Listen to you! *Some*body stole them. Wendell got them somehow. You just want to go straight to Daddy, the male authority figure, so it's out of your hands."

I opened my mouth to argue but I realized she was right. I said, "It could have been anyone. Wendell's teacher. A kid in school. Maybe we should go to the police."

"Oh, that's smart. I'll be the first one they suspect. Working illegally. They'll send me back."

"Hmm. Well, we've got to tell someone. We're in over our heads here." We drove in silence. Then I said, "Maybe my mother's right and the statue is the real object of value. Then the stones could have been used to pay off the thief. If we find the thief, we find the buyer."

Jenny Rose glared at me. "Who are we, Detectives Scott and Bailey?"

I gave her a hard look and she said, "Right. I'll make a list." She ruffled around Morgan's glove box and came up with a ballpoint and paper.

I said, "Clearly, what we're looking for is a collector. Fine arts. That sort of thing." Even as I said it, I thought of Morgan.

"That reminds me," Jenny Rose said, "the day I pulled Radiance out of the drink, there was something suspicious about it. Come to think of it, she wasn't very grateful. And she had marks on her. I thought at the time I'd done them but the more I think about it, it doesn't fit. Now I'm sure of it. See what I'm saying? Maybe she's afraid of someone."

Startled, I looked at her. "You mean like someone threw her in?"

Jenny Rose shrugged. "What the fuck do I know?"

Again I thought of Morgan Donovan. That day I'd met him, his wrist was hurt. I started to tell her then stopped myself.

"Well, what is it?" she said shrewdly.

I wasn't going to protect him, was I? If Jenny Rose and I were partners, we were going to have to be honest with each other. "I was just thinking Morgan's wrist was hurt that day."

"Doesn't strike me as a thief, though," she said and then she looked at me. "Oh, there you go thinking it's Glinty. Just because he looks so . . . what was the word Paige used?"

"Slippery," I supplied.

She gave me a mean look. "He's just hot," Jenny Rose defended him. "Dishy." She struggled to find a word her old auntie would understand. "Hip."

"Write down Patsy Mooney."

"Oh, please. She wouldn't know a work of art from a coupon."

"Look. If we're going to investigate this, we've got to think of everyone who had opportunity and motive," I said.

"Well then, investigate Teddy."

"Teddy?"

"Why not? He's always hanging around. What's he after?"

I tried not to laugh at the thought of wholesome Teddy as a criminal, but I remembered his bitterness toward Morgan. I didn't object as she wrote him down.

"Let's put on the list whoever was in Sea Cliff after the statue was stolen."

"Right."

"How do you want to do this?"

I said, "We can eliminate the two of us."

"No. To be fair, we should head the list."

I laughed. "That makes no sense."

"But it's fair."

I held my head, "Oh, fine. You and me."

"Paige?"

I remembered the pen at Noola's, which I had little doubt was hers. What had she been up to at Noola's? "Yes. Put her down."

"Oliver?"

"Sure. He could have done it. Everybody. And don't forget Glinty."

"Uh! He wouldn't dare."

Don't be so sure, I thought but didn't say. I said, "Come on. Everybody in the pool."

"All right, all right, I put him down."

"Morgan."

"Yes. I wrote his name."

"Mr. Piet?"

"Ah, Mr. Piet. If anyone threw Radiance overboard, it would be him."

"Why do you say that?"

"Because he's always got it in for her. Telling her what to do—and she a grown woman! He thinks Twillyweed is like *Upstairs Downstairs* and she's the parlor maid."

I felt sorry for Mr. Piet. Jenny Rose was so young. She couldn't know what it was like to have an unruly child.

"Nah," she vetoed. "It wouldn't be him. He was off that day."

"He still could have been out on the boat with her." Suddenly, I thought of something. I said, "Jenny Rose, he was fishing, remember? He caught that weakfish we were eating that night!"

"That's right! Good thinking."

I, who forgets why I've entered a room once I'm there, was happy someone thought so. "Put the heat up, will you?" I said. "It's freezing. And Radiance. Don't forget her. I wonder what the real reason she was out sailing was. Fishing! I thought she was a showgirl."

"A *dancer*. She wants to be one of those girls in a line at Radio City. Jake, do move your paw. How can you be in the front and the back at the same time?" She put her head back and closed her eyes. "I don't know. I just don't know. Maybe the stones have nothing to do with any of them. You realize we have no idea what we're talking about?"

"What about that school bus driver?"

"Right." She stopped fiddling with the control panel. "I'll throw him in. I can't stand him."

"And the lady from the rectory."

"Lassiter? Oh, I hardly think—"

"Just write her down. How many is that?"

"Oh, creepy. There are thirteen."

I turned off at Glen Cove Road and we headed north.

Jenny Rose wrung her hands. "I think you're right. We'll have to have a talk with Radiance."

"Now that she's back at her place, we'll go tomorrow while Wendell's in school. We'll say you want to check on her. See how she's doing." I glanced at Wendell asleep in the back. "It could get dangerous."

"Yeah," her eyes lit up.

When we got back to Twillyweed, Jenny Rose carried Wendell in and I waved good night. We were concerned about the gems, but it was all still a kind of mad adventure for us. Had we known what evil lurked, I don't think either of us would have remained in Sea Cliff.

I took off up the steep hill, realigning Morgan's radio buttons to their original stations, then sat for a while in the car while Jake dozed and I watched the distant, dreamy lights across the sound, listening to Morgan's Jonathan Schwarts-style station with its old-fashioned ballads. I touched the dashboard, smelled the friendly leather seats. "Take good care of him," I said to the car, letting Jake out to sniff around. I locked it up and walked to the cottage in the hurling wind, wondering enviously about Morgan's weather stick. When fine weather did come, I'd buy myself a little Hibachi and grill hot dogs, I promised myself hungrily. And tomorrow would be a good day, regardless. I'd put the cushions outside to air on the deck. I shivered and carried my stuff up the short walk to the cottage. Jake was delighted with everything. There's something about putting the key into the lock of your own digs. The door swung open and I stepped in. The place no longer smelled of dust and decay, but refreshed and lived in. The little kitten's head popped out of a sneaker. Jake bounded in and then, spotting her, froze. The kitten's fur stood up in a shriek along her little back. My heart stood still. At that moment it could have gone either way. I said a fervent prayer to St. Francis, who has a way with animals, put down a bowl of water for Jake, and said in as calm a voice as I could muster, "All right, you two, you don't have to like each other but we're going to all have to live together. So draw up enemy lines or have it out now—but somehow we're going to have to get along, got it?" More worried for Jake's eyes than I was for the kitten, I turned my back so there would be no show for my benefit and went into the bathroom. I held my ear to the door. There were no screams or flying fur as far as I could tell. I took a nice warm shower and slipped on my own cozy, flannel nightgown, relaxing immediately. But when I went outside, the kitten was standing up on the table, still as a statue with her tail straight up in the air. Jake had slopped the water dish but he hadn't settled down. He sat in a rigid pose, waiting, I supposed, to see what would happen next. Ignoring them, I opened the old burgundy phonograph and put a record on for company, took the slipcovers out of the washer, and threw them in the dryer. Then I put the curtains in the washer and tackled my next job, sorting through the piles of books and records, working into the night.

Noola had wonderful records, Tony Bennett, Antonio Carlos Jobim, Dinah Washington, Ella in Berlin, Albinoni, Mozart, Claude Debussy, Keith Jarrett's *The Köln Concert*. I put that one on, loud, and wiped the rest of them down with a damp cloth and returned them to their sleeves. When my cell phone jangled from my purse, I almost didn't hear it. "Hello?" I shouted.

"It's me," Enoch said. "How could you just take Jake without talking to me first?"

If he thought this was the way to start with me, he was very mistaken. I lowered the volume on the music and said, "Enoch, you left the dog alone in a dark house with no water—and he had to go! You told me you'd take him to work. When I let him out, he hardly made it out the door!"

He sighed. "Claire. We had a six alarm over in Jamaica. Terrible. Three people—"

"Oh. All right, all right. I'm sorry. But still, don't go blaming me for taking *my* dog when your job interferes with his well-being!"

"Well-being! He had to hold it in for an hour! Jesus!"

"Enoch, was there something else?"

"Well, are you all right?"

"I'm fine. I'm out on Long Island. I have a safe place to stay and there's nothing, really, you need to know after that."

"Whose house are you staying at?"

I looked up at the shelves of dusty books. "Some old woman's house." I didn't exactly lie.

"So what are you doing?"

"At the moment I'm cleaning out that old woman's jelly safe."

"So now you're a cleaning lady."

"Sort of."

"Claire. This is ridiculous."

"No more ridiculous than living with you under false pretenses."

"I keep telling you. I'm not gay. It was so unimportant! Every guy—"

"No, Enoch, not every guy," I said, my lips tight, thinking unhappily of Morgan Donovan and his loyalty to a pledge. "While I'm on my way to the city to get some go-nowhere, stupid job you put me up to so you could have unprotected sex with some man—"

"It wasn't unprotected sex. I wasn't having unprotected sex with anyone but you."

Something about the way he said it rang true. "At least that." I gave a guarded sigh of relief, my chances for survival improving.

"I'm sorry I hurt you," he said.

"Look. I'm not hurt. Not anymore. I don't know what I am, but I just don't want to see you."

He said nothing. He hadn't wanted this, didn't ask to favor men. But, I reminded myself, he'd brought this on himself. I was his cover. I remembered that long-ago man in the park jacking off every chance he got to a young girl at a lonely bus stop. A girl who'd felt too guilty to tell. Well, I was grown up now and I sure as hell wasn't going to spend the rest of my life as somebody's cover. "Look, Enoch, it's over. You and I both know it. Let's just get on with our lives."

"You're just going to dump me?!"

His astonishment was so outraged I almost laughed. Finally, I said, "Look, I'll call you before I come back to Queens to pick up the rest of my stuff." We hung up and I thought, *That's it. My days of devoting myself to inappropriate love are over. Finished. Basta.* A man with a yen for other men. A man engaged to another woman. A man still carrying a torch for the wife who'd left him! What was wrong with me? Well, whatever it was, I was done. I turned up the volume on the music. From now on I was off to a new start. And, as my ex-husband would say, *Let everybody else go get locked up!* So resolutely did I simmer, I never heard the door I'd never thought to lock creak open until Jake went berserk. He jumped up on it, knocking over one of Noola's pretty china vases, banging the door shut with such an intimidating cacophony of barks that whoever it was had to have run down the hill in a sissy fit. I didn't even think to be frightened as I picked up the pieces of china. I was more concerned I'd scared off Mrs. Dellaverna, or maybe a raccoon.

Raccoon would be bad. I went to the door and opened it. I craned my neck but didn't see a soul. Whoever it was had dropped a lovely gray glove on the step when Jake had gone into protection mode. I picked it up and laid it on the mailbox till someone would claim it, went back in the house, and then, with an odd feeling, turned around and locked the door.

It was the sky that had gone crazy, not him. He almost laughed at the churning, whipping treetops, dense and black as pitchforks against the starry sky. And that music. What lunacy! Oh, she was someone he was going to have a lot of fun with.

He tromped easily through the bush and heavy pine, the steep hill propelling him down and along. He hadn't counted on that dog. That was a surprise. But dogs were no problem. Cats were the sly ones. Sinister, *he thought with a smile,* like *me.*

Unconcerned and hatless, he kept on down through the heavy undergrowth. He was just beginning to enjoy himself and then suddenly—foraging through his pocket and remembering he'd forgotten his glove—he slammed to a halt. His shoulders tightened and hunched, his breath came short and rapid. Fir branches swatted and shushed the moldy stone along the Irish fence.

But it wasn't important, he soothed himself. He'd get it back. And then he'd have to go underground for a while. But just for a while. . . .

JENNY ROSE

Jenny Rose sat dwarfed in the blue flowered easy chair. She lit up a cigarette and tried to smoke, but it made her feel sick. She stuck it into a soggy tea bag and listened to it go *sss*. Her mother's family all lived these entire lives and here she'd never known them, never been part of their holidays or meals or any of those things they took for granted. They probably never even thought of her. Never. You could see it on their smug faces when they posed for Christmas pictures. No one thought *If only Jenny Rose were here*. No one had longed for her. She leaned her chin against the windowsill. The paint was so old it was probably lead. And yet . . . she remembered today and her grandfather's face.

She'd turned to see him watching her while she'd trimmed the fruit and their eyes had met. He hadn't looked away as though he were loaded with guilt. His eyes, so much like her own, had said something nice. A little bit like love, she thought. He was her own grandfather, wasn't he? She rocked with a fair dose of pleasure. Her own precious blood.

CLAIRE

It was morning. Jake sat politely before me, his head cocked, his drool forming a puddle to his left on the floor. "Hello," I said, "have you eaten the kitten?" I looked around. There she was, up on top of the fridge, sound asleep. But as I spoke to Jake, one little ear of the kitten stood up to listen. I'd stripped the windows before I'd gone to bed and now I rose, eager to see what had become of the delicate curtains. They looked all right. They hadn't shrunk, anyway. I opened the screen door and let Jake out, hoping he wouldn't frighten Mrs. Dellaverna. The kitten streaked past us and with equal measures of hope and fear I thought, *Oh, boy, I'll never see her again*. The curtains were still damp so I put them in the dryer for a short time and then laid them out flat on the table, now blessedly empty and scrubbed to a sheen. I lugged the ironing board out and touched them up, then the embroidered dishtowels. Those ironed up so prettily, I hung them over the sink window with fish hooks I found in a bait box and stood back to admire my work.

When I went to let Jake back in, I remembered the glove from last night and looked to the mailbox. It was gone. That was odd. Jake lumbered happily over, ready for breakfast now. "What did you do," I said, rumpling his fur, "hide it?" Oh, well, I figured, it'd turn up eventually. We went back in. I navigated him through a bowl of water and wiped his muddy paws, then gave him a dish of dry food livened with Mrs. Dellaverna's leftover manicotti. He devoured this with gusto and when he'd finished, he mopped his snout this way and that on the old Turkish carpet. He came back to me with that drunken sailor gait of his and pressed the side of his warm body against my leg. I stood there for a moment just being with him. One of the bulbs in the pretty hanging lamp over the table gave a notifying flicker and went out. I knew I had plenty of bulbs and went to the closet to fetch one, then stood on a chair and peered into the bowl of stained glass while I had the pack in my hand. My heart sank. Six dead bees. I don't know what it is about me and bees, but to see so many of them dead in there, it just made me feel horrible. I reeled and held on to the lamp and climbed down. But I'm a modern woman and I don't bother with omens. I went into the bathroom and washed my hands and face and brushed my teeth. We were going to visit Radiance this morning and I wanted to organize my thoughts. I fixed myself a percolated cup of coffee and opened the window to the cold and sat down with the view. The clean smell of the salt air wafted in. I didn't know what I'd done right in life to have that view for me alone, but there it was and here I was. I wrapped myself in Noola's old shawl and hugged my hot, milky coffee to my chest and listened to the screams of the gulls and—Was that him? Yes. The man with the doll. I'd behaved terribly. He might be crazy but no one deserved to be made to feel like a monster! I leaped to my feet and raced out the door, hoping to catch him, to apologize.

"Aye!" Mrs. Dellaverna stood at the gate barring my way. "*Buongiorno!*"

"Good morning!" I called in return, relinquishing any idea of the beach. And I got a load of what Mrs. Dellaverna was carrying: a pot of homemade gravy and ravioli, all for me. This would have to stop or I'd be big as a house. I invited her in to get acquainted with Jake and sat with her while she talked. Not once did I look at my watch.

By the time I got to Twillyweed, the sun was high in the sky. When Jenny Rose saw me coming up the drive, she burst out the door. There was no walking out the door for Jenny Rose; wherever she went it was always a bursting, the door slammed and the birds holed up in the bushes took off for their lives. I got a warm hug and a *How's the pooch?* and then she ran back in and upstairs to grab her stuff. I was standing in the kitchen waiting for her to come back down when I heard a car in the driveway. It was Oliver's snazzy red vintage Alpha Romeo. Jenny Rose sort of danced back down the stairs.

Paige came in wrapped in a perfectly ironed lavender bathrobe. She threw open the cabinet over the sink. Without greeting me she said, "Turn off that fluorescent light, will you? I have such a splitting head-ache! Jenny Rose, will you run upstairs and ask Patsy Mooney where the painkillers are?"

Oliver opened the back door and rubbed his hands together. "Man! It's nippy out there."

He looked happy to see me. He was wearing a lightweight navy blue cashmere overcoat and brought the cold in with him. He looked like a diplomat, his blond hair brushed straight back. He was different when he wasn't drinking. Younger. His eyes were bright. I was glad to see him, too.

Paige pursed her lips. "And where have *you* been all night?"

He went to the sink and washed his hands. "Just over in Freeport." He gave me a sheepish grin. "Took the casino boat." He flicked his wrists to dry off rather than disturb the ironed hand towel, purposely sprinkling water on the potted ivy. "Claire," he said, "I was wondering if you'd accompany me to the dance?"

Paige put in hurriedly, "We have to go. It's not a *dance* dance. It's for charity. Everyone sort of has to go."

"When's that?"

"After the big race."

"I'd love to." I smiled.

Paige crossed her arms. Out of the blue, she said, "Look, Claire, I know from Jenny Rose that you're worried about the AIDS thing. I've got a friend over at St. Francis. She's a volunteer. Runs the joint, to hear her tell it. Anyway, she could get you in for a test. In and out. What do you say?"

I tried not to look at Oliver. What must he think? "Absolutely. That's so kind of you. I have insurance. I just . . . haven't had time to do anything about it yet. Thank you so much."

"Not at all." And then, knowingly, "I don't want my brother catching it." She winked. "Oh! That reminds me. Oliver, come inside and help me pull down the crystal punch bowl. It's our contribution. They want to show it off today to raffle it. I asked Patsy to get it down yesterday and she never did." She saw his face and frowned. "Don't look so aghast. We never use it."

"Can't it wait?" He moved her perfunctorily aside.

"No, it can't. Mrs. Lassiter is stopping by to pick it up for the dance. I don't want her coming in and sitting down, wasting my time," she insisted ungraciously. "I really want it done now."

He padded halfheartedly behind her into the dining room. His toes, I was sad to notice, pointed out.

Jenny Rose trailed the rim of the sugar bowl with her finger and cocked her head at me.

"So what now? You fancy Cupsand saucers?"

"It's just a dance, Jenny Rose."

She lowered her voice, "Did you ever notice that Morgan Donovan watches you when you're not watching him?"

I fought the coming blush with all the might of last night's resolution. "Morgan? He's nice."

"Nice? He's worth two of that moron you're thinking of seeing."

"Morgan happens to belong to someone else."

"Who?"

"That 'moron's' sister, as if you didn't know."

"That's not the way I see it. He doesn't love her. And they're not married. Anyway, it's pretty obvious he's got a crush on you."

I looked up, desperate to hear just these very words and yet knowing the hopes they brought with them would ultimately be dashed. Jenny Rose was just a girl. She thought a man's keen interest meant he was stuck on you. She didn't realize that in the end, commitments held men accountable. I was just the new gal in town. Besides—and this I knew for sure—I wasn't about to be anybody's last fling before he tied the knot.

Oliver came back in in his shirtsleeves and Paige, not trusting him, followed carrying the crystal bowl, then rested it on the marble countertop. "How's our boy?" Oliver said.

Jenny Rose leaned over a basket of fruit on the table. "Off to school. And," she added merrily, "he walked the whole way." She took a bite of a green apple with a delicious-sounding crunch.

Irritated, Paige touched her temples. "Jenny Rose. Please. The Tylenol. I'm dying."

"Okay." She trotted off down the stairs.

"Why is it so quiet?" Oliver said. Brother and sister squared off and faced each other.

The atmosphere between them was so thick they seemed about to have an argument. "Well . . ." I stood. "I'd best be off. I'll wait out—"

"Don't be silly." Paige raised a shoulder. "Have some tea."

It didn't take much of a dimwit to realize I was in the way. "If I have any more tea this week, I'll float away."

"It's the clock." Paige stood erect. "No one's wound the clock."

"Oh, that's it," Oliver agreed. "Someone's walked off with the key. Wait, Claire. I'll drive you up. Car's still warm."

I considered what to do. If I told him we were off to Radiance's, I might get Jenny Rose in trouble. Maybe her mornings weren't her own. "I really do want to walk." I smiled insincerely at him. "But thanks."

There was a clunking, banging sound. We all looked up. The cellar door flew open and Sam the cat shot across the room like a bat out of hell. Jenny Rose staggered into the room. Her mouth was in an O. She didn't look at us. She grabbed her throat and with a pitch to the heavens, she screamed and screamed and screamed.

"What's happened?" Mr. Piet hurried in, knocking over the avocado plant and spilling dirt across the white tiles.

"It's Patsy Mooney," Jenny Rose gasped.

Oliver and Mr. Piet rushed down the stairs she'd come up.

"She's dead," Jenny Rose whimpered.

They came back up.

"Call the police," Oliver said. He was pale as a ghost. "She's been strangled."

CHAPTER FIVE

CLAIRE

Jenny Rose came up to the cottage after the doctor and the coroner had come and the police had cordoned off the place. She fell into my arms and I let her cry, then we sat down together on the old couch, which, at last free of clutter, was warm and embracing.

"So you gave them the stones?" I said.

"No," she whispered, like they were listening.

"What? Are you crazy? Now they'll think we have something to do with it!"

"Well, you left!"

"Oliver told me to come here and wait. Did the detective interview you?"

"No, I said I had to go get Wendell."

"But it was you who found Patsy! And Wendell's in school."

"I know. I lied."

I stared at her. "You can't lie to them. They'll find out and think you have something to hide!"

"They'll arrest me. Is that what you want? Whoever killed Mrs. Mooney was after me."

"What! Why?"

"Don't you remember me telling you I changed rooms with her? Somebody went there to get me. And then they found her instead and killed her."

We sat there looking at each other. Then she said, "So what should we do?"

"Being arrested is better than being killed," I said. "Anyway, why would they want to arrest you?"

She yelled, "That's the big story in the media, illegal immigrants who kill Americans! Of course they'll think it's me. Is that what you want, me to go to jail?"

"Of course not. Just . . . Just . . . I don't know. There's a vast difference between a Dominican gang member and an Irish au pair!" But even as I said it I recognized the take a Nassau County detective would have on Jenny Rose with her hip-hop hair and blue nails and tattoos, even if they were fake. She looked like a punk. I said, "Let's just try and think clearly. You came to Sea Cliff and right away Wendell gave you the moonstones."

"Not right away. Well, yes, right away. But it wasn't like he gave them to me. He wanted to and then Patsy Mooney snatched them from him and I demanded she give them to me—"

"Wait a minute," I interrupted, "she had the stones in her hand?"

"They were in a scarf. He had them wrapped up in a scarf. I don't think she knew they were in there. I certainly didn't. I only discovered them when I cleaned out my bag." She looked puzzled.

"We've got to talk to Wendell."

Jenny Rose made a helpless gesture. "Every time I ask him he shuts up."

"What, like he's frightened?"

"No. More like he doesn't know what I'm talking about."

"Look. I know you don't like the idea, but this goes way beyond illegal immigration, toots. This is withholding evidence in a murder investigation, and in this country they don't take kindly to that."

She sniffled into her hanky and pleaded, "Do you think they'll put me in jail?"

"No, of course not," I said but without much conviction. If no one had reason to kill Patsy Mooney, the police probably would look for the nearest illegal immigrant. They'd call her a person of interest and come up with some reason to hold her. Even one night in jail was something to be avoided at all costs. I tried to think of how I could use my ex-husband's connections without getting him involved.

Someone tapped on the door, the dog howled, and we both jumped and grabbed hold of each other. But I knew that shadow. It was Mrs. Dellaverna. I got up and threw open the door.

"I just heard!" She barreled in holding her head. "I'm thinking, what's gonna happen now?"

Ignoring me and simply brushing past Jake, she sat down at the table facing Jenny Rose. "You the one who found Patsy?"

"Yes." Jenny Rose seemed very tiny and young sitting there all hunched up. Jake seemed to sense her distress and went over and sat on her feet.

"Oh, my God, what are we gonna do?!" Mrs. Dellaverna raved and the two of them started crying. Suddenly Mrs. Dellaverna reared up and squinted, gypsylike, at Jenny Rose. "It's a kind of funny. You find the girl drowning, it's Radiance; you find the body, it's Patsy!"

"Wait," Jenny Rose cried, "you think I had something to do with it?"

"I'm not looking for a wage-a-war. All I'm saying is it's funny, that's all."

"Fuck you." Jenny Rose stood in a fury.

Mrs. Dellaverna threw the dishtowel she held up over her face and ran out the door home. Jenny Rose flung herself onto the bed, sobbing. Jake circled, gargling restrained submission. I called him to me and held him tight because he and I were both trembling. Then a soft tapping at the door sent him rigid and yowling with fright. I calmed him down and went to get it. It turned out to be young Teddy. I was so relieved. He stood in the doorway, his skin all flushed and rosy, looking past me to Jenny Rose. You could tell he was crazy about her. And worried. "Come on in," I invited. Because Jenny Rose didn't care a fig for him, she hardly minded that he saw her in such a state.

"Look," he said as he sat cautiously on the edge of the sofa, "I thought I'd better let you know. Patsy Mooney's husband is on the loose."

"Her husband?" Jenny Rose squawked. "She doesn't have a husband! She told me!"

"Well, she does, I'm afraid. Did." He sighed sadly. "She didn't have an order of protection against him because he was a retired cop himself. She thought the police here would have it on file and give her away. Oliver, Paige, Mr. Piet, and myself all knew. We thought he had no idea where she was. And we have no idea how he found her. We knew he was violent. Mooney is her maiden name. She didn't use his."

This let Jenny Rose off the hook. "What's his name?" I asked, more relieved than I wanted to let on.

"Woods," he said the name with little-disguised scorn. "Donald Woods. One of those control-freak, hooplehead cops you think you'll only read about in the paper."

"Oh," Jenny Rose sank back in the pillows, and cried, "that's why she said, she said, '*Thank God that's over*,' about her marriage! I can hear her clear as a bell like it was yesterday! Oh, my God! I can't believe it! Maybe if I'd left her alone in her turret she would have heard him coming up the stairs! Maybe she wouldn't be dead! That fuckin' thick carpet! She wouldn't have heard a sound!"

"Now, now," Teddy comforted her. "There's no stopping these wife beaters. It's no one's fault but his. I won't have you blaming yourself."

I shot him a bemused look because he seemed to have affected a Ronald Colman accent. And then I remembered Mrs. Dellaverna telling me about her friend hiding out at her place. Some *shit of a husband* who'd *beat her up good* . . . I said, "So they're sure it was him?"

"It certainly looks like it. He was seen at the deli, asking around. We know he'd been arrested before for smashing her up. A real violent guy." He shook his head, grimacing. "I'd give a pretty penny to know how he found out she was here."

Jenny Rose sat up. Her expression turned suspicious. "And how he knew she was in the basement. You know, I knew someone was watching the house. I felt it!" She shivered.

I remembered last night and Jake flipping out. Had the fellow come looking for her at the cottage? "Where do they think he's gone?" I asked cautiously.

Teddy raked his hair. "That's just it. He was seen coming into town but no one saw him leaving. He might well still be here."

"Shit," I said.

"So I want you both to lock your doors and windows."

"Well, he's not after us." Jenny Rose quaked in her blanket.

"No, but he might be looking for a place to hide out for a while. You don't know. He could be in someone's garage or—"

"Or break into someone's home and hold them captive till the coast is clear!" Jenny Rose finished for him.

"I'm afraid so."

I'd brought Jake to Sea Cliff at just the right time. I thought of that poor, demented Daniel on his own. He would be easy prey for a man like that. Obviously, someone like him would never think to lock his doors.

Teddy's blue eyes moved around the cottage, taking it all in for the first time. "I love your curtains," he said, trying to lighten things up.

"Amazing what you can do with a little strong detergent and a hot iron," I said, glad he was here. I was sure he'd be happy to look after Jenny Rose while I did some investigating on my own. I lured Jake up onto the bed—he knew any bed was typically off-limits—to keep him happy and left the two kids with a fresh pot of coffee and some Ikea cinnamon buns.

I almost asked Teddy if I might borrow his station wagon but decided against it. Morgan would have my car back to me shortly and it wouldn't hurt me to pedal up and down these steep hills, quiet and swift. I went out to the shed, opening the creaky door with care in case Patsy's murderer lurked inside, and lugged out the bicycle. It was rusty but it seemed to work all right. I was grateful to Morgan. Morgan. His words came back to me and echoed in my brain. *I almost strangled him,* he'd confessed about the seminarian that'd molested an altar boy. I was only halfway down the path into town when my cell phone rang. I bumped onto the side of the road and opened it.

"Auntie Claire?"

"Jenny Rose. What's up?"

"Remember I told you Wendell acted like he didn't know what I was talking about when I asked him about the stones?"

"Yeah."

"Well, I got to thinking. Maybe he really didn't know about the stones."

"What do you mean? You told me you got them from him."

"That's just it. I assumed he was frightened about having the stones. But when I asked him about the scarf, remember I told you he was completely forthright about answering? Maybe the stones weren't wrapped up in the scarf at all. Perhaps they were already in my pocket."

"I don't understand."

"Maybe I swept them from Patsy when I grabbed the scarf from her."

We were both silent, digesting this possibility. "Or," I suggested, "maybe Patsy put them there. Or anybody. Put Teddy on the phone."

"He had to go."

"What? I thought he'd stay with you!"

"No, he had to open a house up on Dosoris Lane for Paige. The police are still questioning her and there's a couple waiting there to see a house. And Mr. Piet is still waiting to be questioned and no one's heard from Radiance. Teddy's going to stop off at her apartment over Gallagher's and check on her."

"Well, I certainly don't want you there alone. We'd better meet."

"Where?"

"Twillyweed."

"Okay. I'll come to you."

"I've got to make a stop or two, first. Then we can talk. Just get there quickly. And, Jenny Rose, *stay* there! Just answer any questions they have truthfully. Really, this changes everything."

"All right," she agreed and she sounded relieved. Little did I know she had her own plans for getting some answers by heading into town.

Meanwhile I bicycled down to the beach and Daniel's house, dead on the water. It was shabby, but you could see how all the real estate agents in town would give their eyeteeth to get their hands on it. It had charm—or it would have with a lot of money thrown in. It was one of those small cottages with a low-hanging roof that resembles a thatch. I tapped on the back door. There was no sound from within. I knocked again and the door just moved open. All right, I pushed it. The kitchen was outdated in the style of the '70s and it was damp. A fly battered itself against one of the windows, buzzing. There was an unopened package of baking soda on the table, some toothpaste, and a cylinder of Comet, like someone had gone to the store and left some things for him. "Daniel?" I called, mentally cursing myself for not telling Jenny Rose, or someone, where I'd gone. I looked out the window into the yard. A decrepit lawnmower stood leaning, suspended, in the half-finished yard. I peeked through to the next room. It was a sort of bedroom–living room, the bed covered neatly with a yellowed chenille spread, a permanent sagging dip in the middle where he must sleep. A toy lay upside down on the rug on the floor: a doll, half covered with a blanky, her arm reaching out. I resisted the urge to go in there. This was a strange and complicated place, but it wasn't degenerate. It was like an empty kindergarten classroom, fizzing with energy that's gone away, vivacious colored boxes on top shelves and viruses and moving orbs of dust in sun shafts from dirty windows. On the kitchen table beside me I noticed a list of grocery items. Something about it looked familiar to me and I skulked closer to peer at it. It was Jenny Rose's and my list of suspects! A thrill of fear ran through me. How in hell had that got here? Steadying my heart, I tiptoed in and picked it up and put it into my pocket. Frightened now that someone was watching me, I slipped out the door. Jenny Rose certainly hadn't been here. Had she? Paige? I wouldn't put it past her to go through Jenny Rose's things. Feeling safer in the light of day, I reread the list. My eye fell to the name Mrs. Lassiter, the woman who worked at the rectory. The snoop in me wouldn't mind checking her out. I got back on my bike, and as I pedaled away I heard the unmistakable clatter of a lawnmower resuming its course. Evidently I frightened old Daniel as much as he'd frightened me.

St. Greta's Rectory was a beautiful place with a mature copper beech, a profusion of birds, and a lovely, well-tended garden. I rang the bell, but it seemed to be out of order. I clopped on the heavy wood.

A bad-tempered lady threw open the door. "I heard you the first time, so!"

She was a skinny, busy lady with a whirl of graying ginger hair, a snub nose, a giant bust, and a mass of freckles all over her arms and face. Her teeth were spaced apart and separate. "Mrs. Lassiter?" I asked meekly.

"What is it?"

"I'm Jenny Rose Cashin's aunt. My name is Claire Breslinsky. I've come to tell you—"

"Claire? You'll be Claire, Mary Cashin's middle girl?"

I was startled. "Yes," I admitted unsurely.

"You're the very likeness of her!"

"You know my mother?"

"Know her? I wouldn't have come to this country were it not for her!"

I was so thrown off my kilter I just stood there while we gaped at each other. I don't know which upset me more—that she knew my mother or that I looked just like her. My mother was old. She was plump. I was . . . I was . . .

She mopped her strong farmers' daughter's hands on her apron and herded me in, saying, "Come in, come in. No sense standing here in the vestibule looking like a pie hit you full in the face!"

I blessed myself from the holy water font and followed her through the cool, timbered archways, over the scrubbed and walnut-oiled tiles, and under a series of handsome naval prints. There would be no doubt a County Cork widow was in residence here. The place shone.

She led me into a white kitchen, fitted out in unfashionable but sturdy oak cabinets, and sat me at the checkered oilcloth. In the tiny window a cactus bloomed an orange wart.

"There now," she said, releasing a happy, eager sigh, and I realized I might be in for a long one. With easy movements she had the teapot up to boil and soda bread whisked from the box, transported butter and jam from the fridge, then carefully sliced a wedge of soda bread and placed it reverently on a doily before me.

"I'm not sure my mother mentioned you were here," I declared cautiously. Had she told me about this woman while I hadn't listened?

Her face fell. "Did she not?"

"But," I hurried to say, "wait a minute, I do remember now! She told me to tell you she was polycoating Jenny Rose's picture in the paper and sending copies off to Skibbereen! That was it. I'm sorry, I forget everything these days. You understand. It's quite an event for us, having Jenny Rose here in the States." I gave up with a heaving breath. "What I mean is, it's not because of her that I'm here."

Suspicious, she looked at me, her freckled face closed and leaning to one side.

"I'm afraid I've come with bad news," I went on.

"Your mother!"

"No, it's none of us. It's Patsy Mooney from up at Twillyweed."

Mrs. Lassiter clutched her heart. "Patsy? My Patsy?"

"I'm afraid she's dead."

She turned red and began to make a strange noise in her throat. I looked around for something stronger than tea. I thought she might be having a stroke, or was choking on something, the way she sat there gurgling and sputtering.

"Mrs. Lassiter, is there someone I can call? Is Father in the rectory?"

She gasped, "He's having a pre-Cana."

"Would you like me to call him?"

Chalk faced, she shook her head then demanded, "How did she die?"

"I'm afraid it was murder."

"Murder?" She stood up and sat down, covered her mouth with her hand. "He got her? Donald, that blaggard, he finally got her?"

"They think so."

She sucked in her breath. "She always said he would! She always said he'd find her one day like he promised and kill her!"

"Can I get you something to drink?"

"Sherry. Under the sink. Hurry."

I went right to it and poured her a water glass full. It smelled like something stronger than sherry. "*Sláinte*," she gasped and drank it straight down. It didn't seem to hurt her. She began to cry. "How did he do it?"

I looked around uncomfortably. "He strangled her."

"Ahh!" She fell again into sobs, her large shoulders heaving up and down.

I sat with her for a good long time. After a while she came around and blew her nose. "But we have such lovely plans! I've got to call my friend Maureen," she said and went into the hallway to call. During this time I swiftly polished off two more thick pieces of her hopelessly good soda bread. Then, feeling guilty, I moved the rest around the plate so it didn't seem so much was gone. She came back in. "I'll have to wait awhile. Nobody's there."

"So you were best friends with Patsy Mooney, then."

"Oh, aye. Grand friends." She peered up toward the little window and shook her head. "Best friends when it comes to that. We're bingo partners. We've been to every jewelry show at the Coliseum. And every fortnight we sit together on the bus to Atlantic City. It leaves from the mall parking lot over at the Americana Mall. She always wins, let me tell you. Patsy can play anything—poker, all of it. Not just the slots like me. I don't know who I'll go with now!" She looked at me with refreshed shock as the atrocity hit her again. "What about all of our plans?" she wailed. "We have so many wonderful plans!"

I let her calm down. "I guess going down there you'd have plenty of time to talk. She must have told you all about her troubles with . . . Donald, is it?"

"Oh, yes. She tells me all about it," she sniffled, still referring to her in the present tense. "I know the whole story, so." She cut into yet another slice of soda bread and pushed it on me. "That's why I have to drive us to the mall parking lot. She won't drive. She thinks if she renews her license, he'll find her, like, what with all his friends on the job. And he did, didn't he? Just like she said!" She burst into fresh sobs. "That's how sly he is. Oh, he's mean. How many times did he beat her up! Kicked her down the stairs when she tried to leave him!"

"I guess you're not surprised to hear the tragic news, then."

She held her arms and her head went down. "It fair breaks my heart." She looked up with sudden clarity. "But I have to say I am surprised. Shocked, more like. It's been some years—so long for him to hold a grudge, isn't it? You'd think he'd have found someone else to torture by now." She shook her head and snuffled into her tissue. "We're good friends, me and Patsy. I always make her laugh."

"She must have been a wonderful woman," I said. "Well, is there anyone I can call to come stay with you? Shall I call Father in?"

"No, no don't do that. It'll all be about him, then, won't it? I'll have to get him ready for a death call, iron his purple stole . . ." She went to budge but couldn't, sipped her drink, her eyes in the past, unable to move on to this new, terrible reality, I guessed. I let her talk. "Buys me little things, too, she does. Soaps and fancy cooking dishes. See this yellow crock from Portugal? She gave me that. And them fancy things are dear, so. She'll leave dollar bills on my ashtray in the car. For gas money. She's that thoughtful."

I got up to go. We walked together down the hallway, our footfalls echoing in the hollow space. "He couldn't leave her alone, could he!"

She shook her head. "You see what it proves? There's a sadist on every street corner. But a good masochist is hard to find."

"What about Mrs. Dellaverna? I could call her to come. I know she's at home."

"Lina?!" She gave me a sullen, cud-chewing face. "Don't know why you'd be mixed up with the likes of her. . . . Don't even think about it. No! Not in my kitchen! Not here! Never!"

My, my, I thought, *such dislike!* "Okay, okay, I won't call her," I promised.

"Telephone Paige," she said, sniffing primly. "Tell her I'll come up to Twillyweed once I've pulled myself together, so." She opened the massive door. "I've got to pick something up there at any rate— a donation for the raffle—and she and I can make the plans for the wake."

"All right. You're sure you'll be all right if I leave you alone?"

She looked at her watch with a capable flourish. "Father will be here in ten more minutes. I'll give him his lunch and then I'll be up. Tell her that."

"All right, and good-bye. I'm so sorry. Thank you for your hospitality at such a grievous time. Your soda bread was a delight." I patted my belly. "One day maybe you'll give me the recipe."

Her pale eyes cheered up. "*Och,* that's what I'm famous for. Father even has me sending it back down to his old parish in Broad Channel just to brag how good he has it, so! Now you'll tell your good mother I was asking for her?"

"Why don't you call her? I'm sure she'd love to hear from you. Especially since you helped Jenny Rose get her position."

She shook her head shyly. "Oh, no. She'll be thinking I'm looking for praise."

"No she wouldn't!"

"Aye, we'll just let that be."

"We'll see." I smiled sympathetically, making a mental note to tell my mother to call.

"Good-bye." She held her long arm up in the air and waved me off with her sodden tissue in a burst of sentiment. "To happier days. And send my regards to Mary." She rocked her head reflectively.

"I will." I hopped on the old bicycle and rattled down the path, once again relieved Jenny Rose's having the moonstones had had nothing to do with Patsy Mooney's murder. I was almost happy. Because that's what this Donald's involvement meant, didn't it? They were separate, thank God. But as I pedaled along the old country path and even before I reached the main road to town, something nagged at my complacence. Just suppose this Donald Woods hadn't killed Patsy Mooney, I conjectured. Although surely he had, if even the police believed it. Still, I scratched my head. The mystery gems turning up in Sea Cliff and then the murder in the same house . . . I kept having the feeling I was missing something. The wind was at my back. I pumped along, my brow furrowed, this niggling occupying me now. A gull flew off in front and gave an excited cry and all at once it came to me. Broad Channel. She'd said Broad Channel, hadn't she? I had more than a nagging suspicion that the two crimes had to be connected. I just didn't know how. Had this Donald Woods clobbered the priest and stolen the statue? No, why would he? Suppose he hadn't had anything to do with it at all? It could just as easily have been Morgan or Glinty or Oliver or Teddy or even Radiance or Paige—someone who knew enough to cast suspicion on a belligerent ex-husband.

It was a hunch, but I couldn't shake the suspicion. I coasted my bicycle into a broad circle and pedaled back to the rectory. I knocked. Mrs. Lassiter, half into her fussy black suit and annoyed again from the look on her face, threw the door open. I was aware that very consciously she put on a martyred, sweeter face for me. "Yes?"

"I'm so sorry to bother you again, Mrs. Lassiter. Would it be all right if I took some holy water up to Twillyweed?"

She was glad, I could tell, it was about nothing else. "Have you got the bottle?"

"No."

"I'll get you a jar," she said and let me stand there while she went to get it. A flock of blackbirds went rushing by.

It was a nice, big mayonnaise jar. "Thanks," I said, then remarked nonchalantly, "Say. Just out of curiosity, what parish was that in Broad Channel your pastor came from?"

"Oh, that'll be St. Margaret Mary's. Father Steger's parish now."

I put on my stupid face "Ah, too bad." I acted disappointed. "I thought it might be my dad's old parish. Oh, well. Just a thought." I smiled weakly and pedaled off. My mind reeled. When I was clear of the place, I let myself think. *St. Margaret Mary's! That's where the priest was clobbered and where the statue was stolen from! Wait till I tell Jenny Rose.*

I caught sight of Daniel's house and turned in the driveway, then left my bike lying on the gravel. "Daniel?" I called in. No one answered. I tickled the wind chimes he had hanging from the sill. They were the big, booming, expensive ones. I waited. No one was there. Still, you never knew. I stepped into the kitchen. Everything looked the same. A cat yowled from inside, half scaring me out of my wits. Then there was no sound. None at all. I crept cautiously across the linoleum. I stepped over the threshold and was in the room with the bed. It smelled so nice, like someone had polished the nightstand with Pledge. And then, for no reason I could think of, I bent over and pulled the blanky off the doll. It wasn't a doll; it was a statue, a statue of Our Lady, her poor eye sockets empty, her arms out extending grace. Hearing my heartbeat in my ears, I picked it up and sheltered it against me. The big cat on the windowsill looked past me, like someone else was there. I started to go. With every step a horror that someone would grab me moved me along with my spine up under me. I made it back outside. I clutched the statue under my jacket and felt tears prick at my eyes. But I didn't cry. It wasn't that. I just stood there thinking, *I've got her.* I made the sign of the cross, took off my jacket and wrapped her up in it, and laid her in my basket next to the big jar of holy water. I looked around and saw no one. No one saw me. I rattled along on my bike, my hand outstretched like a guardian vessel, shielding my booty. I should have gone to the police right then. But I didn't.

JENNY ROSE

Hastily making her way into town, Jenny Rose then stood in the middle of Main Street and took a breath. She would talk to Glinty and find out what he knew. She'd been so worried the police would suspect her that she hadn't given a thought to whether or not he—But no. No, Glinty would never have strangled a soul. She was sure of it. Oh, poor Patsy Mooney! Jenny Rose spotted a shop where they sold crystals and religious items. Surely they'd carry Mass cards. She went in and then, hearing urgent, familiar whispers, busied herself behind a wall of scented candles. It was Paige, wasn't it? She was lecturing Radiance in that schoolmarm, patronizing tone of hers.

"You never even came to Noola's wake! What's wrong with you? You wouldn't go to her funeral and now you won't even come back to the house when the poor woman—!"

"I don't like the dead," Radiance moaned. "They terrify me! Coffins and holes in the ground—"

"Don't start that again. It's not just our duty," Paige reminded her, "she was kind to us all."

That stopped her. "Yes," she agreed in a small voice. "You're right."

"I've got to get back. They want to interview me again. Why are you all dressed up?"

"I'm not."

"Where were you? In the city? What were you up to? I can tell you were up to something!"

Paige said this in such an uncharacteristic, almost savage tone that Jenny Rose decided it was time to make herself known. It wasn't that she minded eavesdropping, but she didn't like them to catch her at it and thought if Radiance whirled around they might. She stepped out and at that moment saw Paige slide her hand up Radiance's shirt back and pull her roughly to her. "There's something you're not telling me," Paige hissed. But Radiance's chin went up, her mouth opened, and her eyes dimmed in willingness. In lust.

Jenny Rose took a quick step backward and turned and slipped, dismayed, around the display shelf and out the door. Blindly she clattered down the wooden steps. *God!* she muttered silently. *Imagine it! Two of the best-lookin' women anyone could think of. Either one of them could have any man she chose. What a waste!* She could understand what it was for Brigid and Deirdre, her own stepparents. No disrespect meant, but let's face it, nobody else would want them, would they? It shouldn't surprise her, of all people, but it did. And how in hell, she puzzled, could those two be carrying on and nobody have a whiff of a clue? Auntie Claire sprang to mind. Poor old sod. How shocked *she* must have been when she'd found out about her fellow! It went to show it was just like she said. You can be living your life and not even know the person closest to you. Not even know where they go in their mind. Jenny Rose huddled away down the street. Uh-oh. There was Teddy leaning on his car in front of the bookshop, drinking a cup of coffee from the deli and paging nonchalantly through a book. Smug bugger. Thought himself fine, didn't he? Smarter than everyone. Figured she'd come around if he just gave it enough time. She went to dart down the alley, but he'd seen her. He kept a blue eye on her until she felt she had to come over and say something. "'Lo," she said as she nodded grudgingly and crossed over.

"You know what I like most about this town?" Teddy mused. "This bookshop keeps its top step like a shelf for books that don't sell. You can take any one of them, free."

She stuck out her pursed lips and slid a reluctant hip against the hood of the car.

"Poor Patsy," he said, shaking his head softly.

"Yeah."

"Looking for Glinty, eh?" He took a knowing sip of his coffee. "Did you talk to the detectives?"

"No to both. It's so horrible, isn't it?"

"Yeah. Horrible. What a way to die!" Teddy sighed, giving the horizon a searching look. "I can't get over Glinty, though," he puzzled, "what with all this going on! For him to go off looking for—how did he put it—the prettiest lass on the planet . . ."

What did he mean? Who was he talking about? Radiance? "Wouldn't have been me then, though, would it!"

"He must have meant you," Teddy blustered, sounding conciliatory, but unable to keep the doubtfulness from his voice. He smiled again, loose with charm. "Maybe he was afraid of the cops. Maybe he knows something we don't . . ."

Jenny Rose tried to smile, not liking him at all just now. She wasn't going to stand here. Forget it! She walked the long way back to Twillyweed.

CLAIRE

By the time I got to Twillyweed there were emergency vehicles and cop cars all over. I hesitated, but Oliver's Alpha Romeo was there and I saw my PT Cruiser, so I left the statue wrapped up in my jacket in the bicycle basket and I walked boldly over the yellow tape. Radiance had just come in and Morgan was grilling her, "Where have you been anyway? Your father's been sick with worry!"

"I was in the city. I walked up from town. They wouldn't let me in the house until just now."

"Well, I want you to calm down. The way you've been acting, you'll be heading for a breakdown!"

No doubt I was gaping at Radiance. I'd never seen her and now here she was—this practically mythological creature, this extraordinary combination of all worlds. You wouldn't see one like her every day.

He noticed me. "Come in, Claire. I've got your car here."

"Yes, I saw it; thank you."

"Thank Mr. Piet. Detective Harms wants to talk to you anyway."

"Me?"

"About Patsy Mooney."

"Well, of course. But I didn't know her, really, just saw her that once at the dinner party."

"Well, then, that's what you'll tell him." He pulled out the strawback kitchen chair for me.

Jenny Rose, a cherry red sweater thrown over her shoulders with one button done, minced through the back door in a conscientious little jig. You could tell she was making a great effort to compose herself and maintain appropriate decorum. She said, "I've got to go pick up Wendell. I don't know if I should bring him back here or not."

Oliver, just coming in from the back porch, a cigar in his mouth, addressed her through gritted teeth, "I went over to the school to get him but we decided it would be better if he stayed until dismissal. You'll pick him up as usual. Oh, and I was hoping you could take him with you to the Great White for a few hours, Claire. Just until they remove the body."

"Of course," she and I said as one.

I whispered in her ear, "I've got to talk to you."

But just then Paige, released from the detective and very pale, came in. Catching sight of Oliver's cigar, she said, "Please put that thing out if you're going to be in the house, Oliver. It stinks. No sense all of us losing our grip."

"I'll get you a cup of sweet tea, shall I?" Morgan put a calming hand on her slim shoulder.

"Yes, thank you." She smiled wanly. "That's just what I need."

Radiance said, "I'll get it. She'll want her Japanese Sencha tea. I know where everything is."

I offered, "Paige, I went and told Mrs. Lassiter what happened. She said she'd come up later and help you plan the wake."

She put the back of her wrist to her head. "That's all I need right now. Nosy Lassiter!"

"That's her, all right." Jenny Rose hoisted herself onto the marble countertop, "She used to stand outside the confessional back in Skibbereen and listen."

Everyone stared at Jenny Rose.

"What?" She wiped her nose with the back of her hand. "She did."

Through the heavy lace curtains, I saw Teddy's maroon station wagon pulling up. He hopped out with his real estate clipboard and came in the door, hesitating respectfully. He sat down. "Radiance, I stopped by your apartment. I was so worried about you. Where were you?"

"I'm all right." She went about setting up the tea things, placing an extra cup and saucer before Jenny Rose on the countertop. Her fingers trembled.

Teddy said, "I can't say I'm happy they found out who killed her, but I feel a sense of peace. There was always something menacing, something tense around the house. And now it's over. Or it will be when they catch him."

I thought of my father who always says *Carry a clipboard and you can walk in anywhere.* I don't know what made me think of that.

Radiance gave her little French shrug. "It doesn't feel very *over* to me."

He returned her look. "All right. Where were *you* all night?"

"If you must know, I had my tryout for the Rockettes this morning." She sank into the chair.

Surprised, Paige reached for her arm, "Darling! Why didn't you tell me?"

Radiance bit her lip. "The worst of it was when I came back to Sea Cliff and I saw the police, I was actually glad something terrible had happened so I wouldn't have to tell anyone."

"Tell anyone what?"

Her head hung. "That I'd tried out and didn't make it."

"Oh, my dear—"

"I'm so ashamed." Her face crumbled. "I was eliminated before they even got started. They took one look at me when I came in. One girl called me a giraffe! I am too tall."

"At least you weren't eliminated because you were a rotten dancer," Teddy consoled.

Eliminated from the Rockettes and—I made a mental note—eliminated from our suspect list. It would be so easily verified.

"Everything's ruined now. Whoever killed Patsy should have killed me instead." Radiance sobbed uncontrollably. "Save me the trouble!"

"That's a terrible, melodramatic thing to say!" Paige knelt and took hold of her. "Stop it!"

A young police officer came in and said the detectives would like to speak to Morgan Donovan.

Radiance wiped her eyes, and Morgan straightened slowly and marched forward dutifully.

I said, "I'd like to speak to the detectives myself actually."

"You'll have to wait your turn, miss." The officer informed me.

"Well, he asked to see me."

"You'll still have to wait your turn."

They left.

Paige stood up and cleared her throat theatrically. "How did it go, Teddy?"

"*Uch*. They want to buy low and sell high."

"They didn't like it?"

"They like it, they just want it for nothing."

"It has a lovely porch."

"And the shade up there. Great old trees."

"Yes. Well, they won't get it for nothing. Dosoris is prime location now."

I thought such a conversation oddly out of place. But then Paige, too, lost it, holding her head in a hopeless gesture.

"Paige! This is too much for you!" Teddy glared angrily at Oliver as though all this were his fault.

Paige babbled, "It's just . . . I remember I looked to check the time and the clock was stopped. I should have known something was wrong! Patsy wouldn't forget to wind the clock!" She pounded her slight fist uselessly on the table.

We all looked at the stilled grandmother clock in the corner.

"I'll do it, Paige." Oliver moved to oblige, then stopped. "But I can't wind it without that red key. We'll have to wait until the detectives are finished down there. She always had it with her. Poor thing . . . She couldn't wind it because she was . . . dead."

I think that's when the horrendousness of what had happened really hit us all. The only sound was Paige's muffled sobs. The teapot shrilled and we all jumped. Radiance pulled herself together and came over and shushed Paige softly, walking her gently from the room. The rest of us just stood around, dazed. Teddy moved the pot from the fire and said uncertainly, "Do you think I ought to wait and talk to the detective?"

"Of course," I said.

"No." Oliver flung out his arm and looked at his watch. "Morgan might be in there for a while. You'd better get going. You'll be late for work. You can speak to them later." Wearily, he added, "We'll never see the end of them, now."

It was the way he'd flung out his arm. All at once I realized with whom Oliver Cupsand had been sitting at Once Upon a Moose my first day in town. It was Radiance. He'd given her money.

Casually, I followed him inside. He had the cold cigar in his mouth and he kept twisting it around with his teeth. "Oliver," I began, "it just came to me. I saw you at Once Upon a Moose when I first came to town. That very day. You were sitting with Radiance. It was during that cold snap and you were both wearing coats." I paused. "You were giving her money."

"For God's sake, I was giving her her paycheck!"

"Oh." I stood there while he gathered a series of papers from his desk. But then I thought, no, he wasn't giving her a paycheck because there was something secretive and clandestine about his movement, the shifty look in his eye that had caused me to look back at their table. And it was cash he'd given her. I didn't move. I stayed behind him and was about to say something when, "All right," he admitted, whirling around in irritation, "I did give her money. But it wasn't what you think." He lowered his voice. "I always give Radiance money. I feel responsible for her, if you must know. Protective. It's nothing to do with *that* sort of love. I'm in love with Annabel. I haven't slept with another woman since she left me. I . . . just can't." He broke down. "I love her so much! I still love her—even after she did this to me! I have no pride. I'd take her back. Even now, if she were here, I'd take her back!" He wriggled his hands in a spasm in front of his face and cried with despair and longing, "Her beautiful Titian red hair!"

It was then the suspicion first came to me: *She's dead. Annabel is dead. He's probably making up those letters. They probably don't even exist!* I left him to himself. There was nothing else I could say. I went up behind Jenny Rose and pulled her into the pantry and we squashed ourselves onto the cushioned bank. I whispered, "Wait till you hear this. The priest at St. Greta's here in Sea Cliff, guess where his old parish was?"

"Well, don't keep me hanging!" she whispered back roughly.

"St. Margaret Mary down in Broad Channel. The same one where the priest was hit on the head the day before you rescued Radiance. In Broad Channel. Remember?"

"Shit!"

"Yeah. Now get this. I went over to Daniel's house and found the statue. The Our Lady statue."

She gaped at me. "Where is it?"

"Outside in my bicycle basket."

"What'll we do? Give it to the cops?"

"If we do, it'll sit on some evidence shelf for months, maybe years. I'm going to go down there and give it to that priest. Then we'll tell the cops."

"I'll come with you."

"No. You stay here with Wendell. Put the statue in my car, the door's open. I'll make up some excuse. Now what was his name, the priest? Oh, yes, I remember; it's Father Steger."

I gave Jenny Rose the key to the cottage and told her to take the bike. Wendell would love to ride on the back and it would distract him.

She hesitated with the key in her open palm. "Patsy Mooney had a fancy little key on a chain around her neck. I think it's the key that winds the clock."

"Why?"

"It was red."

"Well, it won't do her any good where she is now."

"No, but if it's gone—maybe someone killed her *for* it.

I slipped out into the yard and took out my cell phone, dialed 411, and got the number for the rectory at Margaret Mary. No secretary answered when I called there, it was such a tiny parish, but the answer machine tape that picked up was the German-accented voice of an old priest. He gave another number in case of emergency. I called it but it went right to voicemail. I took a chance and left one, saying I had information concerning a missing statue and then I left my number. I realized I'd forgotten to leave my name and started to call back and then I gave it up. I leaned wearily against the fieldstone fence. Enough already. We were in a real pickle here and I was going to have to swallow my pride and ask Johnny, my ex-husband, for help. I punched in his number. There was no answer and it rang right into the message box like when he's off gambling, so I tried the precinct. Johnny is retired, but you'll often as not find him skulking around in his old precinct. "Nah, I ain't seen Benedetto around," I was told. But he hesitated before he said it—like he knew something I didn't, so I got worried.

I called my son, Anthony. He answered the phone with a preemptive, "Ma, I'm in lab."

"I'm sorry, Anthony, I just want to know where Daddy is. I can't reach him and it's kind of important."

There was a moment of silence. Then he said, "You mean you don't know?"

"Know what?"

"He took Portia away to get engaged."

"What?"

"You really didn't know?"

I was speechless and sank down onto a large rock. There was this fieldstone wall covered with lapis blue flowers to the left of me. I couldn't think of the flower's name. Really blue, they were.

His voice softened. "They went to the Riviera Maya, Ma. I can't believe nobody told you."

My mind whirled. Exactly who would it be left to tell me such a thing?

"Ma? You okay? You want me to come home?"

It was his concerned voice and the realization that he'd leave school to see to me that finally clicked me back into reality. Lobelia. That was the name of the blue flower. Indigo blue and now locked in my mind for always representing my ex-husband's new love. "I am . . . I'm fine. I just . . ." I pulled myself up. ". . . didn't know."

After I assured Anthony I was all right—I wasn't, but what good would it do to upset him yet again about his father—I didn't know what to do. So I went back in and told Mr. Piet I *had* to talk to the detective in charge, but he was still interviewing Morgan. I tried to eavesdrop to find out how long it was going to take and overheard them dishing about someone's sailboat. From the tone of their voices they seemed unconcerned. I heard them laugh. God! I had to think. I lied and announced I had to go to Queens. Oliver wanted to come with me and for a moment I was tempted, imagining us together tooling top down in his theatrical red convertible—a girl is, after all, human—but I put him off. Instead I took my car and went back to the Great White.

When I got there, I peered through the screen. Jake was asleep and dreaming, running conscientiously after some bad dog, his front and rear rights digging at the air. The kitten was curled up asleep, right on top of him like a hat bobbing along on a bumpy train. I went for my key and realized I'd given it to Jenny Rose, then opened the door anyway because I hadn't locked it. I went in and my cell phone rang, waking them both. I walked back outside with Jake leaping beside me and answered the phone. It was Father Steger. I sat down on a milk crate beside the sundial.

"I just got your message," he said excitedly in a thick accent. "I was blowing down the boiler." His breathing was labored.

I said right away, "Yeah, look, Father, I found your statue."

You could practically see him close his eyes in relief. "Thank God!"

"I got these two blue stones, too. I'm pretty sure they're the eyes." I walked around the yard, savoring his delight. "I can't come today, but I'll drive over tomorrow, okay?" He didn't seem unnecessarily curious as to how I'd got them. I guess in his line of work you hear no end of stories.

"What can I do to reward you?" he asked, not too eagerly, afraid I was going to ask for money because that was one thing he didn't have. I knew the type. The soles of his shoes would be worn down to the leather and he wouldn't have had a haircut in a while. He'd be sprinkled with dandruff and dotted with canned soup stains. That's the thing. Just because of the bad apples you read so much about, everyone neglects the idea of fine priests. And yet on and on they go, don't they, never complaining, just visiting the sick and giving out Communion and Last Rites, despite the bad rap. You'd really think they'd let these poor fellows have wives.

"Nah, don't thank me," I said, then changed the subject, "Say, Father, you didn't see the guy who hit you, did you?"

"No. He got me from behind. But I fell on his arm. I know that."

"So what else did he take?"

"Some rosaries," he began. I waited. "Several rosaries," he went on. "You wouldn't believe what they charge now for the crystal ones. People are very touchy about their rosaries. I expected to see someone come back for that nice lavender one. From Fatima, I believe. Pity, that was."

"Nothing else taken that day?"

"Nothing of value, no."

Because he hesitated, I went on, "But was anything else missing?"

"Just this and that. It's the statue my parishioners want back."

"What do you mean exactly, 'this and that'?"

"Well. There was some cash. He took that. Forty-two dollars. And he took our old lost-and-found box full of stuff parishioners left. Old things." He was rambling on, "Eyeglasses. Watches. Rosaries. Some jewelry . . . nothing expensive."

My ears perked up. "Jewelry?"

"Well, mostly glasses—they all looked about the same. Magnifiers, mostly. There was a pair with red frames, I remember. You know. Cheaters. Those you find in the pharmacy. Prescriptions people would have come looking for. But I told all this already to the police."

All these questions were making him suspicious. So I told him I'd be down tomorrow and I let him go. The dog jumped up to sniff the package that looked like it might be from the butcher. I put the statue down on the outside wooden table and unfolded the thing. I stood her up. I took the gems from the bag in my pocket and with calm fingers snapped them easily into place where they belonged. One fell right out so I went in and got the Krazy Glue from the fridge, came out, and fastened them both in good. They seemed to move like living eyes. Together, Jake and I beheld the statue. She was complete again, and none the worse for wear. She looked good there. Then out of the blue I started remembering things. Like Morgan collecting antique watches, and his wounded wrist the day Radiance had nearly drowned. I got out my phone and called Father Steger back, and when he answered, I shouted, "Hello, Father Steger, it's me again, Claire Breslinsky, I hope I'm not disturbing you."

"Never mind." He sighed, resigned.

"Father, in the box of stuff that went missing, could there have been a very valuable watch, in there?"

"Oh, I don't think so. My parishioners are not the fancy ones, you know."

"I know, but sometimes antique watches look like gaudy, cheap things unless you're looking for them. Or even one of the plain ones that might seem just old . . ."

"No, I'm afraid not," he said decisively.

"Hmm." I sat there for a minute both relieved and disappointed and gazed unthinking into the blue water shimmering in the distance behind the statue.

He offered, "Mind you, I'll miss that box."

I patted Jake absently.

"That was a lovely old box. Bronze, it was. Heavy."

"How? Bronze?"

"Well, it just had a nice glow about it. The lid was a sort of dial. Ya, a moon dial, Father von Ritasdorf had told me it was. He was German, too, you know, from Schwenningen in the Black Forest. Had all sorts of gizmos in his room when he died. Ya, I'll miss that box."

My ears began to ring. "A really good box?" I egged him on.

"Let me see, what did he call it? A lunar something . . ." Father muttered. "*Ach*, yes, a lunar volvelle it was, some gadget that is said to allow one to tell time by the moonlight. It sat on the top of the box like a decoration, if you can believe it, such a nice thing."

Morgan's very words came back to me and my heart sank. *Moon dials*, he'd murmured, *I'm mad for them.*

"Very old," Father was saying. "Ah, well. We'll all be gone one day."

"Yes, Father." I looked around worriedly. I'd been alone, but now I had the uneasy feeling I was being watched. It was a creepy feeling, and I took the statue and the dog and carried the phone into the house and locked the door. I said, "Say, Father? There's one thing you could do for me . . . would you bless the house?"

"Sorry?"

"I mean this house where I am."

"Over the phone?"

"Well. It's just a little house."

I was waiting for him to object, but then I realized the silence meant he was praying and so I was silent, too. I held the phone up and closed my eyes. When he was finished, he said so.

"Gee, thanks, Father. Maybe you'll come out here when you have some time," I suggested. "Your old friend Father Schmidt lives out here at St. Greta's. You could see him, too."

"Oh, Schmidty, yes," he remembered dismissively. "Still got that floozy cooking for him?"

Could he possibly mean Mrs. Lassiter? "Er . . . I'm not sure." I frowned. "And, Father, thanks."

"Well, thank *you*," he said. "May God be with you."

But it wasn't only God who was with me because I really did hear a noise at the side of the house. And then I remembered Daniel. No doubt he'd seen me at his house. He knew it was me who'd taken his doll. A chill went up my spine. He wouldn't come looking for it, would he? I hid the statue in the button closet and went to the door. No one was there. "Want to go for a ride?" I asked Jake. He gangled to attention. He'd found his own spot here in Sea Cliff right away, Jake had, and he was very cozy, having made a cave for himself under Noola's old hassock with a view out the screen door so he could squeeze his eyes at squirrels. "Have a drink before we go," I told him. And what do you know, he went and slopped up the rest of the water in his water dish. You can have your pedigree dogs. Mutts are the ticket.

I took Jake and we got in my car and drove east along the coast road where the traffic was sparse, and then after a while there was no traffic at all. My head spun. As much as my suspicions kept insisting Morgan must have something to do with it, I longed for this not to be so. And of course I had no inkling of proof. It was all just some dreaded hunch. Motive he would have had. But murder? The sun was high and I stayed in sight of water as long as I could, treating myself to the lush glimpses of prosperity the North Shore offered, turning off onto a charming lane where the sun broke through thick canopies of green. There's something mollifying about wealth: the rolling hills and white corrals like you'd see in Kentucky, private drives up to ghastly miniature French châteaus and Normandy Tudors. I found myself suddenly before a farm with a vineyard and pies for sale. No way I could pass this up. And there was no man in the car to stop me! I pulled over, let Jake run around awhile then went in. There were actual peaches like from childhood, small, fuzzy things hot from sunshine. They looked like they really would taste like fresh Georgia peaches. There were homegrown tomatoes, big and tiny ones all basketed together and—I was helpless now—hand-embroidered dishtowels. In all these things, I lost myself. I forgot about Daniel and Sea Cliff and Morgan and Jenny Rose and even Enoch. I was a young girl again, in a barn with tubs of fresh-cut unshucked corn and blackberry jams, in red-and-white-checkered, pinking-sheared hats.

After spending lots of money and leaving myself with little till the end of the week, I felt no guilt whatsoever. I rather relished my booty; for what is a woman's life without these precious fanciful necessities? I climbed back into my Cruiser with Jake, driving into the sudden, uneasy realization that it was far too early for peaches, tomatoes, or even corn and that everything I'd just fallen for had been carted off some bruising, farting Bronx Terminal market truck. As the road gleaned eastward, my mind—that evidently had kept on ticking while I had shopped, which is the marvel of shopping—had loosened and freed itself and told me to head for one more place. I'd seek out Teddy. I had to talk to someone who'd level with me. He worked at some restaurant with the same bug name as the town, didn't he? What was the name? I'd lost my way by now so I pulled into a garden center in Oyster Bay and it came to me of its own accord. Locust Valley. "How would I get to Locust Valley?" I asked the pleasant, sun-wrinkled woman who seemed about my own age.

"You can't get there from here," she warned me. "You'll have to go back."

"How far back?"

"All the way until you can't go any more."

"Oh, I don't want to," I complained. "I want to keep going this way."

She gave me a curious look. "All right, easy, girl." She laughed. "I've seen this before. It's that combination of fresh paint and antiques. You've hit the gold coast and it's gotten to you." We both laughed. "You can let the dog out here if you like," she told me. "There's no one here." Gratefully, I let Jake stretch his legs up and down the rows of plants and seedlings. After she gave Jake a fresh bowl of water, she drew out a conglomeration of lefts and rights to follow while I succumbed to pots of well-started hollyhocks and foxglove and trailing geraniums. What? They're very hard to find. I lowered my backseat, loaded it up, and Jake and I climbed back in, on our way to being broke but immersed in the heady perfumes of fruits and flowers, curiously aware of being alive and well. And hungry. The road curled this way and that and it was well past lunchtime when I got to Locust Valley, a catch-your-breath-it's-so-pretty town. And the Inn! It was like a scene from a Bing Crosby movie, all charm and wonderland, hunched under a thicket of snowberry. I parked the car any old where in the shade, let Jake out for a quick walk, fed him a quarter of the apple pie, and told him to go to sleep. The restaurant door was wide open, airing out the place, and I walked into the cool dark. There was a bar on one side and the restaurant on the other. Midway between lunch and supper, the place was empty but for a crooked, ravaged old woman in exquisite pearls, who leaned, soused, from a stool at the bar. I saw Teddy right away. He was at work already, standing wiping glasses and chatting with the woman.

"Hi." I smiled and raised my arm to him.

His face fell. He put the glass down and came out from behind the bar. "What happened?"

"No, nothing, Teddy," I rushed to assure him, "I just wanted to talk to you. I was driving around out here and I remembered Paige said you worked here and I thought, let me stop in and say hello."

He visibly relaxed. "I thought something else had happened."

We gave each other a commiserating look, and suddenly I was ashamed of my shopping spree. What was wrong with me, splurging on niceties while Patsy Mooney lay murdered? I was glad I'd parked across the road so he wouldn't see my car piled high with frivolous bounty.

He led me over to a table and we sat down.

"It's some beautiful place," I remarked.

"Hangout of the wealthy," he quipped. "It's like a clubhouse for them. They're in and out like fashion. Have you eaten?"

I made a dummy face that said if I had I could surely go again.

He winked. "I'll be right back." He hopped away into the kitchen and I noticed he was limping. When he came back in, he carried a tray of delicate bits of wild Alaskan salmon strewn over fancy salad and three fresh slices of light, mouthwatering bread.

"That looks wonderful! Teddy," I said. "Why are you limping?"

"*Uch*. Football. Old injury. Every time I carry something heavy it acts up." He poured me a glass of red wine. "Those beer deliveries kill me."

"Mmm." I took a sip. "What is it?"

"Cakebread, 2013."

"Yikes. Delicious. Listen, my budget—"

He put his hand over my purse. "Don't even think about it, Claire. You're my guest."

"Oh, come on, Teddy," I protested, digging into the salad regardless. "I don't want you to have to pay for me."

"My pleasure." Teddy looked at me with that admiring yet respectful gaze we women of a certain age so treasure. "Anyway," he whispered, leaning close, "it's been opened. Last night's happy remains."

"Teddy." I put my hand over his. "I'm sorry my niece is so, well, I'm sorry she—"

"Doesn't care for me? Never mind."

I regarded him thoughtfully. He was young. He'd recover.

He refilled the dent in my glass. From the end of the bar the swank lady suddenly lurched erect and chirped, "*Singing bell-bottom trousers and coats of navy blue; He'll climb the rigging like his daddy used to do!*"

Teddy and I exchanged looks. "Duty calls," he said and hobbled down the bar to where she slumped, chin tucked in pigeonlike, contents of her Hermès purse sprawled across the bar in front of her. With the precision of a contestant in a game of pickup sticks, she managed to extricate a cigarette from the stuff. I heard Teddy try to convince her to let him call her a cab, but she wasn't having any of it. In an uncommon show of impatience, Teddy gathered up her things and literally threw them into her purse, then lit her cigarette with her gold Dunhill lighter. As bad luck would have it, the boss happened to walk in just then and he hauled Teddy off to the office to reprimand him. I hoped he wasn't going to fire him.

Feeling myself watched, I looked up and was surprised to see Glinty in the mirror. He gave me quite a start, sitting there on the other side of the room. Glinty! What on earth was he doing out here? Realizing I'd recognized him, he came toward me with a face that looked as though he'd been busted. He didn't actually shake my hand or greet me, no, he just loomed in my vicinity to convey, I suppose, some sort of acknowledgment without actual greeting. "Here alone?" he asked, eyeing me skeptically.

"Yes. Jenny Rose is waiting for Wendell to get out of school, I think."

He continued to hover.

At a loss, I rambled on to no one, the way you do when confronted with the socially inept. "I never knew anyone with as many jobs as Teddy," I marveled. "He works so hard. You know, when things like this happen, with poor Patsy Mooney, it makes you wonder about, well, important things . . ." I hesitated. "I don't know why Oliver doesn't help Teddy out. Like, you'd think he'd just *give* Teddy some money. Especially when he knows he wants to be a teacher."

Glinty sat down. "Oliver doesn't give him any because he doesn't have any. Anyway, Teddy will never be a teacher. He dropped his classes months ago. He didn't mention it? Doesn't surprise me; it suits his purposes to be thought of as a student."

"Really? Oh. I'm sorry to hear that." How embarrassed he must have been not to mention it. My heart went out to him. I murmured, "Teaching is a wonderful vocation."

"You know what Teddy says about that? 'Those who can, do. Those who can't, teach.'"

I pressed my lips together disapprovingly. "That doesn't sound like something Teddy would say."

"Ask him."

"I will." I smirked, looking around for Teddy. "And if he did say that, it was most likely to defend him against your scornful attitude. Not everyone makes it through college." My first impression of Glinty had been so right. He was a horrible person, selling out his friend like that. I said, "I think it's admirable just to have *tried* to get through school in this day and age."

He began, to my horror, to pick from my plate. "Don't look at me," he said with a shrug. "We all know I haven't spent a day in a classroom since I was fourteen." He wiped his narrow hands down his pants thighs to clean them and his face relaxed into his everyday snarl. He said in his hard-to-understand, thick accent, "But don't you think it must be a little tiresome always being admirable? Did you not notice how everyone out here on the North Shore cries about how miserable life is? But where are they all?" He laughed. "Out sailing over to Shelter Island. I like that." He looked away. "And by the way, Oliver really doesn't have any more money. If he had, Teddy'd get it one way or another."

I sat back. "Well, if his money's tied up, he could always sell any one of his paintings. They're worth a lot."

"Those paintings belonged to Noola, you know."

"Really?" I looked up, surprised.

"Yes." He spat a piece of spoiled fish into *my* napkin and tossed it under the table. "Oliver needs money himself."

Appalled, I made a scoffing noise. "*Tch*. He has all the money in the world, if he wants it. He just has to cash *some*thing in."

"No, he doesn't."

"Of course he does. He's a financial adviser. God, this salmon is delicious. I'm assuming he'll pay for Patsy's funeral, won't he?"

He barked a laugh. "I don't think you understand. He wouldn't be able to keep that house open till next winter if Morgan didn't keep laying out money."

It was my turn to laugh. "Morgan doesn't have any money."

"Morgan? Morgan's worth millions."

I shook my head. "You've got it all wrong. Morgan works in the boatyard, painting boats and things." Why was I telling *him* this?

"Morgan doesn't *have* to work on the boats. He owns the boats. He's got the *Gnomon*, the *For Sail*, the *Corinthian* . . ."

"What? Stop it. Don't pretend that Morgan's rich."

"Of course he is. Why do you think Paige is so desperate to marry him?"

"But . . . but it's the other way around."

"No." Glinty laughed, delighted. "You've got it all wrong. Morgan feels indebted. Responsible. They all grew up together. Paige and Oliver looked after his mom all the while he was in Scotland with me."

I stopped eating and stared at him, stymied.

"And then later when we were in Bosnia."

"But . . . But . . . Look at all Oliver's fancy vintage cars."

"Vintage? Those old pieces of junk? Those cars are from when times were good. They're held together with spit and rubber bands. Wouldn't make it into Glen Head without Mr. Piet's mechanical ability. He's always got one of them up on the hydraulic lift. Calls it his 'Emergency Room.'"

"But then why does Mr. Piet stay there at all?"

Glinty shrugged. "Radiance is nearby. He likes to keep an eye on her. As you're discovering, it's not the worst place in the world to live. He practically keeps the lot of us fed with all the fish he catches. Fixes half the village's cars and lorries with that hydraulic lift that was put in years ago and him the only one knows how to use it. He's probably in the best financial shape of all of us, Mr. Piet is. No room or board. No vices." He gave me an arch look. "Of course he was busted for carrying reefer in from Guadeloupe, years ago. But he did his time. Now, he just keeps socking away any money he makes. I'm sure he has a tidy pile himself."

"And you mean Paige is not . . . She has no money either?"

"Poor as a church mouse. Why do you think she works as a real estate agent? For fun? Prestige? It's damned hard work. Once in a while she has a windfall—that keeps them going for a while—but never near enough to run a house like Twillyweed. Can you imagine the taxes? And then of course she pulls a small salary from her fund-raising, that's all."

If this was true . . . "But, but . . . they serve all those fabulous wines," I protested.

Glinty gave a harsh laugh. "Remains of the good old days. The only reason there's any of that left is Oliver prefers malt whisky. You must have noticed he drinks like a fish."

"But how could this happen?"

"Come on. You really didn't know?"

"Wow. No, I did not. But the paintings . . ."

"All belong to Morgan," he finished for me. "Now that Noola's gone, they belong to him. Noola never wanted to move from the Great White. She loved it there in that wee cottage, which I was hoping to live in when I heard she'd died." He narrowed his eyes at me. "But never mind about that. She had Oliver keep the paintings at Twillyweed because she knew they'd be safe and appreciated there. They're all insured."

"But where did she get them?"

"She bought them. Collected them, over the years."

"Hang on a minute while I digest this."

He went on, "Two generations ago the Cupsands were one of the most prosperous families in the Northeast. You want to know the straw that really broke the camel's back?"

"Of course."

"Oliver's gambling. It's in his blood. Whenever things start to go right, the minute he gets his hands on a little money, he drives down to Atlantic City or the track and pisses it away. And he loves the ponies."

"Oh, I know that game," I broke in. "My ex-husband is the same way!" I heard my voice rise and sat back self-consciously. The wine had gone to my head. Suddenly I was glad Johnny and Portia were getting married. She could have him.

"Annabel couldn't take his gambling, see?"

"But how could she have left Wendell?"

"She didn't leave Wendell. She left Oliver." For a moment he looked at me blankly. Then he said, "I keep thinking she'll come back for Wendell."

I shook myself. "I can't get over it. So Morgan is rich. I can't believe it. I had him set in my mind as a . . . as a—"

"Hard luck case? That's pretty funny."

"But he *acts* so subservient."

"Morgan? Nah, he feels bad for them. He's very kind, Morgan is. He's only one of the most eligible bachelors on the North Shore. No relatives now but the father back home in Invergowrie. Another nut, he is. Lives like a Spartan on marmalade and sheep's cheese and molasses bread. Spends his time puttering on clocks and making lures for fishhooks and boiling up his own marmalade. Won't take a penny from Morgan."

I sat there with my mouth open. "Whereas, Oliver . . ."

"Oliver's all right. Nobody like him. Top-notch sailor."

My mind was racing. If Morgan was rich, he wouldn't have to hit an old priest on the head to get what he wanted, he'd simply buy it. I stared, stupefied, at this slinky, cocky fellow my niece was so taken with and I got the feeling he was enjoying this, categorizing everyone for me, the newcomer.

He went on, "All right, he's a little disappointing . . . acting like he's a financial adviser when he can't keep hold of any loot himself, but he's not a bad person. He's just broke. Living on past glory. I suppose he could always teach sailing at the club if things get any worse." He gave me a sort of leer. "You know, in the old days he was what you'd call a catch."

The *old days*. Ten years ago? I had to laugh. Someone like Glinty was just getting started. He had the whole world in front of him. For him, ten years was almost half a lifetime.

I remembered something. "What about Oliver's apartment in the city? That must be worth plenty."

"*Phh*. That's not his. That's his fraternity brother's bachelor pad. Loans it to him. You know these good old boys."

"God! This is too much." I looked at him sitting there, whittling one finger with another. "Glinty, why did you tell me all this?"

He looked around with a hunched-over, furtive look and shrugged. "I don't like the air in the village right now. Dicey—with this murder and all. Better you should know."

A party of five came into the restaurant, and an attractive young woman in heels minced out with menus to seat them. Glinty sneaked a look over his shoulder and stood. "Do me a favor, will you? Don't mention to Teddy I was here."

I shot him a puzzled look. "But . . . didn't you come here to see him?"

"Uh-uh. I was following you." He stepped away before I could reply and disappeared down the hallway. I went back to my food. By the time Teddy came lumbering back in, the place was filling up. He looked refreshed, as though he'd just washed his hands and face. He winked at me and got right over to some beefeaters in Brooks Brothers uniforms at the bar. I'd finished eating. Reluctantly, I stood. It was time to go. I thanked Teddy for the meal and walked outside into the humid air.

The sky was dark purple. I got in my car. Frowning, I leaned over and gave Jake a halfhearted stroke. In the distance there was thunder. I switched the radio on. Miles Davis, "Take Five." I looked in the mirror. Morgan was rich! This was good, right? If that was the case, what reason would he have to kill anyone? He wouldn't have had to, would he? This was assuming someone other than her husband had killed

Patsy Mooney. Something someone had said kept that idea in my head. What was it? Mrs. Lassiter. I remembered her saying she thought he'd have found someone else to torture by now. Meaning, I supposed, it had been quite a while since Patsy Mooney and he had been together. But no, that couldn't be right. He was seen in town, in Sea Cliff, just yesterday. No. It *was* him. The ex-husband is always the one. The cops weren't stupid. There was no need to worry. They'd catch him.

I took out my cell phone and called Detective Harms at the station house. He answered in a pleasant, no-nonsense way. I got right to the point, "I've found something I believe is pertinent to the Patsy Mooney case and was wondering if we could get together for a talk?"

"Sure. Who is this?"

"Oh. Hi. This is Claire Breslinsky. I'm staying at Morgan Donovan's house, the Great White? My niece—"

"Look, Miss Breslinsky, I'm on the other line. Why don't you come in tomorrow morning and I'll have someone take down your statement. How's that?"

"Good. Good. Ten o'clock?"

"See you then."

It began to rain in a fretful, weary way. *Plunk, plunk.* And then I thought, *If Morgan is so rich, what would he want with me?* I put my wipers on, turned off the lane, and headed down the regular parkway to Sea Cliff in traffic.

JENNY ROSE

That night, when the widening moon crept up into the sky, Jenny Rose sang Wendell to sleep as she straightened his room. She hadn't kept Patsy's death from him, but told him there'd been an accident. She told him quickly, as soon as she'd got him alone and realized Oliver hadn't told him a thing. She couldn't bear that sort of thing, dealing with a problem by not addressing it. It was despicable. It had been done to her as a child and she wasn't having it. No, sir. Patsy had died, she explained without fuss. That was why all the people were in the house. She'd had a terrible accident, she said. He'd taken it at face value, wide eyed and serious, and hadn't questioned her, she supposed, because no one ever bothered to explain anything to him. But then, later, when he lay there cuddling his favorite sailboat, he regarded her trustingly and said, "So, Jenny Rose, I won't have to eat my potatoes?"

She stopped tidying and walked over to him, sinking onto the floor beside the bed.

"Because Patsy says I never can leave the table until I finish up my potatoes. And now I don't have to?"

"That's right, sport." She smiled gently. "No potatoes unless you want them."

"And you're not going away from Twillyweed tonight?"

She gave him a fierce hug. "I'll never leave you unless it's all right with you!"

This seemed to mollify him. She sighed with relief. They'd gotten over the hump. The most important thing was she'd gained the little fellow's trust. She felt a kind of pride. Yes, for the first time in a while, hell, her whole life, she felt as though she were making a difference. "What song will it be, now, tonight? 'The Summer Wind'?"

"No." He made a satisfied wiggle into position under the covers. "'You Are My Sunshine.'"

She sketched him while she sang the same absorbing verses over and over until he dropped off—she'd captured most of him in shadow, just a telling edge of him in light, and, pleased with what she'd done, she rolled the drawing up into a scroll. There was something about pain and sorrow that helped art, leaked the important stuff into your work, made it poignant. It was too bad, but there it was, true. When she was sure Wendell was deep asleep, she crept, shivering, past the yellow-taped basement door and up to her room in the turret. She opened the drawing and put it on the nightstand already splattered with paint, weighting the edges down with Patsy Mooney's left-behind seashells. Nothing would be the same without Patsy Mooney, she mulled. For the moment, Mr. Piet looked after them, and Jenny Rose had to admit he managed things very well. There would have to be a wake and a funeral when they released the body. She sucked in her breath. The poor old soul. She hadn't deserved to die that way. Glumly, she walked the series of windows around the turret and lowered all the slatted rattan shades she'd earlier raised up for her precious light, knotting them shut by their cords, one by one. Patsy Mooney had kept them down all the time. "Begonias don't like too much light," she'd explained. Or had she known even then that he was after her? She remembered Patsy's darty little eyes as she'd assured her about the basement apartment, *No one will get you here.* Had she known then he was that close to finding her? Suddenly Jenny Rose stopped, hearing something. Was someone there? "Hello?" She cocked her head. But who would be coming up at this hour? Wendell? She checked that the monitor was on. So sensitive it was she could hear the soft drone of his snores. No, it wasn't anything, she was just nervous. Anyone would be. She opened her closet door and inspected her few clothes. There was one robe she'd had since she had been in the south of Turkey. She'd never worn it, saving it for a special occasion. It was an antique, gold-threaded wedding garment, a sort of coat. She'd bargained for it in the bazaar, drinking mint tea with shopkeepers who themselves wore long medieval robes as they'd sat around a smoking lantern. She stroked the course gold-woven thread and the slippery corroded lining, stained a bit with rust. She held it to her chest and twirled around the attic floor to no music—then stopped. She *had* heard something. Someone. A chill ran up her spine. But wait—maybe it *was* Wendell, upset from Patsy's death! She unlatched her door, flung it open, and stood at the top, peering down the whitewashed winding staircase. There was the smell of motor oil—and something green. From behind, a hand slipped into the waist of her shirt and another covered her mouth to stifle the beginnings of her scream.

It was Glinty. Couldn't he ever make a noise like a normal person?

Her head fell back onto his shoulder and he rasped, "Jenny Rose. Don't you remember? 'Twas good, was it not?'"

Not knowing if she was all right or not, she nodded her head yes. He let go his grip and maneuvered her into the room. He latched the lock.

"How did you get in?"

"*Ach*, that was easy. Any thief could get into this mad system of wobbly windows."

She rubbed her neck where it always got kinked. "So it's a thief you are now?"

"No. I didn't say that." He leaned his gangly body into hers and she could smell the pot on his breath. His eyes, rich with umbrage, burned into hers. "I'll not have you call me a thief."

Reassured by his taking insult, she lowered her voice seductively, "What would you have me call you then?"

He laughed. Then he grew serious. He pulled her forgotten pair of underwear from his pocket and said, "The thing is . . . I can't stop thinking of you."

She snatched the undergarment and shied away backward. "Look, I know you must think I'm this easy slut but, well, actually I was an easy slut, wasn't I? But—"

"Shut up." He tilted his head and caught her mouth with his and sealed it off with the tip of his tongue. Locked together, they tangoed backward to her bed and fell onto it.

The light winked in the east above Glen Cove when Glinty finally moved to untangle himself. They were both still half awake. He licked the kink in her neck where it always bothered her and Jenny Rose groaned with pleasure. Magically, the kink had disappeared. She turned onto her back. "I'll be missing you when you sail off," she told him, half sweetly, half reproachfully.

He looked away. "I'll not be going anywhere."

"Will you not? Scotland won't call to you when this murder business is over? Or when you've made your fortune?"

"I hate Scotland," Glinty confided. "It's the midges, mostly. They'll eat you alive." He wiped his brow with the inside of his arm. "Don't look at me like that. I'm serious. I'll not go back. I've no one there. No. It's America I love." His eyes twinkled. "Land of the free."

She shot him a look. Was he being sarcastic?

He turned serious. "You feel the way I do, don't you? About us? Because I've got to know . . ."

"I do," she admitted, surrendering, touching her heart with the tips of her fingers.

He ground his body into hers in sheer delight. "Now. Give me something," he whispered.

"What?" she blinked.

"A token. Something with the smell of you."

She smiled, a little love drunk, and burrowed into the pillow. "Take whatever pleases you."

He stood up and climbed into his jeans. Holding her eye, he lifted the Turkish wedding robe.

"Not that," she said with a pout.

"You said anything." He raised a brow.

"Anything else."

He opened her top drawer and came out with a silky black-and-yellow bra. "This?"

"It doesn't smell of me, dodo. It's clean."

He moved toward her and clenched her arm behind her back, then looped the strap through his finger and traced it all across and around her limp body, behind her back and up between her legs then under his nose. "Now it does," he said with a growl. He let her go and she collapsed into a heap. "I'll call you later," he promised.

She watched as his slim, fluid body moved in the half-light. He was cruelly pale, his hairs black and in a fine marking down his narrow front and back. She wondered idly how she would get him to pose for her without insulting him. He finished dressing then stopped at the door and he opened the latch. "Oh," he said, like it just came to him, "and when they ask you where you were at the time of the murder, just tell them you were with me." He smiled at her tenderly. "Tell them I come to you in the night. That way they won't have you as a suspect."

And as she heard the door latch click and he slipped with no sound down the winding stairs, her hand returned unconsciously to the kink in her neck. He might be her alibi—but so would she be his.

CLAIRE

The unfamiliar ticking of the seven wall clocks I'd wound back to business woke me absurdly early the next day. I remembered Patsy Mooney and said a quick prayer for her immortal soul, then one that they'd catch her husband quickly. Whether he did it or not, it was best to know the truth. I brushed my teeth, washed my face, and slipped into a cool white blouse and jeans. Jake sat ready at the door, impatiently moving from cheek to cheek.

"All right, I'm coming." I laughed, looking around the tidy room. All was fresh and clean, and the flimsy white curtains rippled out horizontally. I don't think I'd ever liked a place so much. I grabbed a pale-pink cardigan I'd picked up at a garage sale and was crazy about. It was amazing to be able to go for walks on a beach I hadn't had to drive to. We took our time and luxuriated in the fresh breeze, then strolled over to the docks where there seemed to be a lot going on. Sailors are early risers and the dock was busy with folks scrubbing their decks and mending sails. My heart leaped a bit at the sight of Morgan Donovan sailing up to the dock.

"Ahoy," he greeted me. Then, pushing his cap back, "Where'd you find *him*?"

"It's a long story."

"Come aboard!"

I crouched on the deck to be at his level while petting Jake, "I can't.

Have to go to the station house this morning." I shrugged. "Time for my interrogation."

"I'll take you."

But I was shy now. He was rich. It was different. "I thought I'd walk."

"I'll take you by boat."

That stopped me. "To the station house?"

"Sure."

"But it's too early."

"We'll go the long way. Bring the dog. Here. Take my hand."

Without thinking, I took it. It was as though we latched on to each other. I lowered myself on board, not caring who saw, and he helped me into a life jacket. I held my breath at the nearness. Getting Jake on was another story. He wouldn't come until he pretty much figured we'd leave him if he didn't hop aboard. Morgan and I laughed when he finally flounced, all fours, onto the glistening deck and slid to a safe spot near the mainsail where he huddled for the duration. Morgan went about untying knots, casting ropes, guiding us away from the dock. When we took off, I was surprised at how fast we moved. I leaned myself into the wind the way he did and we scooted away, the force of the wind taking hold and the mainsail filling. In one movement, he secured and coiled the halyard and we skimmed the bright water past a fleet of other boats. Terrified and thrilled, I held on for dear life. Morgan, a cigar butt in the corner of his mouth, eased against the rudder and lay back, at ease. I thought I'd never seen him so like himself, so . . . what was it? Happy. Before you knew it we were out far. It was beautiful. He lowered the sails and let the boat drift. I turned and faced him. He leaned across me and took hold of the tiller and tied it. There's nothing like the clean, sweet smell of a man. I felt like nuzzling my cheek against the reddish fur of his arm. But I wouldn't. Of course I wouldn't. "This is heaven," I said. "What's that over there?"

"Connecticut. One day when you have more time I'll sail you over."

"I'd love that."

"Tell you what . . . I've got some leftover chicken below." He jumped up. "You hungry?"

"I'm always hungry."

"And some wine? You like wine, I think."

"Too early for me." I laughed. "Haven't even had breakfast! I'll make tea." I went below, filled the kettle, and set about lighting the kerosene stove. He went back to the tiller. Jake lay basking in the sun and I thought, *Hmm, this is good; anywhere we go we can take him.* Waiting for the kettle to boil, I couldn't help noticing the wines Morgan had in his little stowaway rack. I pulled one out. A Silvio Nardi, Brunello di Montalcino, Italia 2005. Impressive. I reached for the teapot and mugs shackled up on the shelf. Wobbling and careful not to knock anything over, I took them topside on a tray and centered it on the cabin trunk. I raised the pot to put the tea bags in and it rattled. I lifted the lid to wipe it out and at that moment I saw the frozen look on Morgan's face. My first thought was, he's hidden something in there. A surprise? I looked down. It was a key. A red key.

It took some seconds for my mind to struggle through this revelation, but only one to know it.

I kept looking down at the key, then out at the sea. He'd let his guard down. For me. But of course he remembered the teapot, seeing me with it. The moment I saw it, I knew. I looked to him. He saw it, too. He realized his mistake but didn't miss a beat. Disappointment must have collapsed my face. I remember I must have said something, something about the tea, maybe. We stood there together for some seconds in the sunshine, hovering between pretense and knowing. Then I tipped it over and the key fell into my hand. It was cold and hard. I clenched it and I felt him wince, his plans caved in.

It was damned and we both knew this. We would always know it. Once you knew, you couldn't go back and not know. He checked both ways peripherally, as though to be sure no one sailed near. What if there was no stopping him, no conscience and no honor, just the cunning draw toward what worked best for him? My mind raced. He must have strangled Patsy Mooney to get that key. And a chill lit up like wings, growing from my back to my shoulders. He started toward me and I went rigid with fear. Jake, sensing my terror, leveled off an objection from the depths of his throat. Morgan hesitated and in that moment I watched him reject this idea, change his mind, go on to the next plan. As smoothly as a man in a dance, he moved backward and, still holding my eyes—regret more than anger in his eyes—he left me there and went below. I tucked the key in my pocket. It was only a short while, but it felt eternal. And I knew he was coming back because what I knew threatened his existence. White fear gripped me and blanked my vision. And then, doing what he wouldn't think I would think to do, I flung myself without a backward glance under the short rope and overboard into the fast-moving depths. Right behind me, Jake splattered in.

The boat sped away. The strong current pulled us. Both shores were far away, irretrievably far. I gasped for breath and struggled out of my shoes. My clothes pulled me down and my eyes stung with brine. To my horror I saw the *Gnomon* tilt, then veer and turn. *Oh, no.* Fear clutched me and I reached for Jake, who paddled toward me, but the current was too strong in the other direction. I watched him get carried away, paddling madly, his eyes strained and wild and frantic like a horse in a blood race, and I knew despair. I heard someone call out from somewhere and I saw Morgan at the helm, decisive, leveling off, aiming the boat toward me. He was talking into a walkie-talkie. Desperately I tried to think of a way to get clear, but I knew there was none. I dove under in desperation, my eyes open.

He swept past me and I came up gasping for air. The *Gnomon* turned at breakneck speed to come again, the wind in her sails, but a yawl off course appeared like a ghost and loomed up with tremendous suddenness and I swam toward it. There were two men on board. They were three sheets to the wind, but they were men. Then the *Gnomon* pulled alongside me and Morgan was leaning over the side and reaching out his arm and shouting at me. I mean really shouting. "What the bloody hell are you doing!" he yelled, heaving a line toward me, veins of fury standing out on his forehead. "Are you daft? You stupid woman! What's wrong with you?"

It was his tone. He wasn't acting like a red-handed murderer at all. He was acting like my father when we kids thought we were smart and almost killed ourselves climbing up on the roof and jumping into the raked-up leaves. Had I been wrong? I was wrong, wasn't I, I realized, sputtering. Those men had seen me. He wouldn't kill me with onlookers, anyway. Arms reached out from the other boat, but I let him hoist me up onto the *Gnomon*. I was so relieved to be out of the cold water. They fished Jake out with a shark hawler and held on to him until they pulled alongside. Then he leaped across. You couldn't have stopped him. He crouched beside me, brackish, panting, I could hear his addled breath. My arm went around him and I clung to him.

"You're out of your mind!" Morgan continued ranting while he went to fetch two warm blankets and put them around us.

The two men on the other boat waved us away with doubtful expressions.

"That's the last time I take a lass out on the boat. That's it!"

I was beginning to feel a little stupid. But had he not tried to hit me with the *Gnomon*? Now *I* was mad. I shouted, "I thought you were trying to hit me with the boat!"

He yelled back, "I fucking hell was not! I was trying to come get you, you daft female! Jesus Christ! What happened? Why the bloody hell did you jump overboard? Did you dive in after the dog?" He lowered his voice. "Why would you think I'd hit you with the boat?"

I reached into my pocket and came up with the key. We looked at each other. Then he said, "Are you hurt?"

"No! It's the *key*. The key that was around Patsy Mooney's neck!"

"Well, what's it doing here?"

"That's what I want to know! It was in your teapot, as if you didn't know!"

He drew back. "I didn't."

"The hell you didn't! Why did you give me that look?"

"What look?"

"When I opened the teapot."

"I thought you found a bloody mouse. It wouldn't be the first time. They hole up in there."

I didn't buy it. "Come on!"

"*You* come on! I ask you out on my boat and the next thing I know it's man overboard. What do you think; it's a joke? You could have been killed! Or worse! There are worse things than being killed!" He slumped forward. "Jesus. You'll be giving me a heart attack!"

He did look pale. I moved forward. "You mean you didn't know anything about the key?"

He shook his head. "No. What do you think? If I did, you imagine I'd have sent you to it?"

That made sense. I began to shiver uncontrollably. "Come on." He dropped anchor and hauled me downstairs.

"I just thought you'd forgot about it," I explained as he rubbed my head with a rough towel.

He gaped at me. "*Ach*, I see. I murder Patsy Mooney for a key and then I leave it in a wee teapot for you to find and then I kill you, too." He raised his eyes. "Brilliant."

I hung my head. "Yes. I see what you mean. Come here, Jake." I made him come and sit beside me by the heater. "But . . . but . . ." I was shivering so hard I could hardly speak. I pulled myself together. "If it wasn't you . . . who would have put it there?"

Morgan shrugged. "Anyone could have come on board. She's never locked down. And with the race, the docks are crawling with strangers."

"Someone was trying to frame you and I come along and fall for it." I bit my lip, befuddled. "I'm sorry. I really am. I was paranoid and I panicked. You've been nothing but good to me and I seem to be nothing but trouble."

He made a sound of disgust and turned from me, saying, "What will you do with the key?"

"Give it to the police."

He sailed us back to port in a brooding silence.

CHAPTER SIX

CLAIRE

I made my way to the station house. Detective Harms, I was told by a female officer, was not in yet and would get in touch with me. She seemed disgruntled that I'd brought Jake in with me. I left the key with her and a detailed note. Disappointed—I never did get over my childhood love of station houses—Jake and I went home. I peeled off my damp clothes and put on a cozy nightgown, crawled into bed, and took a nap.

It was the phone that woke me. I was surprised when it was Paige. She sounded absolutely chipper. "Listen," she said, "I spoke to my friend over at St. Francis and she said she could slip us in this morning."

"Slip us in where?" I blinked.

"For your AIDS test, Claire."

"Oh. Uh. Sure. But I'm waiting for the detective to call me back."

"Why? You weren't there when it happened." She paused. "Were you?"

"Very funny. Hey! Jake! Get off me!"

There was loud silence at the other end of the receiver.

"Oh," I explained hurriedly, "it's my dog, Jake. He's my dog."

"You have a dog there?" she cried, and I realized the reason I was so worried she'd mistakenly think I had a man in my bed was because I wouldn't want her telling Morgan. Which is sick. I am odious. I rubbed my eyes. "What time is the appointment?"

"In an hour and a half. I'll pick you up in an hour."

"Paige, is Jenny Rose there with you? I've got to speak to her."

"Look, my friend is doing us a favor fitting us in. You can talk to Jenny Rose any time, all right?" Without waiting for an answer she hung up.

I looked at the clock. I'd have just enough time to feed and walk Jake, take a shower, and have breakfast. I staggered from the bed and padded to the window. A flock of geese were crossing the blue sky, coming home for the summer. A definite good sign. Little sailboats skimmed the water. And there—I leaned out the window—was Daniel! I leaned so far out to wave to him that I tumbled out the window headfirst and into the garbage pail. My legs stuck up in the air and churned like an eggbeater. More embarrassed than injured, I thrust myself over, wiggled to my feet, and lifted the heavy rubber can off me and ran back in the house. I struggled into my mukluks, opened the door, the dog ran out, the kitten ran in, and I took off down the path in my baggy flannel nightgown. He was almost to the end of the strand and I was out of breath when I got to him but, huffing and puffing, I cried, "Hi!"

He turned and looked at me and I thought, *How could I ever have been frightened of this pathetic little man?* He was scrawny as Robinson Crusoe. His pale, diluted blue eyes lit up when he saw me and he gasped, "Did you see the geese?"

"Yes," I said. "I saw them. Means good weather, right?"

He pushed his bottom lip up over his upper and stood there staring at me.

I said, "Daniel, I want to introduce myself. I'm Claire. I'm staying in Noola's cottage."

"Oh, she's dead," he said informatively. "She drank bad tea!"

"Er, yes," I agreed. Bad tea? Is that what they'd told him? We looked together up at the cottage. I went on, politely and sincerely as I could,

"I wanted to say—uh, I'm sorry I screamed last time I saw you. You see I imagined you were someone else and I was just shocked, I guess, to see—" But he wasn't listening. He was, at the moment, petting my hair, which had come undone from its scrunchy back at the garbage pail. And then I remembered just what it was that had made me scream last time. It hadn't simply been that he was the wrong sex. There was definitely something weird going on, some eager, demented cast in his expression that followed me inside and looked for something, something private. Delight suffused his toothless smile and I could feel a lump forming in my beating chest. Trying to be casual, I glanced peripherally to see if anyone else was on the beach. Nope. Just he and I.

"Paige's coming to pick me up." I shrugged nonchalantly. "I'd better get going."

Daniel, however, didn't intend to let go of my hair. He had my arm, too, holding me fast while he patted, *tap tap tap*, on my hair. I gave a little pull to see how that would go. No dice. He held me tight. He had an odd smell, too, like coriander or something. Part of me felt sorry for the pathetic little man he was, so obviously in need of human touch, but the other, more urgent feeling, now, was definitely distress.

"La la la," I sang, making no sense, intending to convey *Hey! This is all okay!* I held his eyes and smilingly sang, *"La la la, la la la la la la. It might have been in County Down, or in New York, or gay Paree, or even London Town . . ."*

He began to turn me, like in a dance or a children's game, round and round we went—

"No more will I go all around the world, for I have found my world . . ." Me in my nightgown and he in his crazy world, stubbing and denting a circle of sand in the sun. *"In yooooou."*

The ferry horn blew from Steamboat Landing and Daniel stood still like it was a signal, then went running off. *Maybe,* I thought, *I'll just move back to Queens.*

JENNY ROSE

Meanwhile, Jenny Rose was throwing back the curtains to let the sun stream in, "Come on, sport, get yourself dressed. No school today. We're off to the boats."

Wendell's eyes flew open and he clattered from the bed, conscientiously smoothing his blanket across the top and tripping over himself getting dressed before she changed her mind.

He frowned. "We have to have cereal first."

He'd forgotten. Jenny Rose said cheerily, "Nah. Know what we'll do? We'll buy ourselves a snack at the deli and take the wee sailboat over there. You'd like that, wouldn't you?"

He was so excited he raced around with his shoelaces trailing, assembling his blue backpack with compass, ball cap, and whistle.

"What's this?"

"I'm not allowed to go on a boat unless I bring this stuff."

"Oh. Okay. That's smart." She wondered who'd thought of that, the mother?

Together they crept down the stairs and past the yellow tape that crisscrossed and held the basement door. He stopped in his tracks, startled, and looked back at Jenny Rose. There. He remembered now. Patsy Mooney was no more. Jenny Rose nudged him forward, grabbed two apples from a dish on the table, and put down a note for Paige. She chose two of the smaller fishing poles from the mudroom, and they scooted out the door before anyone could object. It was already warm and they removed their sweaters and tied them around their waists. Halfway to the dock, they crossed paths with Mrs. Dellaverna, arms laden with greens, on her busy way.

"Top of the day to you," Jenny Rose greeted her pleasantly.

"Watch out!" Wendell shouted to Jenny Rose. "She's got poison ivory!"

"It's fresh dandelion!" Mrs. Dellaverna protested, lowering the bushel and letting him look. "Where are you two off to so early, eh?"

"We're taking out the wee sailboat," Wendell told her excitedly in Jenny Rose's Irish way.

"Oh, yeah? Bring me back a nice fish. What do you say?"

"Okay!" Wendell's eyes shone and he gave her a high five before they continued on.

"Don't sail too close to that old factory; she's condemned!" Mrs. Dellaverna hollered after them. "And there's a riptide runs aside the gat. Don't go out past Teddy's boat. That's a bad tide, now, okay?"

"We won't, we won't," Jenny Rose assured her and they ambled on.

"We'll never go by Teddy's stupid boat," Wendell agreed scornfully.

Hmm, Jenny Rose wondered, *how come?*

It took them quite a while to get the boat out past the fine sloops. There wasn't a trace of wind and Jenny Rose had to row. When they were at last sitting pretty and their rods leaned easily against the rail, Jenny Rose ventured, "Do you not like Teddy, Wendell?"

Wendell didn't answer.

Jenny Rose, trying not to act too interested, slathered the boy with Coppertone. She massaged and wobbled the white liquid up and down the frail little arms.

"That's my very favorite smell," Wendell confided.

"Mine, too! How about that? So . . . I wonder why Mrs. Dellaverna doesn't like Teddy?"

"Because," Wendell offered, "Teddy hurted Noola's cat, Weedy."

"Noola? Oh. The lady who passed away. Morgan's mother, that would be?"

"Yes."

"Hurt her cat? Why would he do that?"

"He did."

"I'm sure he didn't mean to."

"Yes." He nodded his head. "Teddy tricked Weedy and put him in a box and he almost ran him over but he got away. Mama says you can't catch a cat doesn't want to be caught." In his vehemence, Wendell jumped up and tipped over the bait box, sending the worms, avid for freedom, into escape. He tracked the worms down and plopped each one carefully into the box Jenny Rose held.

"Wendell, adults have to restrain cats to take them to the vet, say, for a shot. Or to the groomer. It doesn't do them any harm." She shivered as one worm jimmied up her hand. She lifted it into its doom box, cut it in half, and threaded the smaller half onto Wendell's hook. She felt a sudden pity.

Wendell held his shiny knees. In a rush he revealed, "Mama promised we could go and find Weedy and then she never came back!" He looked around this way and that, his bad eye twisting furiously. "She never came back!"

"All right. That's enough for now. I don't want you to think about another thing. You just sing a little song so the fish will come. All right, lovey? What about that nice one I taught you?

Just then the fishing pole signaled a hit and Jenny Rose was glad for it, glad not to think anymore of a woman who'd come up with promises and then never kept them. She wiped the slime off her knife and rinsed it in the cold, clear water. But now there was something else nagging at her. For which was worse, a woman who would go off and leave this dear little boy, or one who'd never come back because she never could?

After a while, they both caught some fluke and Jenny Rose demonstrated to Wendell how to clean them, how to handle the knife carefully and wipe it and wash it when he was done. They weren't far from shore and they both were tired now. They headed back to Twillyweed, up the sandy slope and at last onto the drive. There was the sound of somebody's radio. A ball game going on. Mr. Piet and Teddy sat at the kitchen table, listening to the Yankees and playing rummy. They loved the Yankees in defiance of Oliver, who passionately revered the Boston Red Sox because his alma mater was Boston College. Mr. Piet was delighted with the cleaned fish and promised to make the fluke with rice, which Wendell loved more than anything, for supper.

"How's that, Wendell?" Teddy ruffled the little boy's hair. "I'll pick up some ice cream if you like. What's your favorite kind?"

Wendell made a face. "Don't want ice cream," he said and ran inside and up the stairs.

"Sorry," Jenny Rose said. "He's exhausted. It's a lot for a little tyke. With Patsy and all."

"No offense taken," he said. "Kids are kids."

Yes, she thought. She must be careful. She mustn't judge him until she knew what the dickens Wendell was talking about. She took the stairs and found him down on the floor in his room, tooling a Hess truck across the rug. She struggled out of her sneakers and chucked them across the room. "Why ever were you so rude to Teddy?" she whispered, crouching down beside him. "Whatever you think he might have done, Wendell, he's still an adult. You must be polite. You might have been mistaken, you know. Sometimes things look one way and they're really another." She plopped onto the bed.

He pushed out a stubborn lip. "Don't like Teddy."

"Why? Because of what happened with that cat? Wendell, I'm sure something like what you thought did happen. But sometimes children see things differently. It might not have happened exactly as you thought. I can't imagine Teddy purposely hurting any animal. He might have meant to take it somewhere. He probably put it in a box to take it somewhere—to get it neutered, perhaps. I'm quite sure he wouldn't try to kill it."

Wendell looked out the window with a sullen face. She'd never let him explain. He closed his eyes and rocked himself back and forth.

CLAIRE

Driving in the car next to Paige was surreal. Just the day before we'd been in her kitchen with a dead body down the stairs. And something else had changed. Knowing she wasn't wealthy leveled the playing field somehow. I know that's a terrible way to put it but it's what I felt. She was still the cool blonde, but it brought her, bad as it sounds, closer to me. Like we were in this together. I got it, understood her motivation. Her quest for Morgan was not based on sacred love, but security. For herself and her brother. And, of course, Teddy. No wonder they wouldn't help him with his tuition; they couldn't. Now that we were on equal ground, we could be—if all went well—chums. No, that was crazy. I was, after all, after her boyfriend. Oops. There. I said it. No going back now. We stopped at the gas station, and I, with my guilty conscience, insisted on paying with my credit card. Unfortunately she let me. As we pulled out, I mentioned meeting Daniel on the beach. "I think I might have upset him the other day. I'm afraid I screamed when I saw him."

"Well, he's not your everyday North Shore citizen," she said. "After all, he's my brother and I love him but—"

"Whoa, whoa, whoa! Hold on. Daniel is your *brother*?"

"Don't look so astonished. He's the first child, Daniel. He . . . stopped growing at one point. I know he looks like a Willy Nelson reject. He's not as old as he looks. It's just some of his teeth had to be pulled. It's because of"—she hesitated—"an accident years ago. He refuses to go back to have the work finished. It's ridiculous. Annabel was taking him there for a while. . . . She was very good with him, I have to say. I can't take him by myself. Oliver's going to have to help me get him there but he's always . . . busy." She grimaced and let her shoulders slouch. "Busy as in gambling. Oh, I know I'm selling him out, destroying his anonymity, as they insist you dare not do, but it doesn't matter at this point. It's not as though he's going to meetings anymore. And you'll find out soon enough. You ought to know. You have a right to know if you're going to date him." She scratched the back of her neck and looked at me appraisingly. "Of course if you were going out with him, he might stop. He gave it up for Annabel, after all. He was really being good when they first got together."

I gaped at her. "Look, Paige, your brother Oliver isn't ready to start dating anyone. Didn't you ever listen to Doctor Joy on the radio? He needs a good year on his own before he can even think about—"

"That's easy for some stranger to say," she interrupted, pooh-poohing this notion, "but loneliness is cruel. Don't you like him at all?"

"Of course I do," I said.

Angry, she inspected her face in the rearview mirror. "Sometimes it's good to have someone near just to keep the hobgoblins away, even if it's the wrong person."

She spoke as though she herself might be consoled this way. But I remembered the short-term satisfaction of Enoch in my bed. Then, because she seemed to be in the mood to call a spade a spade, I couldn't resist asking, "The story of the baby? That was Daniel's baby, right?"

"Oh, you know about that, do you? Well, it's all true."

"But, I never found out what happened to the baby, who adopted it."

She stubbed her cigarette out. "What do you mean? When Daniel's junkie wife overdosed, Mrs. Dellaverna found Teddy and kept him all night. And all the while everyone was out looking for him!"

"Teddy? You mean *he* was that baby with a junkie mother? You mean *Teddy* is Daniel's son?"

"He's my nephew. Well, you know he's my nephew, Claire."

"But I thought that baby . . . Mrs. Dellaverna said—"

"Ha-ha. Mrs. Dellaverna. Let me just tell you where she fits in. That baby, our Teddy, wandered off when his mother shot herself up with so much heroin she died with the needle in her arm. Can you imagine? When Daniel came home, he found his wife dead and his baby son missing. That's right. And it was Lina Dellaverna who found Teddy wandering around the beach. The way she tells it, she was out hanging wash and just happened to spot him. She thought she'd put the baby to sleep and then she fell asleep. I don't think she meant to do anything really criminal—she certainly didn't know Janet was dead. She kept him in her cottage all night long and when she saw them searching in the morning, she came out to see what was going on. That's why no one talks to her."

"My God. How horrible! Why would she do such a thing?"

"She said she wanted to keep him safe. The old witch."

"But surely she knew you and Oliver would look after him."

"We were just kids! No one would have given a baby to us. Anyway, Daniel was demented enough before this from an accident; he was slow, but then he really had a breakdown. He couldn't stop searching for the baby even after he was found. He went into a crazy downward spiral he never came out of."

"Yes," I murmured thoughtfully, "that was terrible what she did, to keep the baby's father from knowing he was alive."

"So now you know why everyone dislikes her. And there are other reasons. She tried to kill Noola's cat, by the way. Just ask Teddy. He was there. He saw her. Look, Daniel might be off kilter but he would never purposely hurt someone. He's one of us."

I leaned back in my seat. "Poor Daniel. Just how . . . uh . . . unstable is he? Does he have moments of clarity or is he always sort of *out* there?"

She shook her head. "Sometimes even I don't know. It's hard to determine where emotional disturbance leads off and physical brain damage begins. You know—scar tissue. Let's just put it this way: He's a dimwit. On the other hand, he can do things no one else can. Noola had him tinkering with watches before he was ten. He can still take them apart and put them back together flawlessly."

"He told me something unnerving when we were on the beach. He said someone gave Noola *bad tea*," I confided.

"That's ridiculous. He's just parroting something he heard."

"And really, Paige, I'm just wondering if there could have been any truth to Mrs. Dellaverna trying to hurt a cat. I've seen her with my little kitten and I can't imagine—"

"Claire," she said, giving me a crippling look, "you don't have to make it all right. You are the most naive person I've ever met!" She turned and looked me full in the face with this seething expression and for a moment I thought she knew everything I felt and was going to hit me. But she wasn't angry; she was upset. She went on, "Look, there's so much you don't know."

"All right, so please tell me."

"My family never received an insurance settlement when Daniel was hit by the *For Sail*. His skull was shattered. Well, Noola couldn't do enough for us, for his rehab—she paid for everything. And believe me, it went on for years! It was very different in those days. You didn't sue your friends. It just wasn't done. At least our sort wouldn't. And back then there was plenty of money."

The significance of what she was saying hit me. I was beginning to understand Morgan's inherited sense of contrition. This certainly explained it.

"Oliver was so young when that happened. So was I. We were just kids." She switched the radio off and sighed. "It's just . . . difficult right now since Noola died and Annabel took off." She held her neck. "Daniel was very close to both of them and seemed to be coming along. He's sort of lost, at the moment. And now with Patsy Mooney—" She turned to me. "Don't think for one moment that Daniel killed Patsy, all right? Don't even think it!"

"I didn't!" I lied. Actually, I'd hoped he had so it wouldn't have been anyone else. We rode in silence. So she, too, suspected someone other than the husband had killed Patsy Mooney. Why, I wondered, was that? Was she just protecting Daniel? So far that she'd let someone else go to jail for what he'd done? I wanted to keep her talking about him. I said, "Doesn't anyone take Daniel out for therapy? You know, like out to sail?"

She gave a scornful laugh. "Who would take him? Oliver? Oliver can't bear to be around him. Daniel's afraid of Morgan—and me. It's all I can do to put his house to a modicum of order! He never lets me take him to a barber. He leaves the tub filthy—"

I said, "I went to see Teddy, yesterday, and—"

"Why?" She shot me another murderous look. "Why are you so interested in— What business is it of yours if—"

"Well, for one thing"—antagonized, now, I finished for her—"my niece is living in a house where murder was committed, okay? For me, that's reason enough. I thought Teddy had no reason to be covering up for anyone and would give me some straight answers. As it happened, Glinty popped up. That's how I found out—"

"Ah! I suppose he told you all our gory financial details. I do everything I can to keep that little monster pacified and he turns around and sells us out at every turn."

Silently, I agreed.

"And Teddy chimed in and backed him up, I suppose!" she continued. "After I did everything I could to make him self-sufficient, to put him on the right track, the little brat does nothing but blame me. Tell the truth. He does, doesn't he?"

"No," I said, touched by her moment of vulnerability, "he didn't blame you at all." I remembered Glinty's peevishness. "It's Glinty who lets loose on everyone, I'd say."

"Yes, of course. Teddy never blames the men. It's always us women who get the brunt of it with Teddy." She turned to me and now I saw the resemblance clearly, wondering how I'd ever missed it. Oliver, Paige, Daniel, and Teddy. They all had those dazzling light-blue eyes.

"I'll bet Teddy didn't mention how he grew up at Guardian Angel House," she spat. "I'll bet he didn't tell you how they would punish him for wetting the bed and I'd have to go and get him, hide him in my closet so Oliver wouldn't drag him back there! And I was young myself!"

"Oh, that's horrible!" We lurched to a halt at a red light.

"Yes, it's horrible. His whole life was horrible. His *good* times were when he was allowed home for holidays to live with his half-wit father. My brother should have died back then when he was smashed in the head. He was meant to. We all would have been better off. Teddy would have gone into foster care and been better off. I know it sounds heathen but it's true!" Hot tears sprang from her eyes and she wiped them away with an angry back of the hand. Then she backed off. "I don't mean it! I don't really wish he'd died!"

"Of course not. It was just all inside and had to come out," I soothed.

The light turned green. She put her foot down on the gas and took off at such an inappropriate speed that for a moment I wondered if she, too, was unhinged. I held my breath. We were coming into Roslyn now, passing the Americana Mall. Neither of us spoke until we got to St. Francis. I was glad to get out of that car. As we walked through the lobby and past the double doors, Paige calmed down. She knew just what to do, where to go. Her college friend, a woman who was a kind of thicker version of herself—the same single strand of pearls and chic, nubby jacket (I was in just such a go-to-get-a-job-jacket of my sister's)—met us at the elevator and walked us right through to the lab. I was put into a chair to fill out a lot of insurance forms and then a comforting, heavyset black lady in mahogany lipstick bumped in transporting a whole collection of blood in glass vials on a trolley. She sat down across from me and, rolling up my sleeve, clucked away my nervousness. It was over before I could break into a sweat. As we walked back to the parking lot, I got the feeling Paige was upset again. "What's up?" I asked her.

She got in the car and pulled her seat belt across. "I mentioned Doctor Varanasi to the tech while you were in the ladies' room—the doctor Annabel ran away with?"

"Yeah?"

"She said he never even stayed down in Virginia. He didn't like it. He came right back."

"Are you sure?"

"Uh-huh. He never gave up his job here."

"Could it be that Annabel didn't actually leave town with him? Could she have left with someone else?"

"Don't be silly! Annabel wrote to Oliver and told him all about it."

"Where were the letters from?"

Paige thought a moment. I could tell she was rattled. "First Jersey. No, first that hotel in the city. Then Toms River. Then Virginia. They were settling there. That's what she wrote."

"Wouldn't you want to call him up and check this out with him?"

"Oh, sure. Let the whole world know she deserted Oliver!" She eased the car onto Port Washington Boulevard.

I said, "I'm beginning to think Annabel never left Sea Cliff at all. I think there might have been foul play."

"What do you mean?" Her fingers trembled as she lit a cigarette.

"I have a strong hunch Annabel might be dead."

"Stop it. You're just paranoid because of Patsy. It's possible they broke up and went their separate ways, but I doubt it. I *read* her letters, Claire. They're in her handwriting. She's very clearly alive. And"— Paige snorted—"having fun, in the biblical sense."

I sensed that she was holding something back. "Someone could have forged those letters."

She avoided my eyes. "You mean Glinty?"

That stopped me. I hadn't been thinking of him at all.

Paige went on, "Why, because he knows how to forge? Oh, I saw how you noticed the paintings were copies. You were shrewd, not saying a word."

Paintings? Forgeries? This was getting better and better.

"But no," she persisted, "I know her handwriting. She has that affected tiny script with all the curlicues. A forger wouldn't have known to mimic them. I might not be good at relationships but I notice things. Small things. Like, she'd put a little sort of squiggle under combinations of vowels. *I* before *E*. Maybe she had trouble spelling and it was a sort of trick to remember. A forger wouldn't know about that."

I wondered how she could be so certain? If someone can forge paintings, he can certainly forge letters. Can't he? Then a thought chilled me. Could *she* have had something to do with Annabel's disappearance? I said, "About the paintings . . ."

"All right, it's true. Oliver hired Glinty to make copies of them. Morgan knew he did it. He looked the other way because he didn't want Oliver to get in trouble with the insurance company."

"Don't we turn here, Paige? Where are you going?"

"I'm sorry. I was distracted. I'll drive around and back. Oh, never mind, I'll just take Northern Boulevard. It's probably faster now anyway with the traffic."

We drove along, both of us longingly eyeing Anthropologie, neither of us able to afford their peppery, stylish clothes.

"There's going to be a town yard sale this afternoon." She looked at the time. "It's still early enough so we can have our pick of the stuff."

"Do you think we should go after all that's happened?"

"Of course. It's for charity."

"Everything's for charity in Sea Cliff," I grumbled. Then I saw her face. "Oh, I'm just cranky because I haven't much money to spend."

She gave me a piercing look. "This is not about you, Claire."

"I'm sorry. You're right. And I am grateful to you for arranging my blood test."

"Good. Let's just hope it works out all right. Come on, we'll go. It'll be good for us to be away from the house." She relaxed, arranging her pearl strands in the mirror. "We wouldn't want people to think *we* felt guilty, after all. And it's a nice walk, the yard sale. Take our minds off . . . things. You'll enjoy it. And Morgan will be there. You like him, don't you?"

"Sure," I answered, overbright. She knew I did. Why would she ask me that? Hadn't she warned me off him at the club? He was hers, after all. Was she trying to rub it in?

"He always comes," she went on, suddenly in a good mood, "and he has a good eye, always finds something valuable for nothing. He has the knack. I could just kill him."

"Coals to Newcastle," I said without thinking.

"Yes," she agreed bitterly.

"Soon enough what's his will be yours," I reminded her unhappily.

She sighed heavily and said, "Nothing's ever that easy, though, is it?"

"Why, what do you mean? Because Patsy's dead?"

She reached across and grabbed my hand. "You will come, won't you? You promise? Things are always smoother when you're around. I don't know why."

"I said I would." I released my hand and settled back into my seat, flattered and insulted in one gulp. I was glad to be going to see Morgan, but disappointed because his fiancée was adamant about having me there. If she wasn't the least bit jealous of me—she who by her own admission was born jealous—where did that leave me?

JENNY ROSE

Wendell was taking his time at the sink. She'd had him brush his teeth to distract him while she waited by the bed with a storybook, hoping she could get him to take a short nap before lunch. It was to be a full afternoon. He wouldn't take off his cap. He was overwrought. It was no wonder. "Come on, Wendell, shake a leg."

He pushed his shoes off and climbed onto the bed and looked out the window. He wouldn't look at her.

"Well," Jenny Rose said, annoyed now. "What *is* it?"

"You don't believe me."

She heaved a sigh. "All right, tell me."

"I *saw* him. I saw Teddy. He put the cat in the box and he put a big stone on top. I was up there at Noola's house. I was in the portyhole cabin, looking out the blue window. I wasn't never supposed to go in unless I told Noola but I had to go for a little attention." Beads of sweat came to his lip and, hot now, he swiped off his cap and threw it to the floor. "I thought Teddy was playing a game. And he . . . he got in his car and started to back up over the box. But Mrs. Dellaverna, she come running out waving a big towel and the hacker and chasing him with the hacker and she kicked the box open and the cat ran off. Weedy. That was Weedy."

Jenny Rose kept her eyes steadily on his. It was the hacker that made it seem true. She'd seen that hacker when they went to the cottage. "He can't have meant—"

Wendell shook his head vehemently yes. "Oh, yes, yes, he did too mean to do it. He put the box down right there in the driveway! But Weedy never come back. Never did. And now everybody's mad at Mrs. Dellaverna."

Jenny Rose stared at Wendell. "Are you sure, lad? Because—"

"I wouldn't fib to you, Jenny Rose." He crossed his heart sincerely and continued heatedly, right where he'd left off, the scenario still unwinding before him. "Mrs. Dellaverna and Teddy had a big fight. Right there in the road. And Teddy pretended like it wasn't his fault; he said that Mrs. Dellaverna put the box on the road and she was crazy. But it wasn't that way. And everybody came out and got yelling at Mrs. Dellaverna but I say it wasn't her fault. And when Mama comes back she'll say so, too."

"Oh, Wendell!" She reached over and took him in her arms. There was no settling him. "Oh, dear one!" She hugged him tightly.

But he wasn't finished. He kept on, nodding and blubbering, "I told Mama everything and she told me not to say another word. Because 'We're going to trap Teddy,' Mama said, 'Just like he trapped the poor cat. . . .' But Mama put her finger here like this"—he pressed his pointer finger on his mouth—"and she said, 'Don't say another word, Wendell. Promise me now!' and she went out and I never did, not until you came and me and you got to be friends." He picked wretchedly at a scab on his leg.

"What do you mean? Is that why you never spoke? She told you that before she went away?"

One large tear fought its way down Wendell's heated cheek. "Yes."

Downstairs, the telephone rang. Mr. Piet was down in the cellar hunting for the rice bin.

Teddy picked up. "Twillyweed," he said.

"It's Glinty, here. May I speak to the fair Miss Jenny Rose Cashin?"

"I'm sorry," Teddy said in his most limpid voice, "she doesn't want to talk to you."

"To me?" Glinty, over the sound of the boats in the background, seemed puzzled.

"I guess not," Teddy said. "Maybe because of something you said."

"I said nary an off word." Glinty searched his mind.

"Or something you promised? I'll bet you must have," Teddy suggested, sounding concerned. He took out a cigarette and lit it with his gold lighter, then slipped the glamorous Dunhill away in his pocket. "I'll bet you used that sharp tongue of yours. So sharp you might just cut yourself. . . ."

"I wouldn't bet too soon, if I were you, Teddy," Glinty shot back, insulted. "What you gain on the horses you lose on the roundabouts." He hung up the phone.

CLAIRE

We pulled into a backup of traffic. There was a line of cars blocking Carpenter Avenue where the series of yard sales began. "Tourists! Already!" Paige fumed then suggested, "We might as well park and walk the rest of the way. Mr. Piet can come and get the car later."

Before I could answer her, Jenny Rose must have spotted us, for she came rocketing over.

"They caught Donald Woods fishing off the pier on Island Park Bridge!" she gasped.

"That's wonderful," Paige exclaimed. "Where's Wendell?"

"Guardian Angel's got it all set up for the kids. Oliver's taken him on the swings." She lowered her voice. "He's dead upset, you know."

"Well, aren't we all," said Paige.

We got out of the car and walked across someone's yard, trampling soft blue pansies and pink lady's slipper. To get out of the way, we segued onto an open lane of card tables filled with beguiling sale items. A lamp made from limestone. Dominoes. Christmas cards from the 1950s. An antique comb and brush set inlaid with ivory. Jenny Rose and Paige hung together and convivially lit their cigarettes. That's the thing about smokers, they get all chummy and you feel like you're not in on something. "This Donald Woods must have protested violently," Jenny Rose was saying. "He swore he had nothing at all to do with Patsy Mooney's death. Made a big scene!"

Paige shook her match out. "Well, of course he would, wouldn't he?"

"Yeah. He swore he hadn't seen Patsy in more than three years and has a new girlfriend now, who owns a gourmet truck down in Long Beach and they're planning to get married. But Oliver found out at the police station that Donald was *definitely* seen in Sea Cliff the day before Patsy Mooney was murdered. He was seen in the deli. They have surveillance video of him. Positively identified."

"That about clinches it." Paige smacked a pile of *Life* magazines.

"Pretty stupid, to let himself be seen like that," Jenny Rose said, offering me a Tootsie Roll.

"Yeah," I agreed, taking it, unwrapping it, and greeting that particular sugary bliss of gummy resistance. "I wonder what he said his reason for being there was."

"Of course he said he had no idea Patsy Mooney even *lived* in Sea Cliff! Said he was here to meet someone who wanted to sell him a motorcycle cheap. Of course there *was* no one. And who cares, right?" Jenny Rose gleamed. "Fuckin' murderer!"

I wondered why he'd come in the light of day? Unless he hadn't meant to kill her but had been carried away by anger. And if that was the case, why hadn't he hightailed off Long Island instead of waiting around in full view for the cops? Unless he thought it made him look less guilty. It just didn't feel right. My ex-husband always told me, *It's not like they say in the movies, you know, how the perps raise a big stink declaring their innocence. Once you catch 'em, mostly they do as they're told nice and easy, walk right into their cell and go to sleep.* And there was something else about this case that kept nibbling at my craw, like a word on the tip of my tongue I couldn't quite catch.

Jenny Rose whispered, "Auntie Claire, we have to talk. It's about Wendell. He—"

But just at that moment Glinty stepped between us, startling me once again with the suddenness of his appearance so that I dropped my envelope of hospital papers. The two of them scurried off. Annoyed, because we did need to talk, I knelt down in the grass to pick them up—and I saw across the yard a pair of boating shoes I knew and liked under an antique school desk. I raised my eyes to his. Both of us held on too long then looked, baffled, apart. The last time I'd admired those worn-out moss green boating shoes they'd belonged to a handsome boat mechanic. Now they belonged to a wealthy North Shore heir. Out of my league. But he strolled toward me. "Say!" he said, sucking in his breath. "Look at this. A copper-lined humidor. Handmade, it looks like!" The canopy of young leaves above us shimmered in a sunlit wind.

Together we bent down, the sun warm on our backs, and peered into the little oven of copper. He was so close I could smell him. Salt. Soap. And the metallic shirk of the box's lining. I turned slightly and he was watching me, his eyes moving down my throat, close enough to kiss. Evidently he'd forgiven me for incriminating him by taking the key to the police. A response to his nearness pulsed inside me and I bumped my forehead on the ceiling and wrenched myself out. Paige had walked off trustingly. It made me feel like a thief. She was standing in the next yard haggling over a sentimental picture when it was the frame she really wanted. She wobbled back over the grass in her heels toward us, all aglow. "Ten dollars!" she sang, disengaging the picture from the frame and tossing the print aside. "It's got to be worth fifty!"

"At least that!" Morgan agreed, admiring the carved, pickled wood, holding it up. They strolled together toward the 99-cent table. He waited tenderly while she scoured each item. "Look, Claire"—she held up a yellowed card of vintage buttons—"something for you!" She chuckled. "Oh, my God. Remember that first night when you came to dinner at Twillyweed? We laughed so hard. Didn't we, Morgan? A lady from Queens with buttons on her ears and a tablecloth for a coat! It was too much. Lord, we were rolling, weren't we, Morgan?" Her eyes twinkled with spite.

Embarrassed, now, Morgan caught my expression and looked away, "Well, we were drunk."

"Ah!" I smiled and smacked my head, pretending I'd just remembered something. "Gotta run home and let the dog out. Paige, thanks so much for taking me, okay? See you later!"

"Hey!" Morgan called after me good-naturedly. "Who said you could have a dog anyway?"

"I'm the mistress of my universe," I shot back over my shoulder, "and no man will wither yon me livestock!" Don't ask me where that came from. It was having all these Scottish men around. When I got far enough away from them, I slowed down, Paige's words ringing in my ears. I made my way unhappily back to the cottage. And Jenny Rose might have mentioned to me she was having it off with that . . . that . . . scallywag! My car was in the drive. I removed Carmela's jacket and folded it carefully. I was getting a little fed up with taking care of other people's things. Suddenly I got so mad, I flung the jacket down on the ground and kicked it. Feeling better, I threw it in the trunk. And then it came to me, what it was I'd been trying to remember. The men from Twillyweed had sailed to Virginia for that chandelier. All four of them. Any one of them could have posted a letter supposedly from Annabel.

In the cottage, Jake greeted me with so much enthusiasm I felt my blood pressure lower. Settling in, we sat together and looked out the window. We admired the fair-weather clouds, and the fleet of slim white sailboats zinging by, all the trappings of privilege. I jumped at the phone ringing in my pocket. "Hello?"

"Surprise!"

My heart sank. It was Carmela, my sister.

"I'm in Lugano," she trilled. "It's gorgeous! Can you hear me, really? I wasn't sure. The mountains are so disruptive!"

"Clear as a bell!"

"So I called Mommy to find out the name of that village Daddy's grandmother comes from, Mairengo? And I went there. Population five hundred and sixty two! Boring as hell. Luckily, I'm not alone. Trurio, my handsome guide . . . well"—she lowered her voice suggestively—"of course, he's young but his father is connected, he works for the government in Milan; you'll meet him because we're *very* close and I wouldn't be surprised if—"

She prattled on. I could see it all. The patent-leather Italian skulking in the background, a ne'er-do-well son of a sanitation engineer, thinking here was his ticket to America. New York, no less! Little did he know our New York was an old house in a once reputable area where temples and mosques now crackled the neighborhood awake over loudspeakers churning out morning prayers, where pigeons reigned and cop cars lurked while high school kids slunk to the park in little herds of cannabis fumes, tossing crack vials like crumbs here and there to help find their ways out.

"Mommy told me all about your saga of woe," Carmela chattered on. "That's what happens when you jump from one relationship to the next without waiting to get to know each other. Surprises. Nasty surprises. That's exactly what happens."

She was right. Then I realized she was talking about Enoch. I was supposed to be upset about Enoch, not someone else's fiancé! And what was this *saga of woe*? No wonder she couldn't get her stuff published. "You're right," I said.

"I am?" She sounded surprised. "Well, now that you realize that, I hope next time you'll look before you leap."

"All right, all right. I get the message." I hung up, relieved that she wasn't in town. Relieved I wouldn't have to deal with her at all . . . and then I remembered Jenny Rose. Why on earth had Carmela called me instead of her? I picked up the phone and hit the green button twice, reconnecting the call.

"Call Jenny Rose," I said.

"What?" I could hear her shifting her phone, see the twinkling lights around the lake.

I started to say something reprimanding and then, thinking better, I said, "Carmela. She's wonderful. She has hazel eyes just like Daddy."

"Yeah?"

"Yes." I could hear her mind ruminating, telling herself all the reasons a knockout like herself should not, definitely not, have a grown daughter around. I could see her as a girl, proud, jealous—as we both were of each other. I knew her so well. I prayed fervently she'd move on to a higher, better level. I waited.

"Stop praying." She laughed. "I can feel you."

"What? I wasn't."

"*Tch!* You're just like Mommy."

"Okay, I was, but for the right reason."

"We're just coming to the border. I'll call you back."

"No! Call Jenny Rose!" But she'd gone.

I stood there for a moment, close to her regardless how far. And then I realized something; someone could have lured Patsy's ex-husband to town . . . but who? I poured the morning's coffee into a cup with milk and ice and Jake and I went out.

Mrs. Dellaverna was standing in her yard. I walked over. "Hi," I said. "What are you doing?"

"I'm tricking the roses."

"Huh?"

"Yeah. You chop off the heads after they bloom and it tricks them into blooming twice."

"Ah. I'll remember that."

"What's the matter? You look depressed. Because Patsy died?"

I shrugged. "I dunno. I can't seem to figure things out."

"Come in my house."

"Just for a sec," I said, following her in. To my surprise, there sat Mr. Piet with his shoes off, his legs crossed and the *Times* folded open in front of his face. "Mr. Piet! How nice."

"Mademoiselle Breslinsky." He bowed his head.

We commiserated about Patsy Mooney. Then I said, "I never thanked you for my headlight."

"So many things have happened." He smiled sadly and his eyes crinkled up.

Mrs. Dellaverna pulled me into her sunporch. Down the sides of an aluminum trellis, hanging almost to the ground, were several incredibly long, skinny green squash.

"It's a *cucuzza*," she confided with intimacy.

"Isn't it too early for squash?"

"Yes, yes." She nodded rapidly. "I plant them early, in March already, here in the house. Look how big! Look how *bellissima!*"

I frowned suspiciously. "You're going to enter them in the contest?"

"No, no, not these. They'll be too many seeds in these by then. They'll be too old and tough. No. Outside I started the others. But I'll make a nice soup. And a little red pepper to make the zest; you have to have the zest!" She motioned me back into the kitchen. There on the countertop was a Tupperware container filled with squash soup and an aluminum foil envelope of red pepper. She nudged them both toward me. "For you." Then she frowned and lowered her voice, "Death . . . it's a part of life, but I don't like this murder. Maybe you need a protection against a *malocchio*."

"Evil eye? Very funny."

"I'm not joking." She yanked my shirt down over my shoulder. "Hold still!" she barked, giving a quick glance toward Mr. Piet—who was pretending to be absorbed in the financial page—and proceeded to fumble with my bra strap, pinning a tiny red ribbon to it. "So nobody gives you the horns!"

"Okay. Okay." I went home and sank into bed, protected now by the Wicked Witch of the Zest. I slept. Then, with something like zeal that I can only imagine came delivered by osmosis from Mrs. Dellaverna, I went to work. I opened the button safe and sat down at the window and polished every little one of the buttons with a spray bottle of hot water and a little vinegar. The summer solstice was drawing near and it took a long time for dark to fall. I welcomed it, the sound of the birds settling in, the boats whistling and groaning into port, and the dark, safe feeling of a cozy dwelling. I lit a candle and some incense and was standing at the stove stirring boiling water into red Jell-O—my mother's daughter that I am—when someone tap, tap, tapped on the screen.

"Hullo, hullo, anybody home?"

Jake let out a bellow and trotted over. My hand went to my hair as I went to the door. It was Morgan. But I'd known it was him, hoped it was him from the moment I'd heard his knock.

"Brought you a weather stick," he said, holding it up in its plastic wrapping. "I got it at the yard sale after you left."

I laughed happily. "I've wanted one since you told me about it!"

"I know. And I've brought you an instruction book on sailing." He ducked through the doorway and handed me a soft cover book called *Basic Keelboat*. I flipped through the pages, filled with diagrams of heavings to and soundings in fathoms. "Thanks," I said, putting it neatly on the end table with other good intentions.

He had an arm up and held the back of his neck, turning this way and that. "I can't believe how much you've accomplished!" He tousled politely and energetically with Jake over the dog's dirty pink Spalding.

Trying not to look smug, I asked, "Time for a cup of tea?"

We stood there for another moment, poised and unsure. I was so happy he was there I didn't know what to do first. But he remained and I realized he was gaping at my feet. I was wearing Noola's mukluks. I could have sunk through the floor. "I'm sorry," I stammered. "I fell in love with them and couldn't resist—"

"Don't apologize." He bent down again and gave Jake a good stroke. "She'd have liked that someone else shared her taste. She walked around like an American Indian half the time, with buckskin skirts and shawls made out of hemp! You mentioned there might be tea?"

"Well, decaf, if you don't mind, at this hour. Yes. Please. Sit. Jake, go sit down. C'mon. Here. Here's a biscuit. Give it to him, will you, Morgan? He won't settle until he's got something to treasure. Make him sit first."

With Jake contented at Morgan's feet—he couldn't get closer if he was wrapped around him—I took out my secret stash of blackberry tea and the prettiest teapot, black-tea brown with yellow daffodils painted on it, and fussed about him as though he were the man of the house come home from a long day's journey. I couldn't stop myself. I didn't want to. The pot in one hand with a dishtowel over my hand, I lowered myself across from him. For a moment there was silence. It would be the first time he'd sat here since Noola died.

"Claire . . . What you've done with this place! I don't know what lucky star I walked beneath when you stomped onto me sloop . . ." Then he said, shaking his head, "I love it so much that you've taken it to your heart. That you seem to respect my mother's memory. Christ, I get so tired of everyone tiptoeing around me so I won't remember my mother's dead. But you see, I'm living her death. I'm in a place of grief. There's no one I'd rather talk about or think about. She's all around me anyway." His voice broke. "I'll not be over it for quite some time—nor do I want to be."

"Well, you're entitled to your grief. Are you hungry?" I asked.

"Sure," he said, as though he'd just remembered food. He touched the teapot and eased his handsome finger gently down the belly of it. "This is the pot she liked the best." A thrill went up me. He said, "Sitting here at this window with you . . ." He shook his head. "I don't want to be anywhere else."

Our eyes met. There it was. That intoxicating fizz of significance. But because it was so new, I was unsure what he meant and feared almost physically to make a mistake and chase him off with my eagerness. I took a sip of tea to avoid saying anything. It was so hot I saw oblivion and had a bad moment taking it down, feeling the wall of pain between my lungs as it scorched my insides. But I'd promised him food. I busied myself, hauling from the refrigerator everything I had worth giving. I had a cheese that was as close to heaven as food can be. Carefully, I peeled away the cellophane and lowered it reverently onto a board, placing beside it a curved silver fish knife. Normally I'll cut it in half and stash the better part for myself when I was alone. Not this night. It merited the center of the table and there I placed it.

"Uh-oh," he lamented appreciatively, taking in the exquisite, firm, grayish crust and just-before-loose insides, "what is it?"

"Brillat-Savarin, it's called. It's named for a famous chef." I sliced some vine tomatoes, sprinkled them with sea salt and black pepper and poured balsamic from Modena and Sicilian extravirgin all over them, eyeing Jake fiercely as I did. Jake is mad for cheese and he's liable to whine until he gets some.

"I am starving," Morgan realized, resting his long fingers over his knees and taking it all in appreciatively. "I love food, really."

"Me too," I said, laying out his mother's creamy napkins and two pretty etched glasses. I'd bought a nice 2010 Côtes du Rhône for a special occasion and hauled it out now. "Water or wine?" I held up the bottles.

"Both," we said together and laughed.

"What's your very favorite food?" I risked, hoping he wouldn't find the question childish.

He thought a moment. "The core of the Boston lettuce, when you just cut it open. I love that," he said while I found an opener in the drawer and joined him. I was waiting for him to ask me what mine was but his head drooped down and he held his hands behind his hips. "I'm going to tell you something. Something I've never told a living soul."

His words frightened me and I wasn't sure I wanted to hear what was to come.

He began, "I don't know how much you know about my past . . ."

"A little. I know a little because Teddy mentioned—"

"Years ago," he interrupted, "at just this time of year, almost to the day it was, right before the race—"

"I know what you're going to say," I stopped him, hoping to spare him. "Your mother ran over Daniel in the water. Mrs. Dellaverna told me. And that's why he's . . . that way."

He looked at me wearily then down at Jake, tickling behind his ear. "Yes, but you see, it wasn't my mother drove over that lad, Daniel, that beautiful young lad." Looking back up, he held my eyes. "'Twas me."

The way he said it. With such sadness in that picturesque way. It broke my heart. "Oh," was all I could say. Then, "I'm so sorry."

He sucked a deep breath in and kept looking at me. I'll never forget that look. He was waiting for me to judge him.

"You were just a boy yourself . . ."

"Ah, but you see, I knew better."

". . . And your mother took the blame. I would have done the same for my son."

"Would you? Do you really think you would have spared him by doing it?"

I didn't know how to answer. He was right. Because it was clear he'd been spared nothing.

"While she was alive, I could never tell anyone. It would have cost her, see?"

"Yes. Is that why Daniel is afraid of you?"

He flinched. The fact of it wounded him; I could see that.

We must have sat there for more than two hours. He talked—oh, he could talk, recounting tales of his youth, stories of Daniel and himself growing up on the North Shore when Daniel was still normal—how grand it had been, fishing and sailing back in those days without the McMansions and the country clubs, Oliver and Paige trailing behind as youngsters, too young to join in their hot competitions. I watched and listened with growing affection. His short hair had lengthened since the first time I'd seen him and now looped around his ears and down his sun-darkened neck and I knew I was sunk. But he must have mentioned five times how good Paige had been to his mother. "All the long while I was overseas, and when I was away at school, it was Paige who looked after her. It can't have been easy for Mother, without me. But she always wrote and told me she was well looked after, then later Annabel came over with Wendell, or Radiance and Paige had stopped by that day or the day before . . . bringing her a package of Lorna Doones or a pint of cream, things she held dear." He squinted, as though he were seeing the past.

I sat there with a smile plastered to my face. It was already perfectly clear to me that he felt duty bound toward Paige and I wished he'd drop it.

"She was so good to my mother, you see. Tended to her all the time." He eyed me steadily. He cleared his throat. "And then there's Radiance. She's very young, of course. One must take care. But we're all very close. Very close."

I understood. He was telling me that while he and I liked each other, he had obligations, commitments. Or was he making a move on me and laying out the rules? Suddenly I was confused. Did he intend to marry Paige and have a little on the side? Is that what this was about? And what did he mean about Radiance? Was he having it off with her, too? Or was that in the plan? I had no doubt he thought he could handle us all. Even if I might not mind being his little bit on the side, I'd be damned if I'd be a little bit on the side of a little bit on the side! I stood ungraciously, went to the sink, and washed and rewashed a couple of dishes, signaling it was time for him to go.

He stood awkwardly, upsetting his chair. "Have I said something wrong?"

"God, look at the time!"

"Oh. Sorry. I was carried away. Will you forgive me? I didn't mean to overstep me bounds. It's just . . . it's so pleasant here." Our eyes were drawn out the window. The sky hung so close and black and thick with stars. "*Ti a braw bricht t'nicht,*" he murmured, then looked up and laughed. "It almost feels like if you leaned out you could grab one of the stars." Then, when I didn't reply, he said, "Ah, well."

"Well," I echoed, "thank you so much for the weather stick. It looks like Pinocchio's nose."

"I'll stop by sometime when I have my tools and put it up for you."

"Right. Thank you." I bobbed an awkward curtsy.

He knocked the chair over again. Suddenly I remembered that crack Paige had made about me and the buttons in my ears. "Oh," I said, "wait just a minute. I have to show you what I've done to your mother's button collection!" I started toward the button safe, but he held me back.

"Please don't," he murmured. "I don't want to see them. You can have them."

"Oh, God. I didn't mean that!" The kitten was at the door, scratching, indicating her needs.

"No, really." He turned his back. "Take them. Take them all. It's not that big a deal." He took his plate and moved tiredly over to the sink and then stood there just holding it, a man with a plate. "Don't you get it? They pain me to look at, each one a hurtful memory, see?"

I gave a sly look into the button chamber. If I emptied it out, I could hook up the sink and turn it into a darkroom. I said, "Look, you might find one day you won't feel the same . . ."

Again he held my eyes. "I'm afraid I'll always feel the same."

I took the dishtowel from him and wiped the few plates and put them up on the shelves.

"She used to sit there fingering them at night," he remembered, "in that chair, when she was thinking of *him*. What she would wear if he came back. Like other people would watch television." He shook his head ruefully. "I used to hate it. I knew who she was thinking of. Always waiting for him. A man who wouldn't think enough of her to come to her funeral." He spat the words then wiped his mouth. "And there was I, the never enough."

"I'm sure that wasn't so."

"That's what it felt like to me. I was the one who'd ruined her life, if you want to know the truth. Stole her blamelessness. That was something very important to her, a religious woman. Before my sin, she was uncorrupted by guilt."

"Morgan, it was an accident, not a sin! You can't think that way."

"But I do. And it's all in the perception, isn't it? I loved both my parents, but they loved me too much, wanted me to see their way. I was the rope they pulled in either direction."

"Morgan. Why are you telling me this? Why don't you tell—"

"Who? Paige? You think she cares about my mother's thoughts? She just wants her wealth. She doesn't understand that my mother's wealth was in wanting good for others. Do you see? She can't understand past the material, Paige. At least that's how it is between her and me. How would you like it if the person you were bound to couldn't bear the touch of you? Didn't want to be too friendly when you were alone because he thought it would lead to what he couldn't bear! How would you like that?"

Oh no. I shrank into myself. This was the worst thing he could tell me. It hurt me so much to think he desired her with all his heart and she didn't want him at all. This crushed my secret hopes; it meant there was no room for me. "Then why—" I almost said *why do you love her?* But I couldn't. The unfinished words hung in the air. If he told me she was *his* moon and stars, if he said it, we wouldn't be able to be friends. I couldn't bear it. And I suppose I'd rather remain just friends with him if only to be around him. That realization shut me up. I gathered my wits and crossed the room and put the kitten out. When I came back, he was sitting in Noola's old chair, his elbows on his knees, his head in his hands. I poured myself another glass of wine, emptying the bottle, and drank it down. Without warning Jake sprang half up on top of the table and swiped what was left of the cheese. "Get away from that table, you rat!" I cried, chasing him. I was furious, but Morgan laughed so hard and so long that I refrained from smacking Jake with the paper. "Just don't do it again!" I shouted.

"He was waiting for his chance the whole time!" Morgan roared with laughter.

Jake eyed us both from under the hassock. He looked so pleased.

"Morgan." I turned and said, "Do you know who killed Patsy Mooney?"

He wiped his eyes. "It wasn't me."

"Good."

He looked up at me, realizing the seriousness of my intent. "No, I'm saying it really wasn't me."

My head wagged. "Double good. I'll eliminate you, then, from my list." It was something in my pronunciation of that tricky eliminate that alerted him.

The corner of his mouth turned up. "Are you drunk?"

"Yes. A little. *Hic*."

He stepped carefully over the carpet, "So, while you're nice and supple, you won't mind *me* asking you a few personal questions?"

I swung an expansive arm. "Go right ahead."

"Good. Because, I'm confused. Are you still in love with your fiancé?"

I scowled. "No. It's like he never was. Like he was a respite from real life."

"And what about the ex-husband? Are you still in love with him?"

I didn't answer as quickly. I decided to be honest. "I'll always love him, somehow." I shrugged. "The kids' father. That's important."

"And I suppose he's handsome?"

"He's the handsomest man I ever saw."

"I see. I guess that leaves me out," he teased, but there was disappointment in his eyes.

I was both taken aback and touched by his vulnerability. "What! You, so beautiful! You shouldn't care about handsome. Just look at your wrists." I leaned over and took hold of one of them, feeling powerful beside his doubts. "Such magnificent wrists." I held one up and wished my lips pressed to it. But I wouldn't do that. Not after what he'd said about the one he loved. I felt his pulse beat against my finger and our eyes met. He pulled back in alarm.

"Oh, listen to me! Never mind," I said. We stepped apart and I heard myself say in exasperation. "See, I think of myself as this slender young romantic figure, and I'm not anymore!" It surprised me that I was crying but I'd started now and couldn't quit. "I'm a big hefty woman who stomps into rooms with a big foolish smile and—"

"Stop!" he demanded angrily. He took hold of my face. With his thumbs he wiped away the wet streams. He leaned and kissed me tenderly on the side of my neck. I don't know about you, but for me the side of the neck is key. That feather at the core of me began its seductive niggle and I felt its resonance to my toes. But then I sensed, rather than saw, the light next door in Mrs. Dellaverna's window go out and the room changed somehow. She could see in. I lifted my head and then like a reply in a song, took a deep breath and, like an idiot, said, "Don't do this."

And of course he listened! He raised his head and tipped it, romantically, watching me. He looked so good, so rugged and everything a man should be. But that knowledge of being observed brought me back to myself. And even swept away by passion and wine, I had to ask. I had to know. I said, "Remember you told me about moon dials?"

His breath was coming faster. "Yeah?"

And then I said, "If I told you about one, would you be interested?"

"A moon volvelle?" His eyes, blurred with passion, became alert. "A real one?"

"Very real. Very old."

"I'd be the one who'd be interested, yeah. An ancient lunar volvelle might be worth a great fortune. Have you seen one?"

"No," I admitted, turning away. "No, I just— I haven't."

"But you've heard about one? A stolen one?"

I didn't answer.

"Because there are unscrupulous collectors who've been known to cover their tracks, who'd be delighted to take a piece like that off your hands, you know."

"But then a collector would have to stay underground. Never be able to give claim to owning it outright."

"Oh, aye," his said, green eyes glimmering, "but many a real collector wouldn't care." Suddenly and in one quick movement he stood and turned away. "*Ach*. I'd best be getting on." He sort of limped to the door and I realized with a thrill that he'd become erect. "I'll thank you for your hospitality." He gave me a wry smile. I moved toward him, meaning to shake his hand and feel again his almost predatory maleness. But he backed away as though he couldn't bear to touch me and at once he was gone. In that moment of ravaging nearness there'd been a palpable heat between us. I hadn't imagined that. His broad shoulders and ropey arms. I'd felt them almost as though they'd encompassed me. You could tell he might have a punishing temper. Hadn't he admitted as much? But was it enough to murder someone? And this time he'd held his impulses in check. Was I to be flattered? I was. I stood there at the door watching the spot he'd left, sobered at once by his leaving. Oh! *Why* did I feel so attracted to this *engaged*, possibly dangerous man?

Halfway down the path he stood still and turned slowly back toward the house.

Oh, my God, I realized with horror and delight, *he's coming back!*

He pressed his nose against the screen. "You'll not believe it. I forgot the reason I've come!"

I cracked the door a hopeful inch.

His hands were on his hips. "I've got your dole."

"Huh?"

"Your wages."

I stared at him dumbly. I'd forgotten I was due any. The both of us laughed and I opened the door all the way. He walked to the table and counted out my pay in cash. Very carefully he laid out each bill and gave a precise, out-loud account. "Now you count it again," he instructed earnestly. This I did, feeling strange. But I'd earned it, I reminded myself, seeing the bad state of my nails as I did. There's nothing like money to cheer you up. I folded the bills into a cracked but still pretty sugar bowl above the stove and walked him to the door.

He hesitated at the screen, then, coming close, pressed his salty sea lips against mine in an ardent kiss. Rapture closed the deal. He stepped back and raked his hair with his hand and, after we gave each other one last look, he went away.

I walked around the room colliding into things. Jake watched me for a bit and then, losing patience, decided it was time for his constitutional. I let him out and stood in front of the mirror brushing my hair.

Lost in thought, it was only after the fact that I perceived his frantic barks. I dropped the brush and, unthinking, flew out the door. Jake was in a corner of the yard, hunched and barking. He wasn't cowering, he stood his ground, but he was freaked out. My eyes scanned the darkness and suddenly I saw it, its eyes, glittering. A badger! It was poised and still, watching. I'd never seen anything like it. It was big as a dog, beige, almost blond, with long fur like a collie. I went rigid.

It was deciding whether or not to spring. I spoke in as calm and seamless a voice as I could, "All right, come on, Jake, we'll go into the house now," and I went toward Jake in a straight line, moving as smoothly as I could, talking continually to the badger without looking at him, "We're not going to hurt you now, we're just going to get out of your way, all right?" and as I spoke I got between the thing and Jake and shepherded Jake to the door and into the house. "Whew!" I leaned against the inside of the house and, sinking to the ground, put my arms around Jake and held him. Trembling, I reached for the phone and put in a call to Twillyweed. It was Oliver who picked up. "Oliver! It's Claire. The most frightening thing just happened. There was a badger out my door. He was huge. Right outside my door! I was terrified it would attack Jake."

"Couldn't have been a badger, Claire," he said, laughing. "We don't have any badgers on the North Shore. It was a possum."

"No, Oliver, it was huge! Big as a dog."

"Possum can be big. Or raccoon."

No, I protested silently, *it* was *a badger*. It had that foxy face, a predator's stance. "And it had long blond hair," I added, "It was . . . well, beautiful."

"Yes, it's rare to see one, but possum are around. They live in the sewers and in the woods on the golf course. Just shine a light out there, he'll disappear."

"That's it, I guess. The porch light's out again. And I just put a new one in!"

"Shall I come up?" he offered.

"No!" Afraid I'd sounded too hasty, I added, "Thank God you picked up the phone. I was so frightened. I'm fine, now, thanks to you."

"Well. All right. If you're sure."

"Oh, I am."

"Call back any time of night if you're frightened again."

There was an awkward silence as we both remembered last time we'd spoken. "I will. Thanks again," I hung up, relieved, but puzzled. I took a new bulb from the kitchen drawer and went to the back and looked out. Of course it had vanished by now, as frightened by me as I him. I let Jake out again to finish his business and I climbed up on the porch railing and reached under the lamp cover. The old bulb hung limply on its thread. I screwed it back in and light flooded the yard. It was crazy. I was absolutely positive I'd screwed it in snugly just a few days ago. I gave it an extra turn, making sure it was tight, and we went back in the house. "Jake?"

He raised his head and tilted it.

"I am so glad you're here."

CHAPTER SEVEN

CLAIRE

Jake and I were inseparable now. He slept, snoring raucously, on the rug at the foot of my bed. Our relationship had deepened a notch. It was like I knew what he wanted and he knew what I wanted. I was so grateful to him for making me feel safe and he was grateful to me from rescuing him from days and days at the window in Queens. For him, this was paradise. As we walked along the cliff early the next morning, my cell phone rang. It was my old editor from *She She* magazine, Jupiter Dodd, the fellow I'd used as a reference when I'd first come. "Darling!" he greeted me effusively, so I knew he wanted something. "How *are* you?"

"Peachy." I reined Jake in from a squirrel's mad dash. "What's up?"

"Well, I'm weekending out in East Hampton and—you know me—I get so carsick on long drives! Can I break up the trip at your little resort B&B? I'd only spend the night."

"Jupiter, it's not a bed-and-breakfast." I remembered my promise to watch Wendell. Jupiter loathed children. "You'd never have to pay at my place but, no, this weekend wouldn't work for me, I'm afraid. I'm babysitting. How about next weekend?"

"What? You deny me?"

"Yes. Just this once. Sorry. Any other time, though."

"Once scorned, never sallied . . ."

"Jupiter. Don't be melodramatic. You know I love you."

"All right, I'll try some other sucker. *Ciao, bella.*"

"*Ciao, bello.*" I took Jake home and walked over to Twillyweed. When I got there, Jenny Rose was sitting at the kitchen table staring into her breakfast tea. I reached through the climbing ivy and tapped on the leaded diamond of glass. She jumped then smiled when she saw it was me. She let me in, fetched me a cup, and we sat down together. You could always count on Jenny Rose for an excellent cup a rosy. Puccini was on the radio. Wendell played on a stretched-out blanket on the floor. "I've kept him home today," she whispered. "He's been whimpering in his sleep, the poor lad. Just feel better keeping an eye on him."

I regarded Wendell, who was dancing tiny parts of Lincoln logs into small structures.

"Those wee bits are the people. The buildings are stores and those are the customers."

"I see." I nodded.

"Auntie Claire," Wendell said, holding a log in the air, "where's Jake the doggie?"

"I left him home in case it rains." I smiled. "He likes it there in his bed."

He stuck one finger in his nostril and wobbled a booger. "What about the kitten?"

Distractedly, Jenny Rose handed over a tissue. "Take it out or leave it in, Wendell. Try not to play with it in company. And put your glasses on."

"The kitten's doing fine," I informed him. "She sleeps on top of Jake's head, between his ears, so I think all will be well. She hasn't got a name, yet, though. That will be your job, remember."

Satisfied, he returned to his play, putting himself into a new pair of red-framed glasses. Jenny Rose said, "Wendell, do me a favor and run up to my studio and find us a chocolate bar." He jumped to attention and was already trotting out the door. "It's next to my bed," she called after him, "or in the drawer. You'll find it. There's a good lad." In the distance, thunder rumbled. She turned to me, "Okay, you're not going to like this, but here goes."

My heart sank.

She twisted a short lock of hair with a paint-stained finger. "I think I might be up the spout."

"Sorry?"

"Preggers. I think I might be pregnant."

"You?"

"No, the bloody queen. Who do you think?"

"But, but, you were the one yelling at me for not using protec—"

"I know, I know!"

"Oh, Jenny Rose, you idiot! Are you sure?"

"No. I'm only a couple of days late. Well. Five days—"

"Well, then, it's too soon to be sure! You've changed continents. Very likely—"

She shook her head then held it. "I been chucking up since three days. Every morning. Then I'm fine."

"Oh."

"I really am, I'm really fine." She looked at me with those hazel eyes of hers and gave me a lopsided grin. "Like, terrific." She shrugged. She did indeed look fine. More than fine.

"But . . . you're so young!" I lowered my voice. "Does he know?"

"Nope."

"Aye-aye-aye-aye-aye."

Out jutted that stubborn chin. "But"—she shrugged—"it doesn't matter, like."

"Of course it matters."

"No, the thing is, I'll have this baby, either way."

"Still. You've got to tell him."

She reached her arms up. "My mother never told."

I froze. "Oh, Jenny Rose. Your mother was fifteen! You're not going to bring a whole new life into the world as a repeat performance! You've got to have a better reason."

"This is the one thing that doesn't speak of reason. A miracle it is."

Wendell trotted back in, tripped, and came over. He clapped two big Cadbury raisin and nut chocolate bars on the table in front of her. She stared at him. "I said one, not two. Whatever are you wearing? Where did you find the red glasses? Those aren't yours. Go put on your own spectacles!"

"They're mine. I found them."

I looked at him. Where had I recently heard of red-framed glasses?

"Well, put them back where you found them. You'll ruin your eyes wearing someone else's specs. You'll be tripping over your own two feet!"

Obediently, he marched across the kitchen and stood before the grandmother clock with his little back to us and stuck his pointer finger into the keyhole. It occurred to me with not a small amount of malevolence that my sister Carmela would have to face not only motherhood now, but grandmotherhood, all in one fell swoop. The low cabinet door swung open with ease and a hoard of glinting things was revealed. Wendell took the glasses off and placed them on the ledge, then foraged around in the pile of sparkling things to find his own. He placed them on his nose and looped the wire ends neatly over his ears, turned, and gave us an obliging smile.

Jenny Rose and I were still, our mouths dropped. On the ledge sat a box of glimmering jewels—its open lid an incandescent lunar volvelle.

At the Tre Sorelle, a cozy place in town where we knew we might talk uninterrupted, Jenny Rose and I sat across from each other. We'd dropped Wendell off at school and now we sat together in the window. The rain came pouring down. I remember hoping Jenny Rose was simply late and not really pregnant. But she looked longingly at the menu and couldn't make up her mind if she would have the Calamari Siciliano or Tartufo or both, so it didn't look good. It was still early and the place was empty but for us. The waiter slipped behind us and we jumped like thieves.

"Just bring us a cheese plate to share and two cups of soup, please," I said.

"What soup would you—"

"Any fucking soup!" Jenny Rose barked and he hurried off.

We both chewed our nails. I said, "So Patsy Mooney *was* up to no good."

"Looks like it," Jenny Rose agreed. "Or Mr. Piet. He's always skulking about."

"They could have been in it together."

"You're right. Meanwhile here's Oliver going mad looking for the bloody little red key so he could open the clock and wind it, then furious because the police have it as evidence so he still can't open the clock, and all the while it's open!"

"Yeah. Unless he knew it all along."

We sat there in silence. She said, "I don't think so. He's too stupid."

We both had a laugh. Then I said, "Why is the key red anyway?"

"Patsy Mooney painted it with her nail polish so it wouldn't get mixed up with the others. When I met her, she was wearing it around her neck. Now I know why."

I had the heavy bag of valuables under the table at my feet. We'd placed everything in a backpack of Wendell's and lugged it with us. The waiter arrived with two plates of heavenly Tortellini in Brodo and a board of fragrant cheeses. I held my temples. "Let's think this through. Obviously they're the family jewels. They must be. Paige talked about emeralds. But the box is from the rectory in Broad Channel. And where does Annabel fit in? Did she steal them and someone took them from her? Or maybe this proves she didn't take the jewels at all."

"Or maybe she was murdered for them?" Jenny Rose said.

"But if she was murdered, where's the body?"

"I think she's dead, Auntie Claire. She wouldn't leave Wendell to fend on his own. I just can't fathom it!"

I said, "So who was the thief? Patsy Mooney? The thing is, it didn't have to be her. It could have been anyone and Patsy could have come across it and was blackmailing him—or her.

Jenny Rose nodded. "You're right. That scenario seems more likely. I can't see Patsy lumbering through a church and banging a priest on the head, but I can make her out acting cute and turning events to her advantage. She might have thought she could get in on a shady deal and make some cash."

"And it cost her her life. She might well have come across the loot and stashed it in the clock for safekeeping. No wonder she wore the key around her neck. The thief might have played along with her attempt at blackmail while he planned to kill her, then called the old boyfriend up to get him to come around. He keeps the jewels and the boyfriend goes to jail for the murder."

"Not a bad plan," she said. "It just might be what happened. Except she never gave up where she hid it. So our thief is still around. And we've got the treasure. It is a treasure, isn't it?

"I think so," I agreed. "All of it feels enormously valuable, especially the box."

"And those emeralds!" She gave a low whistle and we both moved our feet protectively around the knapsack. "But who?"

"Yes, who? Everyone certainly had access. Think back."

Jenny Rose leaned in toward me. "I have to tell you, that Teddy is a piece of work. He's my number one suspect. Do you know he tried to run over a cat? He's not all charming and respectable like he makes out!"

But she would point to anyone before Glinty. I had to say it. "Jenny Rose, it's possible it was Glinty. That is, after all, his business. Jewels."

She reared up in anger. "It could just as well have been Morgan. He's the one who's crazy for all those antique gizmos! Look at the box, that, that—what's it called?—the moon clock thingy."

I dropped my head in my hands. "You're right. A moon dial would be his heart's desire. He even said so. Collectors are known for their unreasonable greed. They could be in cahoots, too. But let's not count out Oliver. He certainly could use a windfall."

"And I wouldn't put it past him," she agreed, "what with his gambling debts."

"And Paige. And what about Daniel? Any one of them could have. But Daniel couldn't have found his way to Broad Channel, could he have? Does he even drive?"

"He's not supposed to, but he's been known to snatch Paige's car and go over to Diane's Bakery in Roslyn. He has a terrible sweet tooth. He lies in wait when Paige takes a nap and he snatches her keys and drives off. He might be nuts, but he's sly. Just when you think he's got bats in the belfry, he'll prove you wrong."

"How do you mean?" I asked.

"I don't know. Like, he'll out of the blue tell you what you're thinking."

"I hate to say it, but Darlene Lassiter seems to run in and out of the picture, too."

"No more than your Mrs. Dellaverna. She's tricky enough to do anything. You know what it is? We're back to Go. We haven't a clue. It's almost like someone's playing with us."

"Hmm. You just gave me an idea. Suppose *we* set some sort of trap?"

"But we can't take a chance with this stuff. It's not ours to risk." Jenny Rose paused. "On the other hand, we'll never know what happened unless we try something. What we need is a lure. We could start a rumor. Suppose we pretended to have found some valuable jewels from Noola?"

"That wouldn't work; Morgan would know it was a guise. Noola didn't collect jewels."

"What about using these?"

"And if the thief grabs them and runs off with them? We'll go to jail."

"All right. What about pretending some *different* antique jewels popped up in Patsy Mooney's possessions? I could have discovered them, say, in her old room . . . in the turret.

I nodded my head. "The thief would think Patsy had been holding out on him. That this wasn't the first time she'd got her hands on something valuable. We could let him have a glimpse, something to stir up his or her interest. Couldn't we make something up?"

"Very funny. What looks like jewels and isn't?"

Our eyes locked as it came to both of us at once. "The buttons!" Her bright eyes gleamed.

I said, "We'd have to gussie them up."

Jenny Rose folded her legs up under her skirt and snuggled forward. "That's where I come in. I'm an artist, remember? A little smoke and mirrors . . ."

"We'd have to get everyone together at once. Radiance. Mrs. Dellaverna . . ."

"How about day after tomorrow, the night before the race? The thief will know the jewels are in the house. We could pretend we've decided to take the jewels to the police right after the race."

I hesitated. "I don't know. It doesn't feel right. Why would we wait? Whoever it is would smell a trap."

We thought while the rain battered down. The waiter took away our plates. Jenny Rose said, "I have a better idea. Suppose we made it known we had some expert coming to value them? You know, an Antiques Road Show kind of guy."

"What, like from Sotheby's?"

"Why not? We could pretend we had someone coming the night before the race. Let everyone catch a glimpse of the 'jewels' in the half-light."

"We'd have to set everyone up in the dining room then, so the treasure could be paraded past them in the distance and then up the great staircase."

"Say! I've got an antique music box just the right size," Jenny Rose cried. "The only one who ever saw it was Patsy Mooney. It was Mrs. Whitetree's back in Ireland so I never bring it out. But it's brilliant. It would make an alluring holdall. From a distance one might even think it's the volvelle. Or one like it. What do you say?"

"We might have a dinner party. It's the only way to get everyone together. Suppose we invited the appraiser to stay for the race and then go back to the city. That would give the thief time to come and snatch the stuff and still go back and join the race and think no one would miss him. He or she wouldn't be able to resist! He'd have to fall for it!"

"It might just work. How would we catch him?"

"I suppose we'd better let the police in on our little plan."

"You think they'll go along with it?"

"We've got to take this to them now, anyway. We've got no choice."

"But who can we get to play the appraiser? No detective would fool a jewel thief."

"You're right."

"Don't you know someone we could pass off as an appraiser?"

"Not likely."

We sat there.

"Wait a minute!" It came to me. "Jupiter Dodd!"

"Who's that?"

"My old boss."

"Is he good and posh?"

"As it gets. If anyone can play the part, he can. And I'll bet he'd love to do it." I opened my cell phone and plunked in Jupiter's number. "I hope he's still around! He might have left for the Hamptons! . . . Oh! Jupiter? Hi, it's Claire. Listen, I've changed my mind about you coming out here on your way out east. And I even have a grand house for you to stay in. Yeah. There's just one catch. You've got to pretend to be an appraiser from Sotheby's. That's right. You would? " I winked at Jenny Rose. "Of course you would! You're an angel! All right, now here's the plan . . ."

CHAPTER EIGHT

CLAIRE AND JENNY ROSE

Jupiter Dodd arrived at sunset in a Bentley convertible, top down. I'd never seen anything so scrumptious: powder blue with cream leather interior. He wore a navy linen jacket, a Troy Donahue yellow ascot under a crisp white starched Irish linen shirt, and he carried a butter-soft attaché case. I trotted down the drive and could have kissed him. Holding his nose up, he ascended from his perch, giving a curt, deliberate bow. "Watch the fingerprints on the car," he said. "It belongs to a Saudi princess. If she finds out I borrowed it, they'll chop off one of my hands!" He twiddled fingernails in the air. "And I've just had them done. Oh, and let's pretend my name is Phillip Montrose. I clipped it from the personnel roster at Sotheby's. He sounded rather high up."

I escorted Jupiter into the library where I introduced Paige and Oliver, praying they wouldn't smell a rat. I needn't have worried. Having worked as an editor in both fine arts and fashion magazines, Jupiter can outsnob the best of them. Oliver had sent Radiance off to the dry cleaner's to pick up his light green Polo sports jacket and then made sure Mr. Piet had his velvet Cole Hahn slip-ons well brushed. Paige, I noticed, had gotten her hair done. They stood there ready as rabbits. I almost felt sorry for them. Paige, perfumed and looking lovely in a fitted luminous oyster sheath and pearls, took Jupiter upstairs to the blue room, once their parents' bedroom and still the best room, quite a tribute in itself, and we now had the lot of them all assembled in the library where they sat around chatting excitedly. Mr. Piet had poached a huge salmon with garlic butter and dill on a cedar plank and the aromas floating from the kitchen were mouthwatering. He'd talked Radiance into helping him serve and she'd outfitted herself in his butler's garb, pinched at the waistline with a thick patent leather belt. It was an odd crew, with Mrs. Dellaverna avoiding everyone and everyone avoiding her. She sat in the window seat with her embroidery, still not sure why she'd been invited. Glinty lounged in and out of the shadows. Darlene Lassiter especially kept her distance. Because Darlene worked at the rectory, she had first dibs on whatever clothes contributions came in from the great North Shore houses and she looked, from her second-hand designer suit to the jeweled pin on her lapel, all the world like a gold coast dragoness.

There was Daniel, his long platinum hair in a stringy ponytail. Paige had put him in one of Oliver's old tweed jackets and it hung piti-fully loose. He refused to wear any shoes but flip-flops, and his horny toenails were atrocious, but he was wearing his teeth, a plus. And, of course, Teddy. Teddy always looked appropriate. And sweet. Everyone gossiped about the next morning's race, except Daniel, who was so cap-tivated by Mr. Piet's aspic canapés that he gobbled them all up before anyone else could get a taste.

Jenny Rose and I had it all precisely planned. When everyone was seated at the dinner table and the room was drenched in candlelight, she was to carry her music box filled with the buttons—the lid under-neath like a Persian serving plate—through the crowded room and up the stairs to the privacy of the blue room for Jupiter Dodd's after-dinner inspection, from which he would emerge in delight over what he would deign a precious find.

We hadn't reckoned on the daylight taking so long to disappear, however, and had to keep urging Mr. Piet to delay each course. At last the crash of yellow sunset oozed into the sea, and the air became soft and lavender. The gloaming, Morgan called it, sitting there on a velvet chair looking like a prince from the highlands. Conversation had grown a little thin. Jupiter said, "That's a lovely grandmother clock you have in your kitchen, Ms. Cupsand."

Jenny Rose and I looked at each other with fright.

Paige said, "Yes, isn't it pretty? And please do call me Paige."

"About 1750, isn't it?" Jupiter said.

"Really?" Paige said. "How can you be sure?"

Jupiter frowned knowingly. "Well, because it has a moon phase, we know it's after 1720. They didn't make them before that. Now, the dials are made of brass and they have those little silver decorations. They kept making *them* only until about 1770. That lets me know it can't be later than that."

Jenny Rose stood. "I think I'll just go tuck our Wendell into bed."

Jupiter continued, "Did you notice how the Roman numeral VI on the clock face is placed upside down? Only the old girls have that. They turned them upright after 1850. And all the early pieces used the Roman numeral *IIII* instead of *IV* for four."

"Really!" Oliver said.

"How enlightening!" Paige marveled, and then everyone was joining in.

"Where did you dig that up?" I whispered when no one was near.

"In the public library," Jupiter whispered back, winking. "Kovels' *Know Your Antiques.*"

It wasn't until after dinner when Mr. Piet danced in the crêpe suzette, its pan aflame, that Jenny Rose made her sudden appearance with the make-believe treasure. Because the flaming suzette was such a hit and warranted everyone's attention and applause, I thought Jenny Rose would have to come close to make sure everyone had a glimpse of the loot. But the room literally stopped at her entrance. She looked, standing there at the threshold until she had everyone's attention, like a younger version of Carmela. I had to blink twice to ascertain it *was*

Jenny Rose. Her short hair was pulled back off her face with gel into a kind of medieval veil and she'd dressed up in some sort of Moroccan costume. She carried a glimmering tumble of what seemed to be antique platinum and gold fitted gems. Just then, something neither of us had anticipated occurred. The music box began to emit a sudden tinkling of "The Waltz of the Flowers." It was so haunting, so utterly theatrical, the tune drifting unbidden across the room. Surely everyone would realize it was a scam. But they didn't, they watched, mouths agape as the glittering "jewels" and Jenny Rose seemed to float across the living room to the hallway. I thought Glinty would fall from his chair. Even Morgan, whom I'd earmarked as sensible, sat knocked for a loop. Jupiter Dodd got up and adopted her by the elbow and they took the grand staircase, she with such Lady MacBethian poise that no one moved until they disappeared into the blue room.

The door opened and Jenny Rose emerged alone and descended the stairs.

"*Chi è quella bellissima ragazza?*" Mrs. Dellaverna marveled.

"It's Jenny Rose," I whispered in her ear.

"Jenny Rose? *No!*" she protested.

Jenny Rose, taking her seat, shrugged with pleasure. "It's just an old thing I picked up in Istanbul."

Everyone began to talk at once. Mr. Piet refilled the crystal glasses with a treasured Sancerre. I was on pins and needles and drank one down and then another. I wasn't the only one. Darlene Lassiter, I noticed, had lost her affected ladylike airs and was reverting back to the barmaid from Skibbereen, slouching with knees obscenely at their ease.

I said to Jenny Rose through gritted teeth, "Why are we doing this again?"

"It's a laugh, isn't it?" Jenny Rose gave me that Irish dare look, which I have to say was contagious—and I tried to relax. We were in charge, right? What could go wrong?

WENDELL

The noise from the party tinkled up the stairs. Wendell opened his eyes just a slit. She was gone. He threw off his quilt. He was already dressed with his shoes on and all. He arranged his toys under his covers and made it look like he was in there, a very good idea he'd observed on TV. He put on his red corduroy jacket, eased the straps of his blue knapsack over his shoulders, and went to the window. Quiet as a mouse, he slid the window open and got up on the ledge. When the two men down past the garage strolled to the other side of the house and lit their cigarettes, he maneuvered himself out and scuttled down the trellis. Halfway down, the wood snapped and he grabbed hold of the vine, landing his feet on the wall of the house with a thunk. The vine was twice as strong as the rotting wood, and he held on for dear life.

Mr. Piet was alone in the kitchen with two orange cakes in the oven and a white restaurant tablecloth wrapped around him. He looked up. What was that? No. No, it was nothing; just those squirrels reeking havoc again on the old roof.

Wendell stirred and then lowered himself in slipping gulps—covered now in blossoms—all the way down to the lawn. As fast as his little legs would carry him, he crossed the yard and made his way down the cliff to the marina—and Teddy's old *Dream Boat*.

CLAIRE

We moved outside and made good use of the veranda despite the damp air, all of us tipsy and talkative. Mr. Piet had dragged out the wrought-iron chairs, and Radiance had strewn twinkle lights and hung paper lanterns from the grapevines on the pergola and lit them with flickering votives. The sky was stars and whizzing clouds. Glinty had a scratched-up violin—a fiddle he called it—and from the corner under the trellis he played with an almost shocking beauty. I was both touched and unnerved by the deep looks he and Jenny Rose dealt each other, the music so moving it seemed somehow wrong for the others to go on talking and laughing. How could such a scamp be so skilled? But I reminded myself of his harsh words about Teddy and resumed my dislike. *He's jealous,* I said to myself. *Just look at Teddy there playing horseshoes with Mrs. Lassiter, as good-natured a fellow as you'd ever want to know.*

We were waiting for Jupiter Dodd to descend after his inspection, the staircase and doorway in full view through the glass doors. It was taking him long enough. We were all getting cold. I was beginning to think he'd fallen asleep and wished I'd never included him in our scheme. Oliver came over with a drink for me. Rye and ginger. He'd remembered. He went over and stood beside Mrs. Lassiter. She remarked, "It's nice to see Daniel here. I didn't know he could be social."

I started to go inside but wanted to hear what he'd say and so I lingered behind them. Oliver sighed. "It's hard to tell with a guy like him. He was such a good kid." He crunched a knuckle. "Before the accident, he was headed for a stellar life. I used to worship him, believe it or not. Still, off kilter as he is, to this day he'd never hurt a soul. There's no real bad in him. It was his wife, Janet. She was rotten. There's no other way to say it. I don't like to speak ill of the dead, but she had no conscience. She was just born without one."

"There's them that are!" Mrs. Lassiter opened her purse and shut it. "At least he has his son."

"Yeah, right." He wiped his lip and looked away.

At last the door upstairs swung open. Jupiter looked more sad than happy, though, and that hadn't been in the plan. I didn't dare look at Jenny Rose. The wind had picked up and the paper lanterns blew sideways, making a noise like fluttering birds' wings. Already I could see Oliver shrink with disappointment, calculating how much he'd lain out for this feast. Jupiter minced down the stairs with such a morose look on his face that my heart began to pound. Carefully he opened and came through the French doors. Glinty stirred and sat beside Jenny Rose, taking her small hand in his.

"I'm so very sorry," Jupiter began, painstakingly taking a seat in our midst. Was he going to sell us out? Paige shivered and Radiance put a caring arm around her shoulder. Oliver threw back his drink.

Jupiter said, "I'm afraid these artifacts are even older and more valuable than I was led to believe. They're quite out of my realm. I've telephoned my secretary. We'll have to wait for my associate to join us tomorrow." He scowled into his drink then looked up through sparse brows. "Would that be all right, do you think?"

"Oh, yes!" everyone effused at once. I sank with relief. Oliver didn't even wait for Mr. Piet but breezed light-footed down to the cellar himself to find a more celebratory bottle. Everyone chattered and cigars were passed around and lit. It wasn't *that* cold everyone agreed. Jenny Rose's wicked eyes glowed and met mine across the starlit night.

CLAIRE

The day of the race broke with a nice, brisk wind. I was up early and trying to enjoy my breakfast—expensive Greek yogurt with a little pot of honey attached—but Jake watched me reproachfully. "Oh, all right." I gave in and let him have the rest. I let him out, washed and dressed quickly, let him in and made my way into town. The linden trees were in bloom and their perfume was intoxicating. Hearing voices and excitement, I went to the overlook, a good location for a broad view of the race. There was still plenty of time before the start, but already I could just feel the high spirits. I watched the villagers hurrying to set up their folding chairs and picnic baskets. At the dock below, sailors aboard their yachts threw good-natured insults at one another. I spotted Daniel down there at the marina, out on the farthermost dock. What was he doing there? He looked so strange standing at the end of the pier gazing out to sea and I figured I'd better go tell Paige. I sprinted off to Twilly-weed, but then something happened that made me forget all about him.

Going up the gravel drive, I stopped in my tracks. An under-cover cop car was parked sideways, all four doors open, winglike. A frightened-looking Glinty, his hands cuffed behind him, was being ushered into a backseat with solemnity, the officer's hand holding his head down like on TV.

I watched them pull away and drive right past me. Not one of them looked at me.

Paige and Jupiter Dodd stood in the doorway. "What's going on?" I hollered.

"Claire!" she called. "You won't believe what's happened! They caught Glinty trying to steal the jewels from Father's room! Our Glinty!" She stamped her foot like a wounded adolescent. "I still can't believe it! I won't."

But Jupiter shrugged and argued, "He didn't raise a peep to defend himself."

Mr. Piet came out drying his hands. Paige demanded, "I don't understand what the police were doing here anyway. I'd like to know. They didn't even look like police, did they, Mr. Piet?"

Jenny Rose pushed through them from the kitchen, her arms akimbo, her face streaked with tears. "You did this!" she fumed at me unreasonably. "You just had to pin it on someone! Are you happy now?"

"Come on, girls, no sense blowing in the wind." Jupiter herded us back into the house. He took me aside. "Oh, my God. It was so exciting. I was in the shower! Suddenly there were police everywhere! It was like on *CSI*! It was heaven!"

"Where's Wendell?"

Paige raised herself onto a bar stool, shaking her head. "He slept through the whole thing, God bless him. He's still up in bed."

"This was all your idea!" Jenny Rose glowered at me.

"But," I protested, "but . . ."

She ran into the powder room and I stood there, listening to her be sick. The foghorn from Steamboat Landing blew. That meant five minutes to go till the race.

I went outside and walked, bewildered, toward the docks. So it *was* Glinty. I ought to be pleased. I was glad. Wasn't I? Well, God help me, I was just glad it wasn't Morgan. I ought to be proud. But I remembered the way Glinty had played the violin so tenderly, and it left me with a hollow, anticlimactic feeling. I could hear the rustling of the sailboats; they were all jockeying for position at the start. I scuffled up and down the length of the crowded dock trying to catch sight of the *Corinthian*, but the gun sounded and the boats took off in a whoosh. I bent over catching my breath.

"Claire!"

I turned. Morgan. Who never raced. Our eyes locked across the span of rocking boats.

"Come for a ride?" He held out his hand.

"Oh, Morgan," I said, jumping on board, "they've arrested Glinty!"

"Arrested for what?"

"Jenny Rose and I set a trap for the thief," I panted. "The whole thing with the jewels last night was a setup. And Glinty went for it. I thought it would happen during the race and I wasn't there and missed the whole thing! I should be glad. But I can't—"

"Whoa! Slow down!"

"Okay. Look. Glinty tried to steal the jewels Jenny Rose had appraised last night."

"What? That's ridiculous!"

I threw my arms in the air. "Except the jewels weren't real. They were your mother's button collection, gussied up. Well, we did put one or two good pieces in just to keep it kosher."

He was utterly baffled. "What are you talking about?"

"It was a gag. The police were in on it. A hoax, to try and draw out the thief!"

Morgan stared at me, grasping this, then burst out laughing.

I said abruptly, "What's so funny? It worked, didn't it?"

"*Ach*. He never did mean to steal your jewels. Glinty's a far cry from a thief. I'd stake my life on it. Look, Claire, the gag is on you. Glinty wasn't up to the house to steal anything. It was me who told him to go there, to find the papers to the *For Sail*."

"What? You're just sticking up for him."

"No, I'm not." He laughed hopelessly. "He was all set to take your niece away with him. Did you not know they were set to run away? He wanted to surprise her with the boat. I hate to be the one to tell you, but your niece . . ." His eyes softened. "She's going to have a baby. Glinty's baby. He went to get the ownership papers to the *For Sail* so he can take her out to sea. She's a fine, brisk vessel for all that. Oliver keeps the papers in his father's desk upstairs in the blue room. *Ach*, the *For Sail* is mine but, ah, well, I never had the heart to actually march upstairs and snatch the papers from the house. Everyone knows she's mine, but the Cupsands always sailed her. Glinty wants to sail her to Maryland and marry your niece straightaway," he explained.

"But . . . then . . . why didn't he say—"

"Didn't want to sell me out, I imagine. Probably thought I'd be in trouble with the family."

My head was swirling. "But, but they've arrested him!" I cried. "The police. He's in *jail!*"

"Oh, I'll just go bail him out," he told me and pulled contentedly on his earlobe. "It won't hurt him much to be locked up for a bit."

We stared at each other across the rolling deck. The wind was making it hard to talk. There were so many boats moving in and out that the water surged choppily.

"Morgan? I don't know. I was just wondering . . . There wouldn't be any significance to a glove, would there? It's just I found this single glove outside the cottage one night a while ago when the lamplight was deliberately put out."

He frowned. "None I can think of."

I looked out to sea.

Then he said, "There was that case of abuse up at Guardian Angel

House years ago. A preacher. Volunteer, it turned out. Used to lock the kids up in the closet to punish them." He said this breezily and then, remembering, grew thoughtful. "But that was years ago. We were worried for a while how it would affect the kids. Yes." He scratched his head. "Played the banjo. He used to wear gloves to protect his hands. Weirdo. They caught him abusing himself right in front of the children! *Made* them watch!"

"He . . . wouldn't still be around Sea Cliff?"

"Naw. He hasn't been around for years. Dead, probably."

I put my sweater on.

"It was Paige who flushed him out," he continued, shaking his head with admiration. "He didn't last long with her around. She cleaned that place out top to bottom."

Paige. Always Paige.

CHAPTER NINE

WENDELL AND TEDDY

Wendell was stowed away nicely now in a pile of supplies and white life jackets. He'd wriggled himself down deep as he could and had slept pretty well, he thought. When Teddy'd come on board, the small boy had jumped with nerves, then burrowed in fearfully and pulled the tarpaulin over his head before Teddy could see him. He would wait here as long as it took. He had all his supplies in his backpack. He knew it was Teddy who was writing those letters. He knew because he'd seen him take the letter paper from Mama's nice desk. He put his ear against the soft cork and he tried to be comfortable, thinking of everything nice, put his thumb in his mouth, and rocked back and forth with the tide. *There was an old man from the west. He wore a pale plum-colored vest . . .*

Teddy sheeted the mainsail to get the boat moving. He wanted to be out of there and back before the winner's celebration. The *Dream Boat* skimmed westerly toward Duffy's Point—away from the regatta, away from the gullible.

He'd get rid of everything implicating him, just weigh it all down and dump it, then slip back into Twillyweed and retrieve the jewels that were rightfully his. Well, they were! Son of the eldest son. If that fat fucking thief Patsy Mooney hadn't come across his hoard, things would have run along so smoothly. Ah, well. It was her own damned fault. Served her right, the bitch. He sniffed the air. Good wind. He smiled. The ex-husband had been a gift. Handy that Patsy was always moaning and groaning to him about how he'd hit her. Getting him to come to Sea Cliff had been a cinch. The timing was perfect. He'd been cutting it close, but it had all worked out. Served her right for making off with his stash. Nosy, fat bitch. It hadn't bothered him a bit to put an end to her. He'd enjoyed it. Almost as much as he'd enjoyed getting rid of Noola. Teddy chuckled. Served her right, too, the old ninny, stupidly announcing there was a priceless lunar volvelle unrecognized for what it was down in that shabby rectory in Queens and no one to care for it! Lucky he'd been there at Noola's with Daniel, delivering Paige's care basket, when she'd come across that German priest's obituary. What an old fool she'd been to think he'd trot right off to do her bidding so Morgan could see it safely wedged onto some museum shelf—never imagining it would appeal to the likes of him. But, no, she'd thought only her precious son, Morgan, would be smart enough to know what to do with a treasure of that magnitude. In her astonishment, she'd spoken too soon. Old fool. Still, he remembered the look of worry and realization that had sprung to her eyes when she realized what she'd said—and to whom she'd said it. She'd always been suspicious of him. All his life. *Janet's son*, he'd heard her murmur once. Like she'd had a bad taste in her mouth. Her skepticism had been like a wall of disapproval he could never get past. Well, he'd gotten past it now, hadn't he? He'd given her a real bad taste. Slipping the pills into her tea was so simple, so quick—even she hadn't suspected he'd think of it.

And now, all he had to do was get rid of the remains of all his mischief, wait till the rest of them were at the race and then go in and walk off with what was, after all, rightfully his; he bobbed his head this way and that and his lips moved as he mused silently to himself. Then to hide it . . . where? Where should he hide it? Somewhere right under their noses, like the basement freezer. No, Mr. Piet might just happen to look there. He'd think of something. Wait till they found it missing! He could hardly wait to see their faces. He would stand there with them, pretending to share their outrage. They'd underestimated him for the last time. Not one of them would even think to suspect him. They were all too stupid.

Teddy smiled dreamily at the helm, relaxed and handsome. He laughed out loud and the laugh caught up in the wind, abandoned and hollow. Atop the hatch, in a lean holding cubby, a pair of fresh dove gray gloves rested neatly one on top of the other, palms down, all set to go.

CLAIRE

It was now or never. I reached up and touched Morgan's cheek, "Answer me this. Are you planning to marry Paige?"

He flinched. At last he said, "I'm waiting for her to tell me she wants out. It can't be me who breaks the engagement. She'll feel like I'm ruining her life. No, it has to be from her."

So that was it. How very noble. I stood. "Fine." I flung my hair mutinously over my shoulder. "Let me know when she's done captivating you."

I scrambled over the cockpit, but he got up and grabbed hold of me. He bent me backward and kissed me right there in the bright of day, holding my arms in his hands to keep me from falling. When he stopped kissing me, my head fell back and he looked down at me, saying, venomously, "Do you like it?"

My head lolled.

He squinted hard at me. "Aye. There's your answer. Because you're straight. Didn't you ever notice that Paige—Don't you get it? She's not."

"What?" I tried to stand and he set me on my feet again.

"She's not straight, Paige. She's gay. Paige is a lesbian."

"What?"

He took a piece of my flying hair and locked it behind my ear. "Look. I wouldn't ordinarily betray a confidence, but you have a right to know. Remember when Jenny Rose saved Radiance in the water? Well, Paige had just told her she'd decided to marry me. You know how Paige is; she thought if she did, she could save her brother, save Daniel, save Twillyweed. She was trying to do the right thing. But for all the wrong reasons. She'd told Radiance down at the dock because she knew she'd make a great fuss. She's so emotional, Radiance. Melodramatic. And Paige told her very gently. But Radiance bolted off in a mad fit and took out the boat.

"But you gave her a ring—"

"The ring was her grandmother's. She weaseled her way into that one and, God knows, I couldn't humiliate her." He looked past me. "The truth is she only ever loved Radiance. They love each other. And Radiance—she's such an idiot—after she went out to sea, she jumped overboard! Don't ask me why. To punish Paige, for all I know. Oh, maybe she made some halfhearted attempt to kill herself. Maybe she did. Although I can't imagine why. More likely fury—and spite, knowing her. And then found herself in over her head."

I stood there, a dodo. This could not be happening again. It was so absurd. It had to be true. "So"—I bit the bullet—"you'd go ahead with this marriage? Out of guilt?"

"She'll dump me."

"And if she doesn't?"

"*Ach*, Radiance is twenty-one now. Paige is not a bad girl. She'll come around on her own. She's afraid—Paige is—afraid to admit who she is. But passion is stronger than propriety. She'll come around."

We neared the dock. Different people floated by and waved and Morgan waved back. I wasn't as convinced as he seemed to be. Paige was as mercenary a female as I'd ever met. But he was cheerful again. He smiled and chose a hard peach and ate it as he leaned his head backward and let out a laugh. There was the buzz of activity and the readying for the finish. It looked like *Seawanhaka* was going to come in first from the tumult and celebration and cries of the onlookers. I spotted Jenny Rose, Mr. Piet, Radiance, and Paige all running toward the dock at once. I cleat hitched the line for Morgan and while he tied her up, I jumped to the dock and made my way through the throng toward the marina. It was strewn with tipsy partygoers and I had to zigzag through. I waved.

Paige called out, "Is Wendell with you?"

"No."

"He climbed out the window." She leaned against the tiers of piled canoes to catch her breath and gasped, "We can't find him."

Jenny Rose wailed, "Oh, my God! I wasn't watching him! It's my fault!" She fell against me.

Then Radiance, in front of everyone, turned around and grabbed Mr. Piet's shoulder and flung him around to face her. "*Non! C'est ta faute!*" she cried. "It's your fault! This is all your fault!"

"It's not," he said, grasping his chest.

"Oh, *mon Dieu*, it's enough! Just admit it! I know you're a thief! I found those moonstones in your room. I even put them in Jenny Rose's pocket to save you from blame!"

"But why would you do such a thing?" He pulled himself free.

"Because I didn't want you to go to jail again. But I'm finished protecting you! *Tu comprends*? Stealing is one thing . . . but murder!" She reared onto a piling and sank to the floor, sobbing. "I'm finished!"

"Radiance!" He fell to his knees "Believe me. I had nothing to do with any stones. I swear to you. On my mother's grave, I swear to you!"

"Yes, you did! Teddy saw you. He saw you at Noola's just before she died. He warned me." Her shoulders slumped. "I only wanted to help you, Papa, but I can't take it anymore!"

Mr. Piet took hold of her. "Teddy told you? And you believed him, *chérie*? You thought I would kill? Why would I kill Noola?"

Radiance looked at all of us. "For the jewels. For the money. Teddy even *gave* me the stones so I knew he wasn't lying! He said—"

He put his arm around her. "But I don't care about the money. I care about you! Why would Teddy tell you such a thing?"

I tried to think. The sun beat down and there was noise all around. Teddy. He would have been a child at Guardian Angel about the time of the abuse . . .

An older fellow who'd been canning bait came toward us. "That your little boy took off on the *Dream Boat*? That little guy wasn't wearing no life vest! I yelled to the captain, but he paid me no mind."

Jenny Rose lamented, "Wendell never trusted Teddy. He would never go off with him!"

The boy selling soft drinks on the dock piped up, "That was the *Dream Boat* just took off, all right!"

"He'd never go with him!" Jenny Rose protested.

Paige cried out and Mr. Piet took her hand. Jenny Rose, pale and frantic, came up behind them.

"Stay calm," Jenny Rose said, trying to steady Paige. "I'm sure they're just out for a sail."

"Where would they go?" I asked.

"Anywhere, could be." The old salt scratched his stubbled chin. The man's wife came up behind him, a beautiful old blonde with skin loose and crumpled as an elephant's hide. "That kid had no one watching him! They went west," she said, pointing, "just around the point. Around Duffy's Point. I seen 'em."

Mr. Piet moved fast. He got up and ran down the dock to stop Morgan dropping anchor. He moved like an athlete, his small legs carrying his broad shoulders in a whiz of movement.

I ran after him.

"Be careful over there past buoy two!" the old man called. "That current's mean!"

Mr. Piet jumped on board and as they pulled off so did I. If anything happened to Wendell, I'd take my share of blame. I was horrified to think how unfairly I'd judged Glinty—and to realize my prejudices were as conventional as my parents'. I hadn't even thought yet of what might happen next, what danger Wendell might be in. I thought we'd just sail out and stop them. If I'd only known what would happen next . . . But

Wendell was out there and we had to bring him back. I figured Morgan
was reliving Daniel's accident all those years ago. He'd rather die than
let anything like that happen again. I shrugged into a life vest and the
men rigged the jib and mainsail. We sailed out into the busy harbor and
headed west, just as a fleet from Hempstead Yacht Club was making its
way in. He was going too fast, too rash.

I shut my eyes, certain we would collide, but at the helm, Morgan
maneuvered us through and we broke free, the sailors' outraged curses
cracking across the wind. The sun shone, blinding me as we flew across
the water. I was so scared I didn't realize the cold. We'd left Sea Cliff far
behind. At last Morgan pulled around. "I've lost them!"

"We must have gone past them," Mr. Piet shouted, scanning the
shore.

"They can't have gone in there. It's a sink bog. Tide's too low!"
Morgan cried.

"There's that old loading dock in there behind those weeping wil-
lows. He could be there."

"No way. That place is condemned. Anyway, it's way too shallow!"
But we couldn't see where else they could have gone.

"He'll run her aground!" Mr. Piet raged. "I'll kill him!"

"He can't be there," Morgan protested again. "It's been locked up
for years."

Mr. Piet was peeling off his sweatshirt. "He shows the real estate,
doesn't he? He'll have keys."

Then, off in the dense grove of willow, practically hidden, something red moved. Silently, we watched, trying to make it out. There were
the cheers off in the distance from the marina, but the slosh of the tide
and the hurling wind was the only near sound. The red figure moved
again.

"It's Wendell," I said, recognizing his jacket.

Morgan looked through binoculars. "It's him all right, and it's
Teddy. He's carrying Wendell."

Mr. Piet reached down and took off his shoes.

"Take care," Morgan warned, "that spot has been sinking for years. It's shallow and if you step down, it'll suck you up like quicksand."

Before I knew what was happening, Mr. Piet dove soundlessly into the water and the back of his head appeared in there near the weeping willow.

"Stay here!" Morgan flung off his shoes and his shirt not a moment behind him. Within seconds he, too, swam through the shallow green water. "You can't leave me here on my own!" I cried out to no one. Trembling, I tugged off my shoes, vest, and sweater and belly-flopped in. The water stung. Disoriented, I came to the surface. The wind was horrific and I lowered back in, dog-paddling toward land. It seemed to take forever. My legs, still dressed, were heavy and sluggish. Finally close, I stepped frantically for land and my foot sunk in muck to my knee. Remembering Morgan's warning, I floundered with horror and fright and yanked myself out, trying to float and paddle my way in now without touching bottom, and without touching the cold air.

Teddy had slipped the boat into a tunnel of shade, camouflaged by draping willow. Where was he? And where were Morgan and Mr. Piet? They had to be in that hollowed lament of a building, the place half sunk in ruin. Skeletons of rusted girders squared off three floors of empty rooms that the wind gored through. CONDEMNED, its peeling signs warned. Backwater trees grew every which way from the moldy openings, its gates and rusty edges jagged. There was nothing but saplings and rubbish, rubber tires flung here and there. I climbed onto a pontoon of dry rotted plank and held on to a piling, then managed to get up on a cement aqueduct. I crept with tentative footfalls, edging along the side of a deep green pond. Chartreuse scum furred the top.

The wind died down, and it was quiet except for a profusion of birdsong. On another occasion, the remote beauty would have struck me. A duck had its head down, fishing underwater. But the duck stayed down, squirming, its tail wriggling in distress. It wasn't fishing. I realized a turtle must be under the scum, pulling it down. I tried not to look, waiting until the duck was gone. It took so long. My heart beat fiercely.

Where had Morgan and Mr. Piet gone? I couldn't see them. Idiotically, I took out my phone. Of course it was soaked. I threw it at the turtle. And then I saw it. A heavy gate, camouflaged with branches, had been moved aside, and a gray cellar door gaped partway open.

I picked up a large stone and edged toward it, lifting the door the rest of the way open. It was dark down there. I sure as hell wasn't going down those broken stairs. No way.

I hesitated. Why didn't they call out? What had happened? The wet oozed up my socks and into my legs. The wind took up again in a frenzy, but the sun shone confidently and I was staying out here with it. On the landing a plastic bag of recent takeout was riddled with ants. I spotted something blue on the ground and bent toward it. A wet knapsack. It was Wendell's. So now I knew I had to go in. I picked it up and fumbled through it. Cupcakes. A juice box. A flashlight. I put the flashlight in my pocket and made sure the door wouldn't blow shut by pushing it all the way open. Shivering wildly, I moved down the steps. They continued down an old stairwell until all light was gone. I held my stone with two hands, edging down, trying not to slip. But the wooden structure was corrupted and weakened, and I didn't trust the walls; pieces of it had already crumbled and fallen away.

Suddenly I heard a distant shout and something crashed and unloosed down in front of me, whacking out a terrible mushroom of dirt and dust. Someone must have fallen through the ceiling. I struggled to see around me. It looked like it once was a parking garage. I could barely make out a series of orange extension cords snaking down the steps and I followed them. I was belowground now. I continued down the stairs, reaching carefully to avoid some broken steps. There was the terrible smell of mildew.

Suddenly the wind rose up with a howl and blew the cellar door shut. I was trapped in darkness!

That was when I realized how wrong I'd been about Teddy. This was a hiding place. My throat closed and I feared for my life. How would we ever get out of here? Oh, God, I realized in panic, I'd never thought to drop the anchor. The *Gnomon* would have drifted to who knew where by now!

And then I caught a glimpse of light moving in front of me in the darkness. Someone was up ahead. I hesitated and turned to go back up to the door. Hearing a far-off voice, I stayed still. It was loud enough that I could make out every word.

"Wendell, Wendell," Teddy was reprimanding, "did you hear that? You made me forget to close the door!" I could hear the exasperation in his voice. "The wind will blow us all to pieces! You never should have come along. Now what am I going to do with you?"

I pressed close against the wall on the landing, shielding myself with my arms—and a cold, wet hand fell on my head with a thunk. I would have screamed had fear not turned me to salt. I slid my hand in my pocket and took out the flashlight. Trembling, I turned it on and light shone onto Mr. Piet's limp body, pressed, eyes closed, against the wall above me. He hung there as though he were hooked onto the wall. I got so scared the flashlight jumped out of my hands—cracking on the cement floor—and fell down the stairwell, down, down, making clanking noises all the way. I froze in pitch-black darkness.

There was a scuffling sound. Then Teddy's chilling voice, "Who is it? Who's there?"

Teddy's limping footsteps came softly toward me, ascending in the dark, and I knew that Morgan had to be wounded. He'd never let Teddy carry Wendell off. . . . And where was he, hoisted against the wall like Mr. Piet or lying knocked out on the ground? If I moved, would I trip on him? I could hear Teddy coming slowly toward me, feeling his way step by step. I didn't know which way to go. Every cell of my body wanted to rush in the opposite direction, but if I stayed pressed against the wall, he might not find me. I stayed put, locked in terror. Again his slow steps and dragging leg, the spine-chilling sound of his confidential, coddling voice drawing near, "I'm just going to have to put you in the closet now, because I have some things to do. The windstorm is tearing everything down. You understand that, don't you, Wendell?"

I heard Wendell whimper.

And then, as if it pleased him, Teddy added in a tone of malevolence, "Time won't keep you in there long."

The hairs on my neck stood. I couldn't let him close that door to the world up there. I had to get out.

And as he came closer his voice continued, ever so gentle, "It's your fault I have to put you in there, you know" he said. "You know that, don't you?"

Wendell answered with a stifled sob.

It came to me that Teddy didn't know Mr. Piet and Morgan were here somewhere. Mr. Piet must have fallen when the steps above collapsed and landed like that, knocked unconscious. But where was Morgan? I could just make out a moving form. Teddy had Wendell in his arms like groceries. And then he muttered distractedly, "You never should have followed me, Wendell. You put me in a very difficult position. You know that, now, hmm? But you see I have my gloves. So it won't be me who's taking care of you, but the nice soft gloves, all right? You're always such a good little boy."

"All right," the little boy answered, trying to buy Teddy's goodwill with polite behavior.

My heart beat loud enough to hear. I thought I heard Teddy going away in the other direction and I felt a moment's relief, but just then he yanked a chain and light from a stark bulb blared, revealing me.

We saw each other.

"Claire!" Teddy exclaimed in utter surprise. The jig was up. The blacks of his eyes became tight pins and I sensed a wolflike fury. "You know," he said smoothly, without missing a beat, "I had the chance to get rid of you the other night."

It struck me that he wore gloves.

I answered. "No, you were put off by my dog."

We remained like that, in a face-off. Just then, a shrill sound pierced the murky corridor. It was Wendell, blowing like mad on a whistle, and it stunned Teddy for a moment. And at just that moment, out of nowhere,

Morgan landed between us. He was wounded and blood trickled from his ear, but he grabbed Teddy. Wendell fell to the ground between them. Teddy, foiled, fought back. They struggled. I tried to get close enough to hit Teddy with the rock but they moved skittishly, twisting one way and then the other. I dragged Wendell out of the way by his paltry arm. To my horror, Teddy had Morgan in a headlock and was strangling him. Morgan couldn't get loose of him.

I left Wendell huddled against the wall and crept up behind them. With all my might I clomped Teddy on the head with my rock. He fell forward and slumped to the ground. "Oh, my God, I killed him!" I cried.

"Don't worry about him," Morgan groaned. "Help Mr. Piet!"

We three scrambled together up the stairs to Mr. Piet and lifted him. Part of the wall came down with him and my right hand holding his back came away warm and wet. "Blood!" I cried. Morgan tore off his sweatshirt, ripped it in half with his teeth, wincing with pain as he did. He propped Mr. Piet's body against me so he could wrap a tight tourniquet around his torso. Mr. Piet wasn't big, but he was dense and heavy.

"Hold this here, Wendell," Morgan instructed. Wendell, gritting his lips, pressed with all his might. Morgan brushed away as much dirt as he could and felt for a pulse. "He's alive," Morgan said and he fell back, hurt. It was his shoulder, dislocated. "We fell through the floor." He groaned in pain. "The steps gave way."

From the corner of my eye I saw Teddy sit up. He struggled to his feet, swayed, and suddenly he darted past us up the stairs. It all happened so fast.

Straining under Mr. Piet's weight, I shrieked, "God help us, he'll reach the top! He'll lock us in, Morgan! We'll never get out!"

Morgan struggled to get up then faltered and seemed about to faint. I floundered with Mr. Piet's slumped form, most of him on top of me.

Teddy heaved open the cellar door and stood up at the top of the steps, menacing, the sun behind him, turning him into a hunched silhouette looking down at us.

"You'll never get away with this," Morgan gasped, fighting to stay conscious. "I'll get you."

"Not this time, Morgan," Teddy sneered. He laughed. "You know they'll never find you here." He struggled to take hold of the storm cellar door and lower it over us. He hovered it there between open and shut, life and death, dangling it like a tease.

Morgan lunged upward but fell short, the effort causing him to writhe with pain. He staggered backward as though he'd been punched and collapsed, unconscious, all the way down what was left of the staircase. I tried to get out from under Mr. Piet.

Just then, from behind Teddy, a raised form—obliterated by the midday sun—silently came upon him, lifting him into the air and casting him down over the ledge and into the pond.

All was still. I'd struggled out from under Mr. Piet's dead weight and lay on the stairs, gasping for breath. I could hear Wendell's little throat rasping. I got up on all fours and then stood and made my way across the landing to Morgan. I stopped when I saw an open door. It was an office, or what used to be an office. There was electricity—a terrible smell . . . there was—I'll never forget it—a preacher's lectern, and on the face of it, a pair of gloves.

And then I saw it: the festering body of a half-naked girl in rubber snow boots on a futon. It was wrapped in a haggle of blankets on a plastic sheet. Her dead eyes were open as though she were watching us, her lifeless body chained by one foot to the wall. I tasted Mr. Piet's blood on my hand as it met my shocked mouth. But no, oh, no. There on the welted mattress lay the body of Annabel Cupsand. The phosphorescent shimmer from the walls wobbled her greenish flesh. The protruding eyes blinked. Wait. Did they blink? I was sure they blinked. I moved closer. A scrawny hand reached out, stilted and grappling. Could it be she was alive?

"Mama!" Wendell screeched from behind me. "Mama!"

I couldn't bear for him to see and I grabbed at him. But he broke free of me and ran and fell, tumbling, then got up and clung, weeping, to her.

I never thought I'd see Annabel Cupsand alive. Never. And now here she was, bound in shock, her long, frizzy red hair in filthy tangles, her white skin mottled.

"Go outside." Morgan's voice came from behind me. "Take the whistle. Flag someone down. Find a cell phone and call 911. Tell them we need three ambulances."

I got to my feet and, shivering with more than cold, followed the wall and climbed up the crumbling stairs, my shoeless, mucky feet stepping gingerly over Mr. Piet's unconscious body. I went on my knees, crabbing like an animal as fast as I could, avoiding the treacherous holes, reaching for the daylight, grasping hold of the heavy door. I thrust it all the way back so it could never close us in; the sound of Wendell's voice echoed up from the damp behind me. That was all I could hear, little Wendell's wailing "Mama! Mama!" through the shattered chambers like hurry-up dice rolling a long shot, insistent with hope.

Outside, I stood on the ledge and saw Teddy's fallen cell phone at my feet. I stared at it. I picked it up. I punched in 911. The blinding sun was in my eyes. I looked down and squinted and saw a human shape there in the green muck of the pool. It was Teddy, sucked in and still, only half of his body sticking out. Speechless, I held the yammering voice of the operator in my hand.

A marigold dinghy was rowing out past the willow and heading toward Sea Cliff. I saw a slim back and a length of long yellow hair.

When they said the place was condemned, they weren't kidding. There were so many police and firefighters at the scene within half an hour that it started to come down on itself and they had to pull half of them out. Then some avid news reporter made a jump from the loading dock to the factory grounds and missed and they had to waste time jimmying him out. It was a mess. You have to give it to those Coast Guard medics; they really know what they're doing. Wendell stayed with me while the medical helicopter flew Annabel Cupsand and Mr. Piet off to the hospital, then a lady officer took Wendell with her in the police boat.

They hoisted Teddy out. I was standing there waiting in an aluminum blanket. He was caked with mud, but as they brought him up, the green muck slipped away and one of his wide-open eyes looked directly into mine. Ice went through me, right through me. He would have let us stay down there in that dungeon. He would have left us there to die.

They started to load him onto a stretcher but then they lowered him into a body bag instead. The police helicopter was coming for him. I was still soaked and went to be close to Morgan, who had turned his back on the pool and Teddy's exhumation—he told me later he didn't go over to look at him because of no other reason than that he was Daniel's son. He felt like he owed Daniel that.

I didn't mention the dinghy. Let them all think the bastard had fallen. The sound of the chopper came close like a scene out of Afghanistan, curling and beating the wind.

CHAPTER TEN

CLAIRE

The human spirit. It's amazing. That day they carted her out—I have to be honest—I never thought Annabel would make it. I thought she'd had it, or at least that they'd amputate her foot. But at that rehabilitation center over at St. Francis, they got her through it.

I was there when we told Oliver she was still alive and had been held captive by Teddy. It was Detective Harms and I at the dock. Oliver had pulled up in a frenzy of boaters, unaware of anything that had gone down. He'd only come in fourth in the race and he looked pretty sore. The detective went on board and I couldn't hear what he said, but all of a sudden Oliver sank to his knees and started up a wail like a banshee and he threw his arms around the detective's knees and held him and held him like he was afraid they'd all go overboard.

Unbelievable.

So Oliver has his heart's desire back and he'll never let her go again. To this day he says he wakes up and checks she's there, so amazing it is to him. He won't gamble anymore either, or so he says. We'll see.

One day I got to sit with Annabel at the hospital, and I had the chance to speak to her alone for the first time. "Annabel," I asked her, looking over my shoulder and hoping nothing would interrupt us, "I know you're not supposed to get upset, but I have to know. That day when you left Oliver, how did Teddy get to you? How did that happen? Do you mind talking about it?"

"No, I don't mind. I never left Oliver." She touched her heart. "That night . . . oh, I was angry at him, all right. He'd gambled away the money we'd planned for refurbishing the bedrooms. I was furious." She shook her head adamantly. "But I would never have left him. And I certainly wouldn't have left Wendell! Teddy had played a dirty trick on Noola and I knew about it. He'd tried to get rid of her cat, and when Mrs. Dellaverna caught him, he tried to lay the blame on her! But I knew what he was up to because Wendell had seen the whole thing and he'd told me. At first I didn't believe him, but he was too innocent to have made it up. I just knew he wasn't lying. I told Wendell not to say a word. I made him promise. I was going to fix Teddy's wagon." She shook her head. "Oliver and Paige were always defending Teddy. You couldn't blame them. They felt guilty. I know they did, because they were always pushing him off. They didn't want him around. The truth is, they were afraid of him. He used to set fires under their cars when he was a kid . . . things like that. I should have known from that how dangerous he was. And he— their brother's son! But that night I wasn't speaking to Oliver or I would have told him I was going down to the marina. I was so angry I wasn't even afraid of the water. I found Teddy on his boat. He pretended he was glad to see me. 'Come aboard!' he said. 'Give me some decorating ideas.' I went on board. I did give him some ideas. That boat is a classic. But then I told him I knew what he'd done and if he didn't make it up with Mrs. Dellaverna and Noola, I'd tell Oliver. He laughed at me, said he was allergic to the cat and was just trying to drive it away, that the cat was making his life a misery. I didn't know what to think. Everything I said he had an answer for. He complimented me. I was flattered."

Yes, I thought, he'd flattered me, too. He knew just how to do it.

She swept a hand through her extraordinary red hair. "He started talking about the jewels, the Cupsand family jewels. He even said they belonged to him! I got angry. I threatened him. I told him he'd never get his hands on the jewels because they were safe in the sea captain's trunk at Twillyweed and Oliver would never let him have them. If only I'd told someone where I'd gone. Anyone! But I made my great mistake. I started to leave. 'Oh, don't go,' he said. I told him I had to get back because nobody knew where I'd gone. I had no idea he would become so cruel. But I thought I could handle everything on my own. And he seemed to change, to become reasonable. He asked me to help smooth things over with Oliver. And then I guess I started to feel sorry for him. Everyone was always so down on him. His life was so difficult. No one understood him. I let my guard down. We had a drink. I don't know what was in that drink." She looked away. "Since then I've tasted that drink many times," she went on, intent, whispering, "You see, he saw his chance. After he knocked me out, he went back to Twillyweed, upstairs into Captain Cupsand's room, and he stole the jewels. Then he went to my desk and took my letter paper. He made me write Oliver that I was leaving him. I was so drugged. I knew what I was doing, but I knew he was dangerous by then. He threatened Wendell if I didn't do what I was told! The next thing I knew I was waking up in that strange, cold place. It was a nightmare. The walls were so damp. I never could get warm." She gripped my arm. "Sometimes it was so cold! When I wouldn't *behave*, as he called it, he would put on his gloves, those horrible, beautiful gloves. He never wanted to get his hands *dirtied*."

Shocked, I thought we'd better stop, but she went on, "The next day after Oliver found my letter and they all were in a frenzy, Teddy made sure they looked to see what I'd made off with."

"To think he had you write the letters! But why did you—"

"He dictated them to me. Oh, it was so horrible. He told me if I didn't write just what he said, he'd bring Wendell there as well. Little Wendell! And he meant it." She dropped her face in her hands, recalling. She blew her nose into a tissue. "And of course he was the one who started the rumor I'd gone off with Doctor Varanasi. When he ran out of my letter paper, he just went back to the house. It just so happened Doctor Varanasi was leaving Long Island when Teddy ran into

him on the train. Teddy was on his way into the city to mail another
letter from me, and Varanasi, asking about me, fell right into his plans.
He was heading down to Virginia to see what it would be like to open a
practice there. Teddy told everyone who'd listen I'd told him I was falling in love with him. He'd already heard Morgan was sailing down to
Virginia to bring back the chandelier Oliver had won in a card game—it
was the perfect opportunity. He volunteered to go down and help him
get it. That's when he posted that terrible letter. Can you imagine? He
told me all this. Oh, yes, he told me everything. He would go on and on.
He would bring me food from the restaurants where he would work
and he would rant and rave. He knew if he laid low for long enough,
he'd be rich. He'd sell the jewels, but not yet. He had to wait and find
an unscrupulous buyer. 'One day,' he would say, 'somewhere overseas.'
But he had time—and he couldn't have suspicion cast upon him. He
couldn't let me go. And he had to keep me well enough to write the
letters." She studied me with those watery blue eyes. "You'll think he
abused me all the time. I mean physically, sexually."

"No," I lied.

"Yes, they all think that. But he never did. I swear it. He was a
voyeur. He only wanted to watch from his closet. He would . . ."—she
closed her eyes—"abuse himself while he would watch me. And he
would only find relief when he saw fear, real fear in my eyes." She shuddered, remembering. "His perversion wasn't only sex, Claire. It was
avarice." She said the word in three drawn-out syllables. "He wanted
what he imagined everyone else had, everyone but him. He would rave
about it. Avarice!" she whispered, her eyes popping, scaring me. "I was
his listening stone. That's what he called me."

Her voice grew hoarse. I had to move closer to hear her.

"In the early days when Teddy had me captive, when I still believed
he'd one day let me go once he had enough money, Daniel went to visit
Noola, Morgan's mother, and Teddy went along. It was an Easter visit.
Daniel took her cake and tea and things from Paige. Teddy always went
along to see what he could get out of it. Sometimes Noola would slip

him money. Noola mentioned she'd read in the obituary that a Father
von Ritasdorf had passed away and she must remember to tell Morgan
about it. Father von Ritasdorf was a horologist—you know, a timepiece
expert—and she had knowledge that the priest kept a fabulous volvelle,
a moon dial from the 1600s, in the rectory in Broad Channel. It was
worth a fortune, she told Daniel. And there it was just sitting there
where any criminal could walk in and take it! The *minute* he heard that
Catholic priest in Broad Channel had this moon dial, Teddy's plan
began to take shape. He'd always waited for an opportunity to get the
family jewels, but, it came to him, why stop at the family's jewels when
he could have Morgan's heart's desire, too? He saw his chance. He was
aware of her weak heart. He and Daniel said good-bye. 'Don't forget
to lock the door' were her last words, but Teddy didn't lock the door.
He left it open and he came back alone, slipped in, and put six pills in
Noola's tea before she could inform Morgan. He killed her to keep her
quiet. He didn't even hesitate. He just did it. That's why they couldn't
place the rest of her medication and thought she'd done it herself. And
then he went down to steal the volvelle. He brought it here for a while. I
saw it. After he told me he'd murdered Noola, I knew he would kill me,
too, eventually, when he was through with me writing letters. He'd have
to. I remember he dumped everything inside the volvelle onto the floor
and held it up like he'd won a trophy. But he foolishly took the lot to
Daniel's house and hid it there. And then something he hadn't counted
on happened. Patsy Mooney discovered his treasure."

"That's about when Jenny Rose and I came to Sea Cliff."

"Yes. Just before."

"But how did she get involved in the first place?"

"One night Patsy was walking home from the rectory where she'd
left Darlene Lassiter. They'd been to Atlantic City on the bus. It was
late. She walked past Daniel Cupsand's house along the beach. All the
lights were off, but she happened to notice a light from the basement.
She knew Daniel was an early riser and couldn't imagine what he was
doing up at that hour. She walked over and peered in the window. But

as she drew closer she saw it wasn't Daniel at all but his son, Teddy. He was sitting at the old model train table. And on the table lay an assortment of odd and compelling items, things that might certainly have been valuable. One of those things was a statue and Teddy was prying the jewels from its eyes. She wasn't sure what she was seeing. She went home and must have thought it over.

"The next day, Patsy made Daniel some custard and returned. While Daniel was busy eating in front of the television set, Patsy went below and found the moon dial. She must have been astonished to see the Cupsand family jewels. Of course she took it all. She put everything in an orange crate and carried it up the stairs. But Daniel had finished his custard and was coming to ask for more just as she was making off with the loot. Daniel blocked her exit and wouldn't let her out of the house. She froze. She didn't know what he would do. But she saw his eyes light up at the statue. She took it from the crate and dropped it down the stairs. He went after it. He didn't want any jewels or the volvelle; all he wanted was the statue because it looked like some doll he used to carry around that Teddy had taken away from him. He stood at the bottom of the stairs crooning to the blind thing. It wasn't worth anything to Patsy, but it was precious to Daniel. Daniel loved the statue but when Teddy saw him with it, he flipped out. He hit him, smacked him hard, until Daniel told him Patsy Mooney had been there. Teddy almost burst a blood vessel when he discovered Patsy Mooney had made off with his stash, the volvelle, *and* the family jewels!" Annabel croaked a bitter laugh and wrapped her shawl closer around herself. "He raved for days and nights! I was almost glad, because he never tortured me during that time. But he went after Patsy. Teddy confronted her and she admitted it. She even taunted him with it. She told him the whole story. But he couldn't do anything about it because he didn't know where she'd hidden the lot. After all I've been through, the worst of it is that Teddy strangled poor Patsy Mooney, trying to get her to tell him where the treasure was when all the while the key to it was on a chain around her neck and he had no idea. The uselessness of it!"

"Yes," I agreed, "but if she hadn't been greedy, she'd still be alive."

"No doubt. He told me she was blackmailing him. Because she didn't want the jewels, she wanted money. She didn't know anyone in that world."

"And in the end," I finished for her, "it would mean her death."

"Death." She tasted the word. "How close I was to that. How many nights I died inside."

I lifted a paper cup of water to her lips. She didn't look too good. But she still had that big red hair that trailed to her waist. I took hold of her cold, small hand. "Don't talk about it anymore," I said.

"It's just a pity Teddy had to die," she murmured.

"Oh, yeah," I agreed, "he should have lived so he could pretend to be nuts and then write a tell-all book they could make into a movie on Thursday night and then one day he'd get out and take some other poor woman prisoner. Come on! It's good he's gone." I held Annabel's hand and squeezed it. Just to look at her, so wretched but alive, was still a kind of miracle. What the human being can be put through, as she'd been, and then to return to normal life—to survive!

She surprised me by saying, "You don't understand. I just would have liked for him to have felt what it was like, what prison is like." She smiled at me, a line of reproach on her mouth, plain and vindictive. She licked her lips, still chapped. "I wanted him to feel what he put me through. I would have loved to visit him. He wasn't crazy, you know. He was sane. He was just"—she paused—"empty. He was evil with a covetousness he could not let go. 'Why must Morgan be the one to have it all?' he would say, again and again. Fixated. It was all about Morgan. You see, he would talk to me all the time, on and on; he thought Morgan was the insidious one, always lucking out, always the accumulator, the collector, and the hoarder, until there was nothing left for anyone else. If I objected—even so much as a look on my face he *thought* was object-ing—he'd whack me with a gloved fist. He was so jealous, eaten up with lust to get that one thing Morgan wanted, the volvelle, the moon dial. One day he was in such a rage he dumped the contents of the volvelle on the floor. All those jewels in a tumble on the filthy floor!" She held up her lavender rosary. "That's how I got my beads. I almost tore my foot off reaching for it before he threw everything back in. I hid it. I clung to it whenever he was gone." Her eyes shimmered. "I begged Our Lady to save me. She did."

"Wendell's faith in you saved you, too," I said.

"Yes."

I looked through the open window at the sky. *And Daniel*, I confided in silence to God.

EPILOGUE

The sun shone golden and a faint breeze stirred the trees. The sky was cerulean blue. It was the seventeenth of July, the day of the new moon, and Jenny Rose and Glinty were getting married. She looked beautiful, Jenny Rose did, in a white Mexican dress we'd bought at Anthropologie then tea-stained ecru in the bathtub. She wore my sparkling button earrings and sat in the backseat of Jupiter Dodd's borrowed blue Bentley, waiting to enter the church. Wendell, the ring bearer, wriggled beside her in brown satin shorts and what he scornfully called a *girl's* ruffled shirt, his brand-new Nintendo game there in his lap to keep him occupied. A burst of organ music filled the church

Father Steger, guest sacramenteur, rocked on pigeon toes, robed and ready at the front of the church. (You should have seen his face the day I took the statue back to him. One sunny morning after we found Annabel, I took a ride down to Broad Channel with Daniel. It was a kind of ceremony for the two of us. There are times Daniel understands more than he lets on. Anyway, that was a good day. I remember we went for Carvel on the way home.)

My parents sat waiting in the first row on Our Lady's side, my mother jittery with excitement, her hair in the tight, fancy marcel of a stringent new perm; my father sat rigidly beside her, wishing they'd get on with it, his mind out in the Buick on his old carpet slippers she'd brought along despite his firm insistence she not do so.

Oliver stood smoking a Cuban cigar out on the church steps,

standing there talking to my sister Zinnie and Johnny, my ex. Johnny always has to be in on all the fun—you get the picture.

My sister Carmela, her silver bangles alerting everyone in the vicinity to her presence, arrived from the airport fashionably late and making a scene as usual, just as the bride was about to walk into the church. She was magnificent in a pink shantung Miu Miu suit and large-brimmed straw hat—looking like a bride herself. She backed out of the cab and paid the driver.

It was an odd sort of driver, I thought. Not odd that he was a turbaned Sikh—there seem to be as many of them driving cabs nowadays in the city and suburbs as there once were in Delhi—but that when he got out of the taxi, he beheld our Jenny Rose in such a significant way.

Carmela turned around and saw Jenny Rose for the second time in her life.

Jenny Rose stood on the floor of the fancy blue convertible she'd arrived in, at eye level now with her mother, the both of them spellbound. Carmela took four steps toward her. *Damn*, I thought, *now Jenny Rose will ruin her mascara*. But that wasn't what happened. Jenny Rose opened her arms and Carmela dropped her purse and fell into them, sobbing. I hadn't seen my sister cry like that since she broke her arm when she was ten. Jenny Rose held her. She didn't cry. She held her. It was funny Carmela was the one to be crying. But not so funny maybe, after all, knowing Jenny Rose. Knowing all she'd been through. When Carmela was finished weeping, Jenny Rose cupped her chin and gazed at her with a dazzling smile. She'd made it. She was here. Her mother was here.

Inside, a restless organ prompted, and Carmela tore herself away. Solemn and jingling, she took the church steps and came in, stealing over to me for a brief hug.

"Carmela," I said with a frown, "your taxi driver is still standing outside."

"I know." She looked back at him standing out there on the street while she straightened her hair. "It's very odd." She grabbed hold of my arm. "Evidently I'm the second girl he's brought all the way out here from Kennedy airport."

Together we watched him praise thanks to the good and mystical God up above, bow charmingly to Jenny Rose, get back into his cab, and sweep away with majesty.

Carmela relinquished my arm, minced inside, and sat with dainty haste beside my father. He patted her hand with his big mitt. It hadn't worked out with her Italian. Just as well, we all thought.

The Irish aunts from Skibbereen sat in a grim knot behind her, looking past her, both of them scented with a lot of lily of the valley.

Annabel was not entirely well yet and wouldn't be for some time, but there she was beside me in the vestibule, weepy, but smiling. I'd been assigned the task of looking after her.

She was swathed in a fringed senorita white silk shawl embroidered with red roses. Oliver had insisted she be warm. They had her in a lightweight, red travel chair. She didn't look too bad for someone who'd been through what she had. It had been touch-and-go at first—she'd been so ghastly thin, but she'd plumped up pretty well, I thought—and she'd been quite firm that she be here for Glinty's wedding.

A burst of organ music filled the church.

"All right." I mopped at her blue eyes with my churchgoing hankie. "You're all right, now."

"It's being here in this place." She smiled through her tears. "It's—I don't know—it's the exact opposite of where I was."

"Sanctuary," I said.

"Yes." She shivered.

Hopefully, Annabel would thrive with so much love coming at her from Oliver and Wendell, from all of us really. She's a survivor. I'm looking forward to becoming friends. And Oliver is a different man, contrite and grateful and counting his blessings for the first time in his life.

I remembered to say an extra prayer of thanksgiving, relieved to have had a clean bill of health come from the hospital. That weight, too, had been lifted. *Breathe*, I kept reminding myself. *Breathe and be grateful!*

Mr. Piet, all sewn together and fully recovered from the horrendous gash on his back, tuxedo sleeves rolled up over his lewd tattoos, had been assisting the chef in the Once Upon a Moose kitchen with all the appetizers. He trotted now past us into the church, rolling his sleeves back down, hurrying to get in before the bride. It hadn't been Teddy who'd attacked him, but when he and Morgan fell through a hole in the floor, he'd fallen onto a broken, gaping flat hook left over from the loading dock. It almost went right through him, just missing puncturing a lung. He'd fainted from the pain and it was a wonder he hadn't bled to death; an inch right or left or if he'd flung himself off and he would have. As it was, now he flinched with every step as his punctured rhomboid muscle painstakingly healed. He was grateful to be alive and had given his blessing to Radiance and Paige.

Thanks to Jupiter Dodd's connections, Radiance has already been offered several modeling jobs and she and Paige are putting a deposit on a condo on Perry Street down in the Village. They love it there, even talk about one day adopting a baby from Guardian Angel House. And as they turned in their pew, their faces shining with goodwill, I wondered how the hell I'd ever missed the most obvious passion of all.

Daniel was in attendance. Paige had seen to that. Jenny Rose had trimmed his hair, but it was still long enough to fill a slithery braid.

I don't know if he'd meant to kill Teddy when he'd flung him off that ledge; I like to believe he'd only meant to stop him. Accidental death, the investigation determined as to cause of death, due to trauma to his head. Or, I've often imagined as I lay in bed, it might have been that crack I gave him myself with the stone. That certainly hadn't helped.

Daniel meditated now, I reckoned, on Darlene Lassiter's soon-to-be-savored pastry.

My two children were in town for the wedding. Good sorts that they are, they sat determinedly at Daniel's side. He would huddle away from them toward the far corner. And they would shuttle back toward him. He would move away. They would wriggle near.

Darlene Lassiter was friends again with Mrs. Dellaverna. After it came to light that it was Teddy who'd pitted them against each other, it hadn't taken them long to make up and they sat together now on St. Joseph's side, the groom's side, where Morgan stood as best man. They whispered animatedly together, having big plans for opening a teashop in town. They were going to take Jenny Rose's idea and hang her paintings on the walls and Tuesday nights they'd stay open late and serve spaghetti; Thursdays, shepherd's pie; and on Friday, salmon. No stress. Nice and easy. It was, by the way, Mrs. Dellaverna who won the charity garden contest money—and kept it, I might add.

The organ music rallied into the wedding march and everyone rose. Oliver looked very dapper walking the bride into the church. Jenny Rose was a picture, her ribbon sash matching the borrowed blue Bentley, all cream and powder blue and thick in the middle, a wreath of rosemary and stephanotis decorating her short, shining black hair. No tattoos today. Glinty looked as though he'd burst with pride as he gently took her hand. They glowed with love. I couldn't help thinking—cynical old thing that I am—just wait till that baby starts squawking all night long with teething. But I heard on the radio that bitterness is just amplified self-pity. That sounds right, doesn't it, when you think about it?

Anyway it was a lovely ceremony, punctuated with my mother's boisterous, happy sobs, and afterward we all walked in a sunlit troupe up the road to the village. Jenny Rose and Glinty hadn't wanted a conventional catering hall with a loud disc jockey and so everyone was to come back to the Once Upon a Moose, whose rafters Paige and Radiance had swathed in peonies and the revived, and astonishingly flourishing, wisteria. Streaming, thick, pale-pink ribbons wrapped the banisters and the doors were thrown open to the street by the new owners. Morgan had arranged for a piper and the music sounded up and down the hills of Sea Cliff. We were just approaching the top of the hill when a nosy, rangy cat with big paws and glassy yellow eyes appeared along the side of the road and strode impudently before us. Wendell let out a cry. "Mama! It's Weedy! Noola's cat! She's come back!"

Annabel clapped her hands in delight from her transport chair. "It *is* Noola's cat!" she cried. Wendell was beside himself with joy and lifted the cat into his little arms.

"What do you know! She came home to Sea Cliff," Mrs. Dellaverna exclaimed. "I'll bet that's the mother of your kitten, Claire. She looks like Sam and Weedy both!"

"You can name your little kitten Sweetie, Wendell," Annabel suggested. "A cross between Weedy and Sam. How about that?"

Wendell stood momentarily transfixed. Then, "Auntie Claire"—he grabbed my hand and pulled me aside in solemn conspiracy. "Sweetie," he explained helpfully to the city bumpkin, as only a country child would. "It's both. Get it?"

"That sounds perfect," I agreed.

Once everyone was inside and had a glass, Oliver, his arm circling Annabel's thin waist, shouted, "Hear, hear! Let's have a toast!"

Morgan, the best man, stood up reluctantly and held his glass in the air. He looked around the room of beaming faces, the white tablecloths, the candles and flowers. He cleared his throat and, in his priestly from the pulpit voice, holding the couple's eyes, said, "All right. Here's one I know that fits. This is from Corinthians." He recited:

"If I speak in the tongues of men and angels, but have not love, I am only a resounding gong or a clanging symbol. If I have the gift of prophecy and can fathom all mysteries and all knowledge, and if I have a faith that can move mountains, but have not love, I am nothing. If I give all I possess to the poor and surrender my body to the flames, but have not love, I gain nothing."

He paused. "Here's to love." With this he lowered his glass to his lips, those sweet lips I have begun to cherish, and drank the cool sparkling wine. And then, in a moment of pure hope, so did we all.

That kitten, Sweetie, will do all right living with Sam and Weedy. A big establishment like Twillyweed can well use three cats. Wendell proclaimed that you have to keep the cat family together and Wendell runs the joint over there, you know. Whatever he says goes, under the watchfulness of Annabel and Oliver. It was Mrs. Dellaverna who came up with the idea they turn their fancy, airy rooms into a hotel when she was at town hall digging up commercial licenses for the teashop. She had noticed that Twillyweed still was registered in the books as a commercial property.

If you ever come to stay at Twillyweed and enter the main hallway, three languid sets of yellow eyes will scrutinize you from antique nooks and any old-fashioned sofa they choose.

Glinty and Jenny Rose have the turret and the rooms below to themselves. Glinty took most of the money he'd saved and together he and Oliver are redoing the place into, I must say, a very grand bed-and-breakfast. Mr. Piet has retained his rooms and bought in with a vested interest as cook. Though *The Black Pearl Is Mine* turned out to be impractical for a family to live on, Jenny Rose and Glinty are going to keep it and use it for holiday tours around the gold coast, a perk of the B&B. The *Dream Boat* has been sold and the money invested for Daniel.

Jenny Rose has a tidy little side business making jewelry from vintage buttons and frame-able hand-painted cards, for sale to all and sundry in the Twillyweed gift shop. They put the gift shop down in the basement in Patsy Mooney's old place. Isn't it said that every great fortune begins with a crime?

Carmela comes out weekends. She and Jenny Rose circle each other like a pair of prizefighters—each of them unwilling to be hurt, yet mad for the prize. Love. She drives out with Jupiter Dodd and Enoch in Enoch's truck.

Enoch and Jupiter Dodd met up at the baby shower. Jupiter took one look at Enoch's big red truck and that was it. "Such transport!" he reportedly exclaimed in hero worship. Of course Enoch says they're just buddies, but I heard from Carmela the three of them are looking for a place out here to rent, so hold on to your hat. I don't know who's more excited about the baby among the three of them. Jupiter had no intention of wasting a good masquerade, he says, and without telling a soul he went and showed Twillyweed's treasure to the real Sotheby's. It turned out to actually be worth quite a bit.

Jenny Rose and Glinty have asked me to work at Twillyweed but, honestly, my days as a hotelier are over. I must say, Glinty bends over backward for Jenny Rose. So you see, you never know, do you? They've only just finished renovations and already have some bookings into next year. They seem to really get a kick out of each other—and laughter floats in bursts from their quarters' open windows. No one could be happier.

Unless, that is, you by chance look in on Morgan and me.

Morgan decided to relinquish some of his money and donate it to Guardian Angel House. Well, we have so much. We've chosen to stay on in the Great White. Neither of us cares much about grandeur. Out of whimsy we've renamed it the Moon Dial. We love the coziness around the fireplace at night, him and me and Jake, the old clocks ticking, two pools of lamplight on our open books. We're not ones for television. Mr. Piet came over and, with Morgan's help, he put on a new roof and remade the deck.

Morgan has an antique clock shop in town now, although you'll find him mostly out sailing. He's more of a pilgrim than a landsman, Morgan is—not to be tied down. I have to ring a big old school bell he's hung on the side of the cottage when I want him for lunch. Sometimes he hears it and sometimes he's too far away. It's Daniel who sits in the shop all day long puttering around with the insides of clocks. You couldn't find a more intent clock fixer. And the thing is, he loves it. Well, Noola taught him. Only sometimes, when I enter the shop, he looks at me with these blue eyes. And I feel like he's got this monopoly on truth. And I don't. And I'm so sorry for all of us.

I have a nice little tomato garden out back. And my *cucuzza*? *Bellissima*. Twice a week I'm Story Lady over at the children's library; they always like the mysteries best, the kids. My days I spend mostly with

Jake; he goes where I go, drawing and painting. You'll find me setting up my easel on any little footpath over Sea Cliff. Funny, because when I was small that's what I liked to do, dreamed of doing—and now here I am, imagination my reality. I don't think I ever really expected to find joy, you know? It was always arbitration and accommodation all day long.

Now, when the evening rolls around, Morgan and I head for our little cottage after our walk. And when we long for space, we have the sea before us—all indigo and sapphire, dazzling endless in the moonlight—and the voyage-worthy *Gnomon* fitted out to take us there.

ACKNOWLEDGMENTS

Heartfelt thanks to Otto Penzler, whose love of a good mystery puts me back on the page, and to Heather Boak, my careful and brilliant editor. Also to Rob Hart, Lauren Chomiuk, and Laurie McGee.

Thanks to my loving husband, Tommy, who keeps the home fires burning; to my sister, Annie, my hero; and to Michael and Kim, my happy ever afters.

Some of the places in this book no longer exist, but they always shall in my memory.

THE
CLAIRE BRESLINSKY
MYSTERIES

FROM MYSTERIOUSPRESS.COM
AND OPEN ROAD MEDIA

Available wherever ebooks are sold

MYSTERIOUSPRESS.COM

Otto Penzler, owner of the Mysterious Bookshop in Manhattan, founded the Mysterious Press in 1975. Penzler quickly became known for his outstanding selection of mystery, crime, and suspense books, both from his imprint and in his store. The imprint was devoted to printing the best books in these genres, using fine paper and top dust-jacket artists, as well as offering many limited, signed editions.

Now the Mysterious Press has gone digital, publishing ebooks through **MysteriousPress.com**.

MysteriousPress.com offers readers essential noir and suspense fiction, hard-boiled crime novels, and the latest thrillers from both debut authors and mystery masters. Discover classics and new voices, all from one legendary source.

FIND OUT MORE AT
WWW.MYSTERIOUSPRESS.COM

FOLLOW US:
@emysteries and Facebook.com/MysteriousPressCom

MysteriousPress.com is one of a select group of publishing partners of Open Road Integrated Media, Inc.

THE MYSTERIOUS BOOKSHOP, founded in 1979, is located in Manhattan's Tribeca neighborhood. It is the oldest and largest mystery-specialty bookstore in America.

The shop stocks the finest selection of new mystery hardcovers, paperbacks, and periodicals. It also features a superb collection of signed modern first editions, rare and collectable works, and Sherlock Holmes titles. The bookshop issues a free monthly newsletter highlighting its book clubs, new releases, events, and recently acquired books.

58 Warren Street
info@mysteriousbookshop.com
(212) 587-1011
Monday through Saturday
11:00 a.m. to 7:00 p.m.

FIND OUT MORE AT:

www.mysteriousbookshop.com

FOLLOW US:

@TheMysterious and Facebook.com/MysteriousBookshop

OPEN ROAD

INTEGRATED MEDIA

Open Road Integrated Media is a digital publisher and multimedia content company. Open Road creates connections between authors and their audiences by marketing its ebooks through a new proprietary online platform, which uses premium video content and social media.

Videos, Archival Documents, and New Releases

Sign up for the Open Road Media newsletter and get news delivered straight to your inbox.

Sign up now at
www.openroadmedia.com/newsletters

FIND OUT MORE AT
WWW.OPENROADMEDIA.COM

FOLLOW US:
@openroadmedia and
Facebook.com/OpenRoadMedia